Praise for Lorelei James's
Cowboy Casanova

"A love story steeped in kinkiness, *Cowboy Casanova* is a story of discovery and domination—the lure of Bennett and Ainsley and the love that would not be beaten...A cowboy story with more whips and chains than a hardware store, the latest "Rough Riders" tale is sure to please series fans."

~ *Library Journal*

"...the heat contained in this story, it was off the charts. The BDSM club scenes were vivid and displayed in exacting detail that left me breathless...Ms. James can write erotica that will leave even the most seasoned reader blushing."

~ *Long and Short Reviews*

"Things I loved about this book were Ben and Ainsley as a couple, the scenes with the family that reminded me why I love them all so much, the laugh out loud moments as well as the teary ones, LJ's knowledge of the BDSM lifestyle with relation to the D/s relationship, the new characters we met, and always a favorite of mine—the panty blazing dirty-talk dialogue."

~ *Guilty Pleasures Book Reviews*

"Oh. My. God. Is it hot in here or is it just me? You'll know exactly what I mean once you get immersed in this sexy, hot, sweaty, erotic, down 'n dirty ride, the latest in Lorelei James' Rough Riders series. Ben McKay is a man you don't mess with. Well, unless you want to be dominated. And like his heroine, Ainsley, I wouldn't mind that one bit."

~ *The Good, The Bad and The Unread*

Look for these titles by
Lorelei James

Now Available:

Dirty Deeds
Babe in the Woods
Running With the Devil
Wicked Garden
Ballroom Blitz

Wild West Boys
Mistress Christmas
Miss Firecracker

Print Anthologies
Three's Company
Wild Ride
Wild West Boys

Rough Riders
Long Hard Ride
Rode Hard, Put Up Wet
Cowgirl Up and Ride
Tied Up, Tied Down
Rough, Raw and Ready
Branded As Trouble
Strong, Silent Type
Shoulda Been A Cowboy
All Jacked Up
Raising Kane
Cowgirls Don't Cry
Slow Ride
Chasin' Eight
Kissin' Tell

Cowboy Casanova

Lorelei James

SAMHAIN
PUBLISHING

Samhain Publishing, Ltd.
11821 Mason Montgomery Road, 4B
Cincinnati, OH 45249
www.samhainpublishing.com

Editing by Lindsey Faber
Cover by Scott Carpenter

First Samhain Publishing, Ltd. electronic publication: December 2011
First Samhain Publishing, Ltd. print publication: October 2012

Dedication

For the readers who always wondered about the mysterious Ben...now you know.

Chapter One

The sound of leather hitting flesh was music to his ears.

He pulled his arm back and snapped his wrist, the movement fluid and familiar. The long leather tail of the bullwhip connected with her quivering flank and a sharp *crack* echoed back to him.

She released a low-pitched grunt but remained still, staring at him with defiant brown eyes.

Stubborn.

Again he lifted his arm. He put more force behind the blow, hitting the same spot, but harder.

Her whole body quivered.

"For Christsake, quit fuckin' around with her. Throw a goddamn rope around her neck and make her come."

Ben McKay squinted at the lone cow, her hooves mired in the mud. He sighed, spurred his horse through the creek and stopped ten feet in front of the immovable cow. After switching out his whip for his rope, he twirled and let fly. The loop circled her neck and he tugged to tighten it. He'd done this so many times he didn't have to spur his horse; Bongo just moved forward.

The cow, given the choice between choking or moving, stumbled forward.

Quinn's horse danced impatiently at the top of the rise, as his rider watched Ben drag the cow up the incline. "Don't know why in the hell she likes that damn creek," Quinn remarked. "She'd stay there until it froze over."

"Probably." Bongo picked up the pace and Ben led the cow through the gate. As soon as Quinn closed off her only avenue of escape, Ben released the rope. He dismounted and approached the cow slowly. "Now don't go getting any ideas about running off." She stood still while he slipped the loop from her neck. Then he slapped her hard on the rump and she lumbered toward the rest of the herd.

Quinn waited while Ben mounted up. They poked along, soaking in the last rays of the sun's warmth. Indian summer had stretched through the first week of October. They'd take temperate days while they could because winter in Wyoming seemed to last more than half the damn year.

"So what're your plans for the weekend?" Quinn asked.

"Goin' to Gillette. I'll be back Sunday sometime." He pushed up his hat and looked at Quinn. "Unless you and Libby need me back early for chores on Sunday morning?"

"Nah. We can handle it. Aren't you gonna be around to watch the PBR Sunday afternoon? It'll be the last time Chase rides in the regular season."

He'd forgotten about that. His bull riding younger brother had pulled his head out of his ass and had made a good showing on the PBR tour the past few months. "Yeah. I'll be back."

"Good, because at the last poker game you volunteered your house as a place for us all to get together to watch."

Ben stopped his horse. "Define all."

"All...meaning all our McKay cousins."

"Jesus. Was I drunk when I volunteered?"

Quinn laughed. "Nope. You were sober enough to exclude kids and wives in the invite. Besides, you own the biggest TV of any of us. And if you sweet talk Keely, she'll bring food."

His cousin Keely loved McKay events with the boys, since she was the only female McKay in their generation. "I'll call her on my way out of town."

When they reached Quinn's place, Ben asked, "We usin' the horses for anything early next week?"

"A couple things we need to check in the northwest corner that's easier to get to on horseback than with the ATVs. Why?"

"I'd like to leave Bongo here until then."

"Not a problem."

Ben dismounted and unhooked the cinch strap.

"Is there a woman in Gillette you've been keeping secret?"

Ben tossed the saddle over the split rail fence. "Wouldn't be a secret if I told you now, would it?"

Quinn dropped his saddle next to Ben's. "Why do you drive to

Gillette to get laid and get drunk when there are plenty of places around here? And plenty of women who'd be happy to be in your bed for more than a weekend."

He snorted and removed the wet saddle blanket, draping it over the rail. "Who'd you hear that from? Tell? Or Dalton?"

Quinn pitched Ben a currycomb. "Neither. I heard that from my wife."

Ben brushed Bongo with long strokes. "Trouble in paradise? Has Libby been hanging out at Ziggy's bar again?"

"Fuck off. No, a couple of the new, single teachers have asked her about you."

"Teachers? Definitely not my type."

"Why not?"

He patted Bongo's withers. "I have a hard time believing a teacher would make a good student."

"What the hell is that supposed to mean?"

Thinking out loud always got him in trouble. "Nothin'. I'm just touchy about all of our damn family members, including your wife, thinking I need to be paired up and married off now that Chase and Ava have tied the knot. Not everyone wants to be chained down with a wife and kids." From the corner of his eye, he noticed Quinn bristle. "Sorry. Between our married relatives lookin' at me like a loser terminal bachelor, and the single chicks at the local bars angling to tame one of the last wild McKays, I'm better off finding my hookups in Gillette."

"I gotta be honest, it's good to hear you're hooking up with women."

"Why's that? You worried I'm secretly craving cock?"

Quinn shook his head. "I wouldn't give a shit if you were. But it's been so long since I've seen you with a date you can't blame me for wondering what kind of woman is worth the drive."

An obedient woman.

Not that Ben could explain that, either. He grinned. "A woman who doesn't want more than a night or two."

His brother laughed. "Daylight's a'wastin'. Get a move on. I'll finish up."

"Thanks, bro. See you Sunday."

Ben sped home. A shower and a change of clothes put him in a good mood and he whistled while he packed for the weekend. House secured, he headed to the barn to refill the dogs' food and water bowls. Ace and Deuce leveled baleful looks at him. "You mutts are spoiled livin' in the house." He petted their heads. "Be good guard dogs, 'kay?"

An hour later, Ben cruised down Main Street in Gillette and parked in the back lot behind the Rawhide Bar. When he crossed the alley, the streetlight sizzled and popped before it flickered out, putting the doorway in shadow.

The left door was the back service entrance to the Rawhide Bar. But the slightly recessed door on the right was the entrance into the Rawhide Club—not that it was marked as such. A keycode was required to enter, a code that changed every weekend. Ben scrolled to the text from Cody and punched in the number, watching as the green light flashed.

A short set of stairs ended at a wide landing. The door was manned by security on Friday and Saturday nights. Because security and anonymity were paramount to club members, Ben was surprised the door was propped open with a barstool and he could wander in, unimpeded.

The large main room, decorated in gold and red, harkened back to brothels in the Wild West. An ornate horseshoe-shaped bar dominated the back corner. The floor to tin ceiling barback consisted of gilded mirrors and glass shelves. A sizeable brick and slate fireplace took center stage on the opposite wall. Several old-fashioned velvet, leather and brocade couches were placed in a semi-circle in front of it. Other chairs and loveseats separated the outer space into individual seating areas. Room dividers also created intimate, hidden spots. At the far back of the room was a hallway that split into two sides.

The high-pitched whine of the vacuum cleaner stopped and Sully strode into view. "Bennett!" He pulled him in for a one-armed man hug. "Good to see you."

"You too. I was beginning to wonder if I was the only one here."

"Nah. Cody's cleaning up a mess in the hallway. Murphy is next door, counting the till. Want a beer?"

"Wouldn't say no."

Sully slipped behind the bar. "It's been a while."

"Sorry I haven't been around."

"No worries. Been slow in the club." Sully popped the top on a bottle of Moose Drool.

Ben settled on the stool. "What about the bar?"

"The bar side always stays busy."

"That's gotta make Cody and Trace happy." He took a pull off his beer. "What's new with you?"

Sully shrugged and loosened his tie. "Not much. Keeping my head above water at the day job. I sling drinks one night a week at the bar to give Cody a break. I've been on overseer status at the club most Saturday nights."

"You still makin' time with that redhead from Sheridan?"

"The last two times I've seen her haven't been on club nights. She comes into the bar side, tosses back a couple of appletinis, we shoot the breeze, and she's gone before closing time."

Ben frowned. "Think she wants to see you outside of the club?" Most female club members didn't hang out in the Rawhide Bar. The reason they'd joined the club was to avoid random, disappointing hookups with half-drunk men after last call. Being a member of the Rawhide Club guaranteed they'd get laid since that was the club's objective—providing a place for no-strings-attached, safe and consensual sex.

"I don't know." Sully rested his elbows on the bar. "I like her. The sex is great. She's not heavy into the Dom/sub stuff, which is fine with me."

Sully's attitude surprised Ben. "Really?"

"In the last couple months I've realized that while I enjoy certain aspects of this club, it's not a permanent lifestyle choice for me. I know Murphy and Layla are happy living the life twenty-four/seven. I suspect Cody and Trace will eventually find a permanent submissive. No judgment from me. But Christ, Ben, I don't wanna put a damn slave collar on a woman. I don't want her to kneel at my feet. All I want is a lover who's sexually open-minded and lets me call the shots when we're getting busy."

Ben pointed his beer bottle at Sully. "Which is why we both joined this club in the first place. Neither of us was finding that open-mindedness in the regular dating world."

"Don't remind me."

"You need a reminder, because I remember those days, pretending

13

a quick fuck-and-suck hookup satisfied me. I got goddamn tired of feelin' like a deviant for what I did want from the women who shared my bed. So while I understand where you're coming from, I also ain't gonna kid myself that I'll ever find the type of woman I want outside of a club like this."

Sully whistled. "That's a harsh answer."

"But it's a no bullshit answer. It was...liberating when I stopped lying to myself that my membership in this club was temporary."

Sully's astute gaze pinned him in place. "You looking for a permanent sub too?"

"Even if I was, I doubt I'd find one."

"That's not an answer."

"Says the lawyer," Ben drawled. "So, why haven't you asked the redhead out?"

"Scared to. What if I find out she's a kindergarten teacher who reads to the elderly in her spare time?" Sully dropped his voice. "Would I be able to fuck her as hard and raw as I did before? Or what if the attraction only makes sense in the club?"

"I hear ya. Which is why I haven't played with a woman from this club, outside the club, for a while."

"A while?" Sully repeated with confusion.

"Can you blame me after what happened with Zoe?"

"No. Hell, I'd forgotten about her."

"Wish I could," Ben muttered. Zoe had been sweet at first, and he'd even taken her to his house—which was a rarity. Didn't take long to discover she needed far more pain in her sex play than he was comfortable dishing out. Zoe preferred to be caned. Not occasionally, but as a prelude to every sexual encounter. And she hadn't wanted the marks only on her ass; she'd demanded them on her legs, arms and back.

When Ben refused to beat her that severely, Zoe turned nasty, threatening to blab far and wide about Ben's sexual appetites. That's when he'd discovered she lived in his hometown. Ben feared how much damage that type of rumor could do to him—a man who fiercely guarded his privacy, especially within his enormous family and within the conservative ranching community. The only reason she hadn't blabbed was under threat of expulsion from the club. And luckily, she'd been scarce in recent months. Still, Ben had asked himself if the misstep he'd made with her had been his fault. If he'd just talked to her honestly, would it have had a positive outcome for both of them?

The incident reinforced Ben's decision to keep the two halves of himself separate: Bennett, the sexual dominant, and Ben, the laid-back rancher. The women who appealed to Bennett would never find a permanent place in Ben's life. Inside the club he never spoke of his life outside the club.

One thing the incident hadn't changed? The fact Ben liked sexual variety. He liked devoting a few nights to a woman, figuring out what she needed, giving it to her and heightening the sexual experience for both of them. He knew that's why he excelled at domination games: he didn't get complacent. Or attached.

"Earth to Bennett. You still with me, man?"

Ben glanced up from his beer. "Yeah. Just thinking. Wondering what's in store for me tonight."

"I'm so glad you asked," Cody said behind him.

He faced his buddy who owned the Rawhide Bar. "Already planned something for me? I'm hoping it involves a hot blonde and a pair of handcuffs."

Cody snorted. "There's a door upstairs that's sticking, floor trim that's come loose, and a couple other things that are beyond my handyman abilities."

"You been saving shit jobs for me so I'll feel useful when I show up?"

"Fuck no. We all know you're useless." He and Sully laughed when Ben flipped them off. "Seriously, I could use your carpentry skills."

Ben drained his beer. "Let's get it done before the club opens, so floor trim ain't the only thing I'm nailing tonight."

Chapter Two

"What does one wear to a sex club?"

"Speaking as a submissive, I wear whatever I'm told to wear. Or more to the point, what I'm told *not* to wear."

Depressed by her dull clothing choices, Ainsley focused on her friend Layla. "But I'm not a submissive, so am I supposed to adorn myself like a badass dominatrix?"

"Well, Miz Hamilton, did you bring a selection of latex and leather?"

"What do you think?"

"I'd be shocked if a bank executive openly admitted owning fetish wear." Layla smiled impishly. "Besides, the Rawhide Club is a private club, like the Elks Club or the Moose Lodge."

Before Ainsley could retort, Layla bounced off the bed and inspected the clothes hanging in the tiny hotel room closet. "Don't you have a corset?"

She doubted a girdle counted. "No."

Layla rummaged inside her mini-suitcase and tossed out pieces of lingerie. "I have exactly what you need to get appropriately dolled up." She draped a red and black polka-dotted push up bra over her shoulder, then a matching g-string, followed by a lacy black peignoir and a red satin kimono.

"Isn't it a little obvious I'm on the prowl for sex if I waltz in wearing my underwear?"

"Girlfriend, what part of looking sexy to get you hot sex is confusing? That's why this club is in existence."

"So it *is* a sex club."

"Yep."

Ainsley groaned and flopped on the bed. Maybe this was a mistake. Maybe she should've stayed home and organized her spice cupboard.

No. You need to add spice to your life—specifically your sex life—not keep it bottled up in your kitchen.

Layla bounced on the bed beside her. "What's really going on?"

"What if I can't? I mean, what if Dean was right?" *Beg any decent man to tie you up and spank you during sex and he'll be out the door.*

"First of all, your ex-husband was a tool. He blamed you for his...ah...shortcomings."

Ainsley snickered.

"Look, sweetie, we've been friends for a long time. You settled for Dean. You were over thirty, panicked about being unmarried and alone, and picked the first guy who wasn't a total troll. Your sex life with him was as predictable as every other part of your life with him. It wasn't a good match, no matter how hard you tried to convince yourself otherwise."

"True. Thanks for the pep talk."

"The club may not be your thing. But you won't know unless you try it."

"Murphy is okay with me just observing?" The other club she'd visited had strict policies about guest expectations. She hoped she didn't stand out like some wide-eyed wannabe tonight, although technically, she was.

Layla smirked. "I handled Murphy. You are my old friend, Angel, from my banking days." Her phone buzzed and she said, "Give me a minute."

Ainsley's thoughts drifted to her failed marriage as she stared at the hotel room ceiling. During the first year of wedded bliss, both she and Dean were so smug about how theirs was a true partnership. Neither had more control financially, emotionally or physically over the other. They were equals. They both held upper level management jobs in the banking industry. They shared the household chores. They took turns cooking and doing laundry.

The only change during their second year of marriage was their sex life became more perfunctory. But they'd talked about it, Dean assuring her that desire fades. Reminding her that friendship, companionship, open communication, common interests and mutual career goals were far more important than sex.

During their third year of marriage, what Ainsley thought she'd loved about Dean began to drive her crazy. His insistence on

17

everything being a joint decision. From where they ate dinner, to the type of wine they drank, to which place changed the oil in their cars. When he asked for her help in choosing a spring vacation destination, she'd suggested that he surprise her. He argued surprises weren't fun. She argued meticulous planning wasn't fun. That's when they started to argue about a lot of other things.

Ainsley realized while she appreciated some aspects of a well-ordered life, there was something missing in hers. Passion. Excitement. Spontaneity.

One night, in year four, she'd decided to rev up their sex life. She stripped in the living room in front of the TV, dropped to all fours and asked Dean to fuck her from behind.

Flustered by her crude demand, Dean refused.

She tried again a few weeks later, on the way home from a cocktail party. Tipsy and feeling naughty, she tried to give Dean a blowjob in their Volvo.

Flustered once again, Dean refused.

The following month her attempt to entice him into light bedroom bondage using his Brooks Brothers' ties netted the same result: a big fat *no*. As did her suggestion that he punish her wanton, wicked ways with a spanking.

At that point Dean suggested she needed counseling.

At that point Ainsley suggested he needed Viagra.

And that's when their supposedly perfect marriage fell apart. Not only because Ainsley craved variety in the bedroom, but the way she'd voiced her concerns to her husband—he wasn't seeing to her needs—had put Dean on the defensive. He became cruel. Cutting. Condescending. What she saw as an attempt to improve the intimacy in their marriage Dean saw as her attempt to force him into becoming a type of man he wasn't. A type of man he'd never be.

So for all her bold talk, in the last year and a half since her divorce, Ainsley hadn't done a single thing to take charge of her sexuality except increase her collection of vibrators.

One night after an extra glass of liquid courage, she'd asked Layla for advice on how to kink up her sex life. Because Layla's relationship with her longtime squeeze, Murphy, was kinky indeed—Layla was a fulltime submissive and Murphy was her dominant.

It'd been difficult wrapping her head around the concept; Layla willingly ceded control to Murphy in all aspects of her life—not just sexually. When Layla had lived in Denver, Ainsley had known Murphy worked in a club, but not what kind of club. But she'd never imagined a sex club, because she had no flipping clue places like that even existed outside fictional novels.

She planned to get a real education about it tonight.

She scooped up Layla's risqué lingerie and slunk into the bathroom. She stripped and added a piece at a time, ignoring the pooch in her belly. Next week she really had to start working out again. The kimono hit mid thigh and adequately covered her jiggly ass. Five minutes after her thirty-seventh birthday her body had started to sag like an ugly old couch. Not that she'd ever in her life been a toned size two.

Now is not the time to revisit your body issues. Think sexy, act sexy, be sexy.

Once she'd tugged on her outfit, she pinned up her hair, securing it with a hairnet. She unzipped the bag and slipped the wig from the Styrofoam dummy's head, settling it onto her own.

After jabbing a million bobby pins into her scalp, Ainsley angled closer to the mirror, smoothing flyaway strands with her fingers. The sleek wig was shoulder length, coal black with jagged ends dyed blood red. It was funky, hip and fun. No one would mistake it for her real hair, but wasn't that the point of tonight? To be daring and eccentric? She was fully incognito in this get-up. She doubted her cats would recognize her.

Two raps on the door were her only warning before Layla burst in. "Are you... My God, what the *fuck* is that thing on your head?"

Not exactly the reaction she'd hoped for. "I'm embracing my inner Sydney Bristow."

Layla grabbed her upper arms and circled her slowly before stopping in front of her.

"So? Do I look ridiculous?"

"No. It just shocked me. But I've gotta say, the wig is perfect with the clothes I brought. Wow, A, you look fantastic."

"Really?"

"Scouts honor. You always look nauseatingly well put together. I like seeing this other side of you."

"What other side? Nuttier? Sluttier?"

"Younger. More playful. Now don't glare at me. I know you're a professional woman and all, but, girlfriend, there's no reason not to show a little skin after that bank vault closes. You're sporting one of those curvy hourglass bodies that men go wild for."

Wasn't that "hourglass figure" phrase a euphemism for...fat?

"Don't hide it. Flaunt it."

Ainsley wasn't the *flaunt it* type.

Or maybe you are. Age and size ain't nothin' but numbers.

"Let's hit the road. The club is about to open and Murphy is getting all snappy and threatening because I'm not there."

Here was the opening she'd waited for. "Layla, can I ask you something?"

"Yes, I have time to do your make-up before we go." She pointed to the toilet seat. "Sit."

Ainsley closed her eyes when Layla hovered over her with brushes, powders and eyeliner. "Thanks, but that wasn't the question I meant. I want to know about your relationship with Murphy. He seems awfully controlling."

"That's the definition of a dominant."

She struggled to find the wording that wouldn't piss off her friend but would also give her the information she'd always been too shy to ask about. "He doesn't like, hurt you or anything if he doesn't get his way, does he?"

"Are you asking if he beats me if I've done something to piss him off?"

"Yes."

Layla swept a long, wet line of make-up across Ainsley's eyelids near her lash line. "Don't open your eyes for a minute."

"Okay."

"Murphy has never raised his hand to me in anger. It would destroy him to hurt me. But you have to understand that his use of whips, floggers and other instruments are part of our life. I ask him to restrain me and leave welts and marks on my skin."

"Why?"

"The pain takes me to a place where I can truly let go of the control I've tried to maintain in all areas of my life since I was a little girl."

Could a little pain really do that? Make Ainsley forget everything? Allow her to exist solely in the moment? Not worry about anything except when the next smack or lash would land? Why did that appeal to her so much? And why was she so embarrassed to admit that to anyone? She'd even led Layla to believe she wanted to explore her dominant tendencies, when submission interested her far more.

Isn't the whole point of this to learn who you really are? If you're capable of letting go? How can you be honest with anyone else when you're still lying to yourself?

"I've had some bad things in my past," Layla said softly.

"Oh, Layla. I didn't know. I'm sorry."

"No one knew because I excelled at keeping stuff hidden. But it was crippling me. I didn't talk about it at all. My way to deal with it was with physical punishment. Making myself hurt as bad on the outside as I did on the inside. That's how I ended up hanging out at hardcore bondage clubs and letting any man or woman use me as their whipping post. But I'd reached the point where I didn't feel pain. One night I hooked up with a Dom who started to beat me severely and I didn't do anything to stop him. But Murphy stepped in. He became my savior in so many ways.

"After he cleaned me up, he took me to his place. This big bear of a man was a total stranger to me and I felt safer with him than I'd felt with anyone. I slept for twenty-four hours straight. When I woke up, he wouldn't allow me to put up my usual defenses. He talked to me. He made me talk to him." Soft bristles swept over Ainsley's cheekbone. "There was something about his voice that encouraged me, soothed me, made me want to please him, made me trust him. Anyway, I told him things I'd never shared with anybody. Things even I'd forgotten. And after I went through a whole box of tissues after sobbing for hours, and my throat was raw from talking for hours, he scooped me into his arms and just held me. For hours."

Ainsley withheld her questions, hard as that was.

"Murphy had been a Dom for a decade at that point. He'd never considered taking on a sub fulltime until he met me. His brother Rafe is a counselor. After my meltdown I spent time talking to Rafe alone, and with Murphy. While all this soul searching stuff was going on, I fell in love with Murphy." She sniffled. "Totally, completely in love with the gentle giant who had such a code of honor that he didn't touch me at all."

"How long did that last?"

"Six months. Murphy took me to clubs where I could see other kinds of play. Play where a Dom administering pain was a preface for sexual pleasure for the sub. Without getting into too many details, it made me hot. And wet. Two things I'd never felt when the whip scored my skin. When he saw my reaction, he knew I was ready to experience the difference with him. It changed my life. So, the long answer to your question is no, Murphy would never abuse me. He gets me. He loves me. We give each other exactly what the other needs." She sniffled again. "You can open your eyes now."

Ainsley looked at Layla.

"Be honest with me. Why are you interested in experiencing any of this? I see a look of revulsion in your eyes, Ainsley."

"It's more confusion than revulsion. I don't know why some of this appeals to me so much." She glanced away with embarrassment.

"There. That wasn't so hard, was it?" Layla asked.

Yes. "I'm relieved your story has a happy ending. I never understood why you just quit your job so abruptly."

"Maybe it seemed fast on the outside, but things hadn't been going well at the bank for awhile. I was more than ready to walk away and start my life over with Murphy. Our relationship might not be the norm, but it works for us. What is normal? And who the hell has the right to define what it is anyway?" Layla smiled slyly. "And yes, I am happy. And I want you to be happy too."

Ainsley doubted she'd ever find happiness in a man whipping her on a regular basis.

Judgmental much? You're just scared of the unknown.

"Let's go. You're driving." At the door, Layla said, "Oops, I forgot one thing." She handed Ainsley a gold wristband. "Since you're still on the fence about what you want, at least try and act like you deserve to wear this tonight."

Ainsley squinted through the windshield at the building across the street. *Rawhide Bar* was burned into a gigantic wooden sign and outlined with rope-like neon tubing. "This is just a bar."

Layla sighed. "What were you expecting?"

"A buzzing neon sign with an arrow pointing the way to a dark and dirty sex club, hidden in an alley. Scantily clad, red-lipped women smoking cigarettes and eyeing their next sexual conquest while the greasy bouncer swigged from a flask."

"Sorry to disappoint you, but the Rawhide Bar has been here for over a hundred years."

"It has? How's that possible?"

"The Rawhide is two separate entities. The club portion harkens back to the days when a brothel operated out of the hotel side. Of course, they couldn't call it a brothel, so they called it a gentleman's club. The owners charged a membership fee, and the city provided the Rawhide with its own charter that's still in effect today."

"Seriously?"

"Yes. Cody and Trace's great-grandfather was the founder. So when the boys of this generation decided to bring back the club aspect in a discreet and exclusive manner, it was all perfectly legal because the charter never expires as long as an original family member owns the building and business inside."

"I wondered how a place like this survived in a smaller town like Gillette without rousing local suspicions. So neither their father nor their grandfather ran any type of club from here when they were in charge?"

"The Depression hit them pretty hard. Then the country went to war. I guess they had a bi-weekly poker club for a few years in the 50s and 60s, complete with cocktail servers who dressed like Playboy Bunnies. Who knows what else went on in the private rooms? They turned the hotel side into a flophouse in the 70s and 80s during the oil boom. Then after the energy bust, that side sat idle until Cody and Trace's dad retired and moved to Arizona."

"And yet the Rawhide Bar survived?"

"Mostly because it is a regular local bar that anyone can wander into and buy a drink. The club part is completely separate."

Ainsley pulled her coat around her skimpy clothes. "And who makes up the majority of the members?"

"A few locals. Most are from out of town. Some from out of state."

"How do potential new members hear about this place?"

"It's not easy, since members have to sign a bunch of privacy and nondisclosure forms. Clientele recommendations come from managers of clubs like this in other parts of the country. Some members will talk to Murphy about someone they think might be a good fit for the club. Then Murphy investigates them. If he has enough interested parties, we host a guest night. In the last two years we've gained thirty new members."

"No problems with Jim Bob blabbing at the town diner that he saw Betty Sue getting screwed silly by a man who wasn't her husband?"

Layla laughed. "Not in the six years we've been here. But there are stringent rules, because a place like this is so hard to find, especially in rural America. The members are very protective of this place and the people they've connected with here. I know several female members who trust a Dom with a flogger or a whip, but they haven't exchanged last names. First names only. No sharing of personal information unless it's mutually agreed upon. And then only if Murphy is aware they'll be meeting outside the club. There isn't a lot of bullshit because all the members are here for the same thing."

"Which is?"

"Sex with varying levels of kink. Sex without strings."

Ainsley met Layla's curious stare. "What?"

"Nice job distracting me and stalling for time. I bet I sounded like a tour guide, breaking down every single thing and providing historical footnotes." Layla struck a pose. "And here we have a spanking bench covered in the softest cowhide. Look at the manacles, lined with rich Cordovian leather. Only the best at the Rawhide Club."

"Did you notice the words to that TV ditty are kinda dirty?" Ainsley belted out, "Head 'em up, move 'em in, move 'em out...Rawhide!"

Layla groaned. "I am so glad there's no karaoke at this place."

She smirked. "Let's mosey on in and find us a cowboy to ride until our hides are raw."

Chapter Three

Ben was contemplating sub choices when a flash of red caught his eye. He swiveled on his barstool to watch the siren in the silk kimono saunter through the room.

Oh hell yeah, his night had just improved tenfold.

She perched on the edge of her barstool, every inch of her so prim and proper Ben's fingers itched to muss her up.

After he watched her for a few minutes, he asked Murphy, "Who is the hot number in red with Layla?"

"Her name is Angel."

"Angel," rolled off his tongue. Perfect name for her. Sipping his beer, he focused entirely on her. Lush body, lush mouth. Great smile. Expressive eyes. She was off-the-scale sexy in his opinion. So why the hell was the woman wearing a wig? Not a subtle one, but a sleekly styled black wig, the last inch of hair dyed candy-apple red. Was she trying to look dangerous? Hip? Naughty?

Be interesting to coax the truth from her. Some very interesting extraction techniques popped into Ben's head.

She must've sensed him staring at her because she turned and met his gaze head on. Their eyes remained locked for several long moments as Ben waited for her to lower her gaze—as he was accustomed. But she returned his intense eye-fuck full bore until Layla demanded her attention.

Holy shit. Dismissive wasn't a reaction Ben usually got, especially not in here. And that intrigued the hell out of him. Casually, he said to Murphy, "Introduce me to her."

Murphy sighed. "She's not for you."

"Why not? Has she already picked someone for tonight?"

"Not exactly."

Ben faced Murphy. "Then exactly what's the problem?"

A devious smile appeared. "She's not here as a sub."

"She's a guest?" Ben frowned.

"Nope."

"She's here as special entertainment?" That'd explain her wacky get-up. Some clubs in bigger cities had themed nights where members dressed up. Cody and Trace had threatened to try it at the Rawhide, but Ben secretly didn't believe that'd fly in Gillette, Wyoming. Then again, he hadn't been around to voice his opinion in the last month.

"No," Murphy said. "And she's not here to bartend, waitress or clean the bar."

Which left one other possibility but Ben couldn't wrap his head around it. "She's here as a...Domme?" After Murphy nodded, Ben's jaw dropped. "No. Fucking. Way. A Domme. In the Rawhide."

"Evidently."

"And you know she's had experience as a Domme?"

"Some."

The woman's defiant stare-down notwithstanding, Ben demanded, "How much?"

That hard look entered Murphy's eyes. "I've told you as much as I can, *Bennett—*" he emphasized Ben's preferred official club title, "—the rest you'll have to get from her. And you know the rules since you had a heavy hand establishing them, so tread lightly. I have no issue throwing your ass out if you think you're above the rules."

As designated club head master, Murphy screened all applicants thoroughly. He kept the club balanced with the ratio of Doms to subs. He ran the club with an iron fist and a closed mouth. Which sucked balls right now, because Ben wanted to know everything about this supposed Domme.

Of course the goddamn rules came back to bite him in the ass the one time he needed to break one. Besides the first rule—everything that happened in the Rawhide Club was consensual—and the second rule—complete confidentiality and discretion among all members inside and outside the club—there was a third rule that stated—the members who wanted to publicly or privately play decided their own roles within the club: dominant, submissive or switch. Each designation had its own power and demanded its own respect.

But then again...the fourth rule—you pay, you play—meant if she came to the club on a regular night, then she was expected to participate.

Oh hell yeah. He could totally push that rule if it came down to it.

"I don't like the gleam in your eye," Murphy half-snarled.

How could Murphy see that? Because Ben couldn't take his eyes off the intriguing Angel. Hot damn. The sensual way she moved screamed of a submissive enticing a Dom, not a confident Domme luring an entranced sub.

"Bennett?" Murphy prompted. "Are you even listening to me?"

"Yep."

"But?"

Ben drained his beer. "I wanna play with her." It'd been years since he'd had such an overwhelming urge to possess a woman. To tempt, to treat, to teach, to punish...all at the same time.

"The gold bracelet she's wearing means I can't let that happen."

Colored rubber bracelets were how members differentiated their designations. Gold bracelets denoted a dominant and required proof of previous experience as a dominant. Silver bracelets signified a submissive. A white bracelet meant the member was a switch—ready to play either role. A black bracelet meant in a committed relationship and off limits.

However, any member could request to change their designation, after discussing the reason for it, with either Murphy or Cody, the only two officially designated Masters at the Rawhide Club.

"I'm aware of what the bracelet means, Murph."

"Are you?"

"Yep." Ben slipped the bracelet over his hand and slid it across the bar top. "Give me a white bracelet."

"Fuck no. This is ridiculous. Come on. What's the deal with you tonight?"

Cody and Sully sensed tension and joined them at the bar, flanking Ben on either side. Cody spoke first. "Problem?"

"Only that Bennett wants to exchange his bracelet," Murphy said.

"Christ, Bennett, you're that bored with the selection of subs tonight? You're willing to let one of these guys beat you and fuck you?" Sully asked with an edge of sarcasm.

"Fuck no." He rested his elbows on the bar and they followed suit to keep their conversation private. "I don't need to point out the woman wearing the gold bracelet, since she's the only woman I've *ever* seen with a gold bracelet in this establishment. But I know better than to violate club rules and publicly question her right to wear it. So I asked Murphy to clarify why she deserved that status and he refused to provide details."

Cody nonchalantly cast a glance over his shoulder. "I gotta agree with Bennett on this, Murph. The woman is out of her element, and I'll eat my fucking keg tap if she's got any real experience as a Domme."

"Better give us the basics on her," Sully added.

The big man stroked his fingers through his long black beard and looked at each one of them in turn, but spoke to Ben. "I told you. Angel is a friend of Layla's. She's here to see if this type of club would be a good fit for her."

"She's been involved in other clubs like this?"

"According to Layla, yes."

"If that's the case, then where does her previous Domme experience come in?"

Murphy sighed. "I argued with Layla about this, especially after she told me Angel's only Domme experiences were in a controlled setting where she...ah...paid the dude so she could be in charge."

Silence.

"So you're telling me this woman waltzed into *my* club, expecting to be given the gold stamp of approval because she paid some dude from a male escort service to let her boss him around for a few hours?" Cody asked tightly.

Murphy nodded.

"So much for being the master of your house." Sully snickered.

"Layla assured me that Angel only wanted the Domme designation as protection; she didn't intend to use it besides to observe."

"That's an even worse reason for bein' here. She's a poseur," Ben said. "She ain't gonna get any real idea if she can handle this, even on a casual basis, if she can't be honest with herself about what she is." For Christsake, she'd worn a freakin' disguise to the club. "I'll bet you each a thousand bucks she's submissive."

A bet no one took, because in six years, Ben hadn't been wrong even one time.

Cody pointed at Murphy. "You know we can't let her in the club if she ain't gonna play. How the fuck did you ever agree to breaking that rule?"

"Let's just say Layla has a helluva distraction technique and she asked at a...ah, a pivotal moment."

Sully and Cody shook their heads.

"How many nights is she here?" Ben asked Murphy.

"Two. Why?"

"That'll be enough. Get Layla to introduce me."

"Only if you inform my little slave that pushing me to admit her friend to the club as an experienced Domme has earned her a hefty consequence."

"Why do *I* have to tell her?" Ben asked.

Murphy motioned Layla over. "Because she'll sass me. But she never gets away with mouthy behavior around you, Bennett."

Layla sidled up to the bar. "A Bombay Sapphire and tonic and a cherry Coke." Her eyes widened when she saw Ben adjusting a white bracelet on his wrist. "Bennett? You're changing your status?"

"Only temporarily so I can fix your mistake." He invaded her space and spoke softly. "You are in big trouble, Layla."

"But why—"

"Don't pretend you don't know why." He watched her gaze skate briefly to Angel's table.

She dropped her gaze to her hands. "I'm sorry, Sir."

"You will convince Angel to play with me." Ben fought a grin when he heard Layla mutter, "Shit. She is so fucked."

"Not as fucked as you are, my pretty," Murphy warned her. "You will do whatever Bennett demands to ensure your inexperienced friend doesn't wind up in a situation we cannot control."

She muttered, "I should've just given her a damn black bracelet."

"Excuse me?" Murphy snapped.

"Nothing, Sir."

"Murphy will decide your punishment for your coercion in getting your friend admitted to this private club under false pretenses," Ben told her.

Layla shot Murphy a contrite look and he snorted. "Puppy dog eyes ain't gonna get you out of the doghouse, woman."

"Whatcha got planned for our wannabe Domme?" Cody asked Ben.

"Charm, tempt, seduce—convince her to let me be her submissive tonight." He lifted a brow at Layla to get her butt moving.

"Putting your plan into play now, Sir." She grabbed the drinks and flounced off.

"I better go help Trace and Riley set up for tonight," Sully said, stepping away from the bar.

"Make sure room four is saved for me," Ben said.

"Will do." Sully disappeared through the side door.

Cody laughed. "You sneaky son of a bitch. You've picked a no-view room. Don't want any of your fan club chicklets to see the almighty Bennett at a woman's feet?"

Ben offered another cocky grin. "Make no mistake. She might think she's giving the orders, but I guarantee I'll be the one in charge."

The first thing Ainsley noticed as Layla sashayed back was her strained expression. "Is everything all right? Looked a little tense up at the bar."

"It was." Layla sank onto the barstool. "See the buff guy with the dark blond hair?"

Ainsley nodded.

"That's Cody. The bar owner. He asked about you."

Her hand froze above her drink. "He did? Why?"

"Well, you're not exactly inconspicuous in that wig. And you're wearing a gold bracelet. So he asked me if you were a lesbian."

She choked on her gin. "Why would he think that?"

"Historically in this club, gold bracelets are worn by men, because ninety-nine point nine percent of the submissives are female. Cody wondered if you were here to perform a public scene with another woman."

"What?"

"He and the other guys—Doms—wanted to know if you had a specific time in mind for that performance so they could watch."

"But...I'm not... I...can't... I don't like..."

Layla leaned closer. "I know that. So in trying to save your ass from, oh, having a woman willing to go down on you in public in front of a couple dozen horny guys, I told them you were choosy. So choosy in fact, that you might not find a man you want to play with at all tonight."

She noticed Layla no longer wore that smug expression for pulling one over on them. "What else?"

"They reminded me of the club rule: if you pay, you play—regardless if you're a member or a guest. No exceptions."

"But you gave me this gold bracelet so I'd be top of the food chain, so I wouldn't have to play."

Layla bit her lip. "Then you'll have to fake it, A, because the consequences of me lying to Murphy and trying to slide you under their noses as a real Domme?" She shuddered. "Not only will Murphy be mad at me for weeks, it could jeopardize his job. If they think I, a lowly sub, can manipulate him into letting anyone into the club, then they won't trust his judgment. In the bar, or with club business, or with club members." Her eyes shimmered with tears. "So you see the position I'm in."

Guilt sideswiped her. She'd never intended to put Layla at risk. "Okay. I'll do it. If you tell me what to do. What are my options?"

"No chance you'll pick up a female sub just out of curiosity?"

Ainsley shook her head. Not something on her sexual wish list.

Layla glanced around. "More members will show up, but if you insist on a man, you're screwed."

"Please don't use that phrase in this context, okay?"

"There's only one guy I know who...um...isn't a submissive but...um...a switch."

"Meaning he likes men and women?"

"Bennett?" Layla snorted. "God no. He worships women with a single-minded intensity that's slightly scary. He's highly sought after here. And he's very, very picky."

"So why is he a switch?" Since Layla took such a long time to answer, Ainsley suspected her friend's response would be a total lie.

"Sometimes he just wants pain." Layla rattled the ice in her glass distractedly before meeting Ainsley's gaze. "An experienced Dom is the safest way to get it."

"Oh." Not the answer she'd expected. She scanned the guys lounging at the bar. Which one was Bennett? Her gaze passed over the buff blond owner, lingered on the tall, dark and handsome guy in the business suit. Probably not him. The enormous man with the buzz cut was either military or law enforcement, so scratch him too. Ditto for the dark-haired, sinful-looking cowboy with the *strip now* stare and the hard-set mouth. The stocky guy who looked away when their eyes accidentally met?

Bingo. Had to be him.

"I've gotta get my collar on. Do you want me to introduce you to Bennett now?"

"Give me ten minutes to freshen up and—"

"Psych yourself up?" Layla inserted.

"Yes."

"Remember two things. Be confident, not bitchy. Use that eye contact thing we talked about. And have fun! You're living every sub's dream, A, getting to dominate Bennett. Embrace it." She slid off the barstool and scampered to Murphy's side.

Ainsley couldn't look away when Murphy hooked the thin leather collar around Layla's neck. Layla kept her eyes lowered, her head bowed.

A sharp sense of distaste arose. How could Layla, a confident, opinionated, educated woman, allow herself to be treated in such a subservient manner?

Ainsley wouldn't have seen it if she'd slunk away in disgust. How lovingly Murphy's big hands cradled Layla's face. His insistent kiss. In that moment, when Murphy whispered in Layla's ear and brought forth Layla's beaming smile, Ainsley felt...jealous at their obvious connection.

Then she felt ridiculous and marched to the bathroom.

After pacing for five of the ten minutes, freshening her make-up for a couple more, Ainsley stilled. Breathed. Adjusted her scratchy wig. She looked outlandish, but that was the point. No one would ever believe uptight Ainsley Hamilton had the balls to wear this flashy garb.

She raised her chin a notch and practiced a cool-eyed stare. Time to earn a ball-buster reputation.

Revved up and ready, she exited the bathroom—just as Layla led Mr. Brooding Hot Cowboy to their table.

Her stomach cartwheeled.

When he aimed his deeply dimpled smile at her, she stumbled in her three-inch heels, straight into his strong arms.

"Whoa there. You all right?"

Ainsley glared at the floor as if it were responsible for her misstep.

Then she looked up into the bluest eyes this side of heaven.

Holy Mother of God. He was striking. She could not wait to tell this man exactly what to do to her. Her gaze slid to his lips. She had an idea or fifty on how he could use his too-pretty mouth.

Layla interrupted Ainsley's contemplation of his oral skills. "I'll leave you two to make your own introductions."

She hoisted herself onto the barstool and thrust out her hand. "An—Angel."

The dark-haired devil clasped her fingers, lowered his head and kissed her knuckles. "A pleasure, Angel. I'm Bennett. Would you care for another drink?"

"No. Thank you."

She looked at him.

He looked back at her.

Awkward.

"Before we get down to business, can I just say that you have the prettiest skin?" He wasn't content with that verbal caress. He dragged a rough-edged fingertip from the inside of her wrist beneath the bracelet to the bend in her elbow and back down.

Goose bumps danced up that limb, fanning out across her shoulder. Bennett scored points for his seductive touch but lost them when she noticed his smirk.

"So let's set the parameters for tonight's play."

"Is this a negotiation?"

His teasing eyes turned shrewd. "Talkin' about expectations is a club rule, in every club I've ever been in." His gaze lingered on her gold bracelet. "Haven't you found that to be true?"

"Of course I know to discuss the play rules." The lie warmed her cheeks.

His expression didn't change.

He kept watching her. "Stop staring at me," she said crossly.

He lowered his eyes with a murmured, "Sorry."

When another bout of silence stretched, she knew if she didn't get a handle on this situation now, she never would. "Can I ask you something, Bennett?"

"Anything you wish."

"Why the dual role of submissive and dominant?"

"For variety, I suppose. How about you? Why the dominant role?"

"It's a power thing."

"Hmm."

She didn't like his half-cocky *hmm*. "What?"

"If that's the case, I find it odd you're a Domme." Bennett raised those compelling blue eyes to hers. The heat and intensity packed a punch so potent she nearly toppled off the barstool.

Way out of your element, Ainsley.

"See, the true power in a dominant and submissive relationship lies with the submissive. Because the sub cedes all control, it's up to the Dom to make sure all the sub's needs are being met. To give the sub what she—or he—wants."

"What do you want?"

Bennett let his gaze slowly slide down to her cleavage, then back up to her mouth. "I want to please you."

Had any man ever said that to her?

"In that I'll gain my own pleasure. But since you brought up my dual sides, I'll admit I'm not a switch very often. In fact, I'm the lone switch here right now. So if you want to play tonight, I'm your only choice."

And what a fine, fine choice. She tempered her eagerness with an offhand, "I suppose that'll work."

"Good. But there is a catch. You're planning to be here two nights so I'll make you a deal."

"I'm listening." God was she ever listening. His deep, rich voice was as mesmerizing as his deep, rich eyes.

"If I agree to let you be my dominant tonight, then I want you to agree to be my submissive tomorrow night."

Oh no. Oh hell no, automatically popped into her brain.

Stop lying to yourself. Isn't this what you were secretly hoping for? To find a man who could see beyond your façade?

Here was her chance to experience both sides. To see if one really fit her better than the other—or not at all. One weekend out of her life. What would it matter? They'd probably never see each other again anyway. "I accept your terms."

Bennett brought her hand to his mouth and kissed the inside of her wrist. "Thank you. Let's get hard limits out of the way."

Ainsley had no idea what that meant. "You first."

"No other guys in the play. No kissing guys, no blowjobs from guys and definitely no sex with guys. Not that you'd probably get any offers of men in this club wantin' to do me anyway."

"Anything else?"

He scratched his jaw. "I wouldn't be crazy about you donning a strap-on and shoving it up my ass."

Geez. That possibility hadn't crossed her mind. At all. She tossed off a breezy, "I'll take that into consideration."

"Thank you."

Bennett appeared to be waiting for her to lead the conversation. "Layla mentioned you're a switch because occasionally you want pain. And I'll be honest, I'm not comfortable with that."

A dark brow winged up. "Ever? That seems unusual for a Domme."

Rookie mistake. "Not ever, but definitely not on the first play date. So if you're looking for someone to take a cane to your butt...I'm not your dominant tonight."

"What about usin' restraints?"

"Is that what you like, Bennett?"

"No. I prefer to be the one doin' the tyin' up."

Now there was an idea. Tying him to the bed and utilizing his very fine body as her personal sexual playground. "So using restraints is a hard limit with you?"

Bennett gave her a considering look. "No, I guess not. With the exception of you tyin' my junk up in knots. I ain't down with that at all."

She permitted a sly smile. "Good to know. Any other hard limits?" She mentally scrambled to remember specific scenes in the BDSM books she'd read. "Hot wax?"

He shook his head.

"Nipple clamps?"

"Not my fave, but not a hell no."

Think. What else? "Anal beads?"

Wariness entered his eyes. "No way."

"Ice, feathers, a blindfold?"

"Ice? Yes. Feathers? Yes. Blindfold?" Bennett's molten eyes drank in every nuance of her face. "No. I'd rather not wear a blindfold because I wanna watch you dominate me. Bein' at the mercy of a beautiful woman is a total fuckin' turn on."

Her belly gave a little flip.

"Now lemme ask you something, Angel. How would you like me to address you?"

"How do your subs address you?"

"Bennett. Or Sir."

"Not Master?"

He scowled. "No. Only two Masters at the club. And I don't reckon I'd like bein' called that. Ever."

"You can call me Angel or..." Mistress sounded as pretentious as Master so she said, "Ma'am."

"Yes, Ma'am. That'll work fine."

Needing a break from the sexual tension arcing between them, she turned her attention to the crowded room.

She'd expected the club would be comprised of young, thin, beautiful people. But the members were an eclectic mix. Although it appeared none of them had dressed incognito as she had.

A striking redhead flirted with the suit-and-tie-wearing guy up at the bar. Murphy and Layla filled drink orders side by side. The owner worked the door and Ainsley knew he was aware of every single thing that went on inside this room. And wow. Some interesting scenarios were developing.

Action behind a privacy screen, which didn't provide much privacy at all, snagged her attention. The low glow of the lights provided a silhouette of a couple in the throes of a passionate tryst. The woman's head was thrown back and she slowly moved up and down. Arching as the man buried his face in her chest. Their faces blurred together as they kissed. When she tore her gaze away, she realized Bennett had been studying her. "What?"

"I wouldn't mind that. You ridin' me slow. Or fast. I bet this angelic face of yours looks beautiful by candlelight."

Ainsley held his gaze. "Are you always like this?"

"Like what?"

"Smooth."

His finger followed the curve of her jaw. "Make no mistake, I'm a very rough man. And if I had to venture a guess, I'd say you'd prefer to see that side of me." He briefly pressed his finger across her protesting lips. "But not tonight."

Chapter Four

"How about if we head to the back rooms?" Bennett suggested.

None of the sexual tension between them had eased in the last fifteen minutes as they'd watched several scenes and negotiations taking place. She stood, butterflies flapping in her belly.

He invaded her space until they were nose-to-nose, belly-to-belly. "What's wrong?"

Ainsley exhaled slowly, trying not to get sucked into the depths of his blue eyes. "I'm not familiar with the club layout so you'll have to lead the way. Will that be a problem?"

The slow, sexy unfurling of his smile was a sight to behold. "Takin' the lead has never been a problem for me." He clasped her hand in his and maneuvered through the throng of people.

She attempted a sort of clinical detachment as she watched the couples engaged in various stages of foreplay. Dancing, kissing passionately, groping, *hello*—one woman was on her knees, hands secured behind her back while her partner twisted his hands in her hair and slid his cock in and out of her mouth. Pausing to trace the outline of her lips with the tip, then gliding back in. He varied the pace, which caused the woman to groan in disappointment when he only teased her lips.

"You wanna stay and watch this one?" Bennett murmured in her ear.

Yes please. "Ah. No. Why?"

"Because you stopped."

The warmth of his chest heated her spine from the top of her butt to her shoulders and she wanted to rest her body against his fully.

Do it. He's yours to command for the night, isn't he?

The millisecond she eased back, Bennett's hands circled her hips, bringing their bodies closer. "I like the feel of you," he murmured.

No one seemed to care they were watching this guy's blowjob. In fact, two other couples joined. One man played with his woman's breasts, murmuring in her ear while she writhed against his groin. The other woman fell to her knees, ripping open her partner's jeans and greedily stuffing his dick in her mouth.

Ainsley turned her head slightly, drawing in the clean scent of Bennett's skin. "Want to takes bets on who finishes first?"

His low chuckle vibrated down her neck.

The first guy rammed his cock fully into his woman's mouth. His eyes locked to hers as he rasped, "Baby, I love how you do this to me every time."

Okay. Ainsley could admit that was pretty hot. And maybe watching it got her a little hot.

Bennett gently tugged her away from the scene. "There's more to see. Come on."

"How big is this place?"

"Not very, compared to other clubs. There are two public rooms, not counting the main bar and lounge area, and nine private rooms. At other clubs, where the members are heavily into all the trappings of the lifestyle, the wait for a public room is long. Here, the private rooms always fill up first."

She had a million questions she couldn't ask because Bennett assumed she'd been in places like this before.

The hallway divided. He waited for her to choose a direction.

Don't be a mouse. Be a...cougar.

Ainsley boldly looked at his crotch then back up at his face. "So, Bennett. Did you dress left or right tonight?"

His blue eyes heated. "Left. Or maybe it was right. Wanna double-check?"

She managed a laugh. "Maybe later. For now, I'll go with your first answer." She started down the hallway, but stopped at the first open room.

The redhead from the bar was naked except for four inch silver stilettos. Draped over a padded bench, ropes secured her arms, her ass was sticking up in the air, and her legs were split wide enough that Ainsley could see the woman's vulva. From back here. In living color.

She ducked out of sight.

Bennett stepped in front of her, blocking her retreat. "Problem?"

"I didn't want to interrupt. It looked ah...private."

"Nope. This is a public scene. And it just started, so we're in luck."

"But—"

"Don't deny us this experience, Angel."

"What is he going to do to her?"

"Spank her."

"Why?"

"Because she wants it."

Her belly fluttered. She took a step closer to the scene and Bennett was right on her heels.

The man wielding the paddle was the business-suit-wearing guy she'd seen at the bar. He'd ditched the suit jacket and the tie. He'd left the top two buttons of his white dress shirt undone and rolled up the sleeves, revealing muscled, tanned forearms. His left hand smoothed over the woman's curves, from her shoulders to her butt and he spoke to her in a low tone. Ainsley couldn't discern specific words but the cadence was obviously meant to soothe the bound woman.

So the crack of the paddle on the redhead's flesh startled her. It startled the redhead too, if her full body twitch and sharp cry were any indication. Before she could catch her breath, two more blows rained down on each cheek.

The woman jerked against the restraints. The harder she fought, the harder he spanked her. She begged him to stop. He didn't even pause.

Bennett must've sensed her question. "An overseer makes the rounds every ten minutes to check that things don't get out of hand."

"She looks like she's in pain."

"She is. But that's what she wants." His lips brushed the top of her ear. "Would you like that? Your beautiful ass bared for everyone to admire? Letting me run my hands all over it before I spank it? And running my mouth all over it to feel the heat on my face after I spank it good and hard?"

"I..." Good Lord, she couldn't even speak.

"Look at her face. See how it's changed? She's trusting her partner to take her to that point where her body craves the connection of his hand on her ass. Where she only feels the warmth, the pleasure, and the care he's showing her, trusting he'll give her the release he built for her."

With the way Bennett offered a sensual step by step, Ainsley mentally traded places with the woman restrained to the bench. *Her* ass glowed bright red. *Her* head spun as Bennett kissed her crazily, one hand fisted in her hair, the fingers of his other hand thrusting in and out of her hot, wet sex. *Her* shuddering, shaking orgasm reverberated in Bennett's hungry mouth.

She groaned softly, intending to turn away, but her face met Bennett's warm neck. She shifted her legs together as she tried to dodge him, but he wasn't having any of it. He flattened his palm on her lower abdomen, holding her in place.

"Are your panties wet?" he murmured. "What would you do if I slipped my hands under your robe to find out?"

"Don't. Please. Not here."

He half-growled, "I'm allowing it only because you're in charge tonight."

The last thing she felt right now was in charge.

"But if I was wearin' that gold bracelet? I wouldn't give you a choice."

Her whole body trembled. And he knew it.

"Come on. Let's see what else will get you whipped into a frenzy." Bennett kept his hand in the small of her back as they moved down the hallway.

The next room was completely open. It contained a throne-like looking chair, except it had shackles on the armrests and the legs. Alongside that chair was a leather footstool and another spanking bench. Restraints hung down. Hooks and pulley systems were embedded in the ceiling. Chains and ropes were attached to the hooks and pulleys.

A naked, blindfolded woman was bound by a set of chains, her arms stretched above her head, a bar kept her legs spread apart. Two men stood in front of her, sucking on her nipples. Each man had a hand between her legs, one in front, one in back. Needy, desperate sounds came from her mouth through the gag.

"This is one of the more extreme things you'll see. For that woman, the more men involved in the scene, the better."

"M-more than two men?" Ainsley stuttered.

"Yep. I've seen her take six men at one time." His lips skimmed the underside of her jaw, sending tingles down the left side of her body. "Wanna know how that works?"

"No."

He chuckled. "Such a bad liar. You're tryin' to figure out where six cocks are gonna go, so let me set the scene. She'd have one in her pussy, one in her ass, one in her mouth. Another would be fucking her tits. The last two? One in each hand."

Talk about multitasking.

"And she really gets off on the guys comin' all over her. On her face, her tits, her ass."

Again, she was speechless.

"Not your thing?" Bennett asked softly.

"Being coated in come? No."

"What about multiple partners? Does the thought of two men touching you, fucking you, bending you to their will send a shiver of want down your spine?"

"No. I'm more of a one-on-one type, I think."

He placed another soft kiss on the inside of her neck. "That's good to know."

With Bennett touching her and kissing her, Ainsley realized she didn't want to watch what other couples were doing; she wanted to experience it for herself.

"Find a room. Now."

"Come on." Bennett tugged her down the hallway and pushed her into a room. He slammed the door and pressed her against it.

She expected he'd kiss her with unrestrained passion. Tear off her clothes and take her hard and fast against the door.

But Bennett stepped back and waited.

For what? A written invitation?

Right, she was in charge of this scenario. Forced out of lust-filled possibilities, she locked her gaze to his.

"Tell me what you want me to do, Angel."

She didn't hesitate. "Make me come. Fast. Use your fingers or your mouth or even a vibrator. I don't care but do it now."

"Drop the robe."

Her fingers fumbled with the knot at her waist. Then Bennett was there, taking over, murmuring, "You really need this, don't you?"

"Yes." The robe slithered down her back. "On second thought, forget the vibrator. I have a whole collection of them at home."

When he tried to kiss her, she turned away so his mouth connected with her cheek.

"No time for kisses, huh?" His big hands cupped her breasts, then he jerked the peignoir aside and pulled her bra cup down. A rumbling noise reverberated against her breast when he bent and sucked her nipple into his hot mouth.

Ainsley kept her hands by her sides, lost in the silken pull of his mouth and the hot lashes of his tongue. She shifted impatiently, her damp thighs rubbing together, trying to create enough friction to set her off. But it wasn't working. She released a frustrated wail.

Then Bennett's mouth was on her ear. "Don't make me guess, dammit. You're in charge. Tell me what you want me to do to you."

She blindly reached for his hand and shoved it between her legs. "Touch me. Please."

He tugged aside her g-string and plunged a finger into her pussy. Then another. Thrusting in and out, a pleased rumble vibrated in her ear when he realized how wet she was. She pushed her pelvis toward him, wanting more.

Bennett trailed sucking kisses down the side of her neck.

Any attention to her neck made her thrash wildly. She used her shoulder to force his mouth away from her skin.

"Hold still," he hissed.

"I can't. Touch my clit. I'm so close."

Muttering another curse, Bennett slid his fingers free and rubbed the wet digits on her clit. He eased back and suckled her left nipple so hard she felt the bite of his teeth.

That set her off. "Yes. Yes!" Her clit throbbed beneath his stroking fingers, sending tremors throughout her body. When her head fell back, Bennett zeroed in on her neck and sucked.

Her whole body vibrated as if she'd swallowed a live current.

He kept sucking and petting her until her knees gave out. "Whoa there, Angel." He pressed his lower body against the door, keeping hers upright.

When he tried to rest his forehead on her shoulder, she twisted free. "I'm all right."

Trying to regain her mental balance, she sidestepped him and took in the private room.

The bland space didn't look like it belonged in a sex club. Well, besides the gigantic bed. And the swing-like contraption in the corner. And the shackles hanging from the ceiling. Maybe her initial impression had been too hasty.

Air blew down from the vents reminding her of her skimpy attire. Why hadn't Bennett enclosed her in his arms?

Because you didn't ask him to. Or tell him to. You're in charge, remember? He follows your lead.

Which begged the question, what now? Now that she'd so easily, so quickly, so wantonly fallen apart in his arms? Begging him to touch her clit, for crying out loud.

A true Domme wouldn't react with embarrassment. A real Domme would probably...reward him for bringing her to orgasm.

Visualizing herself as that ball-busting woman allowed her to face him with a sultry smile. Her appreciative gaze rolled over his body. "Thank you, Bennett. I guess I needed that more than even I knew."

"It was my pleasure, Ma'am."

"Know what my other pleasure would be? Seeing you completely naked. Strip."

The muscle in his jaw flexed and he made no move to obey.

"Problem?"

"No. I just... No problem at all." His leather vest came off first. Followed by his western shirt. He grumbled something as he toed off his boots, but she was too busy gawking at his near nakedness to pay much heed.

Heaven help her, the man had one of *those* chests. Broad, muscular, masculine perfection with just the right amount of chest hair. Ainsley's eyes followed that trail of dark hair down his torso to the top of his jeans. She watched as he unhooked his belt. Watched as he popped the button loose. Watched as he slid the zipper down. Held her breath as those Wranglers fell to the carpet. Holy mother of all saints the man had the largest dick she'd ever seen outside of porn. She finally chanced a look at his face.

Bennett managed a tight-lipped smile. "Like what you see?"

"I'm sort of half-scared by it, if you wanna know the truth."

"I haven't gotten many complaints."

"I don't imagine you have." She sauntered forward. Her eyes snared his. Then her fist closed around his girth and she squeezed.

He hissed.

Ainsley stroked the hard, heated flesh. "Tell me what you like." He sucked in another sharp breath when her thumb swept beneath the cockhead.

"I like that. But..."

Her hand didn't stop moving, her eyes never wavered when she asked, "But what?"

"But I'd rather fuck you. I'd rather watch you get off again."

Something about his response seemed rehearsed. Something about the too-bright look in his eyes told her that he wasn't used to being manhandled. Which made sense, if his reason to switch to submissive was to feel pain. His submissive role tonight wouldn't be the same as other times.

She rolled to the tips of her boots and pressed her lips to his. "As delighted as I am by your selfless sentiment, Bennett, it's not your decision, is it?"

A tiny flare of anger replaced the pleasure in his eyes. "No."

"No what?"

"No, Ma'am."

"Good answer." Ainsley angled her head to feel his downy chest hair brush her cheek. She nuzzled his pectoral, breathing in his warm, earthy scent. He groaned when her questing mouth found his nipple. She licked the disk, dampening the hair around the hidden tip, using her teeth to tease the tiny nub as she increased the stroking motion of her hand.

"God. Dammit."

She upped the tempo, switching to shorter, harder strokes.

"Ah fuck."

"Stop swearing at me."

"Sorry it just feels so... Shit, it feels so fuckin' good."

She smiled against his chest. "Tell me how close you are."

"Embarrassingly close."

"Why are you embarrassed?"

"Because my stamina is usually... Christ, do that again."

"This?" Her middle finger slipped between his damp balls on the down-stroke. "Or this?" Her thumb traced the wet edge of his cockhead above the sweet spot on the upstroke.

"Both. God! Dammit."

She sucked hard on his nipple as she jacked him. "Tell me what you want, Bennett."

"Don't stop. Faster. Yes. Just...like that." He humped her hand and swore a blue streak as he came in hot, short bursts.

Ainsley watched his cock as he erupted, feeling a heady sense of triumph. Triumph and power. And heat. Getting him off had turned her on again.

Then Bennett's hand curled around her jaw, forcing her head back. His eyes were still pleasure-clouded when he murmured, "Thanks."

She playfully squeezed his softening cock one more time just to see that warning look flicker in his eyes. "Stay put. I'll be right back."

After washing her hands, she wet a washcloth with warm water, intending to clean him up. But she handed it to him instead. It seemed too intimate, touching him in the aftermath.

But she did watch. She'd never known seeing a man handle himself could be so sexy.

He tossed the rag aside. "Did it turn you on, getting me off?"

Was it that obvious?

"Let me take care of you. Let me get you off again. This time with my mouth."

Her pussy throbbed a happy *yes*. It'd been a long time since she'd seen any tongue action. A really long time. But she also knew Mr. Charming and Persuasive Bennett would push for more if she gave in without restrictions. "You are such a silver-tongued devil."

"Is that a yes? You want me to prove how well this devil can use his tongue?"

"Of course it's a yes...just as soon as you put your clothes back on."

That stopped him short. "What? Why?" His mouth remained pursed, intending to argue.

"Is that a problem?"

"Not at all."

"Not at all...what?"

"Not at all, Ma'am."

Yeah, she was totally loving this power thing.

She sat in the armchair, watching him get dressed. Such a pity to cover up that magnificent body.

His smooth movements belied the annoyance in his eyes. His boots barely made a sound as he crossed the room. Her heart thumped when he dropped to his knees.

They stared at one another for a very long minute.

"Take off your panties."

In one fast, and hopefully sexy move, Ainsley whisked off the g-string.

Then Bennett circled his fingers around her ankles just above her shoes. His hands glided up her shins, over her knees and up the inside of her thighs. He tapped the outside of her hips. "Scoot down so I can reach all of you."

That's when she panicked, the reality of her wet sex up close and personal in Bennett's face, as well as her fat white thighs, rounded belly and big butt. Shoot. Maybe she should insist he shut the lights off.

"You want a play-by-play?"

Bennett's voice startled her. "A what?"

"Do you want me to talk about how badly I want to bury my face in your pussy? Of how perfect and sweet it tastes? How fuckin' hot it is that you're so wet?"

Instead of purring, "Oh yeah, you can keep up that sweet dirty talk all night," she let her confusion show. "Why would I want that?"

"Just a guess, because you haven't given me any instructions about what you *do* want."

Another rookie mistake. She gave him a haughty, "What I want is to come. Think you can handle that?"

He made a primitive noise and lowered his head to kiss the rise of her pubic bone. The cheeky man looked up at her when his tongue danced across her clit.

At the second swipe of his clever tongue she abandoned the idea she had any control in this situation at all.

He slid his tongue down the seam of her sex. Circling the opening and plunging inside. Licking. Sucking. A wiggling maneuver that made her gasp.

Her body twitched against the barrage of sensations. His rough-tipped fingers spreading her open. His short hair teasing the swell of her belly. His wickedly wonderful tongue was a constant reminder of how much she loved oral sex.

Not that she'd ever experienced oral sex like this.

The man teased and tormented. He built her to the detonation point, and backed down, just because he could.

And then he sent her soaring.

Her clit pulsed against his sucking mouth. She let her head fall back and shamelessly reveled in every glorious throb. Once the storm inside her calmed, she tried to scoot back up to conceal her lower half, but Bennett wouldn't allow it.

"Don't close yourself off from me. Every part of you deserves to be worshipped." He kissed her knees. "I want to worship your body with mine tonight. All night."

That comment sounded far too practiced. She placed her hands on his face to stop his marauding mouth. "Hold on there, slick. I don't know if that's in the cards."

Bennett truly appeared confused. "Why not?"

"Because I'm in charge, remember?"

"Right. Sorry, Ma'am."

The man didn't look the teeniest bit repentant.

Ainsley stood and discreetly put on her g-string. "While I'm considering our options, I could use a stiff drink."

"Let's head back to the main room so we can talk."

She trembled when his warm, insistent lips followed the slope of her shoulder as he helped her put on her robe.

His huskily whispered, "I like the way you tremble in my arms," only caused her to tremble harder.

They'd exited the room and reached the end of the hallway, when the owner shouted, "Bennett! There's a malfunction with the pulley system in room nine. I need your help."

Bennett sighed. "I'll meet you as soon as I'm done, okay?"

Ainsley strolled into the crowded main room, feeling out of place. Her little bit of confidence evaporated. Too many people surrounded her. Too much had happened in such a short amount of time. She needed to clear her head and she couldn't do it here.

Without saying goodbye to anyone, she slipped into the night.

Chapter Five

Ben couldn't believe Angel had snuck out of the club last night.

Yes, you can. And you don't expect to see her tonight either.

That would suck.

After he didn't find her cooling her heels in the bar area, he scoured the entire club for her. Layla had sworn she hadn't seen Angel leave. When he pressed for more information, Murphy stepped in, reminding him of the club rules. He'd managed not to snap, *fuck the club rules*, which would've gotten him thrown out on his ass and banned for the weekend.

He'd nursed a beer, watching dispassionately as two of his sometime playmates ended up with Trace and Riley. Then he'd headed to Cody's place and crashed.

Ben figured it made him a fool, waving off a constant stream of subs tonight, as he waited for Angel to show up. The woman flat out fascinated him. Her boldness in lying about her Domme designation. Her wide-eyed reaction to the scenes she'd witnessed. Followed by her moments of true Domme-like behavior. The way she jacked him off and made him clean himself up. Her insistence he put his clothes back on when he so obviously wanted to fuck her.

But what really tripped him over the edge for her? Her genuine surprise at her body's response to him. Allowing her to believe she'd been in control last night told him exactly what he'd suspected: she was submissive to the core.

She'd be a challenge. Ben couldn't remember the last time he'd been challenged by a woman, inside or outside the club. His last four regular playmates hadn't posed any challenge.

Zoe had been a trial.

Ali had been too eager to please, a lifestyle sub in training.

Lorena had needed submission as therapy; they'd mostly talked.

He considered his one-nighters a fun way to pass the evening. A little bondage, a little practice with his toys, a chance to hone his skills with a whip, flogger, cane and crop.

Talk about clinical. And cynical. Now he remembered why he'd stayed away from the Rawhide in the last month. He needed to shake off his attitude. But if Angel didn't show up tonight, he wouldn't stick around.

Ben looked around the room at the tables of couples, some already in play roles, some still negotiating. Sully, sans his usual lawyerly suit, was propped against the wall in overseer mode. Neither Cody nor Trace was around. Gil was behind the bar.

His gaze scanned the crowd. He froze when he spotted Angel, watching him from a corner table. How long had she been there?

She studied him for several long minutes. Then she stood, gracefully slipping from her chair. She started across the room. Stopped halfway. The distance between them seemed to increase with his every heartbeat.

It was damn difficult not to swoop her up and carry her off, but he waited for her to come to him.

He didn't bother to hide his grin when she threw back her shoulders, lifted her chin and strode forward.

Good girl. See? That wasn't so hard.

Angel slid into the seat across from his. "Hello, Bennett."

"You came." *Smooth, McKay.*

"I said I would. I've been here awhile. Watching you."

"See anything interesting?"

She cocked her head. "Besides the dozen women who approached you? I was waiting for one of them to drop down and lick your boots."

"Wouldn't have mattered if one of them had."

"Why not?"

"Because I'm not interested in anyone but you."

Tension thickened the air.

How was it possible she was more alluring than he'd remembered? She'd donned the wig again, but her make-up wasn't as severe. Her facial structure was a study in contrasts, wide angular lines that emphasized her dainty feminine features. Apple cheeks, big hazel eyes framed by long, dark lashes, an upturned nose. She looked soft and angelic, except for her mouth. Goddamn those pillowy lips were made for nights of red-hot sin.

"You skipped out last night." Ben placed his hand over hers to stop her nervous finger tapping. "But you're here now and that's all that matters."

"I don't have the foggiest idea what that means."

It means you're mine tonight.

She squirmed as if he'd said those words aloud.

He kissed her palm. "It means you and I are about to swap bracelets."

Those bewitching hazel eyes widened.

"Don't look so surprised. That's why you came back, isn't it? You're curious about how it'll be with me."

"And scared," she added softly.

He stilled. "You're scared of me?"

"A little. I'm more scared of my reaction to you. You're just so...different from any man I've ever been with. I mean, look at you." She touched him then, without conscious thought.

He studied her eyes as the tips of her fingers explored his face. Gently sweeping over his cheekbones. Tracing his jaw from the bottom of his earlobe to the dent in his chin. Innocent caresses that instantly gave him a hard-on.

"Such a stern look on such a handsome face," she murmured as her thumb outlined his lower lip. "I prefer your heart-stopping smiles to your scowls. But I imagine I won't see many smiles from you tonight, will I?"

Lightning fast, Ben trapped her face between his hands. "You'll see plenty of smiles from me tonight." He pressed his mouth to hers, letting the kiss linger, but not taking it deeper.

A delicate shiver rippled through her. When she attempted to retreat, he let her.

"It's time." He removed the white bracelet and slid it across the table.

She removed the gold bracelet and exchanged it for the white one.

"Now. Let's talk about hard limits," he said.

"No other players."

"Understood."

"No public scenes between us."

That put a kink in his kinky plans. "You're sure?"

"I'm positive."

"How do you know you won't like it until you've tried it?" he countered.

She shook her head. "That's a hard limit. No exceptions."

"Fine. What else?"

"No anal."

"Have you ever experimented with it?"

Two bright pink spots appeared on her cheekbones. "No. And I don't want to start tonight."

"Okay. What about bondage?"

"Yes, because I assume you know what you're doing with ropes and such?"

"I've had a few years of practice. Anything else?"

"No. But if something you're doing makes me uncomfortable..."

"Use your safe word and I'll stop immediately. But keep in mind it's not for casual use."

"Gotcha."

"The public club safe word is red. You should have a personal one too. So what is yours?"

Her nose wrinkled. "Broncos."

"Why?"

"I hate that team."

Ben grinned. "Guess you and I won't be watchin' football together any time soon, since that's my favorite team."

She didn't crack a smile. She fidgeted as if debating something.

"Ask me the question."

Her startled eyes zoomed to his. "How did you know what I was thinking? Oh right. This isn't your first rodeo, is it, cowboy?"

"Nope."

"What if I don't meet your expectations?"

Like that'd ever happen. "My list of expectations is short. One, complete honesty between us at all times. Two, keep an open mind because I'll push you more than you'll expect. Three, you don't just up and leave when we're done. We *will* talk about everything that goes on between us tonight and how you feel about it. Especially important this first time." He threaded his fingers through hers. "Much of what happens between a dominant and a submissive is psychological, not just physical. I need to know you ain't gonna bail on me the second I undo your restraints."

"I won't run out. I promise."

"Good. Now, would you like a drink?"

"Yes, please. Bombay Sapphire and tonic."

"I'll be right back."

"Don't they have waitstaff?"

"No. Keeps interruptions to a minimum. If members want a drink they can get it themselves."

Gil already had a bottle of Ben's brand of beer out when he approached the bar. "What does the lady want?"

Ben told him and waited, taking a sip from his beer. When Gil returned, Ben asked, "What time are Murphy and Layla doin' their thing?"

"Any minute now. Same place they always use."

"Thanks." Ben wondered if he should tell her about the scene. Could Angel handle seeing her friend publicly whipped and fucked? He took the chair beside her.

She said, "What's wrong?"

"That." He pointed at her drink. "You know that stuff looks like watered down glass cleaner, right?"

"Doesn't taste like it." She sipped. "If the honesty thing applies to you, tell me what's put that wrinkle in your brow?"

Astute little sub. "Murphy and Layla are doin' a public scene."

"That's not normal for them?"

"No. Some couples give up exhibitionism once they're in a committed relationship."

"So why are they doing this?"

"Layla got herself into a bit of trouble last night."

Her eyes widened. "Is it because of me?"

"In a way. Layla never should've lied to Murphy to get you into the club. It was her choice, so she has to deal with the consequences. Their scene will be about punishment."

She paled. "Seriously?"

"Yeah. So we can stay here until it's over. Or we can go find a room right now."

"You suggesting I hide? Even though it's partially my fault she's being subjected to punishment?"

"It's not your fault. Layla isn't a novice to the lifestyle, Angel. You are."

"Will it be bad?"

"I swear to you Murphy won't hurt her beyond what she can handle. But the whole point is to remind her of her submissive, not subversive, role in his life."

Determination flitted through her eyes. She drained her drink. "I want to watch."

Brave girl. "Just as long as you understand you cannot interfere. Period."

"I won't."

Ben left his unfinished beer on the table. Clasping her hand, he led her through the crowd, taking a left at the hallway.

Two dozen people were in front of the medieval room. He nudged her to a space in the middle of the crowd, wrapping his arms around her upper body, unsure if he meant to hold her up or hold her back.

She gasped softly, seeing Layla in chains, arms above her head, a spreader bar keeping her legs apart. Her naked back faced the audience. Murphy wielded a single tail whip.

Layla stuttered, "F-fourteen, Sir."

Welts decorated Layla's back. Murphy didn't move as he cracked the whip again; the tip scored the tender skin on her left side.

Angel jumped and Ben held tight. "This part is almost done," he murmured. "Murphy never does more than twenty strikes."

Layla counted, her voice staying strong. But Murphy didn't look happy when he leveled the final blow. He put the whip aside and stood in front of his submissive, forcing her to meet his gaze as he unhooked the manacles from her wrists. Then he nodded at Sully, who rolled a pommel up front.

Layla said something to Murphy and he snapped, "That earned you another ten." He hoisted her off the floor, placing her torso on the modified pommel horse. Her head and arms dangled on the opposite side, which left her ass sticking up in the air. With her legs spread by the bar, her pussy and her anus were totally exposed to all who watched the scene.

Murphy restrained Layla's arms and snagged a paddle off the cart.

He grabbed a fistful of her hair, raising her head. "Twenty swats. You will count them down from twenty. And if I'm not convinced you've learned your lesson, I will add twenty more from the cane. Are we clear?"

"Yes, Sir."

He moved behind her. He swung, the paddle connected with her skin, high on her left butt cheek.

"Twenty. Thank you, Sir."

The next blow hit in the same place.

"Nineteen. Thank you, Sir."

The next blow lower. Each blow precisely placed so every inch of Layla's ass was cherry red.

But that wasn't all that was red. Ben murmured, "Look at her pussy. See how wet and swollen it is? These last ten aren't punishment for her. They're her reward for takin' the punishment. Understand?"

She nodded against his neck.

Murphy bellowed, "I can't hear you, sub. Louder."

"Three. Thank you, S-sir."

Layla's voice had taken on a dreamlike quality. The last two blows landed so close to her cunt she moaned. When Murphy finished, he tenderly smoothed his hands over her abraded ass. But Layla barely stirred. He dropped his pants. When he reached for the strap-on, murmurs rippled through the crowd.

Murphy squirted lube on his cock and on the phallus centered above his cock and stroked both. He drizzled more lube between her butt cheeks. Using both hands, he aligned the dildo to her asshole and his cock to her cunt and shoved both in deep.

Layla's head came up and she wailed.

"Is he..."

"Fucking her ass and her pussy at the same time."

She said, "Oh God," but she didn't avert her eyes from watching Murphy master Layla. Murphy slowed his thrusts, sped up and reached around Layla's thigh to toy with her clit.

She wailed again. "Please, Sir."

"Say it, Layla. Say it and I'll let you come."

"I'm sorry," she sobbed. "I'm sorry I disappointed and embarrassed you."

"That's what I wanted to hear. You've earned this." He fucked her harder, moved his hand faster. "Come for me."

And Layla did. Her body convulsed. She screamed, but they weren't screams of pain.

Murphy kept reaming her until her body went completely slack. He slowed, leaning over her to place a tender kiss on her back. He pulled out and bent down, releasing the spreader bar from between her ankles. After pulling up his pants, he crouched in front of her and cradled her face in his hands. Wiping her tears, murmuring to her, smoothing her tangled hair from her face, kissing her with tenderness and fire. He unhooked her restraints and scooped her into his arms, kissing the top of her head as he carried her into a private room and shut the door.

Watchers started to scatter.

His sub had craned her head to look at the closed door, so Ben couldn't read her eyes.

When he placed an openmouthed kiss on her shoulder, she tried to get free from him. "Hey now. Easy."

"I can't... I never...God. That was... I have to..."

Then his sub raced down the hallway like the hounds of hell nipped at her heels.

Chapter Six

Ben caught up with her in front of room four. "Whoa. Where you goin'?"

"I don't know."

"Talk to me."

"I can't. Not here."

He herded her into the room.

Immediately she retreated to a corner and sent off don't-touch-me vibes.

This isn't the first time you've dealt with a skittish sub.

"Angel? Are you upset about the scene with Murphy and Layla?"

"Not upset. It horrified me. I can't believe I stood there and watched him whip her. She tried to explain to me why the hurting stuff was part of their life, and I thought I understood, but obviously I didn't."

Ben didn't remind her everything was consensual. He just watched her pace as her mind raced.

"But no one around me was horrified. So when Murphy finished whipping her and switched to the paddle, it didn't seem as horrible. Mostly because I saw the change in Layla's body language. And it wasn't like Murphy noticed it too; it was like Murphy had *caused* the change in her. And each time that paddle connected, I could almost feel her calmness and bliss floating over me."

Sweet sub, you really are starting to get it.

"But Murphy didn't use sex for shock value for the people watching. He used it because Layla needed it. And I'll admit it was pretty hot watching him, especially with two..." she gestured distractedly, "you know. I've never believed a woman could scream from an orgasm. But it wasn't like a porn scream, it was a *you touched my soul* type scream."

She stopped by the door with her hands clenched at her sides, her eyes closed. "But when Murphy knelt in front of her, the gratitude, love and admiration in his eyes for Layla was far from horrifying. It was beautiful. And I never would've believed any of this if I hadn't seen it firsthand. If they hadn't let me be a part of something so intensely personal for them."

Ben had known Angel was smart, but that didn't guarantee she'd be intuitive. It also didn't guarantee she truly knew what she wanted. He waited for her to regain her balance. The longer he waited the more he realized her epiphany wasn't making her happy. In fact, she seemed to have closed herself off from him again.

He crowded her against the door, relying on the power of his voice, not his body, to keep her in place. "Talk to me."

Her haunted hazel eyes burned with indecision.

"Is there something else about Murphy and Layla's scene that's bothering you?"

"Yes. No." Her gaze fell to his chest. "It's something I realized about myself while watching it."

"What?" Ben expected loss of eye contact would encourage her to speak openly, but she remained mute. "Answer me."

Her voice was barely a whisper. "I can't ask you."

"Can't ask me to do what? Fuck you? Whip you?"

"I don't want to be whipped. Ever." She gnawed on her lip.

"Still waitin' for an answer, Angel."

"Fine. I can't ask you to spank me."

"But you liked watching that redhead get her ass smacked last night." That's when Ben understood. "You need me to take the choice away completely. Like Murphy did with Layla. You need me to decide when to paddle your ass."

She nodded, a bit shyly.

"I don't like usin' a spanking as punishment."

"I'm not usually much of a rule breaker anyway, so see my dilemma?" She peered up at him. "I'd be worried you'd use more than your hand on me."

"There's no need for you to worry because it'd be my decision."

She pursed her mouth into a scowl.

"Ah-ah. None of that." His lips grazed the plumpness of hers, hovering a breath away, waiting to swoop in and claim the kiss she'd denied him last night.

This time when she opened her tempting mouth, Ben denied her a kiss. Moving his lips to the tip of her chin and cruising up the left side of her jaw. He nuzzled her ear, licking, blowing, nibbling. The more he nuzzled, the harder she squirmed. Coarse hair brushed his cheek and he itched to remove the wig, so she wasn't hiding anything from him.

Her fingers inched up his chest and she clutched his shirt.

"Hands by your sides," he reminded, nipping her neck.

She gasped, twisting away from his mouth.

"Stay still." His tone turned sharp and he forced her hands back down.

"I-I don't know if I can."

"Not a request." When Ben sank his teeth into the section of skin between her shoulder and throat, her knees buckled and she shoved him away hard.

Her mouth was open in shock when she realized what she'd done. She took a defensive posture, wrapping her hands over herself, attempting to melt into the wall. "Sorry. God, I'm sorry, Bennett. I forgot for a second."

"Then it's time I give you a very clear reminder about who's in charge." He uncurled her fingers from her biceps, forcing her hands by her sides. "Repeat after me. Bennett is in charge of me tonight."

"Bennett is in charge of me tonight."

"Say it again. Bennett is *completely* in charge of me tonight."

A spark of irritation darkened her eyes but she repeated, "Bennett is *completely* in charge of me tonight."

"Good. But because you inappropriately used your hands, you've lost the use of them for as long as I see fit."

"What? No. That's not fair—"

Ben got right in her face. "Keep it up and I just might rethink my stance on not usin' spanking as punishment for talkin' back. Understand?"

She swallowed hard. Then nodded.

"Turn and face the wall."

She didn't hesitate at his command. She didn't move when he unzipped her corset and tossed it aside. She didn't protest when he tugged her leather skirt down her legs, leaving her in a tiny peach lace thong and the three-inch black patent leather pumps.

But she did tremble when he rested his hands on her hips. "You're shaking." He pressed a kiss on the slope of her shoulder. "Why?"

"Because I don't know what happens next."

"But it's exciting, isn't it?" Ben slid his hands up the front of her body. Over the soft curve of her belly. Pausing to cup her breasts. Stopping to place his thumb on the erratic pulse pounding in her neck. "What's your safe word?"

"Broncos."

"Do you want to use it now?"

A pause, then, "No. Sir."

Ben twined his fingers with hers and towed her away from the wall. At the end of the bed was a leather foot bench, the perfect height, length and width for what Ben had in mind. He dragged it to the middle of the room.

"Sit." He opened the top dresser drawer and removed the items he'd need.

She remained in a prim and proper pose. Her head wasn't bowed and her eyes seemed mighty interested in what he held in his hands.

He stepped so close she had to widen her knees to accommodate him, grinning down at her because her mouth was level with his cock. "So, what do you think I'm gonna do?"

Her gaze traveled up his torso until their eyes met. "I think you'll unzip your jeans so I can give you a blowjob."

Ben's smile faded. He crouched until they were eye-to-eye. "Last night, when you were playing at bein' a Domme, whose pleasure were you more concerned with? Yours? Or mine?"

"Mine."

"And that's where you went wrong, Angel. That's how I knew you weren't truly a Domme. Bein' dominant isn't about takin' what you want."

Her cheeks reddened and she looked away.

"Eyes on me, please."

Her gaze winged back to his.

"Bein' dominant is about figuring out what the submissive needs. It's about trust. Tonight, as your dominant, you're trusting me to give you what you need, maybe even when you don't know what that need is."

"And you know what I need?" she asked with an edge of surliness.

He nodded.

"How? You don't even know me."

"That's where you're mistaken. I've been observing you since I first saw you. Before we even talked I watched you. While you were sizing me up, I watched you. And last night when we walked through the club? I studied your reaction to every scene and your response every time I touched you. When I had my hand between your legs getting you off, I watched you. When I had my mouth between your legs, makin' you come? Well, I really watched you then. So I may not know your favorite kind of ice cream, or the name of the street you grew up on, or your birthday, but I guarantee that I've learned things about you that'd surprise...even you."

Her eyes never left his as she processed his words. He could practically see her backtracking, trying to remember how much of herself she'd given away.

"What?"

"I was an awful Domme, wasn't I?"

"Not awful. Just confused about the difference between power and control. So let me show you." Ben smooched her mouth. "Lay back and let your arms fall to the floor."

She straddled the bench and stretched out. "Like this?"

"Nope. Scoot down so your head is almost hanging off the end. Now move your feet until they're right beside the bench legs. Yep. Perfect." Ben dropped the straps on the floor and trailed the ends of the silk scarves up her sumptuous body. Starting at her knees, zigzagging across her exposed flesh, swirling around her nipples, watching the tips constrict. "Such a gorgeous body. I love seein' you nekkid. Once I start touching you I won't wanna stop."

The tensed line around her mouth softened.

Ben lowered to his knees. "Relax your shoulders." He twined the red scarves from her elbows to her wrists, immobilizing her arms.

The height of her heeled shoes only allowed him to tie her legs from mid-calf to ankle. He ran his palms up the inside of her thighs. "Your skin looks so pretty wrapped in red silk."

She lifted her chest when he secured the first strap above her hips. "What are you doing?"

"Tyin' you down so you can't jerk away from me when I touch you." He secured the next strap above her breasts. "Stay still. If you move too much the strap will bite. I don't want these beautiful breasts bruised."

"Will it pinch me more than it is now?"

He traced the edge of the strap from one armpit to the other. "If you arch too high. And the only thing allowed to pinch these sweet babies is me." He tweaked both nipples simultaneously.

She gasped. "Bennett, I don't know about this."

He studied her reaction to being bound. Rapid breathing. Slight trembles. But she wasn't attempting to jerk against any of the restraints. "Are you afraid I'll hurt you?"

"Umm. No."

His index finger trailed from the dip in her chin, down her neck, between her breasts, passing over her belly button, stopping at the swollen folds hiding her clit. "Are you afraid I'll make you lose control?"

When she turned her head away, Ben gently grabbed her chin, forcing her attention on him. "Answer me."

"Yes, okay? I'm scared you'll make me lose control. You've already got me tied up so I can't move. When you start to touch me I'll probably beg you to make me come."

"So?"

"So, that's embarrassing."

"Oh, little control freak, there's no one here but us. There's nothin' embarrassing about you begging me. Every time you come by my hand or by my command, it'll show you how in tune I am with your body." Ben's thumb stroked her bottom lip. "That's not embarrassing. That's how it's supposed to be."

"You won't...build me to the point I'm begging you and then stop? Just because you can?"

Was this a brand-new fear? Or had some mean fucker in her past gotten his kicks by denying her an orgasm? "Makin' you come is a rush for me, so if I deny you that, I'm denying myself. But I ain't gonna lie. Sometimes delaying that gratification intensifies it. For both of us."

They measured each other for another minute.

"Say your safe word if you wanna stop."

"I don't want to stop."

"Then we're done talkin'." Watching her eyes, he slid his finger down her slit. The wetness he found at her core didn't surprise him, but she wore that look of embarrassment. He pushed his finger inside her. "Don't be ashamed of how your body responds to me."

Ben slipped another finger inside, using his thumb on her clit. The feminine heat and wetness made him want to sink his cock into her now. But he painted a trail up her body with his wet fingers instead, lapping the sweet stickiness with his tongue. He smeared her juices on her nipples, then sucked it off slowly. One side at a time. While his mouth was busy, so were his hands. A teasing brush of his fingertips across her belly. Caressing the deeply contoured sides of her body from hip to armpit. Skimming the outside of her legs. Grazing the inside of her thighs. But never touching her sex directly.

Much to her squirming displeasure.

He focused his attention upward and knew the instant she realized his intention.

"No. Stop. I can't—"

"Relax your neck." He firmed his lips and followed that swan-like curve from the sweet spot behind her ear to the hollow of her throat.

A full body shiver rolled through her. "Please. Don't."

"You're really that riled up about me kissing you here?" Ben bestowed a warm, soft kiss to the side of her neck. Then he parted his lips and scraped his teeth across it.

She bucked up with a sexy whimper.

Breathing in the scent of her passion-warmed skin, he dragged openmouthed kisses from the sweep of her shoulder, up and down both sides of her neck, back and forth from her jawbone to her clavicle.

She tried to block him, raising her shoulders and angling her head into his face whenever he got too close. After her cheekbone smacked into his nose, he warned, "Hold still, goddammit."

"No. Don't. I can't take any more."

"Am I hurting you?"

Eyes closed, she nodded.

Liar. "Then say your safe word."

A couple of heartbeats passed before she shook her head.

Which meant her mind protested but her body didn't. That was his goal for tonight—to get her mind and her body on the same wavelength.

Ben cupped her sex. Wetness coated his fingers. Yeah. Her body wasn't objecting at all. Keeping his hand covering her pussy, he zeroed in on the hot spot on the left side of her neck.

She jerked on the restraints, arching and tossing her head, narrowly missing a collision between her sharp chin and his forehead.

Enough.

He pressed one hand to the top of her head; his other hand gripped the base of her throat.

Her eyes were panicked and if she hadn't been restrained, Ben suspected he'd see skid marks on the carpet from her hasty departure.

"Breathe. Do you understand I'm not gonna hurt you?"

Took a second, but she nodded, purposely inhaling slowly and deeply.

But her neck was so rigid he worried it'd be sore. "Relax. Talk to me."

"Take your hand off my neck, unless you plan to choke me out with auto-erotic-asphyxiation for your next trick."

He laughed. "Trying to piss me off to see if I'll give up on you and untie your binds?"

She seemed surprised he'd picked up on her intentions.

"Tough luck. I have half a mind to just let you squirm and thrash around like a bull in a buckin' chute. Wouldn't be long before this wig was laying on the floor. And wouldn't that be interesting?"

That definitely got her attention.

"Why are you so damn squirmy whenever I touch you here?" He stroked the cord straining in her neck.

Her jaw clenched.

He brushed his lips over hers. "This would be a good time to practice that honesty thing, bein's you ain't goin' nowhere unless I let you."

"Fine. My whole neck is super sensitive. One touch on it, one whisper across it and I'm a mass of goose bumps. So when you kiss my neck like you were? I feel like I could come from just that."

"And that's a problem...why?"

"It's embarrassing."

"Huh-uh. Try again."

"My head gets fuzzy. It makes me..."

"Lose control. Guess what? That's exactly what I'm tryin' to do. Because control is mine, not yours."

Ben slid his hand between her legs. Swirling his middle finger in her juices and following the seam of her sex up to her clit. He rubbed the tiny nub until it plumped, her escalating moans urging him on. Then he went in for the kill, suctioning his mouth to her throat as he shoved two fingers into her wet pussy.

Her body jerked like she'd stepped on a live wire.

He felt the vibration of her scream beneath his lips and a jolt of male satisfaction hardened his dick. She was so damn responsive. He imagined spending all night teasing her, driving her to the pinnacle and then kicking her over the edge. Some other time, since he was chomping at the bit to fuck her.

When the tension left her body, he donned a condom. He untied her legs and kneaded her calves. "Any numbness?"

"No."

Releasing the straps, he perched on the edge of the bench. Grasping the backs of her thighs, he pulled her legs straight up and placed her ankles on his shoulders. When he widened his knees, her pussy and her asshole rested against the base of his cock. He twisted his hips, grinding his cock against those hot spots.

She pressed into him for more friction and her eyes fluttered closed.

"Eyes open," he said curtly, waiting until she complied. Then he gradually fed his cock into her, until he was buried to his balls.

"See how I've positioned you? So I can fuck you as deep as possible? So you can't touch me? So you can't touch yourself? You are totally at my mercy. Your body, your pleasure all belongs to me."

Tight, wet warmth surrounded his shaft. "Squeeze my cock with those cunt muscles as I pull out." The increased pressure around his dick felt amazing. "Again."

After the third time, her surprised, "Yes, more," as he withdrew made him grab a handful of ass and hike her pelvis higher. No easing in—he bottomed out on the first thrust.

She arched hard, and turned her head with a drawn out moan.

"Eyes. On. Me."

A bit of defiance showed in those hazel depths when she looked at him.

He answered her unspoken question. "Why? Because I want you to see who's fucking you. Who's making you cry out. I want you to see who's in charge." Ben plunged into her again.

Moisture trickled down his spine. Her chest turned slick with a sheen of sweat. Her breathing became labored. When he kicked up the pace, he wanted to come so bad his balls fucking hurt.

"Are you ready to come, Angel?"

"Touch me. I can't—"

"You will come. Without me touching your clit. Without kisses or whispers in your ear. Without me suckling your nipples or biting on your neck." Right after he said that, goose bumps covered her skin. "But you love the thought of that, don't you? Me sucking on those hot spots that make you tremble. Make you scream."

Ben pulled out halfway to stroke his cockhead against her inner pussy walls. "Arch your lower back." He rocked that G-spot, squeezing his fingers at the root of his shaft into a makeshift cock ring. He felt her body go rigid from neck to chest to belly to legs in anticipation of the orgasm. He rasped out, "Bear down."

She unraveled. Her muscles spasmed around his cock and a long, low pitched wail distorted the air, competing with his grunting breaths and the hard grinding of his teeth.

When the last pulse faded, he unleashed his control and fucked her without pause. Each stroke bringing him closer...and closer. He roared when his balls emptied, each pulse better, hotter than the one before. "Fuck. Fuck!" He closed his eyes and let go.

A cramp tightened his palms. The sexual fog lifted from his brain and he opened his eyes. Ben glanced down, seeing he still had a death grip on her butt. He moved his hands to circle her ankles, resting above his shoulders. Keeping his gaze on hers, he kissed the inside of her calf.

The hazy look of pleasure had softened her face. Although she deserved a break, he couldn't allow that. He needed to keep her in the post-orgasmic state a little longer.

Ben carefully set her feet on the floor. He ditched the condom and knelt by the bench. While he untied her arms, he fed her sweet kisses and murmured against her skin, until she released a contented female purr.

He tilted her head back and peered into her sex-sated eyes. "Get on the bed, Angel. We're not done."

Chapter Seven

Ainsley blinked at him. "What?"

"Get on the bed. Now."

Okay, so there wasn't after sex cuddling. But it'd be hard to complain after Bennett had thoroughly rocked her world.

Three times.

Talk about a rush, a total mind blower, how completely freeing it was to be tied up. Not to have to worry where to put her hands on his body. Or if she should be touching him more. Or mirroring the way he touched her. Or if she'd lose it when he found her sensitive spots. Which he had. In record time. Oh boy, she couldn't believe she'd come so hard just by him—

"Angel," Bennett said sharply. "Are you listening to me?"

His handsome face swam into view. She smiled dreamily. "You are so good looking. Even when you scowl. I just want to lick you all over." She touched the deep cleft in his chin and swayed closer to him. "Would you let me lick you here?"

Strong fingers circled her biceps. He studied her face, a cross between delight and pride dancing in his blue eyes. "Christ. You really are sex drunk."

"If I'm sex drunk, it's your fault."

Bennett bestowed that heart-stopping smile. "Oh, I'll definitely take all the credit," and gently pushed her onto the bed.

She flopped back with a sigh, staring at the gossamer fabric rippling on the canopy above her. She felt like that fabric. Light. Floaty. Beautiful. Her skin tingled. Her pussy throbbed. And she absolutely didn't give a rip she was bare-naked with a man she hardly knew. The hottest man she'd ever been with. With the biggest dick she'd ever encountered. How would she ever get that thing in her mouth?

His amused face hung above her. "So that's what you're thinking about? How you'll fit my dick in your mouth?"

"I said that out loud?"

"Yep. It will fill you up. Guaranteed. It'll be fun helping you bone up on your deep-throating skills." He pulled her to a sitting position. "Gimme your foot so I can take off these ankle-breaking shoes."

"They looked naughty and sexy up by your ears."

He just grunted. Then he patted his thighs. "Come here and sit on my lap."

She walked on her knees, watching as his eyes ate up her body. When Bennett's gaze lingered on her belly, she didn't suck in the pooch, nor did she mention getting back to exercising to tone up her wide hips and flabby thighs. Ainsley just let him look his fill.

He curled one hand around her jaw, holding her in place as he kissed her. These bone-melting kisses were new. Soft, slow, and thorough. He explored every inch of her mouth with his tongue as he urged her to sit on his thighs. Ainsley didn't mind the awkward position if he'd just keep his mouth on hers, devastating all her senses with his drugging kisses.

But Bennett abruptly spun her around, face first on the bed. One of his legs pinned both of hers to the mattress and his hand was in the center of her back, holding her down.

"What are you—"

A sharp smack echoed when his hand connected with her butt cheek.

Ainsley jerked up, her haze of pleasure evaporating. "That hurts!"

"Hold still. Every time you fight me I will add another one to each side."

He smacked the other butt cheek and she automatically reared up. Oh God. It stung. How had she ever thought she'd like this?

Two more stinging swats on her tender flesh. "I warned you. Tell me you understand the consequences."

She said, "I-I understand," almost by rote.

Bennett's hands made soothing circles on her butt. Then he landed two more blows.

Tears prickled in her eyes. Her entire body vibrated with a mix of fear, anger and humiliation.

Then his deep, soothing voice drifted to her. "The first few spanks are hard. You can get through them, Angel. Breathe through them.

Loosen up your body. Count them out loud."

The whole time he spoke his hands caressed her backside. Then he stopped and smacked her left cheek hard, up by her hip. He bit off, "Count."

"One." *Please only let there be one more.*

He mirrored the spank on the opposite cheek.

"T-two."

Her head buzzed. Her butt was on fire. Her face burned like she'd spent the day at the beach. By the time she'd counted twelve smacks on each side, a strange kind of anticipation began to build. She wanted to feel his hard palm connecting with her flesh. Would the next blow be harder? Or softer?

It will be what he chooses. Enjoy it. Revel in it.

Bennett murmured, "That's it. That's what the bite of pain can do for you. Get your mind to shut off from everything but how I can make you feel." Then he administered the hardest hits yet.

By the time she'd reached number twenty-two, that restless need for release had her rubbing her thighs together. She wanted to tell Bennett to finger her clit with his free hand.

"If you've got time to think about tellin' me what you need to get off, then I'm not makin' it clear just who is in charge."

Was the man a mind reader?

Then he smacked the back of the left thigh, up high by her pussy. Oh God. This was torture.

Delicious torture.

"Count!" Another round of rapid-fire smacks.

She'd drifted off into that happy place again and hadn't kept track. "I...I—"

Bennett barked, "Don't. Move." His hand left her back and both hands gripped her hips as he hiked her ass in the air. More spanks. Not as hard as on her ass. He stroked his fingers up her slit before he spanked her again.

Everything stopped. No more spanks. No more barked orders. Ainsley felt Bennett staring at her ass.

Then he caged her body beneath his and that deep voice rumbled below her ear. "Your pussy is wet. Really wet. Do you know what that means? That means you liked your first spanking. And you took every blow so beautifully. Almost regally." His warm lips grazed her neck and she shivered. "Goddamn your ass is hot, woman." He chuckled. "In many ways. I wish you could see how pretty it looks. How your pink thighs and red ass frame your pussy."

Bennett's words sent a thrill through her.

"Good behavior is rewarded. Get on your hands and knees on the end of the bed."

She didn't meet his gaze; she just did what she was told. In that moment of foggy pleasure, she understood she'd needed freedom from choice. How could that feel so freeing? Why did she have the urge to weep with gratitude that he'd shown her what'd been missing?

The bed jiggled. Ainsley chanced a look between her legs when something soft brushed the insides of her thighs. Oh. Wow. His head was right below her...

Bennett yanked her down until her pussy was right on his mouth. He feasted on her, spreading her open with his thumbs. One minute that wickedly talented tongue was fucking so deep she swore she felt the tip tickling her G-spot. The next minute he suckled her pussy lips, then speared them apart with his tongue. He lapped at her delicately, making greedy masculine sounds, teasing the flesh hiding her clit with firm-lipped bites. And finally, he sent her rocketing into bliss when he sucked directly on her clit.

The orgasm blew her doors off. Ainsley threw her head back and practically screamed. The strong pulses zipped from her clit to her pussy to her fiery bottom, making everything—her skin, her sex, her butt—throb in sweet, torturous synchronicity.

She experienced that shivery sensation again. Her head became heavy. Her well-used body whispered for her to lie down. She was vaguely aware of Bennett moving from beneath her.

Then his fingers were under her chin, lifting her face up. "Eyes on me, please."

Took her a couple tries to remember how to open her eyes and Bennett laughed softly. She smiled at him. The way he looked at her made her feel like a goddess.

"Hey, beautiful. Such a blissful look I put on your face."

"It was..." Beyond words because she couldn't finish the sentence.

"Do you remember when you said you wanted to lick the cleft in my chin?" Bennett bent so they were nose-to-nose. "Do it now. You came all over my face, so I want you to lick your taste from me." He tilted his head back, but kept his hungry eyes on hers.

Her tongue darted out and flicked the sexy cleft. She playfully bit down as she lapped her juices from his chin. Once she finished, she dragged her mouth up to his and outlined his lips from corner to corner. She sucked at his full lower lip and let her teeth scrape the fleshy inside as she slowly released it. "I taste good on you, cowboy."

His dark eyes held a dangerous look. "You'd be a real challenge for me, wouldn't you?"

"Probably."

"Good thing I live for a challenge." He smooched her nose. "Don't move."

Ainsley heard him rummaging around behind her. Any desire to sleep had fled. She wanted more time with this man.

More than just tonight? Would you come back to the club if he asked?

The bed dipped and the heat of his body called to hers. "This is cold but it'll help." A sticky substance splatted across the top of her butt like icy raindrops. His callused hands spread coolness over her flaming ass, toning down some of the hotness, and she couldn't help but sigh.

"Know what I normally do, after I've reddened a woman's ass like this?" His finger traced her butt crack. "I fuck it. Hard and fast. While she's in that hazy place where the line is blurred between pleasure and pain." He pressed his finger against her anus and she involuntarily clenched. "I'd like to force this tiny hole open to take every inch of my cock. But you have a hard line on no anal, right?"

"Right."

"So I guess we'll just have to do it this way." Bennett impaled her pussy in one masterful stroke.

Yes. Yes! She loved it from behind. Something animalistic about that male power driving into her, experiencing sex at its most elemental level.

And the way Bennett hammered into her defined primitive. His hips slapped her butt, every thrust a reminder of her stinging ass. Every thrust a reminder this time wasn't about her pleasure. Only about his. He controlled it all. She didn't have to think, just feel.

His voice was hoarse. "Almost there. Jesus, this is so good." A feral groan sounded and Bennett rode her hard as he came.

After he pulled out, Ainsley fell face first into the mattress. When Bennett rejoined her on the bed, she made the time out sign above her head.

Laughing, he stretched alongside her, propped on his elbow, trailing his fingers over her spine. "You did very well."

He'd warned her they'd talk when they were done. But really, what was she supposed to say? A play-by-play so soon after the game ended was unnecessary.

"You'll want to sit in a cool bath tonight. And probably tomorrow."

"Thanks for the tip."

Bennett's hands stopped caressing her. "Don't get snippy. If there's a problem with what happened, let's talk about it."

"That's the problem, Bennett, I don't want to talk."

"Hmm. That is a problem."

Then Ainsley found herself on her back with a grinning Bennett above her. "What so funny?"

"This. I'm not known for bein' a big talker in my life outside the club." His lips toyed with hers. "So I'll just say this straight out: I want to see you again. I can finagle a guest pass outta Cody."

"So I was a good submissive?"

"You were a great submissive. Didn't give me nearly as much lip as I figured."

"You sound disappointed."

"There is something to be said for an inventive punishment scene," he drawled.

Ainsley set her hands on his lean cheeks. Her fingers continued a southerly descent, stopping to trace his collarbone. Her palms rested on his pecs and she glanced up to gauge his reaction. "Is this permissible, Sir? Within the realm of your control?"

"I'll ignore that smartass remark this time. But yes, sub, you may continue."

She ruffled his chest hair and fingered his nipples until he hissed. "I like your body. Sorta sad I didn't get to touch it as much as I wanted." She dragged her knuckles down to his groin. "And this appendage is why the term penis envy exists."

"As much as I love flattery, you haven't answered my question."

"That's because I don't know what to say when you tell me you want to see me again."

"Easy. Say yes."

She frowned. "That's it?"

"Yep. I'd like to explore this pull between us. I have a feeling it'll be explosive."

"Maybe that's what I'm afraid of."

Bennett tipped her face up. "Afraid of me?"

"No. Afraid of myself. Of letting—"

"Go?" he supplied.

"No. Afraid..."

"You don't know what you're afraid of, do you?"

Ainsley shook her head.

"Let's try this again next weekend. Maybe we can figure it out together." He pressed a lingering, gentle kiss on her mouth. "Say yes. Please."

She found herself whispering, "Yes."

"Thank you." He rolled off the bed and dressed quickly. "I'll leave you alone. I know you prefer time to think, although if I have my way, you'll lose the ability to think entirely whenever we're together."

Chapter Eight

Ben's hair was still damp from his shower when he heard the first knock on his door. Who was the early bird? The event didn't start for an hour.

Keely yelled, "Ben? You decent?"

"Yeah. Come on in."

"I need you to help me carry stuff in."

The back end of Keely's black Escalade was open. She handed him a cardboard box containing two Crock-Pots. "Damn, cuz, this smells good. What is it?"

"Pulled pork."

"There's a lot of it."

She slid her rhinestone-encrusted sunglasses on top of her head. "I know how much you guys eat."

Ben smiled. "None of us are gonna complain there's too much food, Keels."

"I'm counting on that because I don't wanna take this home."

"Jack doesn't eat leftovers?"

"Jack is out of town for the next week," she said, a pout in her tone.

Four trips later his kitchen counter was covered with containers of all sizes. Keely bustled about, transferring food from one dish to the next.

He brought her a Bud Light from the bar and a Moose Drool for himself. "Need me to do anything?"

"Nope." She took a swig of her beer and hopped up on the counter. "I wanted time to catch up with you."

Catch up. Right. She intended to grill him until her brothers arrived and forced her to stop. "What's on your mind?"

"Your mysterious older brother Gavin."

Ben leaned against the opposite counter. "What about him?"

"Is he keeping in contact with you guys?"

"He's called me and Quinn a couple times. When the PBR was in Arizona he went to see Chase ride. He met Ava too."

"Any idea when the rest of us get to meet him? It's bizarre that Aunt Vi had Uncle Charlie's baby and gave him up for adoption. And then they ended up getting married years later anyway?" She shook her head with disbelief. "I hoped Gavin's status as an only child in his adoptive family meant he'd be curious about all of us."

He tried to find an answer that wouldn't offend. The McKay family was overwhelmingly large, especially with the influx of babies in the last few years. From the few times Ben had talked to Gavin, the man defined cautious. It made sense he'd test the waters with his newly discovered siblings before he plunged into the gigantic McKay gene pool.

After Gavin showed up on their parent's doorstep a few months back, announcing he was their firstborn son, Ben figured Gavin had satisfied his curiosity about his birth parents and that'd be the end of it.

So it'd shocked him when Gavin called. They'd been exchanging emails since then. Ben kept it casual, waiting to see if Gavin was only maintaining contact out of some level of guilt. But they had more in common than Ben had initially believed. Gavin liked working with his hands and had experience remodeling the rental properties he owned in Arizona. They were both single, although Gavin had joint custody of his fourteen-year-old daughter. But during their conversations, Gavin never mentioned coming to Wyoming and Ben wasn't the type to push.

You had no problem pushing Angel last night.

"Earth to Ben," Keely said.

He looked at her. "Sorry. He's asked about our cousins. It's a lot to absorb."

"Spoken in the diplomatic tone I expected. Bennett McKay, the peacemaker."

He flipped her off.

Keely grinned. "On to the next thing I want to harass you about—I mean talk to you about. You know how much I adore the log bed you made us. It's big enough that I have my own space, in theory anyway—" she snorted, "—if Jack would ever let go of me at night. The damn man is stuck to me like Velcro."

"You're not really complaining."

"True. But I didn't know you'd talked to him about specific modifications to the original bed design. And I've gotta say. Very sneaky, Ben."

"What?"

"Don't play dumb. You built the bed with hidden hook-and-eye thingies so that depraved man could tie me to the bed any way he wanted."

He smirked. "And again, little cuz, you ain't really complaining."

"Yes I am! Why didn't you tell *me* so I could tie *him* up? I'm your cousin, your family, your flesh and blood. How could you let him have the advantage over me?"

"First of all, the submissive is always the one in control, regardless if she's bound by rope or by her dominant's word. Second, those are not special modifications Jack asked me for. But I knew if I added them, he'd put them to good use." Ben pointed his beer bottle at her. "Because I suspect there are plenty of times you need to be trussed up to get your butt paddled."

Keely wore a calculating expression. "I knew it!"

Probably pointless to deflect, but Ben tried it anyway. "Hey, Jack noticed the hardware before you did, when we assembled the bed."

"I'm not talking about that. I'm actually good with GQ learning the ropes, so to speak. I'm talking about you. Tossing out that dominant and submissive lingo like a pro."

Ben shrugged. "Never devalue opportunities offered by good porn."

"Bullshit. I think—"

"I think this is a conversation I never wanna have with you, Keely. So drop it." The way she froze, Ben realized too late he'd used his Dom voice.

"Does that tone always get you immediate obedience?"

"Not with you, apparently," he said dryly.

Keely laughed. "Look, I don't give a rat's ass what consenting adults do behind the bedroom door, but I've gotta ask: is your...proclivity why you go to Gillette?"

Proclivity. Diplomatic way to put it. He studied her, debating on whether to give her a piece of the truth or to lie. The odd thing was, he trusted Keely. She might be a chatterbox, but he'd never heard a whisper of her being a blabbermouth. "Yeah, I suppose it is."

"Huh." She seemed to be deep in thought. "I know someone who hung out at the Rawhide Bar. She'd never tell me why the place had such a pull on her. She was awful secretive. Like it was a private club or something."

Somehow, Ben kept from choking on his beer. "What's her name?"

"Annaliese."

He couldn't help but smile. "I know Annaliese."

Her gaze sharpened. "How well?"

He knew the petite blonde loved to give head after being flogged until she came. "Well enough."

"Ah. Evasion. I'm beginning to understand why your motto is *gentlemen don't kiss and tell.* I'm also beginning to understand why you aren't interested in dating anyone from around here." Keely cocked her head. "Although Jessie told me you went out with her coworker Simone a couple of times."

"I went out with her *once.* Why? She badmouthing me or something?"

"No. You knew within a single date she wasn't your type?"

"Simone was..." Too abrasive. He preferred his women docile. Like Annaliese. Like Angel last night.

"Simone was...what?" Keely prompted.

"Suffering from baby fever. She's lookin' for a man to be her husband only so she can get knocked up and experience the joys of motherhood. That sets off my warning bells."

"What? A woman who wants to settle down?"

"No. A woman who's only interested in getting pregnant. I doubt she'd be focused on me or the marriage, since she's already fixated on babies."

"So you expect your woman to devote all her energy to you? Make you the center of her existence?" Keely demanded.

Ben shook his head. "But I watched my sister-in-law Libby's single-minded focus on having a baby nearly destroy her marriage to Quinn. I hated watching my brother suffer. I hated seeing everything they loved about each other become unimportant. They were lucky and fixed their problems, but that's a rarity because the divorce rate is so damn high. So I ain't gonna sign on for something for the rest of my life knowing ahead of time it ain't what I want."

She started to retort when two raps preceded Quinn walking in. He cast a glance at the dogs snoring in front of the woodstove. "Did you drug my usual welcoming committee?"

"No. They spent the weekend in the barn, pacing, missing their cushy life inside the house, snoozing by the fire. You want a beer?"

"Sure." Quinn placed a tinfoil-covered plate on the counter. "Libby made brownies."

"Ooh. Yum." Keely moved dishes around to make space.

Ben slipped behind the bar and popped the top on a bottle of Coors Light, nudging it toward his brother. "Before we get overrun with family, what's up with Dad? I called him on the way home today and he said he couldn't talk. He was figuring something out." Ben winced. "Christ. Please tell me that ain't married man code for him and Mom havin' sex?"

Quinn laughed. "Nope. He was lookin' at airline schedules."

"Why? They goin' to see Chase and Ava in California?"

"Nope. Gavin invited them to Phoenix."

"Really? That's...good. Isn't it?"

"I hope so."

His cousins streamed in. Kane and Kade. Cord and Colby. Colt and Cam. Brandt, Tell and Dalton. They all gave Keely a rash of shit before bellying up to the bar. He handed Colt a Coke. Then he set out the beer and popped the tops.

"Man, how do you remember everyone's favorite beer?" Dalton asked.

"Must be the time he's spending in the bar in Gillette," Cord said. "Do you have an owner's stake in it?"

I wish. "Nope. Cody and Trace own it. I help out when I can, but I mostly just hang out."

"I don't see why you don't hang out in the bars around here," Dalton said.

"Because the bars around here suck, dumbass." Tell took a drink of his Coors.

"Maybe sometime me'n Tell will head that way since you like the place so much."

Dalton had been saying that for a while, so Ben shrugged it off.

"You should."

"Besides, I'll bet it ain't your buddies that're holding your interest. Got a woman stashed there?"

He looked at Kade, standing next to Colby, and blatantly changed the subject. "Rielle mentioned seeing Skylar last week. She said Sky had been sick. Is that why you weren't around?"

Kade nodded. "Some flu thing. I'm just damn glad the girls and I didn't get it." He knocked on the wooden bar top.

"You sure the sickness wasn't from Sky being pregnant?" Cam said slyly.

"Fuck off, lawman. Some of know when to say when."

"And some of us not so much," Colby muttered.

"No way. Channing is pregnant *again*?" Kane asked.

"God no." Colby also knocked on wood.

"Libby ain't pregnant either," Quinn offered.

"Ditto for Indy."

"Add AJ to the *not* list," Cord said.

"Did this conversation have a point?" Tell demanded. "Or all you gonna whip out baby pics next?"

"Yeah, cause you don't have a picture of your nephew Landon in yours," Keely inserted.

"We're just tryin' to figure out who's pregnant," Kane said. "Cause at least one woman in this family is always knocked up."

All eyes zoomed to Brandt.

"What the hell? Jessie's not pregnant."

A beat passed. Then all everyone turned and looked at Keely.

She bristled. "What did I do now?"

"We're just wondering..." Colt drawled.

"If you've got a bun in the oven?" Cord finished.

"I've got a whole package of them right here." Keely whipped a roll at Cord's head. "Jerk." Then she pegged Colt with one. "Asshole. You telling me I look fat?"

"Put away the dinner rolls, Nolan Ryan. We ain't sayin' you look fat. We're just tryin' to figure out who Ma is knitting the new baby blanket for."

"Not me. Jesus. Jack and I have only been married a year. And after I saw AJ in labor with Beau?" She shuddered. "Maybe never."

"Oh, it wasn't that bad."

Keely threw another roll at Cord. "Not that bad? Didn't AJ threaten to cut off your *big swinging dick filled with demon seed* if she ever saw it again?"

Cord smirked. "She didn't mean it, trust me."

"Kiss and make up with your *big swinging dick*, did she?" Colt said with a snicker.

More laughter broke out.

"How did we get on this subject anyway? I was hoping there'd be no baby talk for a change," Dalton complained.

"We got on the subject because my brother was avoiding your question about the women keeping his interest in Gillette," Quinn said.

Ben scowled at him.

"Or maybe he only wants us to think that. Maybe he really has his eye on a woman closer to home," Keely tossed out.

Thanks a fuckload, Keely.

Quinn's beer bottle stopped halfway to his mouth. "Ah hell. I should've seen that one comin'."

"I'm confused," Ben said. "Should've seen what one comin'?"

"Not what, *who*. You know, your hot, sexy, single neighbor, Rielle Wetzler?" Keely added, "How's she doin' with that bed and breakfast? I don't ever hear anything about it, which can't be good."

Dalton stood. "Count me out of the conversation when it comes to the Wetzler girls."

"And count me out of the conversation where you guys are tryin' to marry off the last of us single McKays," Tell said. "We like livin' the carefree bachelor life."

Ben noticed his married cousins exchanging smug looks after he, Dalton and Tell high-fived.

"Nothin' goin' on between me and Rielle. We're friends. I've built some furniture for her. Done some repairs at the B&B. She keeps an eye on my dogs when I'm gone. Just normal neighborly stuff. Plus, she's at least ten years older than me."

Cord grinned. "Age ain't nothin' but a number. Trust me."

"Maybe she does all that stuff because she wants to be more than just friends. You should ask her out," Cam suggested.

"You might even get to put one of the beds you made her to good use," Quinn teased.

"Very fucking funny."

"Ooh. Someone's sensitive."

Male laughter erupted.

He snapped, "We watchin' bull riding or didja bring nail polish so we could give each other manicures while we gossip?"

Keely rang a cowbell in the kitchen. "Come and get it!"

While plates were being filled, Ben shooed his dogs outside and turned on VERSUS. Once everyone was settled, Ben brought another round of beer before he fixed a plate for himself. He looked around, glad his cousins had put their differences aside and not only worked together, but could hang out together occasionally. They were all too hotheaded and stubborn for their working relationship to always be sunshine and roses, but at least that relationship wasn't combative day in and day out.

A collective groan rippled through the room when a bull stomped the crap out of a rider's leg.

Low stakes betting didn't last more than ten riders because Tell won all rounds. Being a PRCA rough stock judge was an advantage.

Buck-offs were more common than an eight-second ride so the speculation was high that Chase had a shot at the championship round, since his first score put him in the top twelve.

After Keely ended her cell phone call, she squeezed between Cam and Colt on the couch. "Carter and Jack say hey to everyone."

"You couldn't go an entire afternoon without checking in with your lord and master?" Cord asked.

"I don't have to check in, jerkface. Jack called me because he misses me."

"I'll bet he was drunk," Cam said.

Keely elbowed him in the gut.

"Brandt, have you checked in with Jessie yet? It's been at least an hour since you've talked to her." Dalton added kissing noises and Tell muttered about being pussy-whipped. Brandt cuffed them both in the back of the head.

All in all, just a normal McKay gathering.

Chase's match-up was announced. He'd drawn Red Bull Rebel. Chase was on the bull by the time the camera panned to him, helmet on, testing his wrap. Another shift of his hips and he nodded to the gatekeeper.

Red Bull Rebel went nearly vertical right out of the chute. Ben mumbled, "Come on, bro. You got this. Stay on him." Chase had total control during the spin. Ben didn't look away from the screen until Chase hit the eight-second mark and the cheering started behind him.

High-fives were exchanged all around the room. Ben grabbed the remote and rewound so they could watch it again. Immediately after the score of eighty-eight was announced, the camera panned to Ava, Chase's wife, in the audience.

"Chase has really turned his ridin' around," Brandt said.

Ben muttered, "He needed to."

"I've never seen anyone more determined when we worked them bulls last summer. One day, Chase climbed on twenty-five bulls." Colby shook his head. "Crazy damn kid. Me'n Cash kept waitin' for him to say enough but he never did."

"Hey, Ben?" Kane said. "Me'n Kade are goin' antelope huntin' next weekend. Do you still want the hides if we bag a couple?"

"Yeah. Any deer skin you don't want either."

"What are you doin' with them?" Colt asked.

"Tanning them and adding pieces to furniture. I'm not sure if it'll work, so I need extra skins to experiment on."

"I'll pass the word along. I know Trev and Ed got permits to hunt damn near everything."

After Chase placed seventh, the party broke up.

Ben was too restless to sit inside, so he headed out to his workshop. But his thoughts kept drifting to Angel. He hoped she wouldn't talk herself out of returning to the Rawhide.

It'd been a common occurrence, in Ben's experience, that once a woman was out of the club atmosphere, she'd get to thinking about how she'd willingly given herself over to a dominant partner. She'd become mortified by her behavior. In the moment, it'd been a heady experience. In the outside world, it seemed...wrong. Dirty. Out of character. A violation of her feminist sensibilities.

Not that Ben disagreed some dominant/submissive relationships were borderline degrading. It bothered him that some women's foray into the scene only showed the worst side. Not the best side, like Layla and Murphy, who'd been together for years. Their devotion to each other's needs was undeniable. Ben wasn't looking for a lifestyle sub, but a woman who understood this wasn't a phase with him. He was a dominant to the core and always would be. He couldn't be with a woman who wouldn't accept that side of him—no matter where they met.

Planing boards for mission-style nightstands took his mind off constant speculation about the odds of Angel showing up.

He suspected it'd be a long week.

Chapter Nine

Oh my aching ass.

Ainsley's butt still stung on Monday morning. Bad. She'd immersed herself in a cool bath as soon as she'd returned to the hotel after her sexcapades at the Rawhide Club with Bennett. Every time she felt that burning twinge, it reminded her of him. Of how he'd known the pain would morph into something else entirely for her.

And that knowledge had shaken her very foundation.

She prided herself on being a logical woman. But what she'd experienced with Bennett defied logic. A smart, independent, capable female ceding all control, in essence saying, *here's my body, do to it what you please, don't let me think, just make me come.*

Did that make her a mindless slave to pleasures of the flesh?

No. Ainsley knew it wasn't that cut and dried. Logically she understood the difference between giving control and having a man take control away. What amazed her was that she hadn't felt powerless at any point. All she'd felt was relief.

Which gave credence to Bennett's claim: the submissive had all the power in the situation. The dominant was restricted only to the amount of power the submissive relinquished. But that didn't answer the question of why she'd trusted Bennett so easily? So quickly? Which led to the next question weighing on her mind: would there be a next time?

She had until Friday to decide. And heaven knew she'd dissect this scenario and potential outcomes a hundred times before then. The image that kept popping up when the doubts plagued her was Bennett's face and the intense way he studied her. He wanted to know her, inside and out. Her every gesture, her every laugh, her every facial twitch and her every word were memorized and filed away for his future use.

And if she was totally honest with herself, she was less spooked by that than she was immensely flattered.

Tapping on her car window startled her. She glanced at the intruder, slicked up, anal-retentive, nosy Turton Ingvold, the man she'd secretly dubbed *the turd*. Because boy howdy, did the name fit him. Brown hair, brown eyes, and a total brown-noser—to everyone except her. Turton treated her with an air of derision. He'd expected to land the bank president position after the man who'd initially been tapped for the job last spring had been abruptly reassigned. But she'd been offered the plum job for this new branch office, making Turton her second-in-command.

She managed to smile at him after she exited her car. "Morning, Turton."

He walked beside her—right beside her—up the sidewalk. "I trust you'll handle the situation with Rita this week?"

No hello, no good morning, no surprise. Half the time she wondered how Turton had reached management level because he had zero social skills and practically no tact. "Yes. I believe she works tomorrow."

"Good. Because I'd hate to think you were showing favoritism and we'd have disgruntled employees—"

"I said, I'd handle it, so can we please drop it?" She felt him breathing down her neck as they walked single file into the bank lobby and it creeped her out.

She stopped for a minute and took stock of the space. The lobby paid tribute to Wyoming's western heritage. Stacked slabs of native stone, exposed wooden beams, rusty barbed wire used throughout in unique ways. Even the chairs were covered in cowhide. The corporation had invested in local artists for the rest of the décor, large bronzes, painted scenes with cowboys and Indians, as well as a large mural depicting the spectacular and desolate landscape in the Sundance area. The brand new building had only been open for business two weeks and Ainsley already thought of the place as hers.

Evidently Turton had been trying to engage her in conversation, or treating her to a thinly veiled comment about her incompetence, and when she hadn't responded, he'd stormed off to his office.

She ditched her coat and briefcase in her office before heading to the employee break room for a cup of coffee. Leslie, the lone loan officer, sat at the break table, dunking a teabag in hot water while she flipped through the newspaper. She glanced up and smiled. "How was your weekend?"

Enlightening. "Too short. How about yours?"

"Between the kid's activities and the laundry I was happy to come to work this morning."

Jenny, the receptionist, sitting next to Leslie, said, "My car wouldn't start and my dad couldn't figure out what's wrong with it, so I spent the entire weekend carless, at home watching TV instead of barhopping with my friends." She sent Leslie a sly look. "If I can't get my car fixed, I might have to come to you for a loan for a new car."

"You'd have to make an appointment for next week, because I'm full up this week," Leslie said.

"That's always good news to hear first thing on Monday morning."

"So what did you do this weekend, Miss Hamilton?" Jenny asked, giving Ainsley's suit a thorough inspection.

Miss Hamilton. Like she was an old spinster. The twenty-something woman was a tad mean-spirited, but efficient, so usually Ainsley let her barbs slide. Not today. She poked Jenny back. "Oh, I went to a club."

Jenny furrowed her brow. "Like a supper club or a knitting club or something?"

The little snot. "No, to a night club."

"Which one?"

"You wouldn't know it. It's out of town. I had a great time but it was exhausting. I discovered muscles I hadn't used in years." She smiled and sailed from the room.

Her taunt literally came back to bite her in the ass when her butt met the leather seat of her office chair.

Ben ditched his gloves and dug his cell phone from his front pocket after it rang for the third time. "Hello?"

"Thank God you're home. I need a huge favor."

He set aside his ax. "Sure, Rielle. What do you need?"

"My car has a flat tire. When I went to change it I discovered the spare is flat too. I have a meeting at the new bank in fifteen minutes. Is there any way you can pick me up and take me to town?"

Ben dusted off his Wranglers, scraped the muck from his boots and grabbed his keys from the workbench. "Hopping in my truck now."

Rielle's place was up the road three miles. The top half of her one hundred and forty-six acres bordered Casper McKay's land and Ben's portion of the McKay Ranch. According to family gossip, thirty years ago both Charlie and Casper had wanted that section. They'd fought over it to the point the original owner had sold the parcel to the Wetzlers, a family from California.

Ben never put much faith in local speculation that the Wetzler's were dope-selling hippies, but they were an odd bunch. Their housing setup had a commune-like vibe—from the individual cabins spread out from the new main structure, to the acres of gardens, the chicken coops, the animal pens, the dairy cows, the bee hives and the fruit trees.

No one knew how many people had squatted on the land with the Wetzlers' blessing. But in the two years since the deaths of her parents, Rielle Wetzler had built the Sage Creek Bed and Breakfast to supplement her income from her organic farm. Even with all the improvements, there was still much to be done. And those improvements didn't come cheap.

Rielle stopped pacing on the porch and bounded down the steps when he pulled up.

The willowy blonde strode toward his truck with an air of gracefulness. Although Ben knew how strong and capable Rielle was, her waif-like appearance didn't appeal to him. Despite his family's teasing, she never hinted about them becoming romantically involved— a first in Ben's life when it came to dealing with a single woman. So their friendship meant a lot to him.

She gathered her long, tie-dyed skirt and slammed the door. "You are a lifesaver, Ben McKay."

"Happy to help." He didn't speak until they were zipping along the blacktop toward town. "So why you goin' to the bank?"

"Because it's new. They won't know my family history and wonder if I'm asking for a loan for new grow lights to increase my secret crop of marijuana."

Ben laughed.

"Seriously. I'm hoping they'll loan me money to pay off some debts. Like what I owe you."

"I told you not to worry about that."

"I do worry." She smoothed her palm from the top of her scalp down to the ends, trying to tame her baby-fine hair. "I'm so nervous."

"You shouldn't be. Them bankers usually have their minds made up before you even walk in the door. Bunch of controlling bastards. Least, that's been my experience."

"I thought all the McKays had more money than they knew what to do with and didn't owe anyone anything."

"Not all the McKays. Especially not those of us who've built houses or businesses or bought land. I've got monthly payments."

"So what do you think my chances are of getting the money?"

"Most bankers are real tight-asses in this economy. They'll take into account that you own the land. But they'll also take into account if your proposed improvements will actually increase the property value."

Rielle sighed. "Too bad the barter system doesn't still work with everyone."

"No kiddin'. Speaking of...thanks for checking in on the dogs this weekend."

"No biggie. I had nothing else going on. Rory was supposed to be home this weekend but she had to work."

"How's her first semester of graduate school?"

"Good. She's still bartending at Happy John's three nights a week since her graduate assistant grant only covers classes. I wish I could help her out more."

Ben shot Rielle a sideways look. "Is that part of why you're applying for a loan? To give Rory money for school? Because, Ree, I gotta tell ya, your stubborn daughter ain't gonna be happy about that at all."

Rielle smiled. "Like mother, like daughter, huh? Too damn independent for our own good. Don't worry, and don't tattle on me. The loan is strictly for the Sage Creek."

The remaining ride to town was quiet. The new National West Bank was an eye-catching structure comprised of blocks of native sandstone, glass and steel. The wooden beams on the outside added an Old West touch, as did the metal trim that would weather and rust in the harsh Wyoming elements. It was a nice addition to the town, even when he questioned whether the citizens of Sundance could support a second bank.

Rielle checked her make-up in the passenger mirror and slicked on a coat of Chapstick. Fussed with her hair. Mumbled to herself and pushed up the sun visor with a decisive snap. "Okay." She curled her fingers around the door handle. "Ready?"

"You look ready. Knock 'em dead, tiger."

"Aren't you coming in with me?"

"Have you taken a good look at me? The last thing you need is them seeing me tracking mud and shit across their brand new carpet. I'll stay in the truck."

Ben sank into his leather seat and pulled his hat down over his eyes, wishing he could take a catnap. He'd had a restless night, thinking about Angel. Wondering if he'd recognize her without that funky-ass wig. Wondering how her real hair would feel wrapped in his fists as he fucked her mouth. His flashbacks made the crotch in his jeans uncomfortably tight, forcing him to redirect his thoughts.

He studied the building's clean lines. He'd built his log house himself and appreciated how form and function affected design, yet retained an artistic feel. As he thought about art, he remembered his cousin Carter had been commissioned for a large sculpture for this bank. Ben always loved seeing what works his crazy-talented cousin created. He was already here. He might as well sneak in and have a quick look-see.

The inside of the bank was as impressive as the outside. The place was busy and no one took notice of him as he stopped in front of the massive sculpture, prominently displayed beneath a circular skylight. A rusty chain enclosed the art—a horse head carved from wood, surrounded by twisted sections of metal of varying heights, sizes and finishes that gave the impression the horse was running through tall, native grasses.

"It's magnificent, isn't it?"

He recognized that sultry voice immediately. Ben spun around so fast he made himself dizzy and couldn't believe his eyes. "Angel?"

Her jaw nearly hit the floor. "Bennett? You... What are you doing here?"

Before he could answer, a hearty hand landed on his shoulder. "Ben! I haven't seen you in a coon's age."

Dazed, he glanced at Bill, his insurance agent, who'd inserted himself between him and Angel.

Bill said, "What brings the elusive Ben McKay to town?"

"Checking out Carter's latest piece of art." *Now go the fuck away.*

"So you're not shopping for a new bank?"

"Maybe." Ben kept his focus on the woman he hadn't been able to get out of his head.

Bill kept yapping. "I reckon Steve Talbot would take issue with that, since the McKays have always banked with Settler's First. Although this bank president is much prettier than Steve."

"You're president of this bank?" Ben said with total shock.

Her eyes turned frosty.

"Look, Bill, how's about you don't mention to Steve you saw me in here and I won't mention to him I saw you?"

"Deal. See ya around, McKay."

Ben moved close enough Angel had to look up at him. "We need to talk, Madame President."

"I'm very busy—"

"I don't wanna make a scene, but I will."

The pink on her cheeks deepened.

Ben's gaze wandered over her tousled golden-brown hair, streaked with amber that fell past her shoulders. "Don't ever wear that ugly-ass wig again. Jesus, woman, I like the look of you. So real. So pretty and soft."

"Don't."

"Don't what? Pay you a compliment?"

"Don't come into my place of business and act like you control me here."

Stung, he bit off, "Then I would appreciate ten minutes of your time in private."

"No."

"Really? You're gonna turn away business? Because I want to open an account."

"Fine. Bonnie can help you with that—"

"Nope. I want you to help me. Only you. So we doin' this or what?"

Her eyes still held a warning. "Five minutes."

As they headed toward her office, a voice called out, "Ben?"

He faced a miserable-looking Rielle. "You done already?"

"Yes."

"Give me ten minutes." He extracted his keys from his pocket and handed them over. "You can wait in the truck."

Rielle's gaze moved between them. "Okay."

Inside a glass-fronted office, she skirted the desk, offering a curt, "Shut the door and have a seat," and slid into an oversized chair.

"I'll stand, thanks."

"I'd think you were a gentleman, saving the chair for your wife or girlfriend, if I didn't just see you order her to sit alone in the truck."

Any veneer of calmness fled. Ben cut across the room and placed his hands on her desk, looming over her. "First off, I wouldn't have been in the Rawhide Club screwing around with other women if I was married or seeing someone." *Breathe, man.* His gaze dropped to the nameplate. Whoa. Her name wasn't Angel? "Maybe I oughta be questioning you and your motives, since you, oh, *lied* about your damn name and wore that ridiculous wig."

"Given my occupation, I'm sure you understand why I disguised myself. Plus, I had no idea what to expect from an establishment like the Rawhide Club since it was my first foray into such a place. Better to be safe than sorry."

"Fine. I guess I can buy that."

She fiddled with a pen. "Can you please sit down?"

"Am I makin' you nervous?"

"We already established last weekend that you make me very nervous, Bennett."

"Call me Ben," he corrected, perching on the edge of the floral-covered wingback chair. "I only use Bennett at the club. Or my mom uses my full name when she's pissed off at me about something. Which you can imagine is all the damn time."

Ainsley smiled.

"I like it so much better when you're smiling at me, angel. The name fits you, although that's not your name." His gaze tracked over the engraved nameplate. "So, Ainsley Hamilton, you're a bank president."

"So it would appear. You surprised?"

"No. I knew you were sharp, and I figured you had a job where you were used to bein' in charge. You haven't been in Sundance long."

"How do you know?"

"I've lived in this area my whole life. People talk when a hot single lady moves into town. I've haven't been in town in recent weeks... Shame on me for not introducing myself earlier."

"You're part of the infamous McKay family."

"Infamous is an exaggeration."

"Not from what I've heard. Anyway, I haven't been out and about Sundance. There's a lot to micromanage when opening a new branch. I spent the first weekend unpacking and last weekend—" Her blush seemed to annoy her. She squared her shoulders. "I don't need to give you a play-by-play of last weekend's events."

"No, you surely don't, because I've been reliving them in my head every damn hour for the last day."

"Really?"

"Yeah. Were you gonna show up Friday night? Or stand me up?"

"I hadn't decided. It was all so...surreal." She rolled the pen between her palms. "But having you here in my office is surreal too."

But damn fortunate in his opinion. "You can't deny something clicked between us last weekend. How about if we talk about it tonight over dinner?"

She gave him a questioning stare. "Dinner? Where?"

"Without adding more fuel to the infamous McKay fire, we'd better stick to my place, because wherever we go in Sundance or Moorcroft, chances are high we'll run into one of my family members. I'm not sure the new businesswoman in town wants to be associated with a McKay." When more suspicion flared in her hazel eyes, he realized he'd have to take extra care with her, given how they'd met. "No one knows about my life at the Rawhide Club."

"You sure?"

"I make sure. I promise. It's only between us." He leaned closer. "Have dinner with me tonight, Ainsley. It'll just be us talkin'. That's all."

"None of that tying me up and spanking sex stuff?"

Was there disappointment in that snappy answer? "If that's the way you want it." Ben tried hard to reconcile this polished, professional woman with the submissive he'd had beneath his hands only two days ago.

"You can cook?"

"I'm a bachelor. Be pretty sad commentary on my life if I didn't know my way around a kitchen."

Ainsley smiled again. "Give me your address and I'll be there after work."

"It's fourteen point eight miles south on Bridger Gap Road. Turn left at the cattle guard. It's a log house. Can't miss it."

Three knocks and Ainsley said, "Come in."

A tall brunette sashayed into the office. "Public relations from the main Denver branch called. I told them you'd call them back as soon as you finished with your client."

"Thanks, Jenny."

Ben bit back a groan. The brunette was none other than Jenny Timsdale. Town beauty queen, hardcore partier and the last-call bar hookup for his cousin Tell. Or his cousin Dalton. Or both, to hear Dalton brag.

She feigned surprise at seeing him. "Ben McKay. Where have you been hiding yourself? I haven't seen you at the Golden Boot, Ziggy's or the Twin Pines in forever."

"I've been busy."

"Your cousin Tell hasn't been too busy to come out and whoop it up with me once in a while."

He muttered, "I don't doubt that."

Ainsley said, "Jenny, is there anything else you needed?"

"No."

"Would you be so kind as to ask Bonnie to start the new account process? Mr. McKay will be right there, as he's decided to open an account with us."

"Sure thing, boss." Jenny flitted out.

Ben couldn't help but grin. Ainsley was no pushover. But she'd soon learn he wasn't either.

"Thanks for the hard sell, Miz Hamilton. I look forward to you meeting my needs."

"Your banking needs," she corrected.

"That too," he murmured. "See you later."

His week was looking up.

About fifteen minutes after Bennett—Ben—moseyed out of the

building after opening a new checking account, Ainsley called Jenny back into her office.

"You buzzed me?" she inquired with fake sweetness.

"Yes. Do you have that number for the PR department? There are four different extensions."

"Sure. No problem. Be right back." Jenny's small, perfectly pear-shaped ass didn't bounce in the skintight pink leopard print skirt.

Ainsley sighed and swore she'd eat like a bird tonight.

Jenny handed over a slip of paper. "Here you go. I hope I didn't interrupt anything between you and Ben."

"No, we were just finishing up. But as long as you asked, what can you tell me about him?"

"Besides he's as hot as fire? Mama, those blue eyes of his just like...look right into you, know what I mean?"

Yes, she'd been on the receiving end of those soul-pondering looks.

"He's pretty quiet compared to the rest of his family. But like the rest of them, he's involved in the McKay ranching operation. He's not much into the bar scene around here. He probably gets sick of women hanging all over him, but he's too polite and gentlemanly to say anything, know what I mean?"

No, that didn't ring true. Ainsley clearly remembered Bennett telling her exactly what he wanted her to do.

"He doesn't really date, definitely not like his cousins do. Because of that, some nasty people around here whisper he's gay, but I don't believe that for a second."

That man was far, far from gay.

Evidently Jenny realized that Ainsley hadn't responded to anything she'd said. Her baby blues widened. "You aren't involved with him or something? Because aren't you, like, a lot older than him?"

Ainsley let the snarky comment slide. "We were just talking about his cousin's art. He had a couple of general questions about the bank and I convinced him to open an account."

"It'd be a big deal if you could get all the McKays to switch their banking business here. I'll bet you can be very persuasive."

Not nearly as persuasive as Bennett could be

And that scared the bejeezus out of her.

Chapter Ten

Ben's charming, rustic house looked nothing like Ainsley had pictured a big, bad Dom's swinging bachelor pad.

Cradling the bottle of wine, she tiptoed up the flagstone walkway, cursing her high heels, wishing she'd changed clothes after work.

Soon as she neared the door, she heard barking. Snarling barks. And thumps. Like the dogs were throwing themselves at the door to get to her.

Ben's voice boomed. "Dammit, shut up. What the hell is wrong with you guys?"

The dogs whimpered.

"Hang on a sec while I put the dogs out back."

She adjusted the shoulder strap on her purse, watching through the screen door as Ben dragged the dogs by their collars.

He trotted back, swinging the door inward. "Sorry about that. Don't know what got into them. They're usually so friendly they slobber all over ya."

She handed him the wine. "They probably smelled my cats." *And my fear.*

"Can I take your coat?" He set the wine bottle on a beautifully crafted side table.

Ainsley stopped on the edge of the foyer. "Ah. Sure." She passed him her trench. He hung it on a coat tree crafted out of some kind of animal horns.

She swiped her palms on her skirt, wishing she had pockets. Wishing she hadn't come.

Why was this so awkward?

You've had kinky sex with this man. Dinner should be a breeze.

Then Ben was curling his hand over her jaw, gazing into her eyes. "You all right?"

"I don't know what I'm doing here. I'm so...nervous."

"Do you want to leave?"

"No."

"Good. Maybe this will help." Ben kissed her. Sweetly at first. Softly nibbling her lips while his thumb stroked her jawline. He patiently coaxed her to kiss him back. Once she opened her mouth wider, he dove right in, blowing all her circuits with a kiss packed with desire, laced with passion. Her head went muzzy and she wrapped her arms around his neck.

After an eternity of those soul-feeding kisses, he tilted her head back to string hot kisses from her chin to her neck.

Chills danced down her arms and neck and she sighed.

Ben chuckled, smooching her mouth one last time before resting his forehead to hers. "Better?"

"Yes."

"What else can I do to put you more at ease?"

His concern touched her. "I'd love to kick off my shoes."

"Feel free. How about a drink?"

"Sure." Ainsley followed him to a built-in bar. "Wow. This is beautiful."

"Thanks. Bombay Sapphire and tonic, right?"

Of course he remembered her drink of choice. "No, actually, I'll take a soda. Whatever you've got is fine."

"Comin' right up."

Ainsley checked out the rest of Ben's house. Definitely masculine with the animal trophy heads lining the wall and the large room focused on the huge TV, pool table and other man toys. Her gaze wandered to the open kitchen outfitted with stainless steel appliances, mahogany cabinetry, a big picture window overlooking an incredible view of the rolling plains. An eat-in countertop separated the kitchen and conversation area, comprised of two leather recliners facing a wood stove with an antique trestle table centered between the chairs. Maple-colored wood flooring stretched from the front door, through the kitchen, living room and bar. The TV/game room had brown and gold-flecked Berber carpet that continued down the hallway. A hallway that likely led to Ben's bedroom.

Did Ben have hooks and restraining devices in his bedroom? Or did he only indulge in that at the Rawhide Club?

"Here you go."

She faced him. "You've got a beautiful home."

"Took me six years to get it done. Definitely a learning experience as far as adding to my carpentry know-how, but it ended up being exactly what I wanted."

Her mouth dropped open. "You built this place? By yourself?"

"Except for the plumbing and electrical and a few odds and ends. It's a kit house. Kinda like Lincoln logs for grownups. I bought three kits and turned them into one house."

"That makes it even more impressive."

"Aw, angel, you're gonna make me blush."

Ainsley was pleased that he'd reworked her fake club name into a term of endearment. She watched as he poured himself a Coke. "Just because I'm not drinking doesn't mean you can't." *Way to tell him what to do.* "Not that you can't decide yourself whether or not you want an alcoholic drink." *Stop babbling.* "I don't know what's wrong with me."

He squeezed her forearm. "You're probably starved. How about if we eat?"

She looked up right into those stunning blue eyes. She swallowed a girlie sigh. He really was delightful to look at. "Sounds great."

He instructed her to sit at the counter as he set everything up. "It's nothin' fancy. Just chicken and potato casserole. A side salad if you want it."

After they'd taken a couple of bites, Ben spoke. "Given the way we met, seems strange to swap life stories, but I reckon we oughta get the basics out of the way. So go ahead. Ask me anything."

That was a loaded question. "You're part of the McKay family ranching dynasty."

"Dynasty." Ben snorted. "I'm just a simple rancher."

"So your main job is..."

"Cattle. Feeding them, breeding them, moving them, selling them. I work with my older brother Quinn on our section of the ranch. But we all help each other out if need be. Certain times of the year are busier than others. It ain't a nine to five job, like banker's hours."

She bristled until she realized he was teasing. "Funny, cattleman. Have you ever been married?"

"Nope." He shot her a sideways glance. "You?"

"I was married for almost five years. Been divorced almost two years."

"Kids?"

"None."

"So what happened to bust up your marriage?"

Ben's forthright manner was refreshing. "The things that made us compatible in the beginning of our relationship started to wear on me. My ex was set in his ways and didn't understand why I wanted things between us to change. Luckily, I got out of the marriage before I became bitter, but I didn't get out unscathed."

His gaze hooked hers. "To be blunt, you wanted to experiment, sexually, and he wasn't on board?"

"He was appalled. At one point he told me I needed counseling to deal with my *unhealthy* attitude about sex and my desire for deviant behavior."

"What a fuckin' idiot. I don't need to tell you that you're better off without him."

"I get that he wasn't a sexual man. For a few years I thought I was asexual, just like him, but I realized I wasn't. The fear that I'd find myself sixty years old and regret choosing a man with a pension plan instead of finding real passion gave me the courage to end the marriage." She pushed her food around on her plate. "His last shot at me? I was a sex addict, control freak, ball-buster. Which led me to believe I was a Domme. So now I don't know what the hell I am."

Then Ben's hands were on her face. "What you are is a beautiful, sexy woman. Smart enough to get out of a situation that didn't fit you. The real you."

Her eyes searched his. "You really believe I'm submissive."

"Yes. It's not control you want, Ainsley. It's freedom from control. Freedom not to have to micromanage every aspect of your life. Freedom to trust that your sexual well-being will be tended to by a man you trust. Freedom to feel instead of think."

"You are the man who can get me to do that?"

Ben leveled that panty-dampening smile at her. "Oh yeah." His hands fell from her face. "We'll finish this conversation after we eat."

The rest of the meal was quiet, except for the dogs barking. After he cleared the plates, he led her to the oversized corduroy couches. Ben plopped down beside her, and picked up her hand. "Tell me about your job."

"That's guaranteed to put you to sleep."

He chuckled.

"I switched banking corporations during our separation since my ex and I had worked for the same company. Basically I started over."

"So you go around opening new banks?"

"No. This was sort of a fluke. I turned around a branch office in Denver. When this job unexpectedly opened up, they offered it to me. I'm probably in over my head. And since this is a small bank in a small community, they expect me to have a community presence."

He groaned. "A man could go broke supporting all the community causes."

"Two words a banker doesn't like to hear together: *go broke.*"

Ben turned his head, brushing his lips in front of her ear. "Does the stern bank president ever wear her hair up?"

Okay. That was an abrupt subject change. "Sometimes."

"Would you jerk away if I put my mouth on that sexy sweep of skin between your hairline and your shoulder?" Ben blew a stream of air across her ear. "Would I have to pull your hair to take what I wanted?"

More shivers spread across her body. "I thought you said we'd just talk tonight?"

"We are talkin'."

"So why does this feel like a seduction?"

"Because I am trying to get you to feel instead of think."

Ainsley fought the urge to push him away as his mouth wandered over her skin. She'd never let a man know her weak spots, let alone hone in on them.

"I sense the fight in you, angel. Let. It. Go."

Hot kisses seared her neck and she whimpered.

"Drop your head back on the couch."

Ben's voice had become Bennett's. Demanding in that deceptively soft way that only increased its power.

She inhaled a deep breath and...obeyed.

Bennett nestled his mouth into the curve of her neck. Kissing her with tiny pecks. Flicking his tongue over the pulsing vein. Whipping her into such a frenzy that she didn't notice his fingers inching up her thigh until his fingertips breached midpoint beneath her skirt.

When she tensed, he warned, "Don't. Spread your legs."

As soon as she complied, Bennett stroked her slit, while his mouth kept up the relentless assault on her neck.

Ainsley shifted her hips, wanting more contact.

"Be still," he warned sharply, nipping her skin in admonishment.

Hard to be still when her whole body vibrated. When she already dangled so close to the edge. Which was ridiculous because he'd been touching her for like two minutes, tops. Over her panties.

"Stop thinking."

Her breathing became choppier yet when Bennett's free hand cupped her breast. The sensations of his mouth and finger stroking her, almost in tandem, were too good, too much, too intense, too intimate. She needed to wiggle free and find her wits.

"Be. Still."

"I can't. I'm too—"

Bennett sucked on that magic spot the same time he pinched her nipple hard. His thumb pressed against her clit and she detonated. Every pulse point in her body throbbed in time to the blood pulsing in her clit.

Ainsley lost herself then. Her mind became blessedly blank. When she raised her head, he withdrew his hand from under her skirt. He straightened her bra and blouse.

"You respond so well to me," he murmured.

"Yes, you're definitely a master at what you do."

A harsh look darkened Bennett's face. "I don't have a playbook. I'm not thinking, *if I stroke her pussy fourteen more times she'll cream on my hand.*"

Ainsley knew he'd intentionally used crude language to drive home his point. "I'm sorry. That's not what I meant. I meant you should have that designated Master title because...well, you are a master at this stuff. It's a compliment."

When she looked at him, Bennett was gone. Seemed strange to think of him as two separate personalities, but he really did have a switch that turned Ben, the easygoing rancher, into Bennett, the intense Dom.

"I ain't gonna lie. I want more of that with you. I've been kicking this idea around all day."

"What idea?"

"I want you as my submissive."

He wasn't joking. She narrowed her eyes. "I'll never be a lifestyle submissive like Layla."

"And I'd never demand that of you."

"What would you demand?"

"Time alone with you. Conditioning you to learn to let go. Showing you how satisfying it is to entrust me to give you what you need. Proving this is what you've always wanted and who you are."

"I don't know enough about this lifestyle to commit to anything long-term, Ben."

He gave her a considering look. "How about if you commit to it—to me—for one month?"

That was a workable timeframe.

"A month of you turning all control and decisions over to me."

Her heart rate spiked. "I need to clarify that you mean all control and decisions...aside from my job."

"I have no intent of controlling your career, Ainsley. That's yours. Everything else would be mine. If you agree to this, we'll skip the club scene for the month. Especially since I know you've no interest in adding exhibitionism or other players into the mix. No need to drive to Gillette when we both live in the same town, is there?"

"I suppose not." Ainsley twisted her fingers together. "Can you give me a for instance on your 'all control and decisions' comment?"

Ben shook his head. "I set all the parameters when we're alone together. I'm not looking to turn you into a slave to perform household chores, if that's what's put the wrinkle in your brow. I'm only interested in your submissiveness on a sexual level."

"So I'd get no say in anything?"

"Sexually? No. If you can't agree to that, well, there's nothin' else to discuss. Because that's the basis of a Dom/sub agreement."

No surprise he'd taken a firm stance. But was he offering her what she needed? Or taking what he wanted?

"I don't expect you to make a decision on the spot tonight. I'll give you a day to think it over."

"A day is all?"

Ben smirked. "I can see if you agree to this you're gonna try and argue with me. And the key word in that sentence is *try.*"

"You do that big, bad wolf bit very well."

"I've had a lot of practice, but I guarantee I ain't all bark and no bite. I'm lots of bite."

She wondered if it was too late for a drink.

He held out his hands to help her up from the couch. "I know you've had a long day and I figure you'll replay this discussion in that pretty head of yours long after you leave here."

"You sending me home?"

"Mmm-hmm." He pushed her hair back from her face. Then the ragged pad of his thumb traced her bottom lip. "I like seeing your mouth swollen from mine."

Talk about a punch of lust. At that moment Ainsley wanted to drag him to the floor and ride him until she was sweaty, sore and gasping for air.

Ben growled, "Goddamn I love that *fuck me now* look in your eyes."

"But you aren't going to act on it?"

"Nope. You need to make the decision about what'll happen between us, from your head, not your cunt. Because if I take you to my bed, I know which answer will win."

She laughed. "I'd say you were overly confident, but I know you've got the juice to back up that claim."

He held her arm to steady her as she slipped her heels on. He helped her put her coat on. He gave her a chaste kiss on the cheek after he walked her out to her car.

Ainsley buckled her seatbelt. When she turned, Ben was peering in her window. She rolled it down. "Did you change your mind about trying to sway my decision?"

"Huh-uh. I just wanted to say I had a great time with you tonight."

"Me too."

"I'll hear from you tomorrow? Either way?"

"Yes."

"Drive safe, angel." He tapped the side of the car twice and stepped away.

On the way home she considered all that'd been said. A couple of phrases kept tripping her up.

I'm not a master. I'm just a simple rancher.

Right. Bennett McKay was the most complex man she'd ever met.

Chapter Eleven

What were the odds the first time Ben had lunch in town in months, he'd run into Ainsley?

Pretty high, given a town the size of Sundance.

Since she was having lunch with the mayor, he didn't approach her. He took the first empty booth in Dewey's Delish Dish and positioned himself to observe her. She laughed more than he'd expected. Whatever she'd said cracked the mayor up several times.

He tore his gaze from her as Dalton and Tell slid into the opposite bench seat. "If it ain't Tweedle-Dee and Tweedle-Dum."

"Fuck off. Didja order for us? We're starved."

"I should've since you guys are always dragging ass."

"Not our fault this time," Dalton said. "Brandt showed up late this mornin'."

"Again," Tell inserted. "It puts us behind every damn day. Them two are gonna have to do something different than splitting their time between Jessie's place and Brandt's place. Every time they stay at Jessie's, he's late."

"I'd bet Jessie is late the mornings she's gotta drive from Brandt's to her job at Sky Blue." Ben slid his menu to the edge of the table. "What's the holdup on them getting one place together?"

"Money, probably. And Dad hasn't exactly been helpful."

Like that was news. His uncle was an asshole most days. "What's Uncle Casper been doin' in his retirement? My Dad never says much about him."

"He drinks until he passes out. We stop by to check on him."

"To make sure he ain't dead," Dalton said.

The muscle in Tell's jaw flexed. "Mom would have a conniption fit if she saw the state of the house. It's nasty. Dad's been livin' like a drunken hermit since their divorce was finalized."

Dalton scowled. "Even after all the shit Dad did to Jessie over the years, she still tried to help him. Cleaned the place top to bottom. Washed his clothes. Cooked for him. He's such an ungrateful bastard that Brandt won't let Jess go over there anymore."

"Too bad you can't just move your dad's stuff to Brandt's trailer and then he and Jessie could have the house. It's at least fifteen minutes closer to her job."

Tell and Dalton exchanged a pained look. "We think that's what they're waitin' for."

"Waiting for Uncle Casper to die?" Ben said sharply.

"He's killin' himself, Ben. He won't listen to any of us. Believe it or not, Mom had some influence over him, but that's gone. They haven't spoken since the day she left. There ain't a lot we can do."

Ben hated the huge rift his uncle had caused in the family, but it seemed wrong to write him off and let him drink himself to death.

A highly rude waitress took their order and as soon as she stomped away, Tell set his forehead on the table. "Fuck me."

"What the hell did you do to her, bro?"

Tell raised his head. "This is why I don't date women from around here. She'll probably spit in my damn food."

"Who is she?" Ben asked.

"Her name tag said Tara if you don't remember," Dalton offered.

"Fuck off, Dalton. It ain't like you don't have sex amnesia every so often."

Ben lifted a brow at Tell. "Sex amnesia?"

"You know. Where you have sex with a woman, good sex, memorable sex, but then you can't seem to recall her name."

His cousins stared at him when he didn't immediately respond. "What?"

"Fuck you, *gentleman Ben.* You remember the name of every woman you've banged?"

They had him there. "Not the ones from way back. But the ones from last month? Hell yeah." His gaze momentarily strayed to the back of Ainsley's head.

Tell gloated. "See, Dalton, I told you he wasn't a fuckin' monk."

"But that don't mean he's a fuckin' man-whore like you are," Dalton shot back.

"Boys. Play nice. So what's so all-fired important you asked me to come to town?" He frowned. "Since it was your idea, I ain't buying your lunch."

"Cheapskate."

"Is this about Uncle Casper?"

"No."

"Then what?"

"We heard you took Rielle to the bank yesterday."

"Yeah, so?" Then he remembered the conversation on Sunday about Rielle. "Christ. I'm *not* interested in her, okay? I was just bein' neighborly."

"We don't care about that," Tell said. "We wanna know why she was at the new bank?"

"Why does anyone go to the bank? She needs a loan."

"Bet they didn't give it to her, did they?" Dalton said.

"She didn't say and I didn't ask. Why?"

"Well, we've heard she's seriously financially fucked."

Ben's gaze turned sharp. "From who?"

Dalton shrugged. "Evidently she put up her land as collateral when she borrowed the money to build that bed and breakfast."

"It's not uncommon to borrow against equity."

"She borrowed the maximum amount of the equity and hasn't made a single payment on it for over a year."

That shocked him. "Are you fucking serious?"

"Yeah. The bank has given her a lot of leeway, but unless she pays at least six months of the amount she's in arrears, in the next forty-five days, Settler's First will start foreclosure proceedings."

"Holy shit." Ben wasn't surprised Rielle hadn't shared that information; the Wetzlers always had a serious distrust about "the man" and the McKay family. Plus, Rielle already felt guilty about not paying him for his handyman help. Or the new beds he'd handcrafted. "Her money troubles ain't common knowledge?"

Tell shook his head.

"How'd you find this out?"

An unspoken communication passed between them. Then Dalton said, "Rory."

"Rory just told you this?"

Dalton pushed his hat up an inch. "Rory didn't just blurt it out. I went to Laramie last weekend to hang out with my buddies and I saw Rory in the bar. She'd just finished her shift and was takin' advantage of the employee discount by doin' a shit ton of shots. Some assholes were bothering her so I kept 'em away." He sighed. "Rory don't drink, so the booze hit her like a cattle truck. Then she started cryin' about how her mama used every penny they had to put her through college. And she'd wanted to get a job after she graduated, but Rielle told her it was more important she finish grad school since it was basically free."

"Christ."

"I don't think Rory knew what the fuck she was even sayin'. I couldn't leave her there, so her boss told me where Rory lived. I took her home." He scowled. "She tossed her cookies in my truck and on me."

"Just like when you used to baby-sit her, huh?" Tell teased.

"Go to hell. I never babysat her."

"I remember. You ran nekkid through the woods with her playing Tarzan and Jane. Or Adam and Eve. Or...doctor."

Dalton ignored him. "So when Rory called me the next day to apologize for barfing on me, I didn't mention she'd been a freakin' blabbermouth. And if she did remember, I doubt she's gonna confess to Rielle that she told their financial sob story to a McKay."

"While I appreciate you tellin' me this, I gotta ask...why?"

Tell leaned forward. "The way we see it, Rielle would probably rather sell the land, or part of it, than lose it entirely when it gets foreclosed on. So we're thinkin' we should approach her with a business proposition. We'll make the cash payments to catch her up on the bank loan to stave off the foreclosure—if she'll divide up the back half of her land and sell it to us. That way it'd be McKay land, from your place to ours, as it should've been before my dad fucked it up all those years ago."

Ben gave them credit for quick thinking. "We've always wanted that creek front section. But they've always refused to sell."

"It don't look like Rielle's got an option now. The sale of that acreage will give her enough money to keep her bed and breakfast open if she wants."

"Who else have you talked to about this?"

"No one," Dalton said. "Not even Brandt."

"Why not?"

"Because as much as we appreciate that Brandt's a hard worker, he's a damn do-gooder. He'll see even talkin' to Rielle as takin' advantage of her. We don't see it that way. We figured you wouldn't either. So, we'd appreciate it if you didn't mention this to Quinn."

It clicked. "Quinn would feel the same as Brandt."

Tell nodded. "You're practical, Ben. And to some extent, unsentimental, like us. It's just business."

"Good business," Dalton inserted. "It has to be just the three of us, if we can swing it."

"Because you don't want Uncle Carson or Uncle Cal to get wind of this either."

"And buy it right out from under us? Fuck no. But it ain't like the purchase wouldn't benefit the entire McKay ranching operation. It'd just give both our families a little more land, a little more pull, and maybe a little more respect. I mean, yeah, they're treating us better than they ever have, askin' for our input, increasing our shares, but sometimes we still feel like the poor relatives."

Again, Ben couldn't argue with their logic. "Do you guys have the capital?" Not wanting to admit he fell into the *poor relative* category, he added sharply, "Because I sure as hell ain't funding the whole thing." He wasn't sure he could fund even a portion of it. He'd have to hope like hell some of his furniture payments came through.

A fierce look entered Dalton's eyes. "I know you didn't mean that to be insulting, cuz. Yeah, me'n Tell are the youngest, but that don't make us the dumbest. We put up the lion's share of the down payment for that section we bought, more than Brandt. Dad don't even know that."

He whistled. "Impressive. You saved all that?"

They exchanged another look. "Not exactly."

"What have you boys been up to?"

"Poker."

"Excuse me?"

Tell offered a shit-eating grin. "We've become damn good poker players. We hit Deadwood for weekend tournaments. Blackhawk, Colorado, has decent-sized pots once a month. We made a shit ton of money playin' online before most them sites closed down."

"When I was in Vegas with you last December for the NFR?"

"I rocked it at the poker tables. Played a little blackjack. I ended up fifteen grand ahead."

Seemed he wasn't the only one with a secret life. "Does Brandt know about any of this?"

"No. He thinks we're man-whores, hittin' strip clubs all over hell when we're really playing poker."

"Except for the weekends I'm working as a rodeo judge," Tell clarified. "So you see why we don't want him to know about this. Alls we want is a bigger piece of the pie and not to have to borrow money from one of the uncles to make improvements on our land."

"Dad didn't have a problem with that, but the rest of us did," Dalton said sourly.

"I don't blame you. I would've had a problem with that too."

"But we can't just show up on Rielle's doorstep and ask if what Rory said was true. It'd be easier if someone Rielle knows and trusts, someone she owes neighborly favors to, would get the real scoop."

"Seriously? I'm supposed to pop over and say, 'Hey, Ree, thanks for watching my dogs and for the zucchini bread and by the way, how much are you behind on your bank payments?'"

"We hoped you'd use your no bullshit reputation to get the facts, and not act the part of an ass-kissing suck-up like the rest of our relatives."

Ben scrubbed his hand over his jaw. This had caught him off guard. "Look. I appreciate your trust in me. I ain't gonna say nothin' to nobody, but I need time to chew it over. Okay?"

"Okay. But don't forget the ticking clock."

Tara delivered the food. She dropped Tell's hot beef sandwich almost from eye level. The cheeky bastard just grinned at her and said, "Thanks, darlin'."

Conversation ceased as they ate.

Ben made a point not to stare at Ainsley, because his cousins would notice his distraction.

Then again, Tell and Dalton shoveled food like they'd never seen it. "What's the rush?"

"No need to sit around and bullshit when there's work to finish." Dalton dropped a twenty on the table. "Let us know if you find anything out."

As his cousins exited the restaurant, Ainsley and the mayor

headed toward him. Ainsley kept her expression blank.

The mayor, Mark Gilbert, was effusive. "Ben McKay! I haven't seen you in town for a while. Did we tick you off or something?" He thrust out his hand.

Ben shook it. "No, sir, Mr. Mayor. Just keeping myself busy on the ranch. Snuck into town to have lunch with my cousins."

Mark leaned in. "What's with this Mr. Mayor bullshit? We've known each other since elementary school."

Ben held Ainsley's gaze. "Just wanted to show you the proper respect when you're havin' lunch with the president of Sundance's newest bank."

He laughed. "Of course you've already met the lovely and capable Miz Hamilton. The McKays have a knack for knowing when a beautiful new woman arrives in town and mercilessly working her with those cowboy charms."

Slathering on the flattery for Ainsley while taking a small shot at him? Mayor Mark didn't miss a trick.

Ben offered Ainsley his hand. "Good to see you again, Miz Hamilton."

"You too, Mr. McKay."

"Ainsley and I were just discussing ideas for the next community event. We're hoping to have something big to welcome National West Bank to our community. You have any thoughts?"

Ainsley cocked her head. "I'd love to hear your input. I've heard your family is a big part of this community and has been for over one hundred years."

"At the risk of bein' accused of nepotism, I'd suggest a community celebration to honor my brother Chase's accomplishments this past year. He might not be headed to the PBR World Finals, but he's done an outstanding job starting his own advocacy group for mandatory safety helmets in bull riding. The mayor knows any time Chase comes back to town there's always people interested in hearing him talk. Now that he's gone and married himself a genuine movie star?" Ben grinned. "This community event could have worldwide attention."

"That's an excellent suggestion, Ben." Mark said. "Would Chase be interested?"

"I can ask him. If he is you'll have to get in touch with his PR people to finalize the details. I only see one problem with this."

"What's that?"

"The McKays have always been customers at Settler's First Bank. I reckon they won't take too kindly to a celebration for Chase McKay bein' sponsored by a competing bank."

Silence.

Ainsley looked impressed...and a little peeved.

"I'm sure we could work something out." Mark glanced at his watch. "I'm afraid I've got a meeting. Could I drop you off at the bank, Ainsley?"

"No. I'll walk back. I'd like to talk a little more in depth with Mr. McKay about his ideas." She winked at Mark. "Maybe try to sweet talk him into hearing my National West Bank pitch about all the services we offer our new customers."

"Excellent idea. Enjoy." He hustled out the door.

Ben gestured to the booth. "Could I interest you in a slice of pie or a cup of coffee while I hear how well you can service me?"

Her stern look vanished into a reluctant smile. "My God. You are unbelievable."

"That's what I've been tryin' to tell you."

After receiving their coffee, Ben had his first doubt Ainsley would agree to his proposition. She spent a considerable amount of time stirring sweetener into her cup, avoiding his eyes.

"Something wrong?" he finally asked.

"No." She glanced up. "Just trying to grasp how the man who groaned when I talked about community responsibility last night came up with a brilliant idea for my community event that cuts my part out of it entirely."

He shrugged. "I'm not worried. I'm sure you and Settler's First can come to an agreement that benefits both of you equally."

"Will *our* agreement benefit us both equally?"

So she didn't intend to skirt the issue. "Yep."

"Care to elaborate?"

"You wanna talk about this now?"

Ainsley looked around the restaurant, almost comically, before she lowered her voice to a near whisper. "Actually, yes, I do."

"Why?"

"Because I'll be able to think clearly when you're not touching

113

me."

Ben smiled unrepentantly. "Words can be just as powerful as a touch."

She challenged him with an arch look.

He also dropped his voice. "Did you imagine yourself havin' sex with Mayor Mark? I'll admit I imagined you in bed with him."

That threw her off. "Why on earth would you imagine that?"

"Because I saw how he looked at you, and, angel, Mark was definitely imagining you in his bed."

Her response might've been, "Oh please," but she really meant, *Go on.*

"This is how I imagined it. He'd probably undress you slowly. Kiss you, run his hands down your chest. Keep all touches gentle and exploratory. When you give him the signal to move on, maybe by releasing a little moan, that's when he'll put his mouth on your skin. Starting with your nipples. He'll spend way more time licking and sucking on them than even you'd like. He'll kiss straight down your belly and you'll feel that tingle of anticipation. Wondering if he'll put his mouth on your pussy and get you off first. Or if he'll just tease you. Push you to the edge and then slip on a condom to take you the rest of the way. I'd bet he's more of a teaser, more an equal opportunity man. If you go down on him, he'll go down on you.

"When he deems you ready for his cock, he'll gently ease inside you, looking in your eyes. He'll keep up a steady pace, asking you the entire time if it's okay. He'll try to remember to kiss you as the momentum builds and he fucks you faster. You won't demand he slow down and see to your needs before his. You decide you'll let it slide this first time. After he comes, he'll pant in your ear how good it was. You'll tell yourself it was okay. Even if you don't believe it. Even if you have a sense that something was missing."

Ainsley stared at him. "And there's something wrong with that scenario?"

"Yes, goddammit, there is, because that's not what you want. That's the type of sexual encounter you've had your whole life."

Her haughty look vanished.

"Now imagine having sex with me."

She licked her lips.

"You know it's not that civilized with me. Sex with me is raw, dirty and demanding, but you'll never feel there's something missing because I will see to your needs above my own. Every. Single. Time."

"So you're more of a giver than a taker?"

"Don't get me wrong, I take plenty. But never at your expense."

She softly said, "Then my answer is yes. One month."

Relief flowed through him.

Ainsley scooted from the booth and Ben followed her outside. He admired how respectable she looked in a form-fitting gold-colored business suit, and he couldn't wait to thoroughly muss her up. "Be at my place right after work."

"So this is strictly clandestine between us?" she asked. "No public outings in Sundance?"

"Nope."

"Well, I don't believe we'll spend all of our time together naked."

"Don't bet the bank on that." Ben tipped his hat and strode away.

Chapter Twelve

Ben hated putting his dogs outside. But if he wanted to use all the rooms in his house with Ainsley, curious sniffing dogs would put a damper on that real fast.

He wasn't a pacing kind of guy, but he beat a path from his kitchen to the bar, through the game room, to his bedroom and back to the living room. He rarely had a case of nerves, but he definitely was feeling them tonight.

Way to act like a confident Dom.

Finally, Ainsley knocked on the door.

Gone was the bank executive. She'd dressed in a long-sleeved T-shirt the color of summer grass, jeans and puffy, down-filled vest. She wasn't carrying an overnight bag.

"Hey. Come in. Did you eat?"

Ainsley shook her head. "Nervous stomach. I wasn't sure..."

"If I'd make you strip the instant you walked in and we'd go at it in the foyer?"

"To be honest, yes."

Ben took her hands in his. "Ainsley. I wanna get to know you. All sides of you. Not just how you respond to me when you're nekkid and trussed up."

"That's a relief."

"For me too."

"Why?"

"Performance anxiety."

She laughed softly, naturally. "I doubt you've ever suffered from that in your life."

"There's always that first time. Now, I've gotta make an embarrassing confession." Ben hung his head. "I'm addicted to *Wheel of Fortune*. Most nights I eat supper in front of the TV so I can get my fix."

"Well, that changes things between us dramatically. Because I'm more of a *Jeopardy* fan myself."

"That's because you have way more brain power than me, smart girl."

"Because you're just a simple rancher, right?" she teased.

"Yep. So how about if I fix us a bowl of popcorn and you can snicker at me as I try to guess the puzzles?"

"Sounds good. You need help?"

"Why? Do you think I'll burn it?"

"No. I just want to make sure you pour extra butter on mine." She stood on tiptoe and kissed him. "If your goal is to keep me off balance, it's working."

They settled in front of the TV. Ben thought you could learn a lot about a person by how they ate popcorn. The quiet munchers? Reserved in life. Loud crunchers? Enjoyed everything with gusto. Eating a single kernel at a time? Very methodical. Piling on extra butter, extra salt and extra seasoning? A hedonistic bent. So it'd pleased him to watch Ainsley pour butter and sprinkle all sorts of seasonings on her popcorn.

She bumped him with her shoulder. "Have you figured out this phrase yet?"

"Nope. You?"

"Yes."

"Prove it."

"On a chicken wing and a prayer."

He groaned. "I hate the pun ones."

"Aren't they all puns?"

"No. Heh. Look. He went bankrupt anyway. That sucks."

During the next commercial, he casually asked, "Are we usin' condoms?"

She stiffened. "I guess. Why?"

"I just hoped you were on the pill. But no biggie."

"I'm on the pill but I don't know if I'm comfortable having sex without a condom, with a man who frequents a sex club. No offense."

"None taken. I'll just mention I got a clean bill of health three months ago and I could show you the paperwork. Twice yearly testing is mandatory for club members. I've always worn a condom. No exceptions."

"Even when you...play like this, outside the club?"

Ben faced her, but she was busy rooting around in her bowl. "Look at me."

She peeked at him from beneath her lashes.

"In the years I've belonged to the Rawhide I've seen a woman outside the club only a few times. But I've never done this—asked a woman to be my submissive for a month outside the club."

"What about inside the club?"

"No."

She hadn't been expecting that answer. "Do you have normal relationships? I mean, date normal women who don't know about you being involved in the club?"

"I'll ignore your use of the word *normal* because of your lack of experience. I used to date. Then my buddy Cody took me to a club in Denver and it changed my life. I no longer felt like a deviant for what I wanted from my partners. I no longer had to pretend my needs were conventional."

Ainsley blushed.

"Every once in a while I'll meet a woman outside the club and ask her out. But if I can't be myself, why waste my time?"

"What's the longest you've dated a woman?"

"Probably...a month."

"Is that why you insisted on a month with me?"

Astute woman. It'd just seemed like an arbitrary amount of time. "No. As a newbie sub, you oughta know in thirty days whether you're cut out to be submissive, even just behind bedroom doors." He gave her a buttery, salty, smacking kiss. "Quit distracting me from Vanna, woman."

Ben solved the next puzzle. They bantered back and forth. But when the game show ended, he sensed Ainsley's anxiety. He set aside her empty popcorn bowl. "Sit on my lap facing me."

"Aren't you afraid I'll make your crotch go numb? I'm not exactly a petite woman, Ben."

"Don't make me repeat myself."

Ainsley threw her leg over his and straddled his thighs. "I guess Bennett the beastly Dom is back."

He curled his hand around her neck and took her mouth in a heated kiss. No easing into it, just sucking in her surprise like a drug. Holding her in place while he controlled the kiss. Keeping it red-hot until she could scarcely sit still. He backed off the intensity, sliding his mouth to her ear. "Go into my bedroom and get undressed. Then lay facedown on the bed."

She immediately tensed up.

Ben waited for her to ask why, or what he had in mind.

"I..." He heard her swallow. "Which room is your bedroom?"

"The room with the four-poster log bed."

Keeping her eyes averted, she climbed off him and disappeared down the hallway.

He flipped through channels for five minutes before he followed her. He paused in the doorway, his eyes drinking her in. Ainsley's body was an abundance of curves, just exactly the body type he liked best.

After shucking his jeans and shirt, he grabbed a necktie, a condom and a bottle of lube from his dresser. From beside the bed, he ordered, "Spread your arms out." Then he straddled her, his knees bracketing her thighs. His cock stirred when his balls brushed the soft curves of her ass. Ben placed a kiss on the back of her head, inhaling the subtle scent of her shampoo. "Do you have any idea how fucking sexy you look?"

He dug his thumbs into the base of her neck and gradually moved across the tops of her shoulders, using a combination of soft and harder pressure. Letting himself enjoy her supple flesh beneath his hands. Goose bumps rippled across her back every time the rougher skin on his hands glided across her. He kneaded her biceps and triceps. He nestled a kiss in the bend of each elbow before massaging her forearms and hands. When he reversed course and dragged his palms over her arms, Ainsley didn't utter a peep.

"You're awful quiet," he remarked as his thumbs followed the line of her spine.

"I wasn't sure if I was allowed to speak."

Ben stilled. "Why would you think that?"

"Because those are the Dom's rules in books I've read."

"What books?"

"The ones that deal with...BDSM."

To some extent, he hated the way the term BDSM was thrown

around as much as he disliked the casual use of the word Master.

"Have you read any of those books?" she asked.

"Fiction? Or nonfiction?"

"Either."

"Nonfiction. When we first went to the Denver club. One of the owners saw that we were clueless bastards and took pity on us. He gave us a stack of material to read so we knew the differences between what we wanted as dominants and what was expected in certain Dom/sub relationships. And I'll admit, even from the start, I've been on the side of the fence where dominance is used as a sexual tool to heighten sexual experiences. I'm not into debasing a sub by using a cage or a pallet to sleep on or a shock collar. Or extreme pain games. Never been tempted by bloodsport or knife play or piss play or even breath play. If I knew subs who were into that stuff, I'd avoid them. But I'll admit it's practically nonexistent at the Rawhide anyway." He rubbed a spot at the base of her neck. "So the subs don't speak because they're gagged or something in these books?"

"No. A sub isn't supposed to speak unless asked a direct question by her dominant. And in scenes, the sub isn't supposed to cry out in pain or in pleasure unless the Dom permits her to."

Ben tamped down his temper. "Have I ever said you can't talk?"

"Umm. No."

"Think I'll ever forbid you from speakin' your mind?"

"No."

"I might take issue if you argue with me about something I tell you to do, but I don't expect monk-like silence from you."

"Oh."

"And this isn't a scene," he said testily.

She lifted up and looked over her shoulder at him. "It's not?"

"No. Christ. I'm giving you a massage."

"Why?"

"Why am I giving you a massage? Because I wanted to put my hands all over you. And you acted nervous. I thought it'd calm you down."

Ainsley continued to stare at him.

"What?"

"You confuse me, Bennett. This confuses me. The variances in the different types of Dom/sub relationships…"

"Hey, there are no rules for us besides the ones I set—with your input. I suspect this will be a *learn as we go* thing for both of us." He lightly slapped her ass. "Face back on the mattress, so I can finish."

From that point on, Ainsley was vocal.

"So tell me more about these BDSM books you read. What things you read in them that turned you off."

"You're more interested in what I *didn't* like than what I did?"

"I'm pretty confident I can figure out what you like." He pressed his thumbs onto a knot beside her right shoulder blade.

"Oh. I like that. You hit it. Right. On. The. Money." Another sexy moan of delight. "You have magic hands."

"Tell me one sex fantasy that ain't in a book."

Ainsley didn't answer.

He stopped the massage. "Tell me or no more magic fingers."

She groaned and said, "Fine, I have a stranger fantasy. It's dark. I wake up and notice him in the shadows. I'm freaked out and then he starts saying all these sexy things. How he's whacked off imagining how it'd be to touch me. How he knows what I sound like when I climax because he's watched me touching myself. He does all sorts of sexy, naughty things to me and then he just leaves and I never knew who he was."

Ben kissed her temple "See? That wasn't so bad."

"I'd hate for you to think I'm the boring banker type with no imagination."

His chuckle vibrated against her neck. "The last damn thing you are is boring. So tell me more about these books. Specifically what you don't like."

"I don't like the master and slave mentality of the BDSM relationships. Where the subs are always expected to kneel at the Dom's feet. Or when they have to keep their heads lowered and eyes averted, not only for their Dom but also for all other Doms, in a club situation. I don't like how the subs are supposed to walk three steps behind their Doms. I really didn't like the leash and collar thing."

"Were you disappointed that you didn't see any of that goin' on in the Rawhide?"

"God no."

"That's a pretty long list of dislikes."

"I was just getting started."

"I'll keep that in mind."

Ainsley jerked up. "Now that I've told you my fantasy and dislikes, will you use them against me?"

Ben pushed her back down. "You know, I'm a little tired of you jumping to the worst conclusion when it comes to me and who I am as your dominant. I get that you wanna know ahead of time everything I have planned for you, Ainsley, but guess what? It ain't happening." He grabbed the tie and said, "Arms behind your back."

"But, I didn't mean—"

"Now." As soon as her arms were in place, he tied her wrists together. He spread her legs and slicked up his fingers with the lube. "Angle your hips so I can reach your pussy."

She had to push up on her knees, and she didn't look comfortable, but she didn't argue.

Ben's fingers traced her slit. "A massage makes you wet?"

"Only when you give me one."

"A total suck-up answer."

Ainsley moaned when he slipped a finger inside her.

"You need to concentrate on my voice and listen to what I'm telling you."

"It feels so good. What if I can't concentrate?"

Ben didn't stop stroking her wet folds as he spoke. "Then you'll learn the difference between punishment and discipline pretty damn quick."

"Is this punishment?"

"No." He swept his thumb over her clit. "This is discipline." He brushed his lips below her earlobe. "Don't come. No matter what I do, you don't get to come."

"But—"

"This is not up for discussion. You will not come. Not now, not at your house. Your orgasms belong to me. They're my responsibility. You don't control them anymore. Understand?"

"Uh-huh."

Ben pushed two fingers inside her and stroked her G-spot, while gently strumming her clit. "Say yes, Bennett, I understand."

"Yes, Bennett, I understand."

He teased, tortured and tormented her. Taking her to the edge several times, seeing if she'd disobey and throw herself over. He skimmed her jawline with light kisses. "How close are you?"

"Very. God."

Ben flipped her onto her back and started kissing down the side of her neck.

"Don't. Please." Ainsley twisted her head away.

Which caused Ben to grab her hair and pull slightly. "Stay. Still."

She whimpered softly.

"I adore your body, angel." Ben kissed the hollow of her throat. The tops of her breasts. "I intend to play with it, however I want, for as long as I want. Testing your limits and mine." He kept finger fucking her, studying her reactions, from the anxious expression on her face, to the hard tips of her nipples, to the flexing of her toes and the clenching of her jaw. When he heard that swift intake of breath, he removed his hand from between her thighs.

Her entire body drooped against the mattress, but she wasn't relaxed.

"You did good." Ben turned her on her side so they faced each other. She sighed as he continued to intersperse tender kisses with languorous caresses. "You ready to talk?"

Ainsley slowly opened her eyes. "Talk? Aren't we going to..." Her gaze dropped to his crotch and the outline of his fully erect dick.

"Fuck? Make love? Have wild sex? Not tonight."

"Oh."

"You're gonna tell me your hard limit. One thing that's an absolute no."

"Only one thing?"

"Yep. You won't know if other things on your very long dislike list would actually be a like unless you try it. Fair warning: I've only got a month with you, so I wanna give you a taste of everything."

"Everything?"

"Everything but your one thing. So what's it gonna be?"

She blurted, "You using one of those scary bullwhip or snake whips on me is an absolute no."

Damn. No single tail. "Okay."

"You just accept that?"

"Yes. Because you only get one. Everything else is a possibility." Ben smooched the frown between her eyebrows. "Tell me something you've never told anyone."

"Like what?"

"Anything." He traced her cheekbone with his knuckles. "Big secret, little annoyance. Give me a piece of yourself you've never shared with anyone else."

She focused on his chest and those tiny furrowed lines appeared on her forehead. "I had lasik surgery on both my eyes four years ago. People knew about it because I'd been wearing glasses for twenty-two years, but I never told anyone why I did it."

"Why?"

"I thought losing the glasses would make me more attractive to my husband. Obviously it didn't work. He just bitched about the price of the surgery."

"Were you happy with your decision?"

"Yes. I felt younger, freer. I liked the change."

Ben kissed the corners of her eyes. "You should. I'm guessing it was the first of many changes."

"It was. It is. Same question back at you, Ben."

Not Bennett. Interesting. He didn't answer, just kept touching her how he pleased.

"You constantly harp about honesty. You expect mine but don't offer yours? That's crap. Sir."

He held back a Dom-like retort. "You're right."

"So tell me something you've never told anyone."

That's when Ben knew he'd have to up the stakes. Ainsley had given him what he'd asked for, but her answer wasn't anything really personal. Or if that was her idea of exposing an unseen part of herself, he'd need to convince her to mine deeper. She was still far too guarded with him, and he needed to break that first barrier. Show his vulnerability on a level that made him slightly uncomfortable.

"I ran away from home when I was eight. I remember feeling ignored, invisible, that no one would care if I just left. I had these visions of my mom and dad frantically searching for me. They were screaming my name, regretting their treatment of me, while my brothers cried. So I took off early one mornin', making sure I didn't go to any of my favorite spots. I waited for them to come find me. But no one ever did. I spent the night by myself. Alone. Every fear realized. Around dawn, a solid day after I'd left, I snuck into my bed. Nothing had changed for them, but it seemed everything had changed for me. I've always felt that day cemented my place in the family. The middle child but in last place."

A beat passed and warm lips connected with his. Ainsley kissed him with the perfect mix of fire and sweetness. When she angled her head to take the kiss deeper, Ben realized her cheeks were wet.

His brain did a victory dance. Although he never wanted any woman to see him as the forgotten boy in Dom's clothes, he was humbled and touched by her honest tears. And he knew the next time he asked her to share something emotionally personal, she'd be less hesitant. "Let's get you untied," he said gruffly.

Ben checked her circulation, falling back into Dom mode. He remained stretched out on the bed as she put her clothes back on, not caring if his staring made her uncomfortable. She'd said as much. His response? "Tough."

He'd kept her flustered, rebuilding that passion between them as he herded her back to the living room. Kissing her. Biting on her neck. Stroking her nipples through her clothing. Then he helped her on with her coat. "Remember. You don't get to come. And if you do get yourself off? I'll know."

"How?"

"Because you are a bad liar. Don't push me on this, Ainsley." He bestowed one last, hot kiss. "See you tomorrow night."

Chapter Thirteen

Since Ben intended to keep her off balance, Ainsley decided she'd do the same to him. Accepting her submissive side didn't mean she had to be malleable or predictable. She could be a temptress. She could feed the soul of the dominant man. And she could damn well cook him dinner too. They both had to eat.

She arrived at his house, bearing a Crock-Pot filled with a pork roast and potatoes. His rowdy dogs nearly jostled it out of her hands as she waited for him to answer her knock.

Oh my Lord. She watched Ben approach through the glass-paned front door, wearing a towel and a scowl. A tiny shiver worked free. She never wanted that displeased look aimed at her. Luckily his glower was focused on his unruly dogs.

Maybe he wouldn't notice the drool dripping from her chin at seeing him nearly nude.

When he opened the door a crack, the dogs clambered to get inside. He snapped, "Sit." The dogs sat. "Stay." They whimpered. And stayed. Wagged their tails to get their master's attention. He opened the door for Ainsley. Once she was inside, he said, "Take off," to the dogs and they slunk away. He finally looked at her, then at the Crock-Pot she held. "What's this?"

"Dinner. You made me dinner the other night, I'm returning the favor."

"Smells good. You can plug it in by the coffeepot."

Ainsley felt his eyes on her as she fussed with the temperature and the lid. When she turned around, Bennett wore the Dom face.

"Supper will keep for a while?"

She nodded.

"Good. Clothes off."

"Right here?"

That one brow lifted as if to say, *You challenging me, sub?* and she stripped without another word.

He directed her through his bedroom to his bathroom. The rectangular shower had a clear glass door. The back walls and floor were comprised of dark gray tiles. Half a dozen nozzles were placed at different intervals on the side wall, and an enormous showerhead was centered in the middle of the ceiling. In the back corner was a built-in seat and another smaller handheld showerhead on the opposite wall. She'd take a gorgeous space like this over a sunken tub any day.

"You're just in time to help me get cleaned up."

Ainsley had a moment of panic. She wasn't one of those women who looked sleek and sexy under the spray of water. Her hair frizzed the instant a drop of humidity touched it. Plus, she wasn't wearing waterproof mascara. So she'd resemble a fat, fuzzed-out rat with raccoon eyes. Yeah. There was an image to turn him on.

Bennett motioned her inside the enclosure and settled her against the far wall. The tile chilled her back. He turned on the water and stood beneath the spray, facing her. "Watch me."

Like she could take her eyes off his beautiful form. Long and lean, ripped arms, narrow torso, strong legs—his every muscle looked carved from granite. He wet a washcloth and soaped up, filling the humid space with a piney scent. Briskly rubbing the sudsy cloth over his arms, his neck and shoulders. Across his pecs and abdomen to his crotch. Over his fully erect cock. Between his legs, down to his ankles, feet and toes. He tossed the cloth aside and squirted shampoo into his palm. Closing his eyes, he scrubbed his head, turning away to rinse.

The rear view was as impressive as his front. Powerful shoulders and back. Firm buttocks so perfectly round and hard her teeth ached to take a bite.

He shut the water off, but steam still hissed from a pipe low to the floor, keeping the space warm. Bennett said, "Face the wall."

He'd moved in behind her. His mouth latched onto her nape. "Did you touch yourself last night after you left here?"

"No."

"Did you touch yourself this mornin'?"

"No."

"And how did you feel today?"

"Achy. Edgy. Needy."

His hot breath burned her ear. "That's how you're supposed to feel. Last night was about putting you at ease. Tonight is about you proving to me that you're ready for this."

She squared her shoulders. "I am ready."

Sweet, lazy kisses morphed into tiny nips on the fleshy slope of her shoulder. She shivered. Bit her lip against a moan.

He zigzagged his tongue along her spine to the tops of her buttocks and placed a sucking kiss in the middle of each cheek. "Get on your knees."

Again she felt that flip in her belly. That spike of heat in her pulse. That deep throb in her sex. As she got into position, Bennett perched on the edge of the bench seat, his feet planted wide on the tile floor.

She dropped to her knees, allowing her hands to rest on her lap.

"Angel, you are a quick study."

His compliment stirred an odd sense of pride inside her.

"Touch your nipples."

Ainsley pressed her palms over her breasts. Squeezing the fleshy globes, she began to rub the centers of her palms over her nipples in small circles.

Her gaze flew to his when two strong hands enclosed her wrists, stopping the motion.

Bennett brought her right palm to his mouth and thoroughly bathed it with his tongue. Then her left palm. Then he placed them back on her nipples.

The wetness from his mouth coupled with the heat in his eyes tightened the tips further. She rubbed faster. Need radiated from her breasts down her belly to gather between her thighs. She was hyperaware of the incremental changes in her own body as she became aroused. She hadn't taken the time to absorb those changes in the past. She'd been was too busy racing toward the orgasm finish line.

"Pinch them," he said gruffly.

It was almost a relief to add more pressure.

"Harder. I wanna hear you gasp like that again. You can take a little more pain."

Ainsley half-expected he'd reach out and show her what he wanted, but he didn't. He expected her to follow his directions. Using just the tips of her thumbs and forefingers, she pulled her nipples and squeezed. A hot line of pain made her gasp.

A brawny hand cupped the back of her neck, bringing her head forward. She opened her eyes as the head of Bennett's cock touched her mouth.

He painted her lips with the wet tip. "Relax your jaw. See how deep you can take me on the first try." He didn't wait for her to open her mouth fully; he just pushed past her lips.

She sucked when the thick cockhead rested on her tongue, wanting that first wholly male taste of him. She sucked again, harder, attempting to pull more of his shaft into her mouth, letting her tongue explore the sensitive underside.

Bennett's hand curled around her jaw. "As much as I love those fuckin' sexy little moans you're making, you don't get to direct this."

Chastised, she peered up at him.

"Goddamn I like the defiant look you're wearing right now. Like you expect me not to have enough willpower to stop you." He shoved his cock further into her mouth, kicking in her gag reflex. "Wrong. I have more control than you know."

Her eyes watered as she fought the urge to dislodge the hardness filling her mouth.

"Breathe." His thumb stroked her cheek. "It's gonna take some practice for you to take me all the way." His blue eyes glittered with lust. "I'm a patient man, but I can't wait to have your breath on my belly as my cock is buried so deep in your throat I can feel your heartbeat."

That dirty play-by-play absolutely drenched her. Ainsley so wanted to squeeze her legs together to spread that hot slickness between her thighs. Physical proof she was really here and this wasn't just another fantasy.

It wasn't that she broke a rule; she just stretched the boundary a bit when she curled her hands around his knees and let her palms slide up his muscular legs until they reached his hips.

Bennett softly snarled at her. "Just for that, you don't get to use your hands on my cock. Only this wicked mouth." He pulled out and stroked back in, each time coming closer to the back of her throat.

She closed her eyes, wanting so much to make this good for him.

"Don't swallow until I tell you to," he warned. "I wanna see liquid running outta your mouth, making your neck wet."

Every time she settled into the rhythm, Bennett mixed it up.

129

Thrusting faster if he was going slow. Slowing down if he'd been using short, quick jabs. Proving to her that he had all the control.

She loved every second of it. His hand gripping the back of her neck. The hardness of his cock on her tongue, hitting the roof of her mouth, rubbing the inside of her cheek.

"Play with my balls," he rasped, "but only my balls."

The globes were already drawn up when her fingers brushed the seam between them. She rolled the balls on her palm. Her middle finger slid back to tickle his perineum with every upstroke of her mouth.

His thrusts all became short and fast.

Ainsley heard that swift intake of breath. The head rested on her tongue. His guttural, "Suck hard now," was her only warning before hot ejaculate spurted in her mouth. "Swallow. All of it."

She hollowed her cheeks and sucked, moving her tongue back and forth beneath the sweet spot as she swallowed.

"So. Fucking. Good. Christ."

There was an endorsement of her oral skills. But she didn't let up even to allow a small, cocky smile.

He slowly pulled out, using the hand holding the back of her neck to tip her head back.

Ainsley licked her smooth lips and met his gaze. Sated, yes. But something else lingered there. Something primal.

Bennett trailed his finger from the tip of her chin, down through the wetness coating her throat. "Beautiful. Look at you. So fucking beautiful."

She blushed. No man ever said anything like that to her. Even while part of her did the cha-cha that she'd pleased him, she wondered if his compliments were simply because she'd just blown him.

"What was that?"

"What was what?"

"That skeptical look. You frowned at me."

Damn. She did have a crap poker face. "I did?"

"Mmm. But I know what'll fix that. Stand."

Her knees were wobbly. Bennett held onto her hips and nestled his face into her cleavage. Then he kissed the upper and lower swells of both her breasts before sucking on her nipples. Sucking with lazy intent. Showing her that the sucking was all about his enjoyment of her body, not hers. Which made his attentions that much more enjoyable.

He tipped his head back and looked at her when she sighed. "We'll pick this up later. Meantime, feel free to use my robe."

"I can't get dressed?"

"No."

"But—"

"Keep it up and you'll be eatin' supper nekkid."

"Your robe will be just fine."

He smirked and tossed her a towel. "Thought you might say that."

After supper they watched the DVR'd episode of *Wheel of Fortune* and snuggled up on the couch.

Ben liked having Ainsley close. Their legs side by side on the ottoman. Her head resting on his shoulder. Her hand on his chest. His fingers trailing up and down her arm. Touching her without restriction as a Dom was one thing. But touching her like this? Almost absentmindedly just because he could? That gave him a sense of satisfaction on a different level.

"You don't talk much about ranching."

"Not much to say. I get up, I do it, I come home, go to bed and repeat the next day. Pretty much the same day in, day out. Except for when we're calving or haying."

Ainsley drew circles on his pec. "Do you get bored?"

"I don't have time to get bored."

"Tell me one thing you did today that was out of the ordinary."

He smiled because she'd tried to wrest control. Instead of waiting for him to question her about something personal, like he had last night, she'd tried to get the jump on him by keeping her question innocuous. "I got an awesome blowjob in the shower."

She poked his sternum. "Besides that."

"I had a beautiful lady bring me supper."

Three more pokes. "Come on. Tell me something."

Ben tried to remember what the hell he had done today. "How about while I'm thinking on that you tell me something out of the ordinary *you* did today."

Silence. Then she sighed. "I can't think of a single thing."

"So banking is as boring as ranching?" he teased.

"At least it was today. Tomorrow I'm hoping for—"

"A bank heist?"

"Bite your tongue, Ben McKay."

He laughed. "Well, tomorrow afternoon I'll be doin' something out of the ordinary. I'm taking my folks to the Rapid City airport."

"Where are they going?"

"Phoenix."

"On vacation?"

"Of sorts. They're mostly goin' to see my brother Gavin."

Ainsley tilted her head to look at him. "I remember you talking about your older brother, Quinn, and your younger brother Chase, but not about Gavin."

"That's because Gavin is...let's just say Gavin recently came into our family." Ben laid out the situation. "Long story short, we're still tryin' to figure it out. On the spur of the moment Gavin invited Mom and Dad to Arizona. So I won't be around tomorrow night."

"Oh."

Did it make him a bastard for being happy to hear disappointment in her voice? "Which is why you're spending the weekend here starting Friday night."

She blinked at him. "I am? I don't remember agreeing to that."

"Because that wasn't a request." Well, it was, but he didn't want to risk she'd say no.

"Okay. Should I bring anything?"

"Your collection of vibrators."

Her cheeks pinked. "How did you—"

"You told me at the club, remember?"

"No. That's not something I usually share."

Ben kissed her nose. "We're sharing a lot, though, aren't we?"

"Some of us more than others," she snipped.

That stopped him. "You think I'm holding back?"

"I *know* you're holding back, cowboy."

"About what?"

"About how you became Master Bennett."

He frowned. "Master. I hate that fuckin' term."

"I know." Her smirk faded beneath his scrutiny. "You've grilled me about why I believed I was a Domme. You're determined to prove I'm submissive, but you've never explained how you became interested in this lifestyle."

"I don't suppose you'd buy the explanation of pure dumb luck?"

"Not entirely."

He settled back in the cushions. Had he ever explained this to anyone? "About eight years ago, me, Cody, Trace and Trent were drinking at the Rawhide Bar after closing time. Bullshitting about jobs and women. Complaining about not getting laid enough. Them guys were coming up with sure-fire strategies to get laid and what kind of women they were goin' after. When the conversation rolled to me and what I wanted from a woman, I told 'em I wanted a woman who'd give me total sexual control, without question or hesitation."

Ben still remembered that panicked feeling after confessing the truth to his closest friends. His worry something was wrong with him, even when he'd been too chicken to act on the erotic and exotic images constantly playing out in his head. Was he a deviant? A psychopath? A sociopath? Would it be enough if he fulfilled his binding, spanking and fucking fantasy, where his partner screamed and creamed from sexual pleasure? Or would he move on to a violent and twisted scenario? Because from what he could tell, his ideas were very twisted. Nice men didn't fantasize about hitting women with whips and canes. Nice men didn't fantasize about tying women up. Nice men didn't fantasize about doing all of that to women while fucking them like an animal.

"Ben?"

He looked at her. "Sorry. Just thinkin'. Come to find out Cody, Trace, Trent and me were all on the same wavelength. We found a couple of clubs in Denver that catered to what we wanted. Bein' in those places lifted a huge burden off me. I wasn't a total freak. Or a bad man. There was a name for what I liked. For what I was. And a place where I could go to explore all aspects."

"Labels are important to you?"

"I've always been labeled—Charlie McKay's middle boy, the one between Quinn and Chase. But I didn't think, 'Hey, I'll join a kinky sex club to set myself apart'. As relieved as I was to find out who I was, I didn't want anyone in my family to know what I was up to. I still don't."

"So began the secret life of Bennett McKay."

"It was a long way to drive, but we did it regularly for a couple years. Then Cody and Trace kicked around the idea of starting a similar, private club in Gillette. After they remodeled the old brothel space, we brought Murphy up from Denver to run it. We'd met Sully in Denver and found out he lived in Gillette. He brought in Riley. Riley brought in Gil. Gil brought in Bryce. All guys who either had Dom experience or were willing to learn. The ten of us set up the club rules, Murphy screened prospective club members, we opened the doors six years ago. Membership stays steady. But it's never been about makin' money."

"Are you financially invested in the club?" Ainsley asked.

"Typical banker question." Too bad he hadn't invested in it. That might solve some of his current financial issues. But Ben would come across as a fucking pussy if he admitted an emotional investment to the place had always been more important. That for him, it'd never been solely about the kinky sex, but him finding acceptance in himself.

"That wasn't an answer," she pointed out.

Once again she'd tried to commandeer the conversation, which had forced his thoughts to money and how he'd come up with his portion to buy Rielle's place, rather than the fact he had a naked sub sitting right next to him. "Because we're done talking." He allowed his gaze to linger on the curve of her breast peeking out by the lapel. "Ditch the robe."

Ainsley stood in front of him naked, awaiting instruction.

"Face the TV." He unearthed the fur lined handcuffs from beneath the couch cushion. As soon as she assumed the position, he cuffed her.

Ben struggled to shimmy his sweatpants off over his erection. Once he had his clothes off, he rolled on a condom. He said, "Turn around," and crooked his finger at her.

He braced her shoulders as she straddled his lap. He buried his face in her neck, searching for the honey-almond scent that drove him wild.

She shivered but didn't try and squirm away.

Ah. Progress.

Using just his fingertips, he traced the line of her stubborn jaw.

Caressed the corded muscles in her neck. Traced the angle of her clavicle to the edge of her shoulder. Every glorious indentation and plane. Then he followed the plump curves of her breasts past those pretty pink nipples. He curled his hands over her ribcage and stroked his thumbs over the soft, feminine swell of her belly and across that sensitive skin between her hipbones. Sometimes he murmured verbal worship of these amazingly unique female parts as his fingers explored, but tonight he wanted to concentrate on every hitch in her breathing. Every reaction to his touch.

He already caught the scent of her arousal and his dick stood at attention, ready to satisfy the call of her body.

Ben ran his fingers through her hair while he kissed her. Unhurriedly. She matched him kiss for kiss. Never veering from his lead. Giving all of herself over to him.

In that moment she was wholly his. What a fucking rush.

He'd intended to drag this out. Teasing those hot spots on her neck with his mouth until she begged to come and then getting her off with his hand. But now? He just wanted to fuck her.

He released her hair and aligned his cock to the source of that fragrant wet heat. Still feeding her deep soul kisses, he put one hand on her ass and urged her to lower her pelvis to his.

Then he was sliding up into that sublimely tight, hot pussy.

Ainsley briefly broke her mouth free from his to gasp softly.

Ben pumped his hips up to meet her downward thrusts. Each deep stroke drove his need higher. His need to hear her cry out. His need to see the pleasure on her face he'd denied her yesterday. He latched onto the handcuffs, angling her body back. Then he slipped his free hand between her thighs.

Her eyes opened and she groaned.

Using the wetness from her body, he rubbed his thumb over her clit.

She began bumping her pelvis against his hand, trying to get more friction. "Please."

"No."

Immediately her body stilled. Then she surrendered.

"Good girl." After teasing her, reminding her who was in charge of her orgasms, Ben quickened the motion of his thumb, increased the pressure on that plumped bit of flesh and watched as Ainsley came unhinged.

She was a goddess, swamped with pleasure, her head thrown back, her silky hair swaying, her kiss-swollen lips parted as she cried out, the pulse throbbing in her neck in tandem with the pulse throbbing beneath his stroking thumb.

He drew out the climax, and only when she was spent did he drive himself over the edge. Yanking on the cuffs chain, bowing her body backward so he could see his cock pumping in and out of her. His fingers dug into her thigh when his balls lifted.

Ainsley's pussy squeezed his cock as seed shot out of his shaft.

Ben's eyes rolled back in his head. He blanked out as her sex milked him of any thought processes. Zoned out, done in, checked out.

Sweet nuzzling on the side of his face roused him. "Bennett."

"Mmm?"

"I like the cuffs."

He laughed and kissed his favorite spot on her throat.

"And thank you for easing me into this Dom/sub thing."

Ben looked at her. "A forced blowjob and me handcuffing you during sex is...easing you into it?"

She nodded. "Don't get me wrong, your aggressive side really does it for me. Like when you tied me to the bench at the club. But I like this closeness too. It almost felt...like it was more than sex."

Instead of admitting, *for me too,* he said gruffly, "Bend your knees." He helped her stand, removed the cuffs and checked the circulation in her arms before hitting the john to ditch the condom. When he returned to the kitchen, Ainsley was dressed.

"Leaving?"

"I need to get my beauty sleep. Don't you know banker's hours are brutal?"

He laughed.

"Have a safe trip to Rapid City tomorrow and I'll see you Friday after work."

Ben walked her out to her car, ignoring her protests that she wasn't afraid of the dark.

As he watched her drive away he knew he'd have to push her next time. Break down some of those barriers. Even when he understood it'd cause some of his walls to crumble a little too.

Chapter Fourteen

The doorbell rang and Ainsley set the bottle of Pinot Grigio alongside the two wineglasses on the kitchen counter.

As soon as she answered the door, Layla squeezed Ainsley in a big hug. "It's so great to have you living so close."

"I'll admit your phone call this morning surprised me."

"Because I invited myself over? We don't live that far apart anymore, so there's no excuse for us not to hang out. Besides, we would've thought nothing of driving an hour across Denver to have dinner together."

"True. Come in."

The cats observed from the end of the hallway as Layla kicked off her Ugg boots and draped her parka and scarf over the back of the couch.

"Cute kitties," Layla cooed, crouching down to hold out her hand. "What are their names?"

"Wally is the tabby. I found him last spring huddled by a cart return at Wal-Mart. Poor thing was just a baby. And Charo, the calico, was my animal shelter rescue the week before. Some sicko kid scorched her tail and cut off one side of her whiskers. But look at that cute face. I couldn't resist."

"Charo. As in she's been...charred? A, you have a bizarre sense of humor."

Ainsley poured the wine, handing Layla a glass. "I apologize for the boxes all over the living room. I haven't completely unpacked."

Layla tucked herself into the corner of the loveseat. She ran her hand over the peacock blue cushion. "This is a stunning sofa. So bright."

"I swore I'd never have a neutral room again. Nothing boring. Or safe." Ainsley's gaze moved over the spring green chairs opposite the vividly patterned blue and green couch that complemented both the chairs and loveseat.

"I'm glad you're stepping outside that neat little box you've lived in for so long."

"Better late than never." She let the wine rest on her tongue. "So Murphy didn't need you in the bar tonight?"

"Thursdays are quiet. People are gearing up for the weekend. I probably would've sat at home anyway, and Murph agreed I needed to come here to talk to you."

Ainsley's face warmed, recalling the last time she'd seen Layla at the club. Was she here to explain that scene? "I wasn't sure what my reaction would be to watching you and Murphy. It wasn't what I expected. Can we just leave it at that?"

"What are you talking about?" Layla's eyes widened. "Oh. The public scene last weekend?" She waved her hand. "I'm not an exhibitionist, which is why Murphy almost always chooses that punishment when I've stepped over the line. I'm here to talk to you about something else. Someone else actually. Bennett."

"What about him?"

"Let me say I knew Bennett was a rancher. I had no idea where. As a sub, I don't ask questions that will get me in trouble. Murphy and I were talking about you, specifically the changes in your life, including moving from Denver to Sundance. He got really quiet. Which freaked me out. Then he told me Bennett lives in Sundance."

Ainsley swirled the wine in her glass before she looked up. "I know. We've already run into each other."

Layla gasped. "You did? Did he recognize you?"

"Right away." She groaned. "Of course it happened at the bank. He requested my presence at his place that night so we could talk. And..." Why was she feeling shy, telling Layla this?

"And what?"

"He asked for a month of me being his submissive."

"I'm assuming you said yes?"

"Why would you assume that?" Ainsley said a little sharper than she intended.

"Whoa." Layla held up her hand. "Not trying to piss you off, A. I suspected you'd be a good fit for Bennett in the club. Especially since you're not sure if you're interested in participating in this lifestyle beyond a short-term sampling. And Bennett...well, he only does short-term."

"Why is that?"

"Bennett likes variety. He's got excellent instincts with whips, floggers, riding crops and canes, knowing how far he can push the submissive's pain threshold. Seems he's always being asked to show his expertise on another member's partner. When he gets her to that headspace, he returns her to her partner."

"So Ben doesn't have sex with every woman he demonstrates on?"

Layla shook her head. "Hardly any, actually. He's very mindful of boundaries, yet there's never any doubt who's in charge during the scene. There's something about his quiet intensity that draws subs like bees to flowers."

"Or it could be the size of his...ah...stinger that attracts them," Ainsley said.

"Oh man." Layla giggled. "Ain't that the truth. Murph once gave me twenty lashes because he caught me licking my lips during one of Bennett's public scenes."

"Yes, Ben's got a smoking hot body besides his impressive stinger."

Layla squinted at her. "What's up with you calling him Ben?"

"When he's in Dom mode he's Bennett. When we're hanging out, he's Ben."

"How much time *have* you spent with him?"

"The last three nights. We've come to terms on the specifics of his one-month proposal. Since we live in the same town, he suggested we skip the club for the month."

"Are you all right with that? You trust him? Because some subs only want to play where there's supervision in case the Dom goes too far."

"I trust Bennett. Even when the idea of surrendering that much control to him scares the bejeezus out of me."

"Learning to integrate your submissive side will be hard for you, but that doesn't mean you should alter your personality, in or out of the bedroom, just to please him."

Ainsley frowned. "Explain that."

"Doms expect a certain amount of disobedience from subs, especially new subs just learning their parameters. You are a strong woman with strong opinions. If you never act out, either accidentally or on purpose, how will you know the difference between punishment and discipline?"

She vaguely remembered Ben mentioning that, but she hadn't asked specifics. "There's a difference?"

Layla nodded. "Murphy forcing me to do a public scene was punishment for the way I humiliated him. Discipline was the caning I received in private the next three days to reinforce his dominance and as a warning not to do it again."

"So I'm supposed to be defiant to see how Bennett reacts?"

"Not always. But accepting everything Bennett says or does...where is the learning curve? What are the limits? For both of you?"

"I never thought of it that way."

"As happy as I am that you're getting a taste of the lifestyle, even behind bedroom doors, I want to caution you about a couple of things."

Ainsley expected Layla to alert her to the physical pain from spankings. Or reiterating practicing safe sex, or suggesting Ainsley call her if something happened that made her uncomfortable. She hadn't expected her friend to warn her off Ben completely.

"Don't fall for him, A. Not as Bennett, not as Ben. Keep the relationship focused on you embracing your submissive nature with an experienced Dom."

"That's it?"

"You shouldn't look to get involved long-term with the first Dom you meet anyway. Don't expect promises of forever or fidelity, especially not from Bennett. Don't agree to play every night. And for heaven's sake, don't spend the night with him because that's a gateway drug for subs. As soon as you're able to function following his aftercare, leave. Or make him leave." Layla's gaze turned shrewd. "What?"

"Ben's already asked me to spend the night with him."

"Have you?"

"No."

"I see that *not yet* answer in your eyes, Ainsley."

She fidgeted. "But he can just command me to stay over anyway, right?"

"Technically? Yes. Especially if you've agreed to give up your weekends to him."

"We haven't talked about that."

"You need to. Next time you're together before the clothes fly off and the restraints come out."

Ainsley rolled her eyes. "Gotcha."

"I worry about you, knowing he's in the area. You're trying to prove you can handle the bank president's job. You're new in town and it'd be easy to spend all your free time with Bennett. I don't want you to get too attached to him, because it won't last."

As much as Ainsley wanted to protest, she'd be wise to listen to Layla since she'd known Bennett for years. "All right."

Relieved, Layla sagged against the loveseat. "Good."

"Thanks for the advice. I never would've mustered the guts to do this if not for you."

"You're welcome. I'm glad we've reconnected, A."

"Me too." Ainsley stood. "Let's eat. Then you can give me hints on how to keep my Dom on his toes while keeping my butt from getting paddled."

"Don't even pretend you don't want that man spanking your ass at every opportunity."

"I'm blindfolding you tonight."

That was an abrupt subject change. "I guess that's one way to start the weekend," Ainsley said dryly. She'd weighed Layla's advice and ignored it simply because she'd wanted to spend the whole weekend with him. In his house. In his bed. Under his control.

Bennett traced the line of her jaw and stared into her eyes. When he studied her so intently, as he touched her with such familiarity, she felt more naked than when she was actually naked. Stripping her defenses was more intimate than stripping her clothes.

"Will I need to bind your hands so you don't tear the blindfold off?"

"Maybe." Ainsley's heart pounded. How could he make her so skittish with just words? "So you're going to blindfold me, tie me up and then what?"

"Leave you in the barn while I come back inside and watch The Speed Channel."

Her mouth dropped open.

"Isn't that what you're afraid of? I'll take away your choices and leave you powerless and at my whim? Then I'll somehow abuse you, or your trust, which will allow you to get upset and leave, which also lets you regain control?"

"Ben—"

"Bennett," he corrected with an edge. "Answer the question."

"I still don't know...the truth is I'm confused."

"I'll un-confuse you. Because you're not supposed to be thinking, are you?" His smile, usually so sexy and sure, took on a decidedly wolf-like gleam. "Get undressed and bend over the arm of the couch."

Ainsley bit back her question. But the uneasiness wouldn't go away. *Just focus on each step.* She removed every stitch of clothing. She stretched across the couch arm. She tried to concentrate on how the soft cushion molded against her hips and belly. How the fabric abraded her nipples.

Bennett crouched beside her. "Do you know the difference between discipline and punishment?"

Yes. But she had the urge to stall. "No."

"Discipline is what a Dom uses to remind the sub who's in charge. Punishment is to correct offensive sub behavior." He plucked her bra from the floor and quickly bound her arms with it.

Neat trick. Okay, *scary* trick.

When he rolled up her blouse, she understood he intended to use her clothing to truss her up. That made this lesson more personal somehow. He covered her eyes and tied a knot at the base of her neck. Everything turned dark and her anxiety increased exponentially. Why was she naked, bent over, blindfolded and about to let this man do whatever he wanted to her?

Retreat! Retreat now. It's not too late.

"Ignore that voice," Bennett whispered in her ear. "The voice of doubt, the voice of reason that demands you assert yourself has no place here. The only voice you should be listening to is mine."

The deep cadence held a compelling, but rough edge. But when she let go of her fear and trusted him, when she pleased him, those harsh tones mellowed into warmth. Ainsley tried to shut off everything but the reality of him: his voice, his touch, his scent, his presence.

"That's it." A single fingertip traversed her spine. "Don't think. Feel. Anticipate."

Sensual touches zigzagged from her shoulders to the top of her butt in a constant stream of motion. Then the sensation changed into a sharp bite of pain in a dozen separate spots on her body.

She pushed up from the couch, only to have Bennett pushing her down.

"Let. Go."

She did and it was a glorious place to be, completely under his care and control.

Caresses slithered over her back, sending goose bumps blooming outward, increasing her awareness of new erogenous zones. As soon as she became used to the tickling touch of a dozen different points of contact, they morphed into pinpricks of fire that seared her skin.

The teasing stroke followed by several stinging snaps went on for several rounds. The hard/soft combination awakened her nerve endings, sending her to the place where pleasure bled into pain and became one. She existed in the moment, in his attention.

That's when Bennett stopped. Curling his hands over her shoulders, he pulled her upright and unbound her hands. "You're beautiful in obedience, angel."

He tantalized her with erotic kisses that increased the dizzying, floating sensation. She was vaguely aware of moving. Of his callused hands gripping her hips as he guided her backward.

"Up on the bed. Hands on the headboard."

Despite the commanding tone, he helped her into the position. He made her wait, but he hadn't left the room. She heard him pacing behind her.

The bed dipped and his warm, hard body pressed against hers. A hand slipped over the curve of her belly, breaching the curls covering her mound. Two fingers followed the seam of her sex and plunged inside her wet pussy.

God that felt good.

His pleasure rumbled in her ear. "Flogging turns you on."

"That's what that was?"

"Widen your stance."

While Ainsley slid her knees out, he thrust his fingers in a few more times before he moved. The bed jostled. Soft hair brushed the inside of her thighs.

"Lean forward."

Oh wow. It was like she was sitting on his face.

His tongue snaked from the top of her slit to her bottom. A very long, very thorough lick.

Her whole body trembled.

"Goddamn you taste good." He yanked her down and went to town. Suckling her pussy lips, then flicking them with his tongue. Mapping every fold with every part of his mouth. Lapping at the cream pouring from her sex.

A whimper escaped when his teeth scraped her clit.

Bennett stilled. "Did that hurt?"

"A little. It just caught me by surprise."

He pressed several soft kisses over the hood of her clit.

Those glimpses of his care, of how attuned he was to her every response amazed her. His work-honed hands clutched the globes of her ass as he ate at her sex. She was so lost in the intimate attentions of his hungry mouth that she jumped at the first brush of his thumb across her anus.

Which caused him to smack her ass and growl a warning.

That smack made her wetter yet.

Bennett began to plunge his thumb in and out of her pussy as he fastened his mouth to her clit.

Ainsley knew she wouldn't last long with such intense focus. All pulse points in her body were already buzzing as Bennett pushed her closer to the edge of detonation. He didn't retreat when she began to grind into his face, desperate for that rush of release.

Right as the climax hit, he slipped his thumb in her ass. Her clit pulsed against his sucking lips. Her pussy and anal muscles contracted in opposition to the throbbing in her sex, making the orgasm seem endless.

As soon as the last pulse faded, Bennett scooted backward. "Stay just like that."

"I can't think, let alone move."

A couple of seconds later he removed the blindfold as he kissed her nape. A slick digit swept over her asshole. "Don't clench."

A light pressure gave way to a gentle swirling motion that encompassed all those unexplored nerve endings. A constant stroking of the outer ring of muscle and a little inside. The more he stroked, the more those nerve endings came alive. She found herself wanting that invasion. Unconsciously she pressed down, trying to force contact.

He murmured, "Who's in charge, Ainsley?"

"You are."

"Relax and I'll give you what you want."

She expelled a steady breath. As soon as she followed his directive, he slipped something in her ass. A thick something. But it didn't fill her bowels completely. Not a dildo. Probably not even a finger.

Demand to know what he shoved up your butt.

No. Be compliant.

Bennett chuckled. "You are bein' a model sub. Avoiding punishment by doin' what you're told without arguing or without questioning me." He slapped her ass. "Let's see how long you can keep it up."

The swat didn't hurt; it merely caught her off guard because it jiggled the thing in her butt.

"You're wearing the butt plug until I take it out." He trailed his finger down her spine, between her butt cheeks, over her tailbone to jostle the object. "Whatcha think about that, sub?"

"I'm not supposed to think." She tacked on, "Sir."

He laughed again. "Good answer. Come on. Let's shoot a game of pool."

Pool? With her bending over the table and that...thing poking out of her behind? No way. "You're joking, right?"

That penetrating blue gaze sharpened. "You might learn more about the difference between discipline and punishment tonight after all."

Ainsley plastered on a smile. "Would you like me to chalk your stick?"

The crotch of Ben's jeans was strangling his cock.

He hadn't expected to get so turned on by Ainsley's competitive streak. Her cocky attitude.

He suspected she'd downplayed her pool abilities when she'd challenged him to the best two games out of three. But as soon as she started shooting, he realized the woman was a novice. He'd hustled enough games in his youth to be considered a pool shark. He'd easily won the first game without taxing himself.

His amusement morphed into lust during the second game. Watching her naked body contorting to try a shot. So he'd been biding his time. Keeping the Dom hovering in the background, pacing like a caged tiger for the opportunity to pounce.

And there it was.

Ainsley scratched on the eight ball. Which didn't faze her in the least. She beamed at him. "Did you catch that awesome shot?"

"Uh-huh. But, angel, you still lost."

"What? No. I got the black ball in."

Jagged spikes of lightning flashed outside the windows. Thunder boomed. The wind whistled through the house with enough force to shake the rafters. Hard drops of rain pelted the skylights above the pool table.

"Yeah, but the cue ball can't follow the eight ball in. It means you scratched. Which means I win."

An ominous crack of thunder echoed.

Her eyes widened. Her delicate fingers tightened around the pool cue. "We still have one game left."

Ben shook his head. "I've won two. The third game is pointless." He let his predatory gaze roam up her body. "And I've got a much better use for the pool table."

The lights flickered.

"You wouldn't."

"I would." He stalked her until her butt met the edge of the pool table, ignoring the elements battling outside his house, focusing instead on the elements raging inside him. "Don't move." He plucked the cue from her hand and returned it to the cue rack. Then he grabbed a flat sheet from the guest bedroom, a couple of condoms and a bottle of lube.

In the few minutes he'd been gone, a mutinous look had settled on Ainsley's face. "Something wrong?"

"What's the sheet for?"

He tossed it to her. "So your knees don't get skinned up from the felt covering the pool table. Spread it out." He grabbed a cylinder-shaped pillow and said, "Crawl up and lay on your back."

That's when everything went completely dark.

"Bennett?"

"I'm here. The power just went out."

"You won't leave me here to go and check on it, will you?"

"Nah. Power outages happen all the time." He ditched his clothes, put on a condom and dropped the lube in the closest corner pocket. "You wanna tell me why you have such a fear that I'll tie you up and leave you alone?"

Her voice was so soft he strained to hear her. "He did it once."

"Who did it?"

"Dean. My ex. I was shocked when he told me he wanted to try some...stuff I'd suggested. He had me strip and then he tied my wrists together around the banister with some kind of electrical cord."

Ben fought his surge of fury and calmly asked, "Then what happened?"

"He left me tied there. For hours. In full view of anyone who walked up to the front door. It was his way of trying to *cure* me. To show me what I'd wanted him to do with me was sick and dangerous."

"How long after that did you leave him?"

"I kicked him out the next week."

"Good girl." It was one of the hardest things Ben had done, ignoring the anger raging through him to concentrate on being what Ainsley needed now. Comfort her, but not coddle her. Return her focus to them. To this moment. To who they were to each other. Proving he'd never ever be that kind of man and she could trust him without hesitation.

Ainsley twitched when he hopped up on the table and crawled over her body on all fours. Strobe-like effects flashed throughout the room, distorting the shadows, which increased her look of fright. Needing to soothe her, Ben's lips captured hers as a shard of lightning and thunder boomed above them.

She jerked so hard their teeth knocked together.

"Easy."

Lorelei James

"Sorry."

Ben reclaimed her mouth in a passionate kiss, a duel of tongues, the constant glide of wet lips as they kept changing the angle of the kiss. Taking it deeper. Making it hotter. Kissing her for a good long time until she squirmed beneath him.

"The storm sets me on edge too." He nuzzled her cheek. "There's something raw about that power. Something that makes me wild." Ben nipped her neck. "Do you feel it?"

"Your wildness? Yes. Your whole body vibrates with it."

"Does it scare you?" He pulled back to look into her eyes.

"No." Ainsley didn't bother to hide her lust. "It excites me. You excite me." Her hands moved over his shoulders and she scraped her fingernails down his back to his bare ass. "I know what you want, Bennett. Take it. Take me."

Ben rose to his knees, primal need clawing at him. "Roll over and grab onto the edge."

As she maneuvered herself into position, he shoved the pillow under her hips and snagged the lube. He scooted back and placed a kiss on each butt cheek. The pounding of his heart rivaled the sound of the driving rain. His hands shook as he removed the butt plug.

He added more lube to the stretched anal opening and coated his cock. He couldn't watch the head of his cock breaching that tight pink pucker, but he could feel the mind blowing contraction of the muscle as pushed his shaft in without pause, until he was balls deep in that untried channel.

She reared up.

He pushed her flat to the table with his body, curling his hands around hers on the edge of the pool table. "Jesus. You're so fucking tight." His mouth brushed her ear. "It'll get better." He canted his pelvis, slid out a few inches and then back in.

"How do you know it'll get better? Have you had a dick in your butt?" she demanded.

Several booms of thunder rattled the windowpanes.

Ben sank his teeth into the skin at the base of her neck, feeling her tremble beneath him. "And what if I said yes? Would you believe I wouldn't put a sub through something I'm not willing to have done to me?"

"I'd say that's not an answer." She hissed when he withdrew,

148

resting the cockhead just inside the opening.

"You're bein' kinda mouthy for a woman pinned to a pool table with her Dom's cock filling her virgin ass." Ben slammed back in fully.

Ainsley gasped.

"You said you wanted this. You said *take me.* That's what I'm gonna do. Take you. My way."

Her fingers tightened beneath his as she braced herself.

Ben started fucking her. Slowly. Steadily. Trying to keep as much of their skin in contact as possible with each stroke. Despite the chill in the room, he was sweating. He whispered, "You feel so goddamn good."

The wind whistled and shrieked. Sheets of rain pelted the windows.

He withdrew and plunged in deep, aware of Ainsley's changed breathing pattern. Aware of her conflicting feelings of agony and ecstasy. "You like this."

No response except for a grunt.

"Admit this was another of your dirty fantasies. Bein' made to enjoy havin' a cock in your ass."

"Yes, okay? Happy now?" She bucked against him, which shoved his cock deeper into her glove-tight channel.

Ben chuckled. "Very happy, angel." That's when he fucked her hard. His hips slamming into her backside. His toes cramped as he used the inside ledge of the pool table to propel himself into her faster until he reached that point of no return.

He came in a head roaring rush.

She followed right behind him, her inner muscles clamped down as she humped against the pillow.

They stayed like that—sweaty, panting, sticky, spent—for quite a while.

What a great way to start their weekend.

Late Sunday morning Ben rolled over and grabbed his phone from the nightstand. "Hey, Quinn. What's up?" Ben frowned. "That's today? Shit. No. I forgot. Thanks for the reminder. I'll be there in fifteen." He hung up and headed straight for the shower. Then he grabbed his clothes from the closet.

"Where are you going?"

"I told Quinn and Libby I'd watch Adam and Amelia today. Usually my mom volunteers to baby-sit, but she's outta town." He buttoned his shirt. "I don't know how long I'll be gone, so make yourself at home. No reason to get up."

"You expect me to wait here for you all day?"

"Like I said, I don't know how long I'll be gone."

Ainsley threw back the covers and angrily started gathering articles of clothing.

"Are you pissed off about this?"

"Yes."

"Why?"

She held out her arm. A section of rope still dangled from her wrist. "Oh, maybe because we'd barely finished screwing, and you left me half-tied to the damn bed so you could answer your phone!"

Shit. He tried to catch her gaze but she stomped away. What was she trying to tell him by calling that last heart pounding, body-pumping bout of sex...screwing? It'd been more than that. It'd been freakin' phenomenal.

"And then you gave me the impression that I was supposed to lie in bed all day and wait for your triumphant return."

"That's not what I said."

"Not in so many words." Ainsley muttered as she yanked on her clothes.

"Something you wanna say to me? Instead of throwing me dirty looks and mumbling under your breath?"

"I realize I'm your sub. But I'm not some object like your saddle. Hanging around ready to be used when you need me, set aside when you don't."

Jesus. Did Ainsley really just compare herself to his saddle? And what the fuck was up with that "be used" comment?

She flounced to the bedroom doorway.

"Where do you think you're goin?"

Ainsley deigned to give him a mocking look. "I'm going to the fucking opera dressed like this. Where do you think I'm going? I'm going home."

"Like hell."

"I've been here since Friday night. I need to check on my cats. Then I have to finish unpacking and wash clothes. All things I've neglected, because I have a life besides the one I spend bound for your pleasure."

That smartass comment raised his blood pressure. "You trying to see how much hotter you can make the water you're already in, sub?"

"No. Sir, Bennett, Sir," she snapped off with military precision and notched her chin higher. "You told me we wouldn't spend every waking minute together. We have this weekend. I think I deserve a furlough."

And it'd been one of the best weekends he could remember, not that he could tell her that with the anger emanating from her like a poisonous cloud. Hey wait. Had she just compared the weekend to a...prison sentence?

"I've got a busy week, so I'll call you. Or maybe you'll call me when you need to practice your rope-tying skills." She threw the rope at him and disappeared down the hallway.

Maybe you'll call me when you need to practice your rope-tying skills? Oh hell no. That would not fly with him.

Ben heard the door slam. By the time he made it outside, her car was halfway up the drive.

Oh, little sub, you've just landed yourself in a whole passel of trouble.

Chapter Fifteen

Ainsley spent all day Monday on the phone with Chase McKay's publicist and going back and forth with Steve Talbot, president of Settler's First Bank. They'd come to an agreement about co-sponsoring the local event as a platform for Chase to announce his new charity. Steve's attempts to cut National West out of the event entirely displeased Mayor Mark, who championed the idea of both banks providing a united front to the community.

So at the end of the day, she felt she'd accomplished something. So much of her duties as bank president were busy work. Seemed she spent her life on the phone.

Not that she minded. She'd taken the position because the regional manager assured Ainsley that the bulk of her job would be schmoozing locals into switching a portion of their banking business to National West. Ainsley could handle PR; it's what she did best. She figured the event would show the locals that this bank was interested in investing in the community. In the next month she'd approach individual businesses, touting the benefits of diversifying their banking needs.

During her divorce, she'd needed a career change. Intrigued by the management end of banking, she'd taken over a small branch office in a low-income suburb of Denver no one else wanted to tackle. Determined to keep the branch from closing, she'd approached every business, big and small, in the three-mile radius, talking up the benefits of banking locally. She used the bank's allotted community funds to resurrect small community events that were underfunded, but much beloved. She volunteered her time, which had a huge impact on convincing locals of her sincerity. The hard work, the unpaid hours of overtime, had paid off. In that year she'd increased that branch's business banking operation by twenty-five percent and the personal banking business by thirteen percent. Quite a coup for a woman who'd spent the previous six years as a PR assistant.

Now here she was in Sundance, basically starting over again. With her PR savvy and Turton as the bean counter, on paper they looked like an unbeatable team to make this branch a rousing success from the get go. But in reality, Turton was bitter Ainsley had been awarded the job. And she still hadn't figured out the best way to deal with him.

Jenny knocked on her door. "Sorry to interrupt, but there's an extremely agitated woman pacing in the lobby. Turton tried to help her but she refuses to talk to anyone but the bank president."

"I'll be right there." Ainsley set aside the stack of files, and straightened her short suit jacket as she made her way around the desk.

But the agitated woman met her at the office door. "Are you the bank president?"

"Yes. I'm Ainsley Hamilton. What can I do for you?"

"Don't treat me like an idiot, for starters."

Okay. So she was testy. "I'd appreciate the same courtesy, Miss..."

The petite redhead looked up. Her large eyes were a pale shade of blue that made her pupils stand out. A striking combination, given the woman's gamine features. "Sorry. I'm Joely Monroe."

"Well, Miss Monroe, let's talk in my office. Could I get you something to drink?"

"I don't suppose you've got vodka?"

Ainsley muttered, "I wish. We've got coffee. Water. Hot tea?"

"Nothing, thanks."

"Have a seat." After they'd both settled, Ainsley said, "Is there a problem with your account?"

"I don't have an account here. That's the problem." She jammed a hand through her hair, cut in an asymmetrical style few women could pull off. "My accounts have always been with Settler's First. Not by choice, I assure you. But there is no bank in Moorcroft and I didn't want to drive even farther to Spearfish to do my business banking."

"Your business is in Moorcroft?"

"I have a medical practice. Small town doctor-type stuff, it's just me and two nurses. Anyway, we've been having problems with our credit card machine. It locks up, and then it won't generate reports. A big pain in the butt since so much business is done on that machine. Settler's First installed the machine as part of their full-service banking promise. But any time it goes down, their advice? Unplug it from the

153

wall for a couple minutes and plug it back in. When that doesn't work, they claim it's my Internet connection causing the problems, which it's not. The machine has gone down fifteen times in the last month. And not once has anyone from that bank contacted me to see if the problem is fixed, or if they should show up and troubleshoot the problem if it isn't. I'm tired of fighting with them. I'm tired of my office manager losing her mind on me because we've got thousands of dollars in transit every time the machine goes down. So I'm shopping for a new bank. But before I go to the trouble of changing accounts and telling Steve Talbot where to shove it, I'd like some guarantee that I'll get decent customer service from this bank."

Ainsley smiled. "We can do much better than decent on the customer service end. We've got a Denver-based IT team here on Wednesday. I'll send them your way and they can check everything in your office, from the phone lines to the Internet service to the credit card machine itself. And if those guys can't figure out the problem? They'll find someone who can."

Her eyes lit up. "Really? You'd do that?"

"Yes, assuming you open an account with us." Or multiple accounts.

"Done. What now?"

"The usual boring bank stuff. You'll have to fill out reams of paperwork, but it'll be worth it in the long run, I promise."

Doctor Monroe glanced at her watch. "It's almost five o'clock. Don't you banker types lock the doors at five?" She scowled. "I took off early today to address this problem with Settler's First only to find out their lobby closes at four."

"Happy as I am that your unhappiness with them brought you to us, I will point out our goal is to maintain more customer-friendly hours than banker's hours. Our lobby is actually open until six during the week and noon on Saturday."

"So now that you've given me the spiel, lay the paperwork on me and I'll get it to my office manager first thing in the morning. It's kosher for her to swing in tomorrow and finalize everything?"

"Absolutely. If you'll excuse me, I'll grab all the paperwork you'll need."

When Ainsley returned to the office, the doctor gave her a curious look. "You haven't lived here long?"

"A few weeks. I transferred from Denver."

"I don't see pictures of a husband or kids decorating your walls. You married?"

"Divorced. No kids." Sort of a bizarre line of questions. "How about you?"

"Also divorced. No kids. And let me tell ya, that makes us a rarity in this area."

"I haven't had much time to meet many people or soak in the local color."

She popped to her feet. "You have to eat, right? I'll take you to a local favorite hot spot where we can chow down a juicy hamburger, split a plate of onion rings and sip a martini."

"A martini? In Sundance?"

She smirked. "Lettie at the Golden Boot makes a mean lemon drop."

"I'm in. Let me grab my coat and tell my vice president to close up. I'll meet you there."

It wasn't like she had plans tonight anyway. Ben acted shocked that she'd gotten a little huffy with him. Probably not smart to compare herself to an old saddle—broken in and ready to be used when he wanted it, out of sight and out of mind when he didn't.

There's gonna be hell to pay for that crack, sub.

Ainsley whirled around like Bennett had whispered that in her ear. But she only saw Turton giving her the stink eye. She had to find a way to deal with that prickly man, but not tonight.

Ten minutes later, Ainsley slid into the booth across from her newest customer. Before she sipped the yummy looking martini, she confessed, "I have no idea what to call you. Doc? Doc Monroe? Joely?"

"Call me Joely. As proud as I am of my medical degree and my practice, it's good to be reminded I'm more than just my occupation." She raised her glass. "To faulty credit card machines."

She laughed. "This is the only time I'm drinking to that."

Joely was surprisingly easy to talk to. The woman definitely had opinions. They talked about college and places they'd traveled. Even after they'd finished a cholesterol-laden meal and switched to soda, neither was eager to leave. It'd been a while since she'd spent time with another professional woman she didn't work with. Or who wasn't in her circle of married friends.

"So what are you? About thirty-four?" Joely asked.

"Almost thirty-eight, and thanks for that, by the way."

"No red-hot love affair you left behind in Colorado?"

"I was hoping maybe I'd find one of those here." Ben's face swam into her mind's eye, and she shook her head to erase it.

Joely stared into her soda as she stirred the ice cubes. "There are a few single men. If you don't mind younger guys. Or cowboys. Not a lot of professional types."

Ainsley wrinkled her nose. "I've had my fill of those types. The problem I discovered with younger guys? They want marriage and a family."

"You don't?"

"No. I've never had that burning maternal urge." She looked up, not knowing how Joely would respond to that. Most women didn't understand. They always claimed she'd change her mind when she met the right guy. But she knew she wouldn't. She'd accepted that about herself. Why couldn't everyone else?

"I hear you. I've lived in this area for twelve years. So if I'd taken up with the first yahoo that asked me, I'd probably have kids by now. Probably be divorced *again*, and a stranger to those kids since I work all the damn time." Joely gestured to the empty space between them. "This is the first time I've been out on a date in months."

Now that Ainsley thought about it, it was pretty bizarre, Joely just asking her out for...holy crap. Had she said *date*? Was the doc...gay?

"You stiffened up, Ainsley, did I say something wrong?"

"You called this a date. It isn't, right? Because you should know I don't swing that way."

Amusement danced in her eyes. "No, it's not a date. Freudian slip, maybe. I'm not a lesbian. If I had to classify my sexuality, I'd say...celibate. And I'm damn tired of it. You know what bites about being the only doctor in a rural area?"

"No, what?"

"That I have to at least pretend to have a moral code. If I worked in a suburban hospital or practice, I could get away with having a different man or two in my bed every week. Heck, I could have that every day. But here? I have to be Dr. Sexless and Upstanding." She cocked her head. "I haven't heard you chiming in about forced celibacy since moving to the sticks."

"There's something to be said for hook-up sex."

"Now I'm really jealous. You've only been here a month and you've already got a local hook-up whenever you want?"

"Joely?"

They both looked at the dark-haired woman at the end of the booth.

"Libby! What's up?" Joely said, "Ainsley Hamilton, meet my friend, Libby McKay. Ainsley is the president of the new bank."

Of course this woman had to be a McKay. "Nice to meet you, Libby."

"Likewise. Are you the one who's responsible for Chase's event this weekend?"

"I sure am. We hammered out the final details today with Settler's First. How are you related to Chase?"

"He's my brother-in-law."

Ainsley went very still. That meant this woman was Ben's sister-in-law. Why that freaked her out was totally stupid, because chances were very slim Ben was anywhere around.

"Hey, Doc, good to see you."

Then that deep voice that fueled her fantasies was right behind her.

"Ben. Fancy seeing you here," Joely said.

"Poor Ben was roped into bringing me into town. Ginger and I haven't had a chance to catch up with girl talk forever so we're meeting when she gets off work."

Ainsley didn't miss Joely's wistful smile that she hadn't been included in Libby's girl-talk time.

"It was no bother," Bennett said keeping his eyes on Ainsley. "I had another matter I needed to tend to tonight anyway."

Her heart raced. She'd probably be tending to her own burning butt cheeks before the night was over, if the hard look in his eye was any indication of his mood.

And didn't that just thrill her?

"Ben, do you know Ainsley?" Joely asked.

"Yes, Ainsley and I have crossed paths a few times," Bennett drawled.

"Right, probably about Chase's event."

"Speaking of Chase's event, Ainsley, I'd like to run a couple of ideas past you."

Her mouth and brain were frozen.

"I'm gonna snag that table in the back," Libby said. "Nice seeing you, Joely. Nice to meet you, Ainsley."

Bennett said, "Either of you ladies need a drink while I grab a beer?"

"No. I'm good. Ainsley?"

She shook her head.

"I'll be right back. Don't go anywhere."

Damn man, bossing her in public.

As soon as Bennett left, Joely leaned across the table. "Bad poker face. You are totally banging him. The elusive, sexy Ben McKay is your local hook-up, isn't he?"

"What?"

"Don't deny it. Up top." Joely held her hand up for a high-five. "Kudos to you for getting some of that hot cowboy ass while the getting is good."

Ainsley slapped Joely's hand. "This is so far under the radar it's underground."

"No worries. I live my life under the radar." She slipped out of the booth. "Thanks for an entertaining evening. I hope we can do it again soon."

She said, "Me too," and meant it.

"I've got your number, you've got mine. Let's set up something fun once the bank business is out of the way."

"Deal."

Ainsley waited for Ben to return, feeling resentful about his command. In public. Then she thought, screw it, and started to leave.

But he blocked her in. "I wondered how long you'd sit there before showing your insubordination." He swigged from his beer. "Or should I say *more* insubordination."

"We didn't have plans tonight."

"You sure? Did you call me to double-check?"

She refused to back down. "I wasn't aware I needed your approval to have a business dinner with a bank client."

"Which is true. So your bank business with the doc is done?"

Say no.

Bennett leaned close enough to get her attention. "You really gonna lie to me?"

"We just finished. I'm going home."

He shook his head.

"You were serious about discussing Chase's event?"

He shook his head.

"Stop that."

He shook his head. "Know why I came to town?"

Ainsley tapped her finger on the table. "Hmm. Does it involve handing me a paddle since I'm up shit creek? Or are you just going to paddle me?"

"You're not getting off that easy this time." He kept that smoldering Dom stare on her. "I'm still ticked off at you for the way you compared yourself to my saddle."

"If the stirrup fits..."

He growled. "You tryin' to piss me off?"

"No. But this is your pissed-off face? Because it looks the same as when you're happy—or when you're turned on—to me."

Wrong taunt, Ainsley.

"Do you really feel I use you?"

"Yeah. Sometimes I do."

An emotion she'd never seen flitted through those beautiful dark eyes. "Get your stuff and plan on spending the night at my house."

"If I say I don't want to?"

"Then say your safe word. You won't see me again."

She stared at him. He stared back. No surprise she dropped their mind-fuck connection first. "I don't want to say my safe word."

"Then you'd better do as you're told, hadn't you?"

Ainsley looked up but he was already walking away.

She wasn't prepared for this side of Bennett.

He had no time for pleasantries or conversation when she showed up at his house. He simply asked her to repeat her safe word. Twice.

When he told her to strip, kneel at his bedroom door and wait for him, she had her first real feeling of trepidation since she'd agreed to be his submissive. Sometime in the last week, she'd even wondered if Bennett was acting. Playing the part of being a dominant man. That when she really got to know him, he'd drop that aggressive role and just be a demanding lover.

But this man wasn't acting. This man was pure, full on dominant male about to mete out punishment to his sub. Why was she kneeling, waiting for his return? He knew she hated the subservience aspect of Dom/sub relationships. Another thought made her stomach roil. What would she do if he slipped a collar on her? Bennett had only allowed her one hard line. He'd told her anything else he wanted to do to her was fair game. The idea of being collared like one of his dogs had her head screaming her safe word and urging her to run.

No. Stay put, stay calm. You can do this. There's a lesson in here in here for you. Bennett isn't a cruel Dom, you know that.

Did she?

Immediately upon his return to his bedroom, after making her wait for twenty minutes, he'd secured her, naked, and stretched her out, face down, spread-eagle on his mattress. He used a riding crop on her butt, letting it glance across her thighs. Twice he'd stopped to see if she needed to use her safe word. Asking in that firm, gentle voice that somehow offered her reassurance, even as it kept her clinging to the edge.

Ainsley shook her head and bore his punishment, wondering why his attention wasn't having the usual effect of turning her on. Wondering why she felt so disjointed.

Then Bennett changed the configuration of the ropes and kept her bound in his bed, but added a blindfold for variety.

When he maneuvered her body how he preferred, she knew he'd fuck her however he preferred. As many times as he preferred.

The first time he fucked her mouth, angling her head off the bed so she could deep throat him. He came partially in her mouth, partially on her face.

No soothing touches in the aftermath. Usually he touched or kissed her mouth, murmuring how sexy her lips looked swollen from sucking his cock.

The second time he fucked her breasts. Pinching her nipples to the surprising edge of pain she craved that usually sent her soaring. But he'd stopped. He squeezed her breasts around his cock and slid his shaft faster and faster until he ejaculated on her chest. But again, no praise from her Dom, no promises that her compliance would be rewarded. It was all about him.

Ainsley drifted into a place where she almost could see the events happening from outside her body. She felt nothing. No pride, no shame, no excitement, no gratitude. None of the usual submissive high where she knew her acquiescence would please him. Where she knew her total surrender was prized by him and he'd gift her with an explosive orgasm.

The third time he fucked her pussy, bringing her leg straight up as he drove into her from the side. Keeping her blindfolded and bound. But he had fingered her clit, with almost clinical detachment, and got her off.

No sweet kisses, or whispered words or loving touching. Just fucking. His way.

The last time he'd brought her ankles up and attached them to her bound hands. She'd laid face down on the mattress, her body pinned like a butterfly, unable to move at all as he'd lubed her back channel with his fingers and then rammed his cock into her ass without pause.

This was what she'd feared Bennett would become. Unyielding. Aggressive and unwilling to provide her with any type of comfort or explanation as he took what he wanted. Reinforcing to her what it meant to be submissive. Reminding her who had the power and the control.

The scenes had happened in such rapid succession, she had no idea how much time had passed when Bennett finally untied her.

If she'd had the strength in her legs, she might've run.

If she hadn't been so confused by Bennett's sudden change, becoming the caring Dom she recognized, she might've shaken off his loving touches. But he'd shown a Dom's care. Massaging blood back into her limbs. Caressing the spots where the rope had abraded her skin. Running those rough hands over her body, not with punishment, but with reverence.

Ainsley's instinct was to give into the sleepiness. She didn't want to ask him what she'd done to deserve that treatment. He was accustomed to her reluctance to discuss a scene immediately after it ended. But this time she wouldn't let it slide. She swallowed hard and managed to eke out one word. "Why?"

"So you'd know the difference."

"Difference between what?"

He bestowed sweet kisses on her lips. "You accused me of usin' you. What I did to you tonight? That was usin' you. Has it ever been like that between us before?"

"No."

"And it won't be again."

She broke down completely. It was hard to be humbled. But she'd needed it. Needed a reminder of what Bennett really was—a dominant man to the bone. But he wasn't a taker. He wasn't a user. She'd signed on for this experience as his submissive. Bennett was who he was. A Dom. A teacher. A taskmaster. This was how he'd be to the next sub in line after their thirty days together ended. She'd never be special to him.

That made her sob harder.

"Come on, angel. Let it out. I've got you."

Bennett's hands were in constant motion over every inch of her bare skin. He nuzzled, touched and murmured to her. Using his entire being to soothe her.

But it didn't help. When she began to shake, not even the inferno of his skin against hers warmed her. He practically carried her to the shower. Holding her beneath the blessedly hot water as the jets pummeled her sore muscles and the steam thawed her from the outside in.

And when the tremors ended, she let the last tears fall, feeling more vulnerable now than any other time with him.

Run. Get out of here now and don't look back.

"I'm okay," she lied in a whisper against his chest.

"You sure? We can stay in here as long as you need."

"I'm sure."

With those long, muscular arms, he grabbed towels hanging from the racks. He tied one turban-style around her head. Dried her thoroughly with the other, and wrapped a bath sheet around her body. He led her back into the bedroom and wrapped her with his robe before tucking her between the covers.

Bennett gathered her in his arms and piled another blanket on top of them.

"I'm still so cold."

"You're not cold. You're shaken. And it's my..." Resting his chin on the top of her head, he said gruffly, "Never mind. It'll keep. Sleep."

But she couldn't sleep. When she wiggled out of his arms, he let her. When she crept out of his house a few hours later, he let her do that too.

Chapter Sixteen

"What're you so pissy about today?"

Ben scowled at Quinn. "I'm not pissy."

"Yeah, you always stomp around and throw shit."

"Fine. I'm in a bad mood. Can we leave it at that and get this damn thing fixed?"

Quinn sighed. "This is beyond what either of us can fix." He kicked the tire. "Let's load it up and take it to D and F."

Ben bit back a snarl. His brother might've said that, oh, an hour ago when they first started dicking with the ATV. "I'll go get the trailer." But when he got to the backside of the barn, he saw both tires were flat. "Son of a bitch." They only had one spare. Which meant they'd have to take both tires off and see if they were salvageable.

A shadow appeared beside him. "Guess I shoulda checked that before now, huh?"

"Probably." Ben pushed upright. "I'll get the jack."

The tire had settled into the ground on the opposite side, making Ben wonder when was the last time they'd used the trailer.

Out of the blue, Quinn said, "Is it woman trouble? Because only woman trouble puts a look like that on a man's face. Trust me, I know."

The jack clanked. "Why you doin' this?"

"Doin' what? Talkin' to you? I'm pretty sure you ain't talkin' to nobody else about this."

Ben grunted.

"Come on. You don't gotta give me her name, but this is eatin' at you, bro."

Eating at him was putting it mildly. He'd had a hollow feeling in his gut that felt a lot like shame. "I did something...that didn't seem wrong at the time, but now I'm feeling guilty about it." He'd taken the harshest stance imaginable with Ainsley—a new sub—showing her what it really meant to be used. Using sex as punishment.

You think she might've been upset? Since she didn't want you to touch her and she left in the middle of the fucking night?

What the fuck had he been thinking?

Because after seeing Ainsley's flood of tears before she fled, he had an acute sense of failure. As a man. As a lover. As a Dom. For the first time ever, he'd questioned his actions. His rights as her dominant. Whether he'd tried to break a woman, instead of breaking through a woman's barriers. Whether he'd been punishing her out of his frustration with her.

The fact he was so upset he couldn't think straight, or concentrate, indicated he'd stepped over the line. And it sliced his guts to ribbons that she hadn't said her safe word.

"Ben?"

He looked up at Quinn. "Sorry. Did you say something?"

"Just wondering how long ago this happened?"

"Seems a helluva lot longer than just last night."

Quinn crossed his arms over his chest. "Is that why you volunteered to take Libby to town last night? To meet up with her?"

"Yeah."

"Man, you don't give an inch. And people say I'm closemouthed? You've got me beat by a country mile. Have you tried talkin' to her about it?"

"Not yet."

"But you do plan to, right?"

Ben tossed the socket to the ground. "I guess."

"That oughta go over well, if you're as forthcoming with her as you've been with me," Quinn said dryly.

"Asshole."

"Look, I'm just gonna toss this out there. We guys expect women to carry the emotional load in a relationship. I've figured out things go to hell when I'm not doin' my part to tell Libby how I feel. Then she gets upset and won't talk to me. It's a damn vicious cycle and an easy one to get into."

Quinn had hit it dead on. Ben had been so adamant about Ainsley opening up, about sharing her feelings, both in and out of bed, that he'd neglected to share his own. He'd kept her at arm's length emotionally, even while he demanded her absolute physical obedience.

Not only did that make him a bad Dom; that made him a bad man.

But he had no idea how to fix it. He sighed. "So got any advice, Q?"

"There's nothin' a sincere apology can't fix, especially if you just started seein' her, especially if you offer it up front. Then talk to her, really talk to her."

The thought of opening up to her scared the crap out of him. He could handle her rejection of him as a Dom. But what if he let her see Ben and she rejected that part of him? The part he didn't share with women who shared his bed? The side of himself that wasn't the confident dominant? The guy who felt like an outsider even in his own family?

"Flowers would help," Quinn offered, breaking into his thoughts again.

"Thanks."

"Is she worth it?"

"Maybe I'm not worth it," he muttered and changed the subject. "We're all set to ship cattle?"

"Oughta be a good year."

"Be a nice change from the last few years." Ben rummaged through the toolbox. "Have you talked to Mom and Dad since they've been in Arizona?"

"Briefly. Sounds like Gavin is gonna show up for Chase's thing this weekend. Which means he'll meet the rest of the McKays."

Ben grinned. "Poor sucker don't know what he's in for, does he?"

Quinn grinned right back. "Nope. But speaking of McKay family gossip..."

The threat of gossip always put Ben on edge. He carried the fear he'd be outed as a sexual deviant to one of his many family members by someone from the club with an ax to grind—with him personally, or the McKay family as a whole. Discretion was paramount to the Rawhide's survival. But nothing was failsafe.

Then he had another jarring thought. If Dalton knew about Rielle's financial problems, had someone else in the McKay family also found out? And that reminded him that he still hadn't talked to her. But with Rielle, timing was everything. If he caught her on a bad day, she'd likely warn him off her porch with a shotgun and not listen to a single word he said. Rielle trusted Ben as much as she trusted anyone, and that wasn't much. So Dalton and Tell had to trust him to know when the time was right to approach her and he'd tell them that if they nagged him about it. "What McKay family gossip?"

"Evidently Mom, Aunt Kimi and Aunt Carolyn went to Casper to visit Aunt Joan last week, and she's got herself a boyfriend."

"Really? Do her sons know?"

"No idea. I sure ain't gonna be the one to tell them."

"I'm with ya there." Ben released the jack and pointed to the tires. "I'll run these into town. See if they're salvageable."

After the tires were loaded into the back of Ben's truck, Quinn said, "Hope to see you in a better mood tomorrow."

"I hope to be in a better mood tomorrow. Thanks for the advice. If it doesn't work, I'm blaming you."

Ainsley looked totally stunned to see him on her doorstep. Or was that fear in her eyes?

He smiled, knowing it looked as strained as it felt. "Hey, angel."

"Hey, Bennett."

Bennett. Not Ben. Dammit. He didn't want to be her Dom right now.

So tell her.

"It's Ben," he said softly, his heart pounding with fear she'd say something about not seeing a difference.

"And so it is Ben," she murmured, studying his face. "Would you like to come in?"

"Please." He offered her the bouquet of flowers before he crossed the threshold. "I hope you don't have plans. I took a chance you'd be home because I wanted to—*"explain, grovel, apologize profusely, beg you not to walk away from me, "*—talk."

"Do I look like I have plans?"

Her locks were tamed in a ponytail and she wore sweats, not another of those snappy business suits. "You look great. But you always do."

"Smooth talker. I'll get these in water." Ainsley hightailed it to the kitchen.

Christ. Was she afraid to be alone with him?

He followed her. When she turned from the sink and saw him, she jumped back. Not a good sign.

"Would you like coffee?"

"I'll take something stronger, if you've got it."

"Bombay Sapphire or raspberry vodka. Obviously my bar isn't as well stocked as yours."

He flashed a quick smile. "I'll take a shot of the blue stuff."

"It's not really blue, silly man. It's on the shelf behind you, help yourself. Lowball glasses are up there too."

"Can I pour you one?"

"Sure." She plopped ice cubes in both glasses and added tonic. "Let's sit in the living room."

Ben chose the loveseat opposite the couch, facing her. He looked around. "This is a great place."

"Thanks. But I know you're not here to admire my decorating skills."

"Maybe I am, since I haven't bothered to show up here before now." He let his gaze wander. "The space suits you. Colorful. Classy. But not so formal. I'm glad to see you don't mind mussing it up." An afghan hung off one end of the couch. A half-finished crossword puzzle was on the coffee table. Boxes were stacked between the loveseat and chair.

"You do have a way with words."

Regrets that you didn't use your safe word last night?

"Why don't you tell me what's on your mind?"

He forced himself to meet her gaze. "I'm here to make sure you were all right after last night. You snuck out on me. Again. Just like that first night in the club."

"Ben, it's—"

"It's not okay. Christ, it's far from okay. Just hear me out, all right? 'Cause I'm not used to...doin' shit like this." He exhaled a frustrated burst of air. "Not that I don't fuck up from time to time, but I've never had to approach a sub and apologize for my inappropriate Dom behavior."

She said nothing.

"What I did was out of line. I won't make excuses. I won't be the guy who apologizes, and tries to defend his actions after the apology."

"But?"

"But nothin'." Ben studied his drink. "I was wrong. I made the punishment about what I wanted, instead of makin' it about what you needed. That goes against everything I am as a Dom and as a man. Jesus. I..." He looked into her eyes and felt his stomach bottom out. "Ainsley. I'm sorry."

"I know you are," she said softly. "I knew it last night. But I appreciate you coming by and saying it and making sure I was all right."

"So are we okay?"

"You mean am I willing to continue as we were? With me as your submissive for the next couple weeks?"

He nodded, fear clawing at his throat that he'd fucked this up.

"Yes. But I want to point out that although it was an extreme punishment scene for us, I could've said my safe word at any time. I didn't."

"Why didn't you?"

"I trusted you. I still do. Although I was confused during the scene and upset when it ended, I really understand why you did it."

Immediately Ben was off the couch, framing her face in his hands, kissing her with sweetness, passion and gratitude. He murmured, "Thank you," against her mouth. Taking a moment to rest his forehead to hers. Taking a moment to wallow in relief.

"However, I don't know if I'm up for any Dom and sub play tonight."

"We'll put a buffer between last night and tomorrow night." He traced the pulse pounding in her throat. "Because Bennett will be back tomorrow night. Guaranteed."

Ainsley stared at him.

He bristled under her scrutiny. "What?"

"It's not a role for you, is it? Not a once in a while thing. It's who you are."

"What? Bein' a Dom?"

"Yes. You can tone him down. Put him aside for a while. But he's always there."

"Does that bother you?"

"Not as much as I thought it would. Because you're the real deal in this situation. I'm not. I'm...what is the BDSM term? A tourist. I'm gawking around, wide-eyed, wanting to see and experience everything before I go back to where I belong."

His hopes plummeted. "Is that really how you see this playing out?"

"I don't know. I have a few more weeks to figure it out."

He sat beside her and took her hand. "Something else you said last week has been bugging me. You accused me of holding back with you. And I realized you're right. I have been."

Her eyes searched his. "Why?"

Because this thing with you scares the living hell out of me and I don't want you to run out when I open up. "Probably because I've only been on one date outside the club in the last three years."

"Recently?"

"A couple months ago. The awkwardness reminded me why I don't go on dates. She talked the entire time, tellin' me all sorts of personal stuff, and she got snippy when I didn't blab my entire past life history. But it's a habit because I don't share personal things about myself at the club. I just share my body and my expertise. Crude, but true. So when you started asking me questions about what I like to do outside the club and at the ranch, I automatically dodged the questions."

"Do you feel I'm prying into your life beyond the Dom/sub parameters we set?"

"That's the thing, this situation is unlike any other for me too. I can't fall into that same pattern with you." Ben touched her face. "I don't want to."

"What do you want, Ben?"

"To really get to know you beyond those Dom/sub parameters. To let you get to know me. To hang out." He didn't add *like normal people,* because what was normal for other people probably wouldn't ever be enough for them. "It's a beautiful night. Would you take a drive with me?"

She struggled to respond.

So he gave her an out. "It's okay if you say no—"

"I'd love to go." Ainsley pecked him on the mouth. "Let me grab a coat."

Ben opened the passenger door of his truck and helped her inside. The night air held a cold bite, which meant the end of the Indian summer was near.

Neither spoke as the pickup rolled away from Sundance. The sky was full-on dark. Hills and valleys that during the day were lined with fall's glorious gold and red hues were austere shadows at night. The truck's tires clacked against the road's grooved surface and they didn't meet another vehicle for ten minutes.

Welcome to Wyoming.

He turned onto a gravel road. The steep, twisty incline had Ainsley reaching for the strap above the door. "Good idea to hang on. It'll straighten out here in a minute."

As soon as they crested the hill, trees flanked the plateau. A plateau where nothing blocked the magnificent view of Devil's Tower.

She leaned closer to the windshield. "Oh wow."

Ben cut the engine and the lights. "I brought blankets so we can sit outside."

He dropped the tailgate, covering the cold metal with an old sleeping bag. He wrapped a blanket around them, bringing her close to his body. "Warm enough?"

"Yes."

They stayed snuggled together, soaking in the brilliance of the stars, content with quiet.

After a while, she said, "This is such a gorgeous spot. I didn't know it was here."

"It's weird when you're used to living among scenery like this—" he gestured to the sprawling grand vista, "—it becomes easy to take it for granted. So I come here when I need to be humbled."

She threaded her fingers through his. "I'm happy you brought me to a place that matters to you. It is beyond amazing."

"I'm glad you didn't think I dragged you out here because I was too cheap to take you someplace else."

Ainsley snickered. "But I need to ask... Did you bring girlfriends here when you were in high school?"

"Nope. It's always been my private place. Well, as private as a public place can be."

"Did you ever come to any life-altering decisions while soaking in the scenery?"

"Given that my workin' life had been predetermined by bein' born into a ranching family, I'll say no."

"Are you ever resentful that path was expected for you? And then Chase got to go off and do his own thing?"

The depth of the questions surprised him. Like she'd just been waiting for the chance to ask. "There are days, but I'll admit those days are rare. I'll also admit I'd probably feel differently about that life if I hadn't found my place in the club. Besides I've always known my station in life regarding our section of the ranch."

She frowned. "I was under the impression the McKay Ranch was one entity."

"It is. But it's complicated with the additions to the original ranch land. My Uncle Carson and his sons have been buying up land for the last fifteen years. So has my Uncle Cal."

"And your family hasn't added on?"

Not yet. "Not much. First there's gotta be land around us for sale to buy."

"Working with the ag industry will be a whole new experience for me. I'll be taking a course after the first of the year that deals with land lease rights, mineral rights, and how it can affect the added value of the land."

"We've owned land lease rights for over a hundred years, in some places."

"So how does it work? Dividing the work and the money when there are so many family members involved?"

"We divvy up responsibilities. Technically all the cattle belong to all of us. We divide them up according to land size. Out here it takes about thirty-five acres to sustain one cow. So those in the family who've bought more land run more cattle, so they make more money."

"Land equals money?"

"Yep. As far as the rest? We've got common ranch equipment to use. Feed is divided up between us because we work together to get the haying done. We're all paid out of the expenses account. Gotta watch those pennies bein's we're only paid individually once a year after the cattle have gone to market."

"I don't know if I could handle only getting a check once a year."

He shrugged. "It's just the way it goes. So I'm glad I get some extra cash from my furniture makin' sideline." Which reminded him he needed to check on what the holdup was for payment on his last completed furniture order. He'd need that money sooner rather than later.

"Does Chase have any stake in the ranch? Seems like he's not around to pitch in."

"He opted out last year and took a cash settlement. I did talk to Chase today. He's excited about the event Saturday."

"Really? Lucky for us it fit into his schedule so last minute."

"He's done with the PBR tour for the year."

"What's it like? Having your sibling a celebrity?"

"Chase is Chase. He's the same way now as he was when he was a kid." He smiled. "A spoiled brat. But he's a good guy." That's when Ben realized Ainsley was doing it again, directing the conversation. "Here you're asking all about my family. You must think I'm a total dick because I've never asked about yours."

Ainsley started to swing her legs on the tailgate. "Not a lot to tell. My parents are missionaries. They're out of the country for a couple years at a time so I don't see them much. Everything changed between us after I escaped to college."

"Whoa. *Escaped?*"

"I spent my childhood in third world countries. All I ever wanted was a normal life. Living in the suburbs, going to school with kids my age, hanging out at the mall with friends, having sleepovers talking about boys, clothes and other girls. Even when we were in the States I didn't have that."

"Why not?"

"My dad requested assignments in rural areas, so we lived on various Indian reservations. I was the outsider white girl everywhere, even in my own country."

"That must've been rough."

"I'd had visions of reinventing myself when I started college, but I played it safe. I didn't want to become a clichéd wild child, rebelling against my father being a minister."

Ben's thumb traced circles on her palm. "Is that why you're goin' wild now?"

"I'm not wild. I'm exploring whether I have a wild side, remember? I'm not sure this Dom/sub thing is more than an experiment. I think

I'm too old to be learning new tricks."

Had she brought up her doubts because of last night? Or was it a warning that no matter how much he opened up to her, there wasn't a chance this could last longer than the thirty days? Ben asked, "How old are you?"

"Teetering on the edge of thirty-eight. Why?"

"This ain't me sucking up, but I thought you were younger than me."

"How old are you?"

"Thirty-two."

Ainsley groaned. "Great. Now I *am* a cliché. Not a wild child daughter of a preacher man, but a cougar."

"Age don't matter. I'd still be the boss of you even if we were the same age."

"I remember saying that to my older brother. *You're not the boss of me.*" She shot him a sideways glance. "That totally takes on a different meaning now."

He laughed. He seemed to laugh a lot with her.

The first edge of the moon peeped up over the top of Devil's Tower. "Look."

"It's breathtaking. Now I understand the phrase moon glow."

"Just wait. In another hour you'll barely see the stars because the sky will be lit up."

Once again silence fell between them, allowing Ben to study her covertly. He was captivated by the play of moonbeams highlighting her face. "God, you're beautiful."

Ainsley looked at him and then away.

"Did I say something wrong?"

"Not at all. It's just...disconcerting. You've given me more compliments in a week than...I deserve."

"That wasn't what you were gonna say." He tugged her closer by the collar on her coat and got right in her face. "Tell me."

"There's Bennett. I wondered if he'd make an appearance."

"He gets pissy when you rip on yourself. So tell me."

Her exhalations puffed against his lips. "You see me in a different way than I see myself. You can make me feel sexy and pretty."

"You *are* sexy and pretty." He pressed smooches to her lips.

"And when you give me such awesome compliments? They're sincere. Not toss off comments because you want to get laid." She rubbed her mouth over his. "You know I'm a sure thing. So I appreciate them even more."

"The only sure thing about you, angel, is you keep me on my toes. I don't take for granted that you're a sure thing because you can stop this at any time. And after last night...I was really afraid you would."

"Ben." Ainsley placed a kiss on his chin. "I can't promise you that this won't end, but I want to see it through until the end date we agreed on. Okay?"

That was more than he'd hoped for, but not nearly enough, and it'd have to do for now. He said, "Okay."

Chapter Seventeen

Ainsley had expected a decent turnout for the community event National West and Settler's First had co-sponsored for Chase McKay and his foundation. But she hadn't expected standing room only. She'd had to restock her bank information brochures and giveaway items within the first fifteen minutes. The fishbowl overflowed into a cardboard box with entries for the five hundred dollar drawing.

Forty-five minutes remained until the golden boy himself, Chase McKay, made an appearance.

She'd seen Ben, not that he'd sought her out. He couldn't—being surrounded by a bevy of beauties limited his movement. Really, it was ridiculous. He was good looking. And he did have that sexy dimpled chin. And those expressive blue eyes. And a great body. And that deep, commanding voice. Those women were enticed by the pretty packaging. But those women didn't know him, the real him, not like she did.

Jealous much?

Truthfully, she hadn't expected to see him, with his brother being the guest of honor. Several tables had been reserved for the McKay family near the stage. Kids of varying ages, with the same black hair and blue eyes as Ben, pawed through the freebie bin until they all came up with matching whistles.

Leslie brought her a soda and an oatmeal raisin cookie during a lull. Turton had volunteered to make the presentation, but Ainsley feared his monotone would put the audience to sleep. She wasn't a nervous speaker. She'd given many presentations in her career, so it bothered her she had the heart pounding, stomach-churning attack of nerves today. She couldn't remember the last time she'd been this jittery.

Yes, you can. That second night with Bennett in the club. And the first night with Bennett in the club. And every night since.

Not exactly the best timing for those reminders to pop up.

Steve Talbot, the bank president from Settler's First, wandered over, holding his fishbowl full of entry slips. "Shall we get this started?"

"You bet." Ainsley grabbed her cardboard box and followed Steve up to the stage.

"Ladies first."

"You the closer?"

He shrugged. "We've got seniority."

Mayor Gilbert quieted everyone down. "Before we get to the main event with Chase McKay, we'll hear from today's sponsors. Ainsley Hamilton, president of National West Bank, will say a few words about Sundance's newest bank."

Polite clapping.

"Thanks, Mayor Gilbert. I'm Ainsley Hamilton, a recent transplant to Wyoming, and I'd like to thank everyone for the excitement and support in welcoming National West Bank and its employees to the Sundance community. We're honored to sponsor Chase McKay's appearance and to support his foundation. Since National West Bank is the new kid on the block, we wanted to show our pride in being part of this great community, alongside with Settler's First, in providing Sundance residents with banking choices. If you're interested in more information, visit our booth, or better yet, come on in to the bank and see what National West can offer you." She exhaled, glad she'd kept her speech short and concise. "Now onto the money drawing portion, which I know is why you're all hanging onto my every word." That comment brought laughter. "I'll need a volunteer to pick a name out of the box."

Immediately five kids rushed to stage. Four boys and one girl. Tempting to pick the dark-haired girl since she'd elbowed three bigger boys to wind up in front. But Ainsley chose the smallest boy with the biggest hat, who trailed behind the others. She pointed at him. "Come on up here, young cowboy."

The kid didn't go around and take the stairs. He took a running jump and threw himself onto the stage.

This amused everyone in the tables off to the left.

Ainsley bent down. "What's your name?"

"Miles McKay." The kid practically shouted the last part, which incited more laughter.

Didn't it just figure she'd pick a McKay? "So, Miles, what do you want to be when you grow up?"

"A bull rider like my daddy and like Chase."

"I've always admired a man who knows what he wants and goes after it. Have your dad and Chase given you any advice?"

He nodded. "Stay on eight seconds."

More laughter.

What a charmer. "Okay, Miles, stick your hand in and pick out a winner."

Miles stirred the pieces of paper before he found the one he liked. When he looked up from beneath the brim of his little black hat, with those vivid blue eyes and serious expression, Ainsley immediately thought of another dark-haired, blue-eyed cowboy charmer. She almost said, "Thanks, Ben," but caught herself and said, "Thanks, Miles. The winner of the five hundred dollars is...Alison Toomey!"

After she exited the stage, Steve grabbed the microphone. "Thanks to National West Bank and Ainsley Hamilton." He addressed the people at the front tables. "Watch out for that one, McKay family. Don't be fooled by her charm, she's only out for your banking business."

Ainsley plastered a smile on her face.

"Let's get down to it." Steve did his spiel.

When he finished, Mayor Gilbert took over. "Now it's time to bring out the man we're proud to call our own, the man who represents the great state of Wyoming and our western way of life, the man who honors his family and his ranching heritage, the man who is bold enough to take a stand for what he believes in. Ladies and gentleman, please welcome home to Sundance, Chase McKay."

Thunderous applause echoed in the room.

Ainsley watched Chase saunter onto the stage. He was shorter than she'd expected, but more powerfully built than Ben. He had a quick smile and quick wit. His smooth confidence in front of a crowd didn't come off as rehearsed, but polished, as if a PR department had groomed him. As Chase spoke, she recognized similarities he shared with Ben. Hand gestures. Thoughtful pauses. Not to mention those rugged good looks.

She was so lost in thought about Ben and his family dynamic that she nearly missed being called to the stage. Leslie pushed her with a, "Go!"

"Now the sponsors of this event, National West Bank and Settler's First Bank, are contributing five thousand dollars each to the Chase

McKay Foundation."

Ainsley and Steve stepped forward with the big, fake checks. Flashing light bulbs nearly blinded her, the applause was deafening. Where had all the camera crews come from?

Chase seemed genuinely stunned by the donation. When it quieted down, Chase took the microphone and looked at the tables on the left. "Ava, darlin', did you get all that?"

She said something, which he didn't hear. "Why don't you come on up here and say hello?"

More raucous applause.

A stunning brunette bounded onto the stage and stood beside Chase. She was a good six inches taller in spike heels. Chase swept her into his arms and laid a passionate kiss on her that made the crowd go nuts. He finally set her down, but wouldn't let go of her hand. "Have y'all met my beautiful wife? Ava Cooper Dumond McKay. Ava is workin' on two documentaries about bull ridin', and she's hopin' to have at least one of them done next spring. Thank you all for comin' out this afternoon." Chase and Ava left the stage and a swarm of photographers followed them.

The crowd vanished quickly. She, Leslie and Rita tore down the display and loaded it in Rita's Suburban. She returned inside to double-check she hadn't forgotten anything. She noticed the poster tacked to the backdrop, but she couldn't quite reach the pushpin.

A warm, familiar body moved in behind her and murmured, "I've got it."

Ainsley didn't budge for several seconds. She just closed her eyes and absorbed the feeling of having him so close.

Then he stepped away.

She straightened her sweater and skirt before she faced him. "Thanks."

"You did great up there. Everybody was real impressed. But I bet you're used to doin' presentation stuff like that?"

"I've done it a time or three hundred."

His gaze moved from her gray pumps, up her calves and over the black wool skirt that clung to her thighs and hips, then lingered on her breasts molded by the gray angora sweater. The palpable heat in his blue eyes made her thighs clench. "Goddamn you look good enough to eat." He grinned. "Twice."

Ainsley grinned back. "That can be arranged. Do you have plans tonight?"

Ben shoved his hands in his pockets. "Ah, my folks are havin' a family thing at their place since Chase is in town, as well as our brother Gavin."

"Of course your family wants to gather and celebrate Chase's success. I'm sure you'll have a great time."

"If you think dodging screamin' kids and nosy relatives is fun," he muttered.

"Excuse me?"

"Nothin'. It's just all the McKays are comin', which means all of their kids. God love 'em, but I'm ready to schedule a vasectomy after about an hour. And guaranteed this shindig will last much longer than an hour."

"Large families are almost another culture to people like me, who have one sibling and half a dozen cousins, total."

"I don't suppose you'd wanna come with me?" he blurted.

That shocked her. "Really? Me?"

"Why not?" That too-blue gaze pinned her in place. "Do you have plans?"

"Well, no, but won't your family think it's odd that you're showing up with me?"

He shrugged. "Steve Talbot will be there. It's only fair the rep from the other bank gets an invite too."

So this wasn't personal. She wouldn't be showing up on Ben McKay's arm as his date. Another shard of disappointment sliced her. "Although I appreciate the invite..." She fiddled with the sleeve of her sweater. "I'm sure—"

"Look at me."

Her gaze zoomed to his at his command.

"That was a lie, okay? I don't want you to come because your bank contributed to Chase's fund. I want you to come for me. I mean, I'd like it if you came with me. Not as my girlfriend or anything, because Christ, no one in my family would leave either of us alone, and I wouldn't put anyone through that." He offered her a shy smile. "So would you consider goin' as my...friend?"

Why did Ben's honesty surprise her? Even when it hurt her a

little? And was he trying to kill her with that sweet little boy smile?

"I'd like that. Do I need to change?"

"Why? You look fantastic."

"Flattery won't get you anywhere, *friend*." A thought occurred to her. "You aren't using me to fend off questions from your family about why you're *not* in a relationship?"

He hung his head. "Busted."

"Ben!"

"I'm kiddin'. Sounds like you've had the same 'when are you gonna find a nice girl and settle down?' questions from your family that I've had from mine."

"No, mine are more along the lines of 'don't let the bitterness from your divorce keep you from finding a good man' and then my mother asks how many cats I've got."

Ben chuckled. "If anyone asks, let's tell them we're too busy fucking like rabbits to find someone decent to settle down with."

"I swear if anything remotely close to that leaves your lips, Bennett McKay, the only thing you'll be fucking in the very near future is your fist."

"Understood." He smirked. "Come on. You can ride with me."

"Wouldn't it be better if I drove? So if it gets too uncomfortable I can leave?"

"Why do you think I wanna give you a ride? That'll give me an excuse to leave too."

Ainsley convinced him to stop and pick up flowers for his mother, so they were late.

As he sensed the questioning looks from his family members, Ben realized it'd been fucking idiotic, lying to Ainsley, telling her that he didn't want to show up at his folk's place, acting like she was his girlfriend. He wanted to hold her hand and lead her through the maze of relatives, introducing her as his. He wanted to sneak a kiss from her in the food line. He wanted...so much more than she did, apparently, because his question about her going just as his friend had been a test of sorts, but he wasn't sure which one of them had failed it.

He watched as she made the rounds with his family, so beautiful and confident and real. For the first time he allowed himself to wonder what would happen when the month was up. Would Ainsley be interested in seeing more of him? And if so, did she want him as Bennett, the man who took great pleasure in awakening her darker sexual needs? Or would she want Ben, the rancher? Maybe she'd want neither and she'd just walk away. That made him want to punch something.

Ben stared out the dining room window to the darkness beyond, mentally planning his weekly to-do list instead of obsessively watching Ainsley. A hand clapped him on the back and he stiffened. He hated Steve Talbot's fake show of camaraderie.

"Ben. Good to see you."

"Talbot. Thanks for comin'."

"I wouldn't miss it for the world." Steve tossed a glance over his shoulder. "But I'll admit I'm surprised you brought my competitor to a family event."

Ben couldn't very well point out the fact Steve wasn't family and *he* was here. "The community event was Ainsley's brain child, so she should be here. Besides, Chase wouldn't have had any local recognition if not for Ainsley's efforts on behalf of National West."

"She is...determined to fit into the community right away, isn't she? That might be seen as trying too hard. Being too aggressive. Few folks around here like a pushy woman like that."

His brain urged him not to take the bait, but his mouth had already gulped the hook. "That's a damn sight better than not tryin' at all."

Steve's laugh was forced. "I see the lovely Miss Hamilton has a champion in you, Ben."

"I just don't find fault with supporting a hard worker—regardless of gender." A phrase that had never applied to Steve Talbot. With that, Ben walked away.

Hopefully his prickly behavior with Talbot wouldn't bite him in the ass if he needed to call on the man for a loan. Made Ben shudder to give that man more power and leverage over him.

He snagged a soda and found a spot in the dining room where he could keep an eye on Ainsley in case she needed rescuing.

Right. You just wanna watch her ass wiggle in that sexy tight skirt.

As soon as Tell and Dalton saw he was alone, they approached him. Tell spoke first. "So you got any news for us?"

"I haven't talked to Rielle yet."

"Why the hell not?" Dalton demanded.

"Because she can be prickly as a damn cactus. Any time I've seen her, she's in one of them moods."

"That's because everything is closing in on her." Tell leaned closer. "You need to get this deal done, Ben. Soon."

He was half tempted to tell them to take a shot at talking to her if they thought it was so fucking easy. "I get that."

"Do you?" Dalton's gaze flicked to the banker. "What were you and Talbot talking about?"

"Nothing important. Why?"

"We were just wondering if you were asking him about a loan, to cover, you know, your portion. Because if this is about money, we can front you some cash—"

"It's not about money. Jesus." His cheeks heated. "I said I'd take care of it."

"See that you do because we don't wanna lose out on this," Tell warned.

Then they took off, leaving Ben to brood.

Fifteen minutes later, Chase slumped against the wall next to him. "You been hidin' over here the whole time?"

"Hiding." Ben snorted. "As if anyone could hide in here. I'm glad Mom and Dad built that three-season room or we'd only get to invite half the family."

"Neither of us would've minded that."

"True. But Mom's really happy everyone is at our place for a change. Seems we've always had to go to Uncle Carson's house for get-togethers."

Chase sipped his beer. "How much do you think Mom's happiness has to do with Gavin showing up?"

"Some, I reckon. But I also figure that's the reason the whole fam-damily is here. To get a good look at him. No offense, bro."

"That's what I thought too. I still think it's weird he ain't stayin' here. Especially since Mom and Dad stayed at his place in Arizona."

"You and Ava ain't stayin' here either," Ben pointed out.

"You can't fault me'n the missus for wanting to stay in Kane's trailer, since it holds special significance for us." He waggled his eyebrows.

"Right. You and Ava are afraid Mom and Dad will hear you two havin' loud sex all night long."

Chase shot him a sideways glance. "We *are* newlyweds. Besides, maybe me'n the missus are afraid we'll hear the folks havin' wall-thumping sex all night long."

"Now I'll have to scrub my brain with scotch to erase that image. And gee, ain't it cute how you're always calling Ava *the missus* now?"

"Fuck off. We'll see how you act when you fall in love with the woman of your dreams. You won't wanna wait to put a ring on her finger and call her yours." Chase hadn't let grass grow under his feet where Ava was concerned. As soon as she'd agreed to marry him, he'd whisked her off to Hawaii for a private ceremony on the beach.

"I doubt I'll ever get married." Ben's gaze automatically sought out Ainsley. She was talking animatedly with his Uncle Carson and Uncle Cal. And she didn't miss a beat when Steve Talbot horned in on their conversation. What a rude asshole.

"You seem to know the new bank prez pretty well."

"Sundance is a small town."

"So there's nothin' goin' on between you and the banker?" Chase asked.

Ben curbed his intent to remind Chase that Ainsley had a name beyond *the banker*. "Nothin' worth mentioning."

"That wasn't really an answer. You lyin' to me? Or just lyin' to yourself?"

Both. "It's not something I can talk about, okay? Can we just leave it at that?"

"I guess. But I'll remind you of all the times you felt entitled to poke your nose in my love life." He laughed. "Although, to be honest, it only became a love life after I met the love of my life."

"Don't you mean *the missus*?" Ben made soft kissing noises.

"Jesus, you're an asshole sometimes. And nice try, deflecting my questions. I just wanted to throw out that anytime you wanna talk about this, or anything else...just call me. I owe you, for all the times you pulled my head outta my ass."

"Thanks, Chase. I appreciate it."

"I ain't one to brag, but I've gotten good at this touchy feely shit since meeting my Ava Rose." Chase belched. "Speakin' of...gotta see what my missus is up to."

Ben had a strange pang of jealousy when Chase swept Ava into his arms and plopped her on his lap, kissing her soundly. They were so in love, so attuned to each other—so oblivious to assorted family members shouting at them to get a room.

He had time to study how his family clustered together. His cousin's wives, Channing, Macie, AJ, Ginger and India had babies propped on their hips. His mom, Aunt Carolyn and Aunt Kimi were carting around their grandkids. Tell, Dalton, Brandt and Jessie had formed their own group in the living room corner. The rest of his cousins were outside because it was damn hot in here. The horde of kids running in and out every ten seconds hadn't done much to cool the place off.

No one bothered him. The groups shifted. He saw his sister-in-law Libby bustling around in the kitchen with Domini and Skylar. No surprise Keely had cornered Gavin, but from the looks of it, Gavin was holding his own.

He realized while amusing himself with his family's antics, he'd lost track of Ainsley. He turned and there she was. "Hey. I was wondering where you'd gone off to."

"I've been behind you the last fifteen minutes."

"Really?"

"It'd be easy to get overlooked in this family, wouldn't it?"

Ben let her insightful comment pass. "You're welcome to share my section of wall if you don't mind bein' overlooked."

"Thank you." She scooted next to him, but not right next to him. "You're pretty quiet around your family."

"Sorta hard to get a word in edgewise, if you hadn't noticed," he said dryly.

"I met Quinn. He's...reserved."

"Only around people he doesn't know."

She blinked at him. "He doesn't know his family? Because he hasn't said much to them either."

He shrugged. "It's always been that way with us."

"Do you two talk at all when you're working together?"

"Sure. If something needs said. But neither one of us jaws on and

185

on just to fill the silence." He let his arm dangle by hers. "What enlightening things did you learn about other McKays?"

A panicked look crossed her face. "I'll never keep the names straight. I asked your cousin...Keely? If they'd developed a smart phone app for the family tree. I was kidding but her husband seemed serious about it."

He leaned closer. "To be honest, I'd buy one. Then I'd have a reference point for each new baby and that baby's siblings. I think I called Colby's second boy the wrong name for the better part of a year."

Ainsley laughed softly.

"God I love to hear you laugh."

"Ben."

"Ainsley."

"Don't look at me like that."

"I can't help it. I've been thinking about the first thing I'm gonna do to you after I peel off that sexy skirt. It makes your ass look amazing, by the way."

Her gaze fell to his mouth and she licked her lips. "What idea is winning?"

"It's a tie right now between smacking your ass until you come, or fucking it until you come."

"I can't believe you said that. Here in your mother's house, with all your relatives within earshot."

His smile held no guilt whatsoever. "But I didn't hear you sayin' no."

Ainsley cocked her head, acting coy. "Because I'm trying to decide which option holds more appeal for me, Bennett. Not that you'd give me a say."

Without breaking eye contact, Ben reached for her hand and squeezed before releasing it. "I'll give you a say, but there is a condition."

"Which is?"

"We leave right fucking now."

Her hazel eyes heated to a molten gold. Those ripe lips curled into a smirk. "I *am* feeling tired, now that you mention it."

It took ten minutes to say goodbye, and Ben knew he'd missed people. If it'd been up to him, they would've just left, but Ainsley was too polite for that.

Once they were finally in his truck, he said, "Straight to my place?"

"My car is still at the community center. I need to get it and I'll follow you out."

He kept hold of her hand, absentmindedly running his thumb over her knuckles. He'd thought the simple touch would soothe him, would lessen his overwhelming need to pull his truck over and fuck her blind. But it only made him more impatient. He shifted in his seat, trying to combat the pressure from his jeans on his already hard cock. Trying to combat the pressure inside himself he didn't quite understand.

He'd been with her last night. Pushing her limits. Mixing it up. Not holding back on his Dom side, but keeping their slap and tickle more focused on the tickle side, than the slap. Using the flogger on the front side of her body. Holding her on edge, waiting for the multi-point sting that never connected. She hadn't acted frustrated, especially not when he'd set the flogger aside and fucked her, face-to-face. Taking his time, building up, pulling back, dragging out the pleasure for an hour before letting them both come. Afterward, Ainsley had been so exhausted, she'd crawled in his bed and had fallen asleep. And like some kind of lovesick sap, he'd crawled in bed beside her and watched her sleep, unable to stop from touching her even when she wasn't aware he was doing it.

He had no fucking idea what was wrong with him.

He parked next to her car, noticing it wasn't the only one left in the lot. He took her hand and helped her from the cab.

She surprised him with a kiss. "Can I just say that I really love how you always open my door? And walk me to my car?"

"It's my pleasure."

Her fingers toyed with the snaps on his shirt. "I can tell you're antsy. My place is closer than yours. So since I have some say in tonight's fun and games, can we play there? You could even keep your truck parked here, if you're worried about someone seeing it parked in my drive."

She was worried about his reputation? Right.

But he was too horny to care.

"Drive."

Chapter Eighteen

Wally and Charo usually greeted her at the door no matter what time she rolled in, complaining loudly, and sniffing her shoes. Not tonight.

Ainsley flipped on the lamps in the living room. She shut the shades. She fought the need to tidy up—straighten the fleece blanket draped over the couch, gather the newspaper and mug on the coffee table. How could she be so nervous in her own house?

"Ainsley."

She looked at him, definitely in Dom mode now, nonchalantly leaning against the wall. With that look in his eye. The man knew how to smolder. "Yes?"

"Come here."

A mere twenty steps across the small space and she stood in front of him. More nervous than before.

Bennett ran his knuckles down her cheek. Then he cupped her chin and traced the outline of her lips with his thumb. "Put your mouth on me."

Ainsley didn't move. Didn't think. He'd tell her exactly what he wanted her to do. And that was exactly what she wanted. After being in charge all day, she'd gladly let Bennett take charge of her.

His hand fell to his waist and he worked his belt buckle, his midnight-blue eyes remained locked on hers.

She lowered to the carpet. She unzipped his jeans and yanked the denim until the jeans were around his ankles. He'd gone commando. His cock bounced against his belly.

He threaded both his hands through her hair and brought her face to his groin. "Take all of me."

Closing her eyes, she let Bennett guide her where he wanted. The wet tip of his cock brushed her lips. She opened her mouth wider, as the hard flesh slipped over her tongue. When the cockhead bumped into her soft palate, she fought the gag reflex until she took his entire length.

He held her head in place and said, "Swallow."

Her throat muscles constricted around the head and he groaned.

"Again."

Ainsley exhaled and swallowed twice in rapid succession.

"Christ that's good. Enough." Bennett slowly eased back. "Suck me hard."

Her hands clamped onto his butt cheeks to bring his body closer. His balls bumped her chin. Then she started to suck.

Bennett broke that tight suction each time as he pulled back until the rim of his cock scraped against her teeth. He permitted her to moisten her lips before he slid his shaft in, again lodging his cock in her throat. "Ah, fuck. I could watch you all night. You're hot as fire on your knees with my dick filling your mouth."

She looked up at him. Not feeling passive, but powerful.

"So pretty." His fingers lovingly mapped every plane and angle of her face. "So obedient. Make me come, angel." He kept his hands on her cheeks as he pumped in and out of her mouth with short, fast jabs.

Ainsley worked the tip, flicking her tongue beneath the head as she sucked in opposition to his thrusts.

His hands tightened, his breath quickened and he made a guttural sound as he came in hot spurts.

A haze of satisfaction coursed through her as she swallowed. She kept tonguing and sucking until he squeezed her jaw, forcing her to release him.

Bennett slumped against the wall with a heavy sigh.

She remained on her knees, running her fingertips up his naked flanks as she nuzzled his belly. Enjoying touching him.

"Ainsley," he said in that sex-roughened voice. He wrapped his hands around her biceps and brought her to her feet. His gaze was firmly fixed on her mouth. "I love seein' your lips lookin' so shiny and full after you blow me. It's goddamn sexy." He leaned forward and brushed his mouth over hers. Twice. Then he murmured, "Get your vibrator."

She hesitated long enough that he quirked the one eyebrow that said, *Why you still here questioning me?* and she hustled to her bedroom nightstand.

Since Bennett hadn't specified which vibrator, she chose the most basic silver bullet model. She returned to the living room to find he'd rearranged the furniture, placing a straight-backed kitchen chair across from one of the green parson's chairs. He'd yanked up his jeans and kicked off his boots. His posture as he rested his backside into her couch might've been standoffish—arms folded over his chest—but the heat in his eyes nearly set her clothes on fire.

"Underwear off. Pantyhose off." He grinned ferally. "But go ahead and put them high heels back on."

After she strapped on the heels, he held his hand out for the vibrator and pointed to the kitchen chair.

"You know what I've been thinkin' about since I saw you up on that stage, looking so damn professional in that sexy-assed skirt?"

Ainsley shook her head.

"How much I wanna see your hand up that skirt getting yourself off." He studied her. "Have you ever done that? Been so horny that you had to take care of yourself in your office?"

"No."

"Don't lie to me."

"No. I haven't done it. I swear."

"Good." Bennett parked himself on the parson's chair less than five feet from where she sat. "Think about it. You're dressed so prim and proper, but your thoughts are so naughty. You're so desperate to come you've locked your office door. No one can see you. No one knows what you're doin'. Show me what you'd do."

Her pulse skyrocketed. Bennett liked to play games. Her hands trembled as she inched her fingers down the silky fabric covering her legs. When she reached the hem, she tugged the skirt upward, not in a strip tease but trying to keep her thunder thighs from joggling. Once the material circled her hips, she glanced over at Bennett.

"Touch yourself."

She palmed her mound, separating her pussy lips with her middle finger. She swirled the tip around the opening, slid it back up and performed the same swirling motion around her clit. Then side to side. Following the slit back down, she pushed her finger inside her pussy.

"Did it make you hot when my cock was in your mouth?"

"Yes."

"Fuck yourself. Use two fingers."

Ainsley spread her knees wider and pressed both fingers deep. She moved them in and out, trying not to be embarrassed by the wet sucking noises her body made. She ground her clit into the hard flesh at the base of her thumb.

"That's it, baby, come on. Take it. I can tell you're almost there."

She arched back, removing her hand so her middle finger could flick her clit. So close. So close... Right...there. She gasped, enjoying that sweet, sweet throb of orgasm. In that moment her thoughts were purely selfish. She didn't think of Bennett at all.

As the last pulse faded, warm lips landed on hers. Impatient fingers fumbled with the buttons on her sweater. She wanted to sink into the kiss, but Bennett murmured, "Off. All of it."

Ainsley stood and draped the sweater over the back of the chair. She unbuttoned her skirt and it slithered down her legs to the floor. Bennett's hands were on the bottom of her lace shell. He pulled it over her head, tossing it aside and attacked the hooks on her bra. Then she was stark naked except for her shoes. And Bennett's hungry eyes ate up every inch.

He led her to the bathroom and flipped on all the lights. "Up on your knees. On the counter. Facing the mirror."

She actually blurted, "But why?" before the two hard smacks stung her backside.

"Now."

Not only did her face heat, but her whole body burned as she scrambled onto the low countertop. She did not want to see all her body flaws in what felt like stadium lighting. Her head fell forward of its own accord and her hair obscured her face.

Bennett grabbed a handful of hair and jerked her back up. "Look at yourself."

"I-I don't want to."

"Not a request." She watched his big hands in the mirror. His roughness to her softness. Those hard-skinned hands roved over her body. Holding her breasts, teasing her nipples, following the wide shape of her hips to her thighs. "You're gorgeous, angel. So bold, yet so compliant. There isn't anything sexier to me. No question you're all woman. And how lucky that you're all mine."

A different type of heat, a melting sensation, filled her chest. Bennett knew her so well. Knew when her confidence needed bolstering. Knew when to force her to stop thinking and just feel. Just obey.

He put her vibrator in her hand. "Get yourself off with this. See how beautiful you are when you let go."

One good thing about this scene—the vibrator would get her off quickly. Ainsley braced her left palm against the wall and turned the silver bullet on high.

As she placed the vibrator tip above her clit, Bennett's hands cupped her breasts. His fingers toyed with her nipples. Then his mouth connected with the curve of her waist.

Oh. That felt fantastic. The string of openmouthed kisses down to her lower back. The sharp bite of his teeth and the sweet, soothing kisses he pressed over the skin he'd nipped.

When goose bumps danced across her body, he chuckled and tweaked her nipples hard.

She gasped. Then she realized she was supposed to be using the vibrator and set it directly on her clit.

"Huh-uh. Not yet. Fuck yourself with it. I wanna see it disappearing into that tight pussy."

She rested the length against her slit before she inserted the buzzing object, allowing her head to fall back as she lost herself in pleasure.

A hard whack on her ass returned her focus to the mirror.

He bestowed such delicious agony on her back with that wicked mouth of his. She watched in the mirror as she shoved the vibrator into her hole, realizing what a turn on it was to see her swollen, glistening sex swallowing it.

"Come for me, angel. Show me again."

She pulled the bullet out and held the tip directly on her clit. The sights, sounds and vibrations were overwhelming. She moaned when the blood-plumped tissues pulsed and moaned louder when Bennett pinched her nipples.

"Watch," he demanded.

And she did. She didn't hate the reflection of herself; she reveled in it. She was unapologetically wanton, a sensual woman riding the wave of ecstasy brought about by her lover's command.

"That's it, beautiful. See yourself as I see you."

Those sweet words had more impact than back-to-back orgasms.

Bennett kissed a path up her left side, pausing to nuzzle the bottom of her breast. "Give me the vibrator."

Ainsley held out it. Keeping their gazes locked in the mirror, he sucked the bullet into his mouth. Then he licked it clean with long strokes of his tongue, making happy growls before releasing it.

Okay. That was hot. Talk about stirring her juices again.

Bennett helped her down from the counter, making sure she was steady on her high-heeled shoes before letting go of her. He whipped off his shirt. Shucked his jeans. Rolled on a condom.

His eyes were wild with lust. All that masculine impatience was for her. She raised her chin and smirked.

"Ooh. Girl is getting cocky. I'd take that as a personal challenge if my cock wasn't about to burst. Bend over. Hands on the floor. Spread your legs wide."

That commanding Dom voice did it for her in a bad way. Once again her blood raced fast. As soon as her fingertips touched the cold tile, Bennett was behind her, canting her hips to his liking. His fingers pulled her pussy open and he plunged his cock inside to the root.

Her wet sex closed around his shaft in an intimate kiss.

He rammed into her, his pelvis pistoning faster with each deep stroke. Taking her how he wanted. Full throttle. No holding back, just hard, quick fucking that left her breathless in its ferocity.

He went beyond coherent speech. Grunts, groans and ragged breathing were his communication. And Ainsley understood him perfectly.

His pace slowed and his fingertips dug for purchase on her ass cheeks. She felt his cock lengthen, felt the violent pulsation against her channel. He came in a drawn-out, full-body shudder that she felt down to the tips of her toes.

Bennett drooped over her, his hand braced against the bathroom door. "Goddamn, woman," he rasped in her ear. "You...I..." He laughed. "Hell, I can't think straight. Hang on." He pushed up and withdrew. He curled his fingers over her shoulders and slowly brought her upright. "Stay there."

From the corner of her eye she saw him ditch the condom. Then he spun her around and kissed her. Not gently. Not playfully. His kisses were ravenous.

He opened the door without missing a beat. He herded her backward into her bedroom and didn't break the seal of their mouths until the backs of her calves hit the mattress. Then he gently sat her down and dropped to his knees. "Now I know why these are called fuck-me shoes. When I saw them today all I could think about was fucking you."

"And now I see that they were worth the money."

"Definitely." He unhooked the buckle and slipped off the right shoe, taking a moment to massage her arch. Then he did the same with the left shoe.

She couldn't hold back the moan of delight when he massaged her left foot. She flopped back on her puffy quilt with a sigh. "A great event, two orgasms, fab sex and a foot massage? I could die happy right now."

He chuckled and kissed her cheek, settling next to her, letting his calves dangle off the bed beside hers.

In that moment she knew Ben was back. She reached for his hand. "Are you staying with me tonight? Or do you need to get back to your truck?"

"Not yet. I wouldn't mind getting under the covers, though."

After they slipped between the sheets, Ben ended up spooned behind her, tucking her against his body, almost completely immobilizing her.

"Thanks for inviting me to your folks' party."

"You're welcome. You deserved to be there. You fit right in."

"Which is odd, given I'm never around my family, and rarely around so many kids."

"The McKays were out in full force today."

"You were...scarce."

His rough-tipped fingers trailed up and down her arm. "That's the way it goes. I'm considered one of the quiet ones, a man of few words, and usually none of importance, so no one pays much attention to me."

"But that gives you the opportunity to pay attention to them." She paused. "Is that why you're so in tune with...people? Because you've spent a lifetime observing?"

"Probably. And without goin' all psychobabble, I've been the middle boy. Even now that Gavin is around I'm still in the middle. Quinn...well, Dad thinks the sun rises and sets with Quinn. And Chase is the superstar golden child. Kinda hard to stand out. So I've always figured it's better to blend."

Ainsley tried to roll over to look into his eyes, but he held her in place. "Blend? Hate to break it to you, but you don't blend. You are..." Maybe he wouldn't appreciate her insight so she held back.

"I'm what?"

"Forceful. You're easily the most forceful man in the room. In any room. Whether at the club or amidst your relatives."

"Oh yeah?"

"Yeah. We kept our distance today. But I knew where you were at all times. Your body was the moon, I was the tide and you had a pull on me. Which I had to resist, you jerk." She lightly elbowed him in the gut.

Ben chuckled.

"I will say you were sporting a pretty serious *back off* aura today. I didn't see many of your relatives approach you besides Chase. And the two younger guys, but they didn't stick around long."

"That'd be Tell and Dalton. There's a family dynamic that'd take me the rest of the damn night and part of tomorrow to explain." He traced the backs of her knuckles. "I guess I wasn't aware I had that vibe today."

"I'm glad to hear it's just today and not every day." She fell silent again.

"I hate when you do that, angel. 'Cause I know them wheels are churning. Tell me what's on your mind."

"I just wondered how much of that standoffishness happened after you accepted your dominant nature. Like if you let the people closest to you see that part of you, you were afraid they wouldn't accept it."

He muttered, "They won't accept it." He stroked her skin. "You came up with all of these observations just today?"

"I'm a pretty good judge of people, Ben. My ex-husband notwithstanding. I worried about that same kind of stuff with him. He didn't accept that sexual part of me. And I never asked him to do half the things to me that you've done to me. So I understand your need to keep that part of your life secret. Dean...actually threatened to tell our

195

friends, my boss, our coworkers, and our parents about my kinky sex requests. For months, every time I saw our coworkers snickering, I worried he'd over-shared at the water cooler."

Ben rolled and brought her on top of him, clamping one hand on her ass to keep her from squirming away. The other hand held her jaw. "One—I don't do things *to* you, I do things *for* you. Big difference. Two—I'm proud of you for realizing his hang-ups are not yours and for takin' a chance to live the life you want. Three—if I ever meet that self-serving motherfucker, I will beat his ass bloody. There's no bigger sin than breaking a confidence. He was your husband for Christsake. He was supposed to be a safe haven for you, not lead the charge in ridiculing you."

This man, who'd known her three weeks, had a better grasp on her, on who she was at the most basic level, and yet embraced her complexities and understood her insecurities, better than any man ever had. No one in her past—man or woman—had ever stood up for her like Ben. No one had ever built her up by knocking down the walls she'd been hiding behind. That knowledge both buoyed her and brought despair, because this thing between her and Ben had an end date.

Didn't it?

She closed her eyes, feeling those stupid, unwelcome tears trying to break free. She jerked from his hold. And he let her go.

But Ben didn't release her. He merely returned her to her previous position and held her while she composed herself. He let the brush of his hands on her skin soothe her in ways words couldn't. Sometimes being a man a few words had its benefits.

She whispered, "Thank you."

"Anytime."

"I'm tired."

Ben kissed her temple. "Go to sleep."

"Are you staying?"

"For a little while."

She punched her pillow. "I know we haven't spent the night together much, but I'm glad you're here."

"Why is that?" He bumped his pelvis into her backside. "'Cause I'm likin' this a whole bunch."

How could she tell him sharing the same bed seemed more

intimate than sex? Sleeping she felt even more vulnerable. Had Layla been right? Being in his bed surrounded by his warm body was a gateway drug to wanting more? More of what she couldn't have?

"Ainsley?"

"Sorry. I started to doze off." She kissed his biceps.

"Liar," he whispered in her ear. "And just so you know, you're welcome in my bed any night. I'll even kick the dogs out for you."

She laughed. "Well, I doubt my cats will be so accommodating."

Chapter Nineteen

Before he got busy filling his day cutting logs and boards for a furniture order, Ben loaded up his dogs and headed to Rielle's.

Unlike Chase, he didn't consider it strange Gavin had chosen to stay at Rielle's bed and breakfast. It was neutral territory and he wasn't beholden to anyone's schedule. He hadn't talked to Gavin much yesterday, and he realized he'd never had a one-on-one, face-to-face conversation alone with his oldest brother and it was past time.

Plus, he had to approach Rielle about her financial situation, as Tell and Dalton had reminded him last night, regardless of what kind of mood she was in, regardless if he was uncertain about where his portion would come from.

The dogs jumped out of the truck bed and raced off into the trees with Rielle's three mutts.

Rielle met him at the front door and held open the screen. "Hey, stranger."

"Mornin', Rielle. Something smells good."

"There's fresh coffee and warm muffins inside."

She was in a good mood, which boded well for him. "I didn't stop over here expecting to be fed, but I ain't gonna say no now that you offered." He followed her into the kitchen.

"I don't imagine you stopped over to talk to me anyway." She pointed to the mugs. "Help yourself."

"Is Gavin up?"

"He hopped into the shower as you pulled in."

Ben sat at the counter, poured himself a cup of coffee and set two blueberry muffins on a plate. "I did want to talk to you about something."

"Sounds serious."

"It is. I wanted to bring it up in private."

"Now you're really scaring me."

Ben looked Rielle in the eyes. "I won't beat around the bush. How much financial trouble are you in?"

Rielle's cheeks turned bright red and her hands squeezed her coffee mug. "I told you I'd pay you for the furniture. Are you here to repossess it?"

"God no. That's pretty inconsequential, considering everything else you owe on, doncha think?"

She nodded.

"So tell me, Ree, how bad is it?"

"Bad," she whispered.

The bitter taste in his mouth wasn't from too strong coffee.

"Can I ask how you found out?" Rielle asked.

"Besides that I took you to the bank and know they turned you down for a loan?"

Her lips formed a sneer. "So is everyone in town aware of my financial predicament? Is everyone whispering that the hippie chick doesn't have a clue how to manage money?"

"No. And if I ever heard anyone say shit like that about you, I'd bust them in the mouth."

"I know you would. You're a good friend, Ben. One of the few friends I have in this town, despite the fact I've lived here my whole life." Rielle knocked back her coffee like it was whiskey. "So how did you find out?"

No reason to sugarcoat it. "Rory."

Her eyes turned to chips of ice and she slammed her cup down. "My daughter called you?"

"No. Evidently she talked to Dalton when he was in Laramie, and Dalton came to me. He's worried about her."

Stunned silence.

Rielle made a wounded sound. "She can't... It's why I..." She covered her mouth and tears pooled in her hard eyes.

Christ. He hadn't meant to make her cry. Ben went to her and pulled her into his arms. "Hey. Rory is a terrific kid, Ree. You've done a great job raising her into a thoughtful, responsible adult. This fucked up situation hurts both of you, but we'll get something figured out, okay?"

It took a minute or so, but Rielle said, "Okay."

"Good. 'Cause I'm too fuckin' old to have new neighbors move in here."

She laughed. And sobbed. And hugged him tighter. "Thanks." She stepped back and wiped her cheeks. "I assume you wouldn't have brought this up if you didn't have a plan?"

He peeled the wrapper off the bottom of his muffin. "I've got a plan. But I'll be honest. I don't think you're gonna like it much. You're in arrears to the bank...eleven months on your loan?"

"Ten," she corrected. "I've got about thirty days left before I default."

"How much do you have to pay to get caught up in the next thirty days to keep them from foreclosing?"

"I have to pay the first six months and all the penalties. Then I have sixty days to pay the remainder to bring the account current."

"How much we talkin'?"

Rielle closed her eyes and took a deep breath. "One hundred and twelve thousand dollars."

Shit. That was way more than he'd anticipated. He didn't have that kind of money. Could Dalton and Tell come up with that much cash? Plus more to put a down payment on the land once they'd kept her foreclosure at bay?

"So please tell me more about this plan of yours, because right now, I'd sign a deal with the devil rather than lose everything."

He looked at her. "The McKays have been called agents of Satan and devil's spawn before, by your own father, if I remember right."

"Sounds like him, since he constantly referred to me as the Whore of Babylon."

It really surprised Ben that Rielle's father and Casper hadn't gotten along better, they were both cut from the same mean cloth. "Here's the deal. Me, Dalton and Tell would give you the funds to catch up to make the back payment. That'll give you a little time to decide if you want to sell us the whole parcel of land, or just part of it."

"You want the creek front section, don't you?"

"Yes. It'd be great grazing land and it's the section that's closest to the rest of our land. Look, if you wanted to subdivide it, we'd be open to that, because we don't wanna chase you off. But we also figured you'd rather sell the land to us and end up with money in the bank, rather than the bank owning all of it and you ending up with nothin'."

"You have the money right now?" she asked skeptically.

He tried to gauge the best response to her mood. If he told her getting that much cash wasn't an issue, would she be resentful? Probably. He told a half-truth. "Not all of it, but I know where I can get it." Jesus. He hoped he could figure out some financial wheeling and dealing —and soon.

"I...I don't know. It sounds like a great solution, but I need some time to wrap my head around it."

"Don't take too long." Isn't that what Tell and Dalton had warned too?

"I won't."

"And promise me you won't do anything until you've talked to me first."

Rielle nodded.

The swinging door from the back set of stairs swung open. "I should've eaten before I showered because the—" Gavin stopped and looked from Ben to Rielle. "I'm sorry. Am I interrupting something?"

"No. I actually came by to talk to you since we didn't get a chance yesterday. Rielle insisted I eat while I waited, and well, I'll never say no to good cookin'."

"Spoken like a bachelor." Gavin helped himself to a cup of coffee. "But that doesn't explain why it appears Rielle's has been crying."

She laughed a tad too cheerfully. "It's from chopping onions for the quiche we're having for lunch."

Gavin looked like didn't believe her, but he smiled at her anyway. "Good to know. I'd hate to have to pound on Ben if he somehow maligned your muffins."

Rielle rolled her eyes. "Ben would never do that. He's a good guy, honest as the day is long."

Ben made a gagging noise.

"Plus, he knows what side his muffin is buttered on." She winked. "If you need anything else, holler. I'll be in my office."

Gavin refilled his coffee and loaded his plate with a muffin and a banana.

"You seem to get along with Rielle," Ben remarked.

"This is the third time I've stayed with her."

Like that explained it. "So how long you staying?"

"I leave at six tonight on the direct flight out of Rapid City to Phoenix." He cut the banana into precise quarters. "I'd like to stay longer, but my ex-wife can't *handle* our daughter for more than a weekend so I have to be back to take Sierra to school tomorrow."

"Don't have a friendly relationship with your ex?"

Gavin separated his muffin into four equal sections. "If friendly fire counts, then, yes, it's friendly."

Ben laughed. "Sorry, you probably didn't mean that to be funny."

"So little is amusing about the situation that I'll take laughter when I can get it." He chewed and swallowed a piece of muffin, followed by a piece of banana.

"Tell me about—" my niece, "—your daughter."

"Sierra is a typical teenage girl. Lots of drama and angst in her daily life. Her mother just adds to it by refusing to be Sierra's parent—she prefers to be Sierra's shopping buddy and confidante. So when Sierra comes to my house after a weekend with my ex, she argues incessantly, breaks the rules and drives me so fucking crazy I want to send her to boarding school."

"No offense, but I'm glad I don't have kids."

"Ah. Therein lies the rub. After a couple days, Sierra is back to being my sweet, funny, wonderful, only slightly annoying, typical daughter."

"At least she isn't bratty all the time."

Gavin ate a third bite of the muffin and banana combination. "That's what Rielle tells me to focus on. Since she survived her daughter's teen years, I'm hoping to survive it too."

Ben couldn't help but stare at Gavin as he shoved his hand through his short hair. That was the most obvious difference between him and his brothers—they all had the almost black hair color from the McKay side. But Gavin's hair was brown and slightly curly, like their mother's. And it was sort of freaky, to realize he had facial characteristics of Quinn, Chase and their father, almost in a perfect blend, so he didn't look exactly like any of them, but like all of them.

"You'd think I'd be used to such scrutiny after last night."

"Sorry. How was your portion of the dog and pony show anyway?"

"Chase was the Thoroughbred and I was the mutt they dragged home that everyone expected to do awesome tricks. I was most likely a severe disappointment."

Whoa. That was a harsh assessment.

Gavin sighed and looked at Ben. "That was uncalled for. It's just... Can I be blunt? I don't know what the fuck I'm doing here. It's all still pretty surreal, this, *hey, you've got a whole 'nother family.* Especially last night. I felt like I was standing in front of one of those small clown cars, and more and more people kept pouring out, and I'm somehow related to all of them."

The McKay family overwhelmed Ben sometimes and he'd grown up around them. He couldn't imagine how Gavin felt. "Did anyone give you a hard time?"

"Not really. Keely was the most obviously curious. But she disappeared fast when Jack and I started talking business."

"Keely might come on strong, but she's fiercely loyal to all her McKay cousins. Just because you don't have the same last name, you have the same blood, so she considers you hers too now."

"Great. She isn't by chance the mother of the ringleader of the McKay kid posse?"

"No. You're probably talkin' about Kyler. Keely is his aunt. Why?"

"That kid cornered me and asked if I was rich."

Good thing Cord hadn't heard that or he would've kicked his son's butt. "What'd you say?"

"I told him no and asked if I could borrow five bucks."

Ben laughed. Gavin had a better sense of humor than he'd given him credit for. But he could just tell by looking at him that the man was stressed out. "What else is goin' on, on the family freak-out front?"

"I've enjoyed spending time with Charlie and Vi. Here and when they came to Arizona. It was great going to the PBR and watching Chase ride and meeting Ava. I spent yesterday morning over at Quinn's and he gave me a tour of the ranch. Libby's definitely got her hands full with those two kids. But as far as the rest? Sorry."

"Don't be. I get what you're saying. You're tryin' to figure out where you fit in just our lives, and then you get thrown a hundred other puzzles pieces."

"Do I sound like a whiner?"

"No, you sound like a man who ain't about to get railroaded into doin' something you're not ready for."

Gavin leveled a serious look at him. "I hope your family appreciates your insight, Ben. I know I do. I'd intended to swing by

203

your place this morning to catch up, but you beat me to it."

That mollified Ben some, although he was aware of being the last on the list since he was the least interesting of his brothers.

A muffled ringing sound became louder as Gavin pulled a cell from his front pocket. He said, "Give me a second." Then, "Hey, sweetheart. Why are you up so early on a Sunday? Uh-huh. No. I didn't know. Sounds like you had a good time. What're you doing today?" He was silent for a minute and his face turned red. "No. Absolutely not. Stop. Right now. Don't threaten or bribe or try to sweet talk me because it won't work. My answer is no. I don't give a sh— damn what your mother thinks. Because you are fourteen years old! Put her on the phone. Now."

Ben wondered if he should leave the room.

A pause. "You listen to me, Ellen. If you sign the consent form, I'll be at my attorney's office first thing tomorrow morning, filing for sole custody of Sierra, without visitation rights. Because she doesn't need to get her goddamn eyebrow pierced! Or her nose or her lip or her belly button. Don't try that bullshit argument with me. End of discussion. And I'd better not see one fucking piercing on her body anywhere when I pick her up tonight, we clear? Put her back on." Gavin paced. "Hey. No, honey, slow down. Sierra-bear, you know how she gets. It's all right. I'm glad you called me. Of course. I miss you too. See you tonight." He calmly shut the phone and braced his hands against the counter, letting his head hang down.

"Mother-fucking-sonofabitch-goddamn-it-all-to-hell-I'm-going-to-fucking-kill-her-with-my-bare-hands."

That was unexpected from Mr. Calm and Refined.

Gavin took several deep breaths, before he glanced up at Ben. "Sorry. Sometimes my ex's sheer stupidity still astounds me. I try and get my frustration out of my system before I'm around Sierra."

"So that wasn't...directed at Sierra?"

Gavin looked appalled. "God no."

"Oh." Ben had no idea what to say.

He sighed heavily. "Great impression. Not only have I showcased my whining and sarcastic side, I've proven I have a quick fuse, a bad temper, a love of curse words and..."

"And?" Ben prompted.

"That's it. Isn't that enough?"

"Nope. I'd like to see how you act when you're shitfaced. I bet that's when you really let fly."

He laughed. "I could use a shot of tequila right about now."

"You're in luck. It just so happens I have a great selection of tequila at my place."

"I've heard all about the house you built. Charlie is really proud of you."

His dad had been bragging on him? That was weird. But cool. "We could head over there now if you've got time."

"I'd like that." Gavin picked up his dishes and rinsed them in the sink.

That surprised Ben too. He assumed a rich guy like Gavin was used to having maids around and people picking up after him all the time.

And what would Gavin assume about you?

He was hoping the time for assumptions was a thing of the past.

Chapter Twenty

After his monumentally shitty day, Ben didn't bother going inside his house. He headed straight to his woodshop, needing to connect with a part of his life that gave him joy. An activity that was solely his, a talent that owed nothing to the ranch, or to his family or even the club.

He tried not to think about Rielle's evasion when he'd asked her where she was in the decision process. He shoved aside his worry he'd somehow fuck up this land deal and his cousins—no, his whole family—would blame him. He tamped down his resentment that Dalton and Tell didn't balk at all when he'd shared the amount of cash they'd need to get Rielle's loan current. When had he become the poor relation? And why the hell did that bother him so much?

Don't think about it.

The smell of wood soothed him. Whether it was pine burning in the woodstove, or the scent of freshly cut lumber, or the aroma of cedar curls beneath his feet. The best way to combat his bad mood was to carve. He chose a small piece of walnut and turned it over in his hands, studying the swirls and whorls in the wood grain.

Some carvers could look at a chunk of wood and see the form inside. Ben's brain didn't function that way. He just started chipping away, keeping the possibilities endless.

He secured the wood in a block vise and lined up his chisels. By the time he finished setting up, he'd noticed the coloration of the wood was similar to that of a barn owl.

Maybe it was the mark of a simple man that all his tension from the day simply vanished when he began carving. He didn't listen to music. His thoughts were focused on the next mark in the wood and what removing it would reveal about the piece. In that concentration he found his own peace.

A loud voice said, "Knock knock."

Ripped out of his creative space, Ben spun on his chair and faced

Ainsley. "How long have you been standing there?" came out sounding more accusatory than he'd intended.

She sauntered forward. "Long enough to admire your deep level of concentration and your skill with a chisel. Long enough to become jealous of that piece of wood because of how you've got your hands all over it."

Ben was uncomfortable that she'd barged into his private space. Over the years he'd grown more protective of his "little carving hobby" because no one knew how much expressing his creative side meant to him, especially since his cousin Carter was the artist in the family. He had no concept of time in here, which was intentional. No criticism besides his own, which was intentional too. "Sorry, I didn't hear you come in."

"Am I interrupting?"

A polite lie sprang to his lips but he couldn't give voice to it.

"I should've called first, but I was feeling restless, so I drove out."

He repeatedly scraped along a deep line. "I reckon it might be a wasted trip for you."

"Why?"

"I'm not in a real sociable mood."

"Bad day?"

He grunted noncommittally.

Ainsley stood right next to him. "Is this what you do to unwind?"

Ben's gaze met hers since her body was blocking his light. "This is one of the things I do to unwind." He let his eyes slowly travel over her body. "You're familiar with the other."

Those warm hazel eyes chilled. "I didn't come out here to ask you to tie me up and fuck me, Bennett."

He couldn't stop the surly, "So why did you come out?"

"Honestly? I missed your dogs. The whole snarling, slobbering, jumping on me with muddy paws thing really makes my day."

His lips twitched. "So you must've been disappointed when they were locked in the house."

"I'll say. It was a total wasted effort to line my pockets with raw meat to win them over."

Ben laughed. Damn woman. Trying to cajole him out of a bad mood.

She wandered around the room, not touching anything. "So even your dogs are banished from your sacred space?"

"Yeah."

"I can't blame you. Between us? I've found Deuce to be hypercritical about any type of art. And Ace? Well, Ace just goes along with whatever criticism Deuce barks about."

"You are hilarious."

Ainsley moved close enough to brush woodchips from his shirt. "I am sorry I assumed it was okay to barge in here."

"Ainsley—"

"Let me finish. The last thing I intended was to add more stress to your day." Her fingertips whisked away more shavings. "Here's the truth, Ben. I missed you. Not Bennett. Not who you are as a Dom, but you." She nuzzled the side of his face. "Thank you for stopping by last night. It was totally unexpected. Completely amazing. And exactly what I...needed. I never understood how much I need to access that submissive part of myself until you showed me how good it could be."

The red splotches on her cheeks indicated how hard that'd been for her to admit. It touched him. And flustered him because she was beginning to mean a whole lot more to him than he'd ever imagined. "I don't know what to say to that."

"Say, I'm happy to see you too, angel."

Ben tugged her between his knees and reached up to frame her face in his hands. "I'm happy to see you too, angel." This woman constantly surprised him. This woman seemed to get him. All sides of him. And that was almost too much to hope for.

She broke the kiss. "Mmm. I needed that too. Tell you what. Why don't we switch roles tonight? I'll wrassle the dogs and then whip up something for dinner. You can come inside when you're done out here. So, if you play your cards right and are suitably submissive to me, I'll wrassle you and whip you too."

"And what will you be doin' while you're waiting on me to hit a creative rut?"

"I brought my e-reader to keep me occupied."

"Some of them naughty books?"

She smirked. "You know it."

Damn. That was sexy as all get out, imagining her getting all wet and squirmy. "Don't be touching yourself if you get to a hot part, understand?" he half-growled.

"And there he is," she murmured, "the beastly Dom."

Ben clamped his hands on her ass and jerked her forward. "The beastly Dom never left, angel. I just tone him down when I'm carving."

"Why?"

"He can be a controlling dick."

She laughed. "As I well know."

He smacked her ass.

"Seriously, though, when you're ready, I'd love to hear more about Ben McKay, master wood carver. I'd love to see the beautiful things these wonderful hands create."

That wasn't a bullshit, throw-away comment. Her genuine interest in yet another side of him was strangely humbling. "Thank you."

"For what? Because I haven't cooked dinner yet and it might be inedible."

He smiled. "I doubt that. Thank you for—" *being exactly what I needed tonight,* "—barging in."

"You're always pushing my boundaries, it's only fair I push yours right back."

"That's probably true. But as far as us switching roles tonight?" He grinned. "No chance."

Christ. He'd made her cry. All he'd done was give her a piece he'd carved last year. A weirdly shaped cat straight out of a Dr. Seuss book that'd been in his scrap pile because he hadn't figured anyone would want it.

Wrong.

His cat-loving sub had gotten all choked up and thrown herself into his arms, peppering his face with smooches, muttering about his sweetness and talent to such an extent that Ben had to kiss her just to shut her up.

The kisses caught fire. Wasn't long before they were rolling around on the floor laughing, Ainsley unsuccessfully jockeying for a dominant position.

Clothes flew and they went at it right on the floor in front of the wood burning stove. He pinned her arms above her head and wrapped her legs around his waist and he drove into her. Looking at her face as the pleasure crashed over her. Burying his face in her neck as pleasure consumed him. Being roused from that happy place by her hands stroking his hair and his back. Damn that felt nice. He oughta leave her hands free more often.

"You know how I never want to talk afterward?"

"Really? No. I'd never noticed that."

Ainsley drummed her heels into his butt. "I'm serious."

"Okay. I'm listening."

"The reason why I don't want to talk is because I don't want to dissect whatever barrier of mine you've breached. I just want to bask in the way you make me feel. Because no matter how we get to that point, with cuffs or ropes or just by your command, it's always exactly what I need. I don't know how you know that much about me, Ben, in the short amount of time we've been together. I'm just really glad you do."

He wasn't expecting that. She'd surprised him for the fifth time in so many hours. "You're welcome. And I don't push you to talk to be a pain, I do it so I know for sure I haven't caused you pain. You're new to this and I can be rough."

"Well, I'd tell you if you were being too rough. But I'm a lot sturdier than you give me credit for."

"Before I forget to say it, thanks for comin' over and dragging my broody ass out of the woodshed." He pecked her on the lips. "Thanks for makin' that taco thing for supper." He gave her another peck. "Thanks for letting me win at *Wheel of Fortune* again." And another soft smooch. "Thanks for the boost to my ego for loving that ugly-ass cat I carved." He dove in for an openmouthed kiss that ramped his need back up and made her squirm beneath him. "And thanks for the spectacular blowjob."

Ainsley eased back and frowned. "But I didn't give you a blowjob."

"You haven't...yet."

Chapter Twenty-One

Ben was financially fucked.

His big payment for the last furniture order hadn't come through. But it wouldn't have mattered anyway. After he did a quick calculation, figuring out how much money he'd need to buy Rielle out, not just pay down her debt, he realized he needed a shit ton more cash.

He refused to admit to Tell and Dalton he didn't have enough to fund his third. He couldn't go to Quinn for the money, because Quinn and Libby weren't living high on the hog and Quinn wouldn't approve of their method of trying to secure the land anyway. He could ask Chase for a loan because Chase had plenty of extra cash, but that crossed a line and quite frankly, made Ben feel like a loser, a broke bum needing a handout from his younger brother. Asking for an advance on his wages from the McKay Ranch fund from their accountant before the cattle went to market would alert his family, which he, Dalton and Tell were trying to avoid. Getting a loan from Settler's First would pose the same problem.

So he chewed on it for a day and came up with a solution. Not ideal, but workable. Okay, it sucked ass, and it crossed another line, but he had no choice.

Late Tuesday morning Ben ironed his plain white shirt, slipped on a bolo tie embellished with the McKay brand and donned his tan suit coat. He added a western belt, centering it between his jean-clad hips. He settled the black Stetson on his head, grabbed his duster and headed to town.

He hadn't set up an appointment with Ainsley at the bank, too many snoopy people would report back to his that family Ben McKay had applied for a loan. So he was planning to take her to lunch and spring his loan request over a good steak.

Ben strode into National West Bank. He tipped his hat to the teller and made tracks straight for Ainsley's office—only to get intercepted by Jenny.

"Ben McKay. Fancy seeing you here again. Is there something I can help you with?"

"Yes. I need to speak with Miz Hamilton."

Jenny sauntered to her desk and tapped her fingers on a large day planner. "She's a busy woman. She's on a conference call right now. She's scheduled a meeting after lunch, followed by a staff meeting, so if you could come back tomorrow—"

"Nah. I'll wait until she's off the phone since we're having lunch today."

Jenny squinted at him skeptically. "It's not on her calendar."

"Huh. I swore we set the lunch date when she was at my brother Chase's event. Guess I'll hang out until her call is done to make sure we didn't get our wires crossed." He leaned against pillar so he could watch Ainsley in action. Something about seeing that smart, sexy woman in her element got his juices going.

"We have a sitting area—"

"I'm good. I'm sure she won't be long."

Jenny harrumphed at his dismissal.

He waited for that moment when Ainsley realized he was there.

Bingo. There it was. Her spine straightened and she swiveled in his direction. Their eyes met though the glass and Ben felt that hard punch of lust. Which increased tenfold when she offered him a sexy smirk and ended her phone call.

The woman had a pull on him like he'd never experienced. He was just as fascinated with who she was out of the sub role, as he was when she trusted him with full control.

Ben about choked on his tongue when Ainsley sashayed out of her office, wearing a form-fitting black pinstriped skirt and a matching suit jacket that skimmed her hips. The lacy red camisole peeking above the jacket's lapels kept the outfit from looking too mannish—as if that were possible with her abundance of curves. When he noticed the red stilettos, his mind zipped to the fantasy of the sharp points of those heels digging into his ass as he fucked her on her desk. Or holding onto them as he fucked her over the desk.

She raised an eyebrow as if reading his wicked thoughts. "Ben McKay. What brings you to town?"

"He claims you have a lunch date," Jenny inserted with a sneer.

Ainsley didn't miss a beat. She snapped her fingers. "That's right.

We were going to discuss some things that came up after Chase's event. I believe you mentioned taking me to Fields."

Sneaky woman picked the newest, most expensive restaurant in town. Ben looked at Jenny and smiled. "Told ya."

"I'll just grab my coat," Ainsley said and ducked back into her office.

"I still find it odd the woman who obsessively writes everything down forgot this date. Makes one wonder why she's hiding that you two are...friends."

Ben wouldn't let this smarmy little bitch take shots at her boss when Ainsley was out of earshot. He leaned closer to Jenny. "Or maybe Miz Hamilton and I are discussing personal bank business and she didn't want it broadcast. I understand your job is to ensure her schedule runs smoothly, just as I'm sure she can count on you to maintain the discretion that comes along with your position."

Ainsley sailed out of her office, saying, "Jenny, would you make sure all the paperwork in my outbox is filed?"

Jenny flashed her teeth. "I'm on it. But remember Turton becomes my lord and master after one."

"Excuse me?"

"Oops. I meant to say taskmaster." Jenny flitted off.

Ben helped Ainsley with her coat. He opened doors but didn't reach for her in any way that might be deemed intimate. It about killed him too. She'd worn her hair up and he wanted so badly to press his lips to her bared nape. To taste that fragrant section of skin and watch her body tremble.

Fields was a new restaurant that utilized locally grown food. The owners only served organic beef, chicken, pork and game. Everything was homemade from ingredients found within sixty miles of Sundance, so the menu selection was limited. This place wouldn't have been his first choice, but he admitted liking the privacy of the high-backed wooden booths and the fact there were hardly any customers to interrupt them.

Ainsley set aside her menu. "So, Ben, why did you really show up at my office today?"

"Were you worried I'd drag you back to your place for a naughty nooner?"

"Worried? No. Disappointed? Yes."

He swallowed a primitive growl. "You get off taunting me in public, doncha, angel?"

"Maybe a little."

"Maybe I'll make you pay for that later."

"Bring it on."

The waitress wandered over to take their order. And as usual, Ben knew the woman. He hadn't dated her, but it wasn't for lack of trying on her part. He kept up a light banter but he was relieved when she disappeared into the back.

"Does every woman in town have a thing for you?"

Might make him a dick, but he was happy to see a spark of jealousy, even when it was unwarranted; he only had eyes for her. "I'm surprised by it too. Used to be the single ladies only talked to me in hopes I'd introduce them to Chase."

"I don't believe that."

"It's true. Which is another reason I've stayed away from dating those types of women. I was never sure if they were interested in me for me. I'm just a plain, boring rancher. I don't have interest in bein' anything else."

Something like sympathy spread across her face.

"Besides. Aggressive women like that don't take direction well."

"And you're all about that."

He grinned. "Yep."

"Okay, Ben. What's up? Why the surprise lunch date?"

Ease into it? Or just say it. "I need a loan."

Any warmth in her eyes evaporated.

"Look, it's a...delicate situation so let me explain before your eyes slice me to ribbons."

"I'm listening."

Rather than admitting the truth—he had his eye on a piece of land about to be repossessed—Ben did something he rarely did: he flat-out lied. Not only had he promised Rielle discretion, he'd promised his cousins that same discretion. Ainsley wouldn't question this reason for needing the money since it was personal. Given all he'd told her about McKay ranching practices, she'd know something was off that he wasn't including his entire family on the possible land deal. "You know I dabble in carpentry. I've built custom furniture for different places.

Some previous customers have contacted me, wanting other pieces. Seems I have a chance to expand and get the challenge of creating something new. To do that I'll need more equipment and keep a wider variety of building materials on hand. And that is expensive."

"When did you decide this? Because didn't you just tell me you're happy being a simple rancher?"

"Yes, I am. But my woodworking hobby has become something more. It's personal."

Her eyes softened, no doubt thinking of the carved cat he'd given her, so he laid it on thick. "That's why I don't want to go to Settler's First. Because I know Slim Jim Beal, who handles the loans, will tell Steve Talbot, who will contact my uncles or my cousins and give them a head's up."

"That's against the law."

"But that's how it works here. Sucks, but it's true. I can just imagine my cousins confronting me, worried I won't be pullin' my weight on the ranch because I'm too busy building furniture."

"I can see where that might bring up questions."

"Questions I'm not ready to answer. But I don't want to lose out on a good opportunity. I've got equity in my house. A steady income. Ties to the area. I'd be a good bet."

"I imagine. And you came to me because..."

Her hard expression said, *Because you expect as your sub I'll automatically say yes.* "Christ, no. Don't look at me like that. I came to you because I trust you'll be discreet. I'm not askin' for any special favors beyond discretion in the loan application process."

Ainsley had on her shrewd bank president face. "Say I agree to help you. Would there be a chance I'd get any of the other McKay banking business?"

That question brought him up short. Was what Steve Talbot said true? She had her eye on his family's coffers? "You'd have some of mine. Isn't that a start?"

"I suppose, but I am first, and foremost, a businesswoman so I'd really like the chance to pitch National West's financial benefits to your entire family—"

"Hey, Ben."

Startled at the interruption, he glanced up and bit back a groan. He hadn't seen Michelle Littlefield, a woman he'd dated right out of high school, for several years. This was one of his least favorite things about living in Sundance—he always ran into someone he knew. "Michelle. How are you?"

"Great. When Gloria came back into the kitchen to tell me you were in the dining room, I had to come out and say hello."

"It's been a while."

"About eight years since I left to attend cooking school. I just recently returned to Sundance."

Then it clicked. Littlefield. "Fields is your restaurant?"

"I always knew a smart guy lurked beneath that handsome face of yours," she teased.

Ben felt his cheeks warm beneath Michelle's admiring gaze and Ainsley's curious one. "Ah, Michelle, this is Ainsley Hamilton. She's the bank president at National West. Ainsley, Michelle Littlefield."

"Pleasure to meet you, Michelle."

"Same here. Sorry if I interrupted a business lunch. I wanted to say hello and mention I'd love to catch up with you sometime, Ben."

Luckily Michelle left before Ben had to formulate another lie about how much he'd enjoy that.

Ainsley raised an eyebrow.

"Sorry."

"Not your fault. But I'm beginning to understand why you prefer spending your free time at the club in Gillette."

"And why's that?"

"Because you can whip the women who annoy you."

He chuckled.

"Back to the loan issues. I'm not trying to discourage you. But you need to be aware loans are very hard to come by in this economy. Even for people like you, who I'm assuming has established good credit. Taking on additional financial burden without a guarantee you'll have increased income? I want you to consider very carefully about applying at your regular bank first."

"I have. And I can't."

She studied him. "I'd have to delve into your financials, Ben, and I don't know how comfortable I am with that."

"It's nothin' I wouldn't tell you if you just asked me."

"You're that open about your finances with everyone?"

"No. But we're more than just casual acquaintances, Ainsley, way more."

She turned her gaze away from his.

"Look at me."

That command grabbed her attention but she glared at him. "Don't do that."

"Do what?"

"Go beastly Dom on me."

He held up his hands in surrender. "Sorry."

"At least you didn't say, *sorry, habit*."

Ben smiled. "So touchin' you right now is out, too? Because I missed it last night."

Ainsley stared at him, her eyes conflicted, but also resolute. "Touching me at any time is out."

"What?"

"You do understand this—" she gestured to the empty space between them, "—ends if I take your loan application."

"What? Why?"

"I can't compromise my position at the bank. Any hint of professional impropriety will have long-term repercussions on my career. So while I'm willing to help you secure a loan, once the paperwork is underway, we will only have a business relationship. Period."

Christ. He hadn't considered it'd come down to that. He hadn't considered how much her casual dismissal of him would sting. "It has to be that black and white?"

"Yes." The firm set to her jaw meant this was nonnegotiable. "Even if we were in a normal dating situation, I'd end it the instant business entered the equation. You have the choice to keep our original agreement intact."

"By askin' Settler's First to lend me the money."

She nodded.

He stretched across the table, and reached for her hand, hoping charm would have some effect on her. "I need the loan. I want you. I want you like fuckin' crazy. I can't have it both ways. For a man used to havin' his way in all things? This absolutely sucks balls. Why can't we—"

217

"Sneak around more than we already are?" she supplied coolly. "We both knew this would end. You're just choosing to end it sooner."

And with that comment, she'd put the ball squarely in his court. Ainsley could chalk up their time together as an experiment. She wouldn't have to consider going into a long term Dom/sub relationship with him. Goddammit, this wasn't fair. The first time he'd found a woman who could—

"Ben?"

Fuck. Not again. He looked up and casually eased back, hiding his annoyance at how quickly Ainsley jerked her hand away from his. "Rielle. What are you doin' here?"

"Dropping off the last of my okra and spaghetti squash in the kitchen."

"Rielle, have you met Ainsley Hamilton? We were just wrapping up a few things from Chase's event." Why did he have to qualify that?

"Rielle Wetzler. Ben's neighbor. A pleasure to meet you. We did briefly cross paths at the new bank a couple weeks back."

"Yes. I remember. Nice to meet you too. So do you run a farmer's market?"

"A small one. This time of year I'm about tapped out. I'm down to root vegetables, apples and some herbs."

Ainsley sighed. "I've been wanting to make some fall soups and the A&P doesn't have a huge selection of vegetables."

"What are you looking for?"

"Turnips. Parsnips. Leeks. Do you have beets?"

"Actually, I do. Three different varieties."

"Please, please, please sell me some. I'm desperate to make a batch of borscht."

Rielle laughed. "I'll sell you anything you want. Come by anytime. I run the Sage Creek Bed and Breakfast out on Bridger Gap Road. I'm usually there or in the gardens."

"You'd better swing by tonight after work, Ainsley. In case there's a run on beets tomorrow," Ben suggested dryly.

Rielle whapped his arm. "Such a smart aleck. I'll leave you to enjoy your lunch. Nice to meet you, Ainsley."

"You too, Rielle."

The waitress dropped off the food and several minutes passed before either spoke.

"You are coming to my place tonight after you stop at Rielle's." Not a question.

Ainsley pointed at him with her fork. "You've got a short attention span, cowboy. No slap and tickle between us any more."

"You said this would end *after* I've filled out the loan paperwork and you've submitted it. Even if I get everything filled out today, the soonest you can get started on it is tomorrow. Which means I'll expect you at my place tonight as soon as you get off work."

"Ben—"

"Bennett," he corrected. "This is not up for discussion. The parameters of our agreement change tomorrow."

"Yes, Sir," she snapped off.

"That smartass response just earned you an extra ten."

"An extra ten what?"

"Ask me again and I'll add ten more."

A mulish look flattened her lips.

After he paid, they walked back to the bank. He intended to come in for the paperwork, but Ainsley tried to hold him off. "It'd be easier if I bring it tonight."

"We won't be spending our last time together filling out a loan application," he half-growled.

She murmured, "That thought hadn't even crossed my mind."

Chapter Twenty-Two

The main structure of the Sage Creek Bed and Breakfast was crafted of rough-hewn lumber and stone. The steps were constructed from railroad ties, set at jaunty angles and filled with marbled concrete, which led to a large front porch. An eclectic mix of furniture created intimate conversation areas. Pots of flowers abounded—surprising, given the late time of year. The sun's last golden rays reflected in large windows stretched to the rafters on both the first and second story. The rustic nature brought to mind old hotels from the Wild West days.

That made Ainsley think of the Rawhide Club, which made her think of Ben. And were her eyes playing tricks on her, or was that Ben's truck parked in front of the barn? She climbed out of her car, following the sounds of laughter to the back of the building.

She called out, "Hello?"

Rielle looked up and smiled. "Ainsley. I was hoping you'd come by. I dug up a bunch of root vegetables." Her gloved hands pawed through the wheelbarrow of dirt. "So far I've found beets, turnips, parsnips, a few carrots, late potatoes and some pink Peruvian sweet potatoes that are too big for the chef at Fields to use."

"I did not expect all this, Rielle, thanks. Will these keep awhile in a dark cabinet?"

"Everything but the carrots. I also snipped some dill, chervil, chives and the last of the lemon basil."

"Sold. I'll take all of it."

"Great! I'll just knock the worst of the dirt off and get them bagged."

"Lemme help ya," Ben said, digging his hands into the wheelbarrow.

Ainsley wished she'd changed clothes so she wasn't standing there useless in her business suit. It seemed strange Ben would be here. "Do you help Rielle with her harvest a lot, Ben?"

"Not usually. I stopped by for something else and—"

"I roped him into helping me. Poor man. Ben is always getting stuck doing things around here. No wonder he doesn't come around as much as he used to."

Ainsley fought the odd spike of jealousy. "It's good to have neighbors you can count on. I lived in a condo in Denver for almost five years and I had only a passing acquaintance with anyone in our neighborhood."

"The McKays and Wetzlers have been tied together for thirty years. We know all of each other's family secrets." Rielle winked and went back to digging.

"You didn't know about Gavin," Ben pointed out.

"True. But I always wondered why your mom went out of her way to check on me when Rory was a baby."

That surprised Ben enough he stopped digging. "Really? Vi did that? Without preaching about the high price of sin?"

"Jerk." Rielle whipped a clump of dirt at him. "Vi never was like that toward me. Or Rory. And you don't give your mom enough credit, Ben. She might've made some mistakes in her life, but she's owned up to them. She's changed a lot."

"I didn't realize you were so buddy-buddy with my mom."

Rielle shrugged. "Vi's a damn sight more interesting than Joan McKay, who was the only other woman close by besides Libby."

As Ainsley shifted her stance, feeling woefully out of place, three dogs came bounding out of the treeline. Ace and Deuce made a beeline for her, barking happily, no doubt remembering her last doggie bribe. There went this brand new pair of pantyhose.

"Ace! Deuce! Sit. Stay," Ben commanded.

The dogs obeyed. Heck, she had the urge to obey.

Rielle's dog cowered by her feet and stared balefully at the man with the *obey now* voice.

Ben smiled at Ainsley. "Kept them at bay this time."

"That you did."

"Not a fan of dogs?" Rielle asked.

"They're fine. I'm just more of a cat person. Cats are more self-sufficient and easier to leave at home alone for a few days."

221

"But not more forgiving," Rielle said dryly. "Rory had an ornery cat that would shred every roll of toilet paper in the house if she was gone for more than a day. Which is why all our kitties are outside cats."

"Rory is your..."

"Daughter. She's getting her master's at the UWYO."

Rielle did not look old enough to have a daughter that age.

Ben tapped the side of the wheelbarrow. "You got bags for these someplace, Ree?"

"In the mudroom. I'll grab them."

Ainsley watched her duck around the corner. Then she focused on Ben. "I'm surprised to see you here."

"Why?"

"Just seems...coincidental you're here exactly the same time I am."

"I swing by and help Rielle occasionally."

"You have a standing date with her on Tuesdays at five thirty-five?"

Ben's eyes narrowed. "If you've got something to say, spit it out."

"Are you trying to hide something about her? Maybe your feelings? Because you're awful abrupt whenever she's around. Always trying to get rid of her."

"You're imagining things."

"Like the first time we saw each other at the bank? You shooed her away pretty fast. Then at lunch today, you were uncomfortable when she approached us. And now, you're here, running interference again. Why?"

He dusted the dirt from his hands as he closed the distance between them. "Because your bank turned her down for a loan. She's a little sensitive about it and I thought she might try to corner you when you stopped to get produce. So yeah, I'm running interference. Not for her. For you."

Ainsley got in his face. "Back off, Ben. I don't need you playing mediator. I'm perfectly capable of dealing with customers who've been denied financing. And I resent you riding in here to rescue me, acting like I can't handle myself in a professional capacity. I can handle myself just fine."

"Or you're just snippy because you're jealous."

"I am not jealous." *I'm pissed because you said you wouldn't use me again. So far today you've used me to help you get a loan and now you plan on using my body one last time before moving on to the next sub.*

An amused smile quirked his lips. "Sure you are."

She wanted to slide that smarmy look right off his face, because this was about so much more than her female jealousy and he refused to see it. "Don't flatter yourself. Don't you think if Rielle wanted to burn up the sheets with you, she'd been tied to your bed years ago, wearing a custom collar? Since you've been such close neighbors and you know each other's secrets?"

Silence. "Angel, you are gonna regret that smart comment."

"Stop looming over me like the beastly Dom. We're not in those roles right now."

"It's not a role for me. And it looks like you need a reminder that I am *always* the beastly Dom."

"You trying to scare me, cowboy?" She purposely taunted him with a label that meant nothing to him. To show him she could turn off her connection to him any time—just like he could.

He put his mouth next to her ear. "The name is Bennett, sub, and your night just got a lot more...interesting."

Ainsley swallowed hard. The heat of him, the scent of him, the overwhelming power and masculinity made her head spin. Made her want to plaster her body to his and lose herself in him. Beg him to take his loan business elsewhere so they could continue this. Beg him to understand she'd never had—maybe she'd never find—another man who knew what she needed like he did. And that pissed her off. Stupid traitorous body. Stupid sex-addled brain. "You can't just—"

"I can, I will, and I did. I want you nekkid and sitting on my bar when I get home."

"This is unfair." Why was she pushing him? Because he pushed her into a corner first? Or because she wanted their last night together to be memorable?

"Says you. I think I'm bein' more than fair."

"I won't do it."

Bennett eased back, fire dancing in his eyes. "Gonna run rather than face the consequences?"

"No. I didn't do anything wrong."

"You insulted me."

"Maybe I was insulting Rielle."

He half-snarled, "That earned you another ten."

She backed up a step. Then another. And he stalked her.

"I thought I heard you sneer that you weren't scared," he said in that low, dangerous voice.

"I'm not." Such a liar. "But I've done nothing to warrant punishment."

"Guilty until proven innocent in my world. So you'd better have a convincing argument against punishment to present to me when I get home."

"Why should I bother? You're going to make it hurt anyway. Hurt worse than it already does." *Stupid move, Ainsley, you aren't supposed to tell him that. You're supposed to be the cool-headed professional and the obedient sub who won't let him see your disappointment on any level.*

Ben gave her a look she'd never seen before. "Ainsley. I never meant—"

"Found them." Rielle waved a stack of paper bags. "I also grabbed the herbs. They should be refrigerated."

Grateful for the interruption, she practically ran to Rielle. "Thanks. How much do I owe you?"

"Twenty bucks oughta cover it."

Ainsley figured that was a low amount after she loaded the four heavy bags into her trunk. She ignored Bennett's hard, hot stare that seemed to liquefy her bones as she chatted with Rielle.

She didn't look his way when she climbed in her car. She hesitated at the end of the driveway.

A right turn led back into town. A left turn led to Ben's house.

She knew his eyes were on her vehicle as she turned left.

Ainsley wasn't naked when Ben walked in the door. Something smelled good, and while the thought of a homemade meal awaiting him stirred a weird longing, she hadn't followed his instructions.

And she didn't seem particularly perplexed about that.

She sliced cubed potatoes and dropped them in a pot of boiling liquid. She tossed in a handful of herbs and nestled the lid over the steam. Then she looked up at him. "Now that I've got that started, we can talk about your—"

"No talkin'."

"But you always want to talk about this stuff."

"Not today." Ben's gaze swept over her fully clothed body. "Strip. Now."

"You said I could convince—"

"Huh-uh." He crossed his arms over his chest. "I'm waitin'."

"I'm supposed to strip right here in the kitchen?"

"You can strip over by the bar, which you're supposed to be on, nekkid, if memory serves. Every time you open that pretty mouth to argue I'm takin' note."

"But—"

"You are surely tryin' my patience today, woman, and that will reflect in your punishment."

"Fine." Ainsley stomped across the room, throwing clothes over her head like confetti as she peeled them off her body.

Ben would find it funny if he wasn't so damn annoyed with her.

Oh hell, there was a fine sight, her luscious butt shaking as she climbed atop the bar. She faced him, arms crossed, legs crossed, wearing a very cross look.

"I don't like your attitude. And I think maybe I've been too lenient on you. Or maybe in the two days we've been apart, you've forgotten who's holding the reins."

The woman actually rolled her eyes.

"Stretch out on your belly."

"Why—"

Then Bennett was in front of her, his hands curled around her face, pulling her forward until they were nose-to-nose. "Do you want me to get a gag?"

Her eyes went wide and she shook her head.

"Then do what I tell you."

Her flesh squeaked against the bartop she obeyed so fast.

"Hands clasped above your head." After she complied, he ran his hand across her body, from her ankle up to her shoulder. "Stay put."

Ben retreated to his bedroom and set his bag of toys on the bed.

He transferred the riding crop, the ping-pong paddle, the medium-sized curved vibrator, the vibrating butt plug, the leg and arm restraints, and the small bottle of lube to a smaller bag. Just for shits and giggles, he grabbed the ball gag and his single tail whip.

Ainsley wasn't meekly stretched out on the bar like a good sub, awaiting his return. She was in the kitchen messing with the stove.

"Are you *still* defying me?" he roared.

She yelped, dropping the metal lid. The loud clank after it hit the floor made her jump again. She bent down to retrieve it, then slammed it on the counter. "I can explain. I didn't want the soup to boil over while you were playing with me so I got up and turned it off." She aimed her gaze at the floor. "I'm sorry."

"Not acceptable behavior," he snapped. "When I say stay put, I mean stay put. You could've asked me to turn off the soup. Instead, you chose to ignore my instructions and did whatever the hell you wanted. Bad choice. Get back on the bar as you were."

When Ainsley peeked up at him with those less-than-remorseful eyes, but didn't move, he pulled out the whip and snapped it in the air. "Now."

Another yelp and then she was running across the room, making all of her girly parts jiggle very nicely.

Christ, his dick went hard and he hadn't even touched her yet. He put the whip, the vibrating butt plug, and the ball gag within her view. He stretched her arms above her head and secured her wrists to the brass rail running along the inside and outside of the bartop.

She didn't utter a peep when he restrained her legs in the same manner, but her breaths were coming much faster.

"Oh and for the record? This isn't playtime. You are bein' punished." Her body shuddered as his fingertips skimmed the curves of her ass. "Do you know why you're bein' punished?"

"Umm...initially? No. Now I know my punishment will be because I disobeyed you. God forbid I put safety first by turning off the stove and preventing a fire hazard."

"Are you still arguing with me?"

"You have to admit—"

"Silence!"

Ainsley sighed. Wearily.

"You disrespected me at Rielle's place. Then you flat-out insulted me. That alone was enough to earn you a few licks. But your absolute disobedience after the fact, in your Dom's home, has earned hefty consequences, Ainsley."

"I understand. And I am sorry."

Like hell you're sorry. "Since we agreed early on spanking wasn't a punishment, I'm improvising. By my count you earned forty marks."

"F-forty?"

"I'll split them—twenty with the paddle, twenty with the ridin' crop."

She exhaled. "Thank you for not...just thank you."

Ben didn't like it that she flinched when he touched her. And why was she shaking so hard? "You wanna tell me what's goin' on?"

"I'm f-fine."

"No, you're not. Tell me."

"Don't use the whip on me. Ever. Please. I-I'd use my safe word before I'd let you."

He froze. Hadn't they discussed her hard limits? Didn't she know he'd never... Christ. This was fucked up. "Ainsley. Look at me, please."

She lifted her head, but her hair obscured her face. He gently brushed the silky strands aside. "I'd never use the single tail on you. I know it's a hard limit."

"Then why is it on the counter?"

He felt like a total dickhead for using it as a scare tactic. "It was just in the bag," he lied.

She relaxed slightly. "Okay."

Part of him wanted to call this punishment off. But a stronger part knew Ainsley needed this lesson.

Why? So the next Dom she hooks up with will reap the benefits?

The thought of another Dom touching her made him insane.

Ben did grant a soft kiss on her forehead as he ran his palm up her bound arm. "Count loud enough so I can hear or I won't count it. And I better hear respect in that tone, understand?"

"Yes. Sir."

Using the paddle, he smacked her left butt cheek. The *thwack* bounced off the bar mirror in an erotic echo.

"One. Sir."

By the time he reached twenty smacks, Ainsley was very squirmy and his cock was painfully hard. What a gorgeous sight, her ass a bright pink border between the white skin of her back and thighs. He traced her butt crack until his fingers connected with her pussy. Her wet pussy. Oh hell yeah. His angel was a sub through and through. She needed this as much as he did.

Pity she'll walk away from this lifestyle and from you at the end of the night. You'll just become a memory of the weeks she dabbled on the wild side.

Ben had to toss that unsettling thought aside. He turned the vibrator on the lowest speed, rolling it across those flaming butt cheeks. He said, "Lift up," and slid the phallus into her cunt.

Ainsley gasped and tried to squeeze her legs together.

He brushed his mouth across the shell of her ear. "Half done. But if you come before you get the next twenty lashes? I'll give you ten more with my hand, understand?"

"Oh God. It's...vibrating right on my G-spot."

"I know. And be warned, I ain't gonna go fast with these last twenty. I like takin' my time with the crop."

She moaned. And wiggled that pretty pink butt.

"Get ready to count." He knew these would sting twice as much because the tissue was already swollen and he braced himself for her reaction.

She reared up when the blow landed. "Oh, you bastard, that hurts!"

Ben waited for her to realize her error.

"Sorry. Sir. It just...stung. Crap. That was...ah... One. Sir."

"Good girl." Ben smoothed his hand over the hot skin, as if deciding where to place the next mark. Her entire body vibrated in anticipation. The next lash hit the crease of her thigh.

"Oh, I...fuck...you...shit... That's two. Sir."

By the thirteenth mark, her body still trembled but she'd fallen into a deeper breathing pattern. Her voice had taken on that dreamy quality as she counted.

At number seventeen, her hips began to bump up and she tried to grind her crotch into the wood. Ben gathered her hair in his hand and raised her head. Her eyes were glassy with that mix of pleasure and pain. He wanted to fuck her so bad he could practically taste the scream she'd release on his first deep thrust. "Don't come. You come and I start over, remember?"

"Please."

"No. You can take three more, Ainsley. And these three are gonna sting."

She shuddered, but whispered, "Okay."

He'd gone into that Dom zone, where their every breath seemed synchronized. Where he felt sweat breaking out on his body in the same places he saw it on hers. Where he felt each blow travel from the crop, up his arm and down to the exact spot on his body where he'd just hit on hers. He swung. Connected with her flesh. She cried out. Not in pain.

"Come on. Two more." As much as he wanted to level the blows *boom boom*, he spaced them out, hyper-aware the anticipation would make the release so much sweeter.

As soon as she rasped out, "Twenty," he shucked his jeans and rolled on a condom. His hands shook as he untied her ankles. She moaned, "No," when he eased the vibrator out.

Ben crawled up on the bar and hiked Ainsley's hips into the air. Keeping hold of her knees, he plunged into that tight, wet heat, and an animalistic snarl burst free.

Ainsley whimpered. He pumped twice more and slipped his hand around to finger her clit. Jesus. She was so primed. As he rubbed that plumped nub, he stretched over her lush, bound body, hissing as her scorching hot butt pressed into his lower abdomen.

"Oh God. Yes. Oh please."

"Come on, baby, take it. You've earned it. It's right there." He withdrew, slammed home, and pinched her clit at the same time he opened his mouth wide and sucked the sweet spot on the back of her neck.

Ainsley released a primal scream. Her cunt spasmed so powerfully around his cock he thought the contractions might suck the seed right out of his balls. He held on through the fierce bucking of her body, through her gasping sobs, through the potent aftershocks that were clusters of tiny orgasms.

When she lowered her face to the bar, trembling and spent, Ben pulled out of her pussy, gritting his teeth as the muscles clamped down, trying to keep his cock inside.

He ditched the condom and closed his fist around the base of his shaft. His eyes focused on the sexy sight before him. That beautiful red butt in the air, her inner thighs slick with her juices, spread to reveal her swollen sex. His hand pumped harder. Just a couple more. His shaft swelled. His balls tightened. Ben roared as he came, aiming each hot spurt at her ass. He gloried in pure male satisfaction at seeing her so thoroughly, so intimately marked by him. First by his hand and then by his seed.

He could not tear his eyes away from watching those milky spots turning into wet stripes on her pinked ass.

But his knee joint cracked loudly, reminding him where he was. Dazed, he patted Ainsley's thigh and backed off the bar. His legs were awful damn rubbery as he walked to the kitchen. He washed his hands, his face and soaked two hand towels with cool water. When he returned to take care of Ainsley, the thought of this being their last night together tied him up in knots. Tied him up so completely he thought about calling off the loan. He could get the money from Settler's First.

You're gonna gamble this chance to own the land your family has always wanted for a piece of ass? Even a prime piece of ass? Wrong. You can have this scenario every weekend at the club. It's nothing special. The land is. Get with the program. Stay on track. Stay focused.

Ben shut out the warring voices in his head and focused on his sub. He wiped her clean with gentle strokes as his free hand caressed her hair. He released her restraints and helped her find her balance as she slid off the bar.

Ainsley leaned on him as he led her to the couches in front of the TV. He draped her across his lap, nestling her head into a cushion, offering her a bottle of water, which she declined.

When he placed the cool towel on her abraded skin, she hissed. Then sighed.

"Anything I can get you?" he asked, drawing random patterns on her back.

"No."

He brought her down from the orgasmic high with soothing touches and gentle caresses. Eventually he urged her to turn on her side so he could see her face.

Ainsley looked at him without his asking.

"What?" he asked.

"Will you kiss me?"

Ben leaned over and captured her mouth. He fed her flirty kisses, tickling kisses, kisses laced with passion, kisses tempered with sweetness. When he nibbled on the inside of her lips, she pulled him closer. Threading her fingers through his hair, holding him in place as she took a hungry kiss. All at once she remembered her place and abruptly released him.

"Sorry. I just needed...you to anchor me."

"I'm glad you asked me for what you needed, instead of making me guess." Wasn't it ironic she opened up to him on their last night together? He brushed his hand over her silky hair, from her scalp to where it curled against her shoulder. "We've come a long way in a few weeks, haven't we?"

"Mmm-hmm." Ainsley pressed the side of her face against his chest. "I'll miss this."

It hit him then, the finality. It wasn't just the Dom/sub relationship he'd miss; he'd miss her. Everything about being with her.

They stayed wrapped together for so long the room grew cold and Ben knew the fire had dwindled to cinders. He smooched her forehead and slipped away, covering her with a fleece blanket.

Ben restocked the wood stove. He crouched and warmed his hands, his thoughts racing a million miles an hour. His gaze moved to the loan paperwork waiting on the counter. It wasn't too late. He could toss the envelope into the fire. They could continue exploring this thing between them.

Then what happens? You spend time together and you fall for her even more than you already have? You've no guarantee she won't end it anyway, because you know she's not convinced this is sustainable. She hasn't acted like she's bothered you're ending it, besides the snippy comments she made at Rielle's. So either way, you've still lost her and you've also lost the land.

"Ben?"

He turned around. "Someone took a little cat nap."

"Sorry." She yawned. "Did you eat?"

"No." He seemed to have lost his appetite. "Are you hungry?"

"Not any more. But I'll leave it for you."

"You're taking off?"

She nodded and wrapped the blanket around her nakedness and

headed for her clothes, which he'd picked up and placed on the chair. As she finished dressing, her gaze landed on the envelope on the counter. "Did you finish the paperwork?"

"Yep."

"Will you be around tomorrow if I have specific questions?"

"Should be."

She grabbed her purse and hastily threw on her coat.

Go to her. Tell her how you feel.

But he couldn't.

"Goodbye, Ben. I'll let you know when I hear about the loan."

"I'd appreciate it. Drive safe."

Then she was gone.

And for the first time in his life, his dogs didn't provide the companionship he needed.

Chapter Twenty-Three

She'd probably get cauliflower ear from the hours she spent on the phone. Ainsley rubbed the sore appendage and switched ears. She didn't get a chance to leave her office until lunch, and when she returned she noticed the blinds in Leslie's office were closed, which was unusual. She knocked and heard a scratchy, "Come in."

Leslie looked awful. Pasty skin, vacant eyes, red nose. She started to say something and ended up having a coughing fit. But she waved aside Ainsley's concern and croaked, "Just a cold. Nothing to worry about."

"Why are you here today? You should be home in bed."

Leslie sneezed. Coughed. Then blew her nose. Twice. "Sorry. I'm behind. I can't afford to miss a day."

"How much are you accomplishing today anyway?"

"Probably not much." She let her head fall back into the headrest. "I feel like death."

"You should've called in sick."

"I tried to, but Jenny transferred me to Turton instead of you. Turton said sick pay didn't kick in for thirty days. So if I didn't show up, my check would get docked. You know Roger and I are still trying to get on our feet after both of us being laid off for six months. I need this job. I'll be fine. I've gone to work far sicker than this."

"I don't care. You're going home. And I don't want to see you back here until you're really better. I will handle the sick pay issue with human resources, understand?"

Leslie sneezed and reached for a tissue. "Thanks, A."

"Anything pressing I need to handle for you today?"

"No. Just cancel the loan appointments for this afternoon."

She'd pass that job to Jenny. "Consider it done. Are you okay to drive?"

"I'm fine. It's not that far. I might squeeze in a few hours sleep before the kids get home from school." She handed Ainsley her appointment book. "The names and numbers are in here."

Ainsley passed Turton's office. His door was shut, as were his shades. She checked the time. He should be back from lunch by now. She wandered to Jenny's desk. "Where's Turton?"

Jenny stopped flipping through a magazine. "He's taking the afternoon off as a personal day. Why?"

So it was fine for him to screw off? But he expected Leslie to stick around when she was hacking up a lung? "I hadn't seen him since this morning." She dropped the appointment book on Jenny's magazine. "You'll need to politely cancel Leslie's appointments for today as soon as possible and tell the clients she'll call them to reschedule."

"But—"

"No excuses. And from now on, you will transfer all employee calls dealing with sicknesses and absences to me, not Turton. Understand?"

She lowered her gaze to the planner. For once, Jenny didn't have a smart remark.

Ainsley finished verifying Ben's financials. She should probably wait to send it off to the main office, but since Leslie was already behind, she didn't want to add to the burden with a straightforward loan request. After she made copies, she stuffed the originals in a next day envelope.

Sealing that envelope gave her a strange feeling of finality she wasn't ready for. She'd liked how things were growing and changing between them. Not only when he slipped into Dom mode, but when he was just Ben.

She'd miss the way he called her *angel.* The way he'd growl it against her skin. She'd miss the way he pushed her to accept what she was. The way he wouldn't let her hide from herself or from him. The way he gave her what she'd needed for so long but hadn't the guts to admit it she'd wanted.

This was temporary. And he'd rather have the money than you.

How long had he known he'd needed a loan? And what would he have done if she'd refused to help him? Would it have strained their Dom/sub relationship? Or ended it completely?

No way to know now, but she couldn't help but feel a little used and a lot disappointed.

Through all her questions and doubt about what could've been, she still felt his pull. She wondered how long she could stay away from him.

Not long, as it turned out. But she'd convinced herself it was a matter of necessity, not personal choice.

She paced, clutching the phone. "Ben? Are you really busy right now?"

"Why? What do you need?"

Then she felt ridiculous and almost gave him a breezy, *Oh no reason, just calling to see how you are,* rather than coming across as incapable.

"Ainsley? What's wrong?"

"I don't want you to think I'm inept or that I only called because I needed something, although both those statements are true—"

"Take a deep breath, angel, and tell me what's goin' on."

"My bathroom sink is leaking and I can't figure out what's wrong and I can't get ahold of the landlord."

"I'm on my way."

"Really? Just like that?"

"Just like that. Be there in fifteen."

She gathered the wet towels and tossed them in the tub. After piling clean towels on the toilet, she sat on the floor, listening to the *drip drip drip* of water into the plastic pail beneath the sink.

When her cats tore down the hallway she knew Ben had arrived, even before he called out, "Ainsley?"

"In here," she yelled back. Her heart flipped over when he entered the bathroom. The man looked even sexier carrying a toolbox than he did carrying his toy bag.

Ben flashed her a brief smile and, "Hey," before crouching down with his toolbox. "When did you notice the leak?"

"After work. I was in that cabinet this morning and it wasn't leaking then."

He turned on a flashlight and the beam arced inside the cabinet. He stuck his head under the sink. "Looks like the nut to the cold water valve is loose. Here. Hold this." He handed her the flashlight and he rummaged in his toolbox. When he found the tool he needed, he scooted under the sink. "Can you point the light where I've got the pipe wrench?"

"Sure." In such tight quarters, she pressed her body to the outside of the cabinet and held the light steady.

A couple of hard clanks, a loud screech and then water spewed forth.

Ben jerked back, hit his head under the sink and yelled, "Fuck."

"You okay?"

"Hold that flashlight steady."

Water was still spraying everywhere.

Another loud clank and the water stopped abruptly.

"What happened?"

"Some idiot forgot to turn the water off before he started fucking with the pipe." He grunted. "That was fun. Can you hand me a towel?"

"Here."

"Thanks." When Ben backed out from beneath the sink, Ainsley gasped because he was soaking wet—hair, face, neck and shirt.

"Look at you. I'm so sorry." Ainsley ducked into the cabinet and used a bath towel to sop up the mess. "What's the diagnosis?"

"The pipe threading is stripped because the calcium deposits are abrasive. You'll have to use the kitchen sink until your landlord can get this fixed. I don't have the right plumbing supplies."

When she backed out and stood, she noticed Ben had removed his shirt. Look at that. Broad shoulders, pumped-up biceps. Smooth skin. Even as her brain yelled *stop*, her fingers heard *go*. She traced the hard ridge of pectoral muscle. "You never really let me touch you however I wanted."

Ben tipped her chin up and gazed into her eyes. "I didn't?"

"No. You were always making our...encounters about furthering my education about the Dom/sub relationship."

He brushed his thumb over her bottom lip. "I'd let you touch me now."

"Ben."

"But you'd much rather I commanded you to touch me, wouldn't you? Should I? Ainsley, put your hands all over me."

That deep, Dom voice traveled through her ear and unfurled inside her like liquid heat, like a drug. She had to twist away from him to hide the longing in her eyes. But longing for what? "I can't."

"I know." He kissed the top of her head. "I should go."

"But your shirt is soaking wet. You might catch cold if you go home with a wet head. The least I can do is wash and dry it for you, while saving you from possibly getting sick." Did that sound like a flimsy excuse to him?

"I never get sick." He raised an eyebrow. "Besides, you think that's a good idea, given what we were? Just last night?"

Of course he reminded her of his Dom role at every opportunity. "I believe we can keep our hands to ourselves for an hour or so, don't you?"

He shook his head *no* and said, "Yes."

Ainsley laughed and snatched the shirt. She was surprised Ben followed her to the small laundry area.

"On the way over here I was kinda hopin' you'd answer the door in heels and an apron. Then you'd say something like, *I need a guy with a big tool to check out my plumbing.* And I'd reply, *I know how to plunge deep.*"

"You imagined I'd lured you over here with a fake porn scenario?" It boosted her ego Ben believed she could conjure up such a sexy scene. "I didn't know you watched porn."

"All guys watch porn." He grinned and towel dried his hair. "Them guys that say they don't are lyin'. We never watched porn together. Pity. There are lots of scenes I would've loved to act out with you."

She started the washer and her focus caught on his incredible chest again. Right. He needed to cover up. "I'll find you a shirt."

Just to be ornery, she picked her Cat Lover T-shirt.

Ben caught it one handed and slipped it over his head. "Speaking of cats...they raced outta the room the instant I stepped foot inside. They hate me."

"Because you smell like dog. Your dogs hate me because I smell like cat."

"Mmm. But I like how your pussy smells."

"Bennett McKay."

He laughed. "Hand me the remote. We've already missed ten minutes of *Wheel.*"

Ainsley sat next to him, like she always did. Bennett jerked her close to his body like he always did. Only when the show ended did she remember they weren't supposed to be twined together. He wasn't supposed to be touching her. She wasn't supposed to have her head on his shoulder.

Almost as if he'd read her mind, he murmured, "Sorry. Habit." His fingers trailed across her forearm three more times before he released her.

She stood and retreated to the kitchen. He followed. Closely. "Look, your shirt still isn't dry. Why don't you stay for dinner? It's nothing fancy. Just a skillet pot pie." When Ben didn't respond, she backtracked. "But don't feel obligated. I'm sure you have better things to—"

He growled that Dom-like warning, curling his hand around her jaw, destroying her protests and her mind with a prolonged, soft-lipped kiss packed with sweet heat. His kisses alone could rocket her into that sublime floaty space.

Her lips tingled when he pulled back. His face was pure Dom. "I want you. Now. Bent over the table with that kitchen towel tyin' your hands together behind your back."

She tumbled backward into the counter. "No."

"You don't get to say *no* to me, sub."

"I'm not your sub anymore, remember?"

Immediately Ben froze. He shoved his hands in his pockets and took two big steps back. "Have I mentioned how much I fucking hate that?"

Remind him he brought this on himself. Reset the boundaries and make this about business. "I sent your loan paperwork off today."

"Find anything in my financials worth mentioning?" he asked tightly.

"You make a lot more off your furniture sideline than what I'd expected. So that's on the plus side of getting loan approval, since it's enough income to make the monthly payments."

"Any idea on how long it'll be before you know for sure?"

She shrugged. "Next week probably."

Then he was invading her space again. "And then what, Ainsley?"

"What do you mean?"

"Our official business will be over. Can we pick up where we left off?"

"Oh, you mean us sneaking around? You bossing me around in private?" She shook her head. "That ship has sailed for us. Our month would've been up next week anyway." Ainsley realized she'd literally let him back her into a corner. "Back off, Ben, or I will snap you in the crotch with this dishtowel."

He put his hands up and looked at the towel twisted in her hands. "Fine. Sorry. But we will talk about it later."

It was telling how comfortable they'd gotten with each other that no awkwardness lingered even after that exchange. She told him a few funny stores from her vagabond childhood. He told her about being raised with his McKay cousins. It was weirdly like they were on a first date. It was...nice. Normal. Relaxing.

Ben peered through the clear lid on the skillet. "That's it? Two big cans of condensed vegetable beef soup, a cup of cream and plop a can of biscuits on top?"

"That's it." A tickle started in her nose and she reached for a tissue. She sneezed. Loudly. Three times in a row. "Maybe I'll lay off the pepper next time." She sniffled. "I forgot to ask if you wanted a beer."

"Didn't think you were a beer drinker."

"I'm not. I bought it for you last week, in case you ever dropped over."

He offered her a deeply dimpled smile. "I'll drop over more often."

Yes, please. And oddly enough, him cuffing her and ravishing her until she came screaming wasn't the first scene that popped into her head.

And what does that say? That you'd be happy to have a dating-type relationship with this man?

Could they try it? She shot him a look from beneath lowered lashes. He'd said he'd be interested in dropping over for a beer. They'd cooked together. Watched TV together. They'd done...normal stuff. He'd asked where this relationship could go after their official loan business was behind them. He'd even backed off when she'd become more aggressive than usual. Could that be his way of hinting he wanted to try a plain old regular relationship with her but didn't know how to go about it? Could they start simple? Start over?

That might work. She'd broach the subject and see how he

responded.

After they'd eaten, she said, "So I'm thinking that we could be...friends."

"Friends?" he repeated like it was some sort of disease.

"Sure. You have friends, don't you?"

"Define friends."

"You could come over here for dinner. I could go over to your place. We could kick back. Shoot some pool." Crap. She shouldn't have tossed that last one in. His expression was a heated reminder of how they'd used his pool table the last time.

"You haven't said anything."

"Because I don't know what the fuck to say to that."

The dryer buzzed.

Ainsley got his shirt and helped him put it on. She automatically started buttoning him up, like she'd often done. Something about redressing him was almost more intimate than undressing him. She focused on smoothing wrinkles from the cotton as an excuse not to look into his compelling eyes as she touched him. Even when she wasn't supposed to be touching him.

Command me to stop, Bennett. It's always been your job to set the physical parameters between us.

When she finished buttoning, Ben pressed her hand against his chest. Right beneath his thundering heart. Was this side of him more dangerous than his Dom side? She had experience dealing with brash Bennett. This dateable Ben? Not so much.

But she wanted to see this side of him too. Maybe he just needed encouragement that she'd accept this side of him.

Their eyes met. Then their lips. The kiss wasn't much more than a simple peck.

"So, call me tomorrow, friend," she murmured.

"Ainsley, I don't know if I can be—"

"That was not a request." She kissed him again, then firmly shoved him out the door.

Chapter Twenty-Four

Ben rang Ainsley's doorbell again. He'd tried calling her cell several times and she hadn't picked up.

Maybe it was an excuse, showing up on her doorstep, but something felt...off. Something besides the bogus friendship she was trying to force on him.

Jesus. He didn't want to be her fucking friend. In the last two days he'd already seen her pulling away. Not only from him, but from her submissive side. Trying to remake him into the type of guy he wasn't, denying her nature and attempting to change their relationship into something it never had been and never would be: normal.

Ben was starting to lose her. That thought had driven him batshit crazy all day after she hadn't returned any of his calls. Hopefully she hadn't reverted to old habits, like that post-date game mind-fuck where the woman waited a certain amount of time before returning her date from the previous night's calls, so as to not appear too eager.

Fuck that. They weren't goddamn dating. She needed a reminder of what they were together. Of how right it was. And if he had to wait until the loan went through, to prove it to her, so be it. But he wouldn't lie to her and he wouldn't allow her to lie to herself.

So yeah, he was going all beastly Dom on her ass.

Frustrated, he turned the door handle. Locked. But the door snicked open because it hadn't been fully latched. That wasn't good. Ainsley was vigilant about locking the door.

Ben stepped inside.

The cats stared at him from the end of the hallway.

"Ainsley?"

No answer.

He scanned the living room. Her purse was on the chair, along with her coat. Her car keys and cell phone were on the side table.

He peeked in the kitchen, no sign of her. He headed down the short hallway. When he flipped on the lights in her bedroom, he noticed the sheets were twisted, the quilt thrown back, pillows scattered across the floor.

His heart damn near stopped at seeing her curled up on the bathroom floor. "Shit." He crouched beside her body and found her pulse in her neck, thank God. "Ainsley?" Ben placed his hand on her forehead. "Baby. You're burning up."

"Ben?"

"I'm here, angel. Stay with me. I need to get you to the emergency room."

"No doctors."

"Tough shit."

"I won't go." She tried to roll away.

He held her still and tamped down his fear. "Then what should I do?"

She mumbled, "Call Joely."

Ben grabbed Ainsley's cell and scrolled until he found Joely's number. He dropped to his knees beside her on the tile as he hit Send.

The doc picked up on the second ring. "Doc? It's Ben McKay."

"Ben. Why are you on Ainsley's phone?"

"I stopped to see her and found her layin' on the floor in the bathroom. Her skin is on fire. She won't go to the ER. It's freaking me out because she was fine yesterday." His words came out machine-gun fast.

"Calm down. Can you tell if she's been throwing up?"

"There's none on the floor or in her hair or anything."

"Can you ask her?"

"She's pretty out of it."

"Put me on speaker."

Ben poked the button and held the phone lower. "You're on."

"Ainsley, it's Joely Monroe. Ben says you're sick. Have you been vomiting?"

"No." She shuddered and Ben's stomach roiled. He smoothed her damp hair from her face.

"When did you first start getting sick?"

"Right after I went to work this morning. I couldn't stay so I came home."

"Tell me your symptoms."

"Hot. Cold. Chills. Headache. Body aches. Sore throat."

"She sneezed a lot last night," Ben inserted.

"Have you taken meds for any of the symptoms?"

"No."

"Okay, here's my on-the-fly diagnosis. She has the flu. Probably the twenty-four-hour variety. Hopefully it already hit its peak."

"Do I need to take her to the ER?"

"Not unless she gets markedly worse. Right now, she needs to take two Tylenol and in another hour, two Motrin. That should drop her fever. If she's awake, make her drink lots of water, but don't wake her to drink. Put cool cloths on her face. That'll at least give her the impression of coolness until her fever breaks." A pause. "You are able to stay with her tonight, Ben, or is there someone else she can call?"

He tempered his initial response, *No fucking way am I ever leaving her*, to a calmer, "I'm staying." He was freaked the fuck out. He'd never taken care of a sick person before in his life. Sick calves? No problem. Sick person? Not ever.

"This is a pretty quick bug," the doc said. "But I'll warn you: it's highly contagious. You should expect to get sick."

"I never get sick," he scoffed at the dial tone.

Ben tried to move her off the bathroom floor. "Come on. Let's get you into your own bed."

"It's too hot in there."

"It's cooler. I promise. Let me help you up." Ben practically carried Ainsley to her room. "Sit on the bed."

"You're always so bossy."

"Part of bein' a Dom."

"Well, you're not my Dom anymore, so let me lay down."

He resisted the urge to snap, *The fuck I'm not your Dom*. He breathed slowly and deeply, completely out of his element on so many levels. "First you need to swallow your meds."

Ainsley screwed up her face.

"They'll make you feel better."

Once she'd choked down the pills, she stretched out on the mattress.

"Close your eyes." He placed a cool washcloth on her forehead.

She sighed. "That's nice. You're nice."

"Thought I was bossy?"

"You are both nice and bossy. I like that about you. Two sides of the same coin."

He couldn't help but ask, "Which side do you like better?"

"The nice side. I think you're afraid of showing that side of yourself to me, more than you are of showing me the Dom side."

Bullshit. You're fighting the truth that you like that bossy side of me better.

Ben kicked off his boots and stretched out beside her. He wanted to fix her now. Scoop her up, race to the doctor and demand she be healed. He forced himself to calm down and watch her settle into sleep, reaching for her hand just as he began to drift off.

Ainsley's restlessness roused him. He glanced at the clock. Only an hour had passed.

She started to push up.

"Easy. Anything you need I'll get."

"A drink."

Ben moved to the edge of the bed and held a glass to her lips. "Here."

She drank every drop.

"Better?"

"Yeah."

He switched out the skin-warmed washcloth for a cool one.

Ainsley sighed when he placed it over her forehead. "Thanks, Ben. You don't have to stay."

"I want to stay."

"Why? It's not like I have any new loan information for you."

That sounded a little cross. "Thanks for the update."

"I'm surprised you'd be interested in hanging out with me, especially if we're not having kinky sex," she said snarkily.

Ben's voice was pure Dom. "The lack of kinky sex was your choice. And it's a damn mystery why I'm obsessed with hanging out with a woman like you who's beautiful, adventurous, smart and sexy as hell."

She slid the washcloth down and squinted at him. "You really see me that way?"

He ran his hand down her arm. "Yeah, angel, I do. You know I do. I see you a lot clearer than you see me."

"Why did you come over tonight?"

To remind you that I'm not some pussy lap dog who will be happy with whatever scraps of friendship you toss at me. "Because I thought you were ditching my calls so I came over to chew your ass."

"And you probably wanted to spank it too, huh?"

"Like you wouldn't believe."

"Ben. That's not...who we have to be."

Yes, it is. That's who we are. And there's nothing wrong with it. But she didn't need to deal with that issue now. "Christ, Ainsley, it scared the crap outta me when I saw you on the bathroom floor."

She reached out and blindly patted his arm, soothing him. "I'm glad you checked on me. It's a very sweet, friend-like thing to do."

Sweet and friend-like my ass. Ben nudged the washcloth back into place. "I need to buy you Motrin as per Doc's orders. Is there anything else you want from the store?"

"Cherry flavored throat lozenges and 7UP."

"Got it." Ben tucked the covers around her. "I'll be back."

When he returned, Ainsley had fallen asleep again. He puttered around her kitchen. Putting the flowers he'd bought in a vase. Finding a saucepan to heat up canned chicken soup. He bribed her cats with treats and chuckled when the fur balls became slightly less standoffish.

He heard the toilet flush and booked it to the bathroom. "Ainsley? You okay?"

The door opened. "I'm tired of being in bed. I think I'll sit on the couch."

She had a pained expression. "What's wrong?"

"My head is pounding."

"Maybe it's the lights." Ben flipped on a lamp and sat beside her. "Come here." He placed a pillow on his lap.

Ainsley rested the side of her face on the pillow and practically purred when he gently stroked her hair. "God. I love how you touch me. No matter how you touch me."

I know you do. "So...I made nice with your cats."

"Had to bribe them, did you?"

"Yep. Shamelessly. With multiple treats."

Her low laugh sent her into a coughing fit. She sat up, blew her nose, took another drink of water and popped a lozenge in her mouth. "Sorry. I hate being sick. You probably were one of those healthy kids, Mr. I-never-get-sick."

He touched her forehead. Her skin was much cooler.

She snuggled more deeply into him. "I'm tired." Her breathing changed and he was certain she'd crashed again, when she muttered, "Thanks for taking care of me."

Ben wrapped a curl around his index finger. "It's a first for me. I'm more the 'sorry you're sick, gotta run' type of guy."

"Well, you're definitely more the 'I'm your boyfriend and I'll take care of you' type now."

Boyfriend? Was that what he was to her? The role she'd demoted him to?

Oh hell no. Fuck no. The kid gloves he'd been treating her with the last few days were about to come off. Just as soon as she got over this fever-induced delirium.

Naturally, Mr.-I-never-get-sick...got sick.

He swore he was dying. He'd contracted bubonic plague. Malaria. Leprosy. Typhoid. Ben McKay was a horrible patient. But Ainsley stayed with him from the onset of the first sniffles. Fussed over him. Took care of his dogs. And when he reached for her in the middle of the night, she willingly went into his arms and comforted him as he shook from his fever, not from passion.

But even in sickness he'd been in total Dom mode. That's when the reality of this situation with him began to sink in.

They were at an impasse. Not friends, no longer lovers. They'd be at this turn in the road anyway, even if the loan business wasn't hanging over them, with the thirty days at an end. So why was she still at a tipping point? Unsure of what she wanted and afraid to tell him?

No. You're not afraid of Bennett; you're afraid he'd see right through you when you lie to him.

So an hour later when Ben returned from his trip to town and plopped next to her on his couch after his shower, she had a hard knot in her throat, wondering how she'd keep this discussion matter of fact.

"You're sniffling. You feel like you're getting sick again?" he asked with concern.

"No. I was sniffing because you smell nice."

He lifted a brow. "I'da showered sooner if you'd told me I was stinky."

"You weren't. I just like the scent of your soap." *That type of comment is not keeping this neutral, Ainsley.*

"Duly noted." He grabbed the water bottle from the coffee table.

"So your mom stopped by while you were in town."

He choked on his mouthful of water. "She did? Shit. Sorry about that. She probably was a total pain in the ass."

Ainsley had wondered how he'd react to Vi's surprise visit. "No, she was great. We talked about our backgrounds growing up with a father in service to God."

That startled him. "Guess my grandfather was a real bastard. Kinda sucks that I was named after him. Is your dad like that?"

"No. Just set in his ways. Your mom is an interesting woman. We have a lot in common. I liked her. She asked me out to lunch."

Ben harrumphed. "She's a meddling woman."

"Your mother was a lot warmer to me than Rielle."

"Jesus. Rielle was here too?"

"Evidently she heard you were sick and brought over a basket of muffins to send you on the road to recovery." An edge of jealousy crept into her tone despite her intent to curb it.

"Huh. That's weird." He pointed to a colorful ball on the chair. "What's that?"

Why did he blatantly change the subject whenever Rielle was mentioned? "My knitting."

"Knitting. You knit?"

"Yes. I had to have something productive to do while you were feverish and thrashing around." She crossed her arms over her chest. "Why? Do you think it's a lame hobby?" *Not the right type of hobby for a sub? Are my hands supposed to busy tending to your needs all the time?*

Not fair.

Ben shrugged. "Not lame at all. You've never mentioned it."

"We haven't exactly spent our time talking in the last month."

"Careful, angel, I might take that as a complaint. Especially when you're the one who doesn't wanna talk about stuff."

Ainsley rested her cheek on the couch cushion. She'd rehearsed this conversation in her head and now was the time to have it for real. "Not a complaint, Ben. Just an observation."

"I don't think I'm gonna like this observation, am I?"

"Probably not." Her eyes searched his. "I like how it's been between us the last couple days, almost more than I did when we were Dom and sub."

The wounded look on his face made her feel as if she'd sliced him in two. "You don't really mean that."

"Maybe you're right. But that's the issue. I don't know what I mean." She sighed. "Sex with you... God, I never dreamed a physical relationship could be that all-consuming. And it was between us. Every single time. The amount of intensity varied, but it was always there." She glanced away, unsure how to finish.

After a minute or so, Ben said, "Can you look at me, please?"

Not a Dom command. She looked at him. In his eyes she saw fear, honesty, trust and power. She saw everything she needed. She saw everything she shouldn't want. Everything she was too...scared to reach out and take.

"What's really goin' on? Did my mother say something to you?"

She shook her head.

His blue eyes snapped fire. "Rielle? Did she open her big mouth? Because—"

Ainsley put her fingers over his lips. "Nothing like that. They were both just curious about why I was at your house. And I didn't know what to tell them."

"How about the truth?"

"Which is what, Ben? We met at a sex club? And we were taking a test drive as Dom and sub couple?"

He growled.

"I just...can't do this anymore. We aren't lovers." She smiled sadly. "You don't want to be my friend, do you?"

"No."

That hurt. "So, it's all sex or nothing?"

"Yep. I've been following your parameters, Ainsley. But when we're through with the business aspect of this loan? I want a chance to put things back the way they were."

"You Dom, me sub."

His hard gaze pinned her in place. "Really? That's how you saw what we had together?"

"No." This was not going as planned. "I thought I wanted to talk to you about this and now I see why I don't." She pushed off the couch.

"What are you afraid of?"

Ainsley didn't answer. She just gathered her things and headed for the door.

Ben hadn't kissed her at all since that night at her house when she'd suggested friendship. When he helped her put on her coat, she wanted to melt into him. She wished he'd go full Dom on her. Demand she stay.

But he didn't say a word. He didn't even walk her out to her car.

That's when she knew it really was over.

Chapter Twenty-Five

This bullshit situation with Ainsley sucked ass. Stuck in fucking limbo. In purgatory.

Waiting, waiting, waiting.

He hadn't seen her for two goddamn days. He'd even called her yesterday at the bank to check on the status of his loan, which was a legitimate reason to contact her because it was getting down to the wire and he'd need the money by the end of the week. For some reason him calling to ask about the loan pissed her off. Then his...request to take her to lunch ticked her off too. She'd said no, she'd be in touch, and hung up on him.

Ben had called her again today. First thing. He'd been nice. Polite. Purposely un-Dom-like. And he'd gotten the same damn response. A polite fucking brush off.

It'd taken every ounce of strength not to march into her office, throw her over his shoulder and drag her to his place, where he could tie her to the bed, and make her listen to him. Make her understand that he fucking loved her. And this waiting to tell her what she meant to him was killing him.

His phone rang. He'd barely said hello, when Kane barked, "Ben? Hope you ain't busy, but we're in need of your peacekeeping abilities."

"What's goin' on?"

"Tell and Colt got into it, and now Brandt and Dalton jumped in. I can't hold 'em all back from beatin' the shit outta Colt."

"Where are you?"

"Uncle Casper's place."

Ben hit the brakes and spun a U-turn in the middle of the road. "On my way."

Seven minutes later he reached the turnoff to Casper's place.

Tell stood nose to nose with Colt. Brandt and Dalton flanked Tell on either side. Kane had positioned himself to Colt's right. Their focus shifted when Ben skidded into the driveway. He jumped out of his truck, noticing Colt had seized the opportunity to step back a couple of feet.

"Hey, guys. What's goin' on?"

"It's none of your fuckin' business what's goin' on, Ben, so back the fuck off and go home," Tell snarled.

That threw him off. Tell was the most even-keeled one in the family. "Fine. Me'n Colt and Kane will go."

"Colt ain't goin' nowhere until he gives us some fuckin' answers."

Tell started to push into Colt's face again, but Ben stepped between them. "Back off, Tell."

"No. Move outta the way."

"I said. Back. Off."

That tone caught Tell's attention. Some of the rage in his eyes momentarily cleared.

Ben pointed to Colt and Tell. "Now someone start talking."

"Yeah, Colt, you heard what Ben said. Start talking," Dalton sneered.

Colt's arms were folded across his chest. "This would be easier for all of us if you'd just move aside and let me get what I came for."

"Where is he?"

"Where is who?" Ben asked with total confusion.

"Our dad," Brandt said. "He's been gone five days."

"Five days? Why's this the first I've heard of it?" He looked at Kane.

"Hey, it was the first I've heard of it too. How come no one told us he was gone?"

"Don't pretend you give a shit about Casper. None of you even bothered to come by and see him after Mom left," Tell said.

Ben disputed that statement. "Quinn came by about six months ago and Casper threatened to shoot him. So I'll hazard a guess you don't know everyone that stopped by to check on him."

But Brandt, Dalton and Tell were focused on Colt. Fists clenched. Eyes hard.

"Go ahead and take a swing at me," Colt said. "Won't change nothin'."

"Nobody is takin' a swing at no one," Kane said. "And quit fuckin' taunting them, Colt. It ain't helpin'."

"Will somebody please tell me what the fuck is goin' on?" Ben demanded.

Colt said, "I stopped by to get something Casper asked for. These guys won't let me in the house to get it."

"Because he won't tell us where Dad is."

Kane drawled, "Ain't this fun? Been at this point since I called you."

Ben addressed Colt. "So is Casper staying with you or something?"

"Or something would cover it."

He sensed Colt wanted to talk, but their cousins had pushed him in the corner and he wouldn't be the first to back out. "Come on, Colt, give 'em more than that. Obviously they're worried."

"Coulda fooled me," he muttered.

"You are such a smug asshole," Tell hissed.

Ben glared at his cousin. "Not helping. And I wouldn't talk to you either if you said shit like that to me, so shut it, Tell."

No one said anything for a solid minute.

Colt dropped the defensive posture. "Fine. Casper is in alcohol treatment."

Stunned silence.

"Are you fuckin' serious?" Brandt said.

"Yes."

"When? How?"

"He called me." Colt rubbed the back of his neck. "Actually he called Indy because she's one of the only family members Casper hasn't crossed. But I ended up answering her phone and talking to him."

"When was this?" Tell demanded.

"A couple weeks ago. He was drunk as hell. I told him no one could help him until he walked away from the booze. I didn't figure he would. If you knew how many phone calls I've gotten, from folks wantin' my help..." He sighed. "So to be honest, I didn't put much store in it. Until he showed up at my house."

"When?" Dalton barked.

"Five days ago."

"Where'd you take him?"

"To get dried out."

Tell wouldn't let it go. "Where?"

Colt remained mute.

When it appeared all three of Casper's sons intended to beat the answers out of Colt, Ben stepped in. "This macho bullshit posturing is pointless." He addressed Brandt, Tell and Dalton. "Jesus, guys, stop and think. Colt can't tell you because of AA confidentiality rules."

"Without bein' a dick, if Casper would've wanted you guys to know where he was, he would've told you," Kane added.

"Wouldn't be the first fuckin' time Dad's kept us in the dark," Dalton retorted.

"You just...helped him? No questions asked?" Brandt asked Colt. "After all the bad shit he's done to the family?"

Colt simply said, "Yes."

"Don't matter where he is, 'cause you can bet he won't make it through treatment. He'll be back home, same mean SOB as before, same drunken asshole as before," Tell said.

Colt shoved Ben aside and pushed Tell with enough force he almost fell on his ass. "*That's* how you react after your father acknowledges he has a problem? By expecting he'll fail? Fuck you. This is why he didn't—wouldn't—come to his sons. It's why he came to me, because I travel this path every fuckin' day. I know exactly where he is, in more ways than one. It's also why I'm goin' in the goddammed house, getting his bible and getting the hell outta here. But you can bet your ass I won't burden him with tales of your overwhelming concern." Colt shouldered his way through Brandt and Dalton and stormed up the porch.

Kane followed him.

Ben really didn't know what to say. This family shit tore him up. He and his brothers never had the volatile relationship with each other and their father that Uncle Casper had with his boys, and to some extent that Uncle Carson had with his. Because Ben hated conflict and tried to cut through it as quickly as possible, he'd gotten the reputation in the family as the peacemaker. He felt far from that today.

Colt wasn't inside long. He bounded down the porch, holding a burgundy book.

"So who knows about Dad bein' in rehab?" Brandt asked Colt.

"My dad, Uncle Cal and Uncle Charlie. Casper asked me to tell them."

"But not us," Dalton said.

"It ain't like our dads said anything to us either," Kane pointed out.

"And now that I think about it, you sneaky bastards have no right to get up in *my* face about keeping secrets," Colt said. "Did you really think we wouldn't find out that the three of you planned to buy Rielle's place? Without discussing it with the rest of us?"

Brandt frowned. "What the hell are you babbling about, Colt?"

It took Colt all of four seconds to see the guilt on Tell and Dalton's faces. "You didn't include Brandt in on this scheme?"

"Scheme is a little harsh," Ben said.

Colt whirled on him. "What about Quinn? Does he know?"

"There's nothin' to know. Just something that Tell, Dalton and I discussed."

"Since you've been squawking about wanting an equal say in the operation, this is the type of thing that oughta be discussed by all of us," Colt said.

Pissed off, Ben shot back, "Like the acquisition of the Foster place was discussed by all of us? Or how about the acquisition of the Hackerly place? Or the acquisition of the Borden place? Or how about the separate section up north that Kade ran for a year? Were we part of that discussion, or did Carson and Cal decide to do that on their own? Oh, right, they didn't even fuckin' ask us." His gesture included Tell, Dalton, and Brandt. "Any of us."

"Not the same and you know it, Ben."

"Bullshit. Alls I know is that it's perfectly fine for your families to add to your sections whenever the fuck you feel like it and run it as a separate operation. But when we wanna do that? It's like we're tryin' to short shrift the entire ranch." Ben forced a slow breath, trying to drop his blood pressure from the boiling point.

Kane said, "I know it probably don't mean shit, but for the record, Ben, I agree with you. And if you can get the Wetzler place, or part of it, and be fair to Rielle, then do it. Me'n Kade won't begrudge you."

"Well, it's a moot point because Rielle has already sold it," Colt said.

"What?" Ben, Dalton and Tell said at the same time.

"When did you hear this?"

"Just this mornin' from Cord and Colby. We heard last week from someone at the bank Rielle was behind on payments and about to be foreclosed on. So we stopped by to talk to her. Pissed her off. I've never seen Rielle like that. Woman had a damn shotgun pointed at us. Said she was tired of the McKay vultures pickin' at her bones before she was even dead. So we took that to mean you all knew about her situation, and made an offer, which apparently wasn't enough."

"Yes it was!" Dalton protested. "We were just waitin' for her to give us the go-ahead."

Colt shook his head. "She said she'd hadn't seen money, and the time was closing in on her. So she sold it to someone else."

"Fuck." Dalton turned his anger on Ben. "What the hell did you do? You assured us you had it handled with Rielle."

Ben threw up his hands. "I did."

"Did you let her know we were serious? Or did you just mention it in passing?" Tell demanded.

"I told her we'd make the payments to catch her up and then we'd discuss division of property. She said she needed time to think it over. So I gave it to her."

Dalton stepped forward and poked Ben in the chest. "It's been three goddamn weeks, Ben. This should've been wrapped up two weeks ago. What the hell have you been doin' with your time? Goin' to that bar in Gillette?"

He knocked Dalton's hand away. "Back off. I didn't have as much cash as I needed so I had to get a loan for my portion and that took time." Jesus, he hated to admit that.

"You should've been able to get a signature loan. We've been dealin' with Settler's First for years." Tell's eyes turned accusatory. "Or are you in hock for something we don't know about and they wouldn't give you the money?"

His cheeks burned, not from embarrassment, but from pure anger. "I didn't go to Settler's First because it's pretty fuckin' obvious that our cousins have someone inside the bank feeding them confidential information. And you can be guaran-damn-teed if I'd waltzed in there, asking for a loan for some land that would be comin' up for sale soon?" He jerked his thumb toward Colt. "They would've known about it and acted on it. So I had to go to the new bank. And like I said, that took time."

"Which is the one fuckin' thing we didn't have. You should've come clean with us about your money issues and we would've given Rielle a down payment, or good faith payment, or something! Instead of givin' her time to think us right outta that chunk of land. Jesus. I don't fuckin' believe this."

"Me neither," Tell said. "This is your fault."

No one disputed Tell's statement.

Colt and Kane wandered to their trucks.

"So you really ain't gonna tell us where he is?" Brandt shouted.

Colt faced Brandt, Tell and Dalton. "Casper will contact you when he's ready. Let him be until then."

No one said anything until Colt's pickup was a black speck in the plume of dust.

"As fucking awesome as this was, I'm getting the hell outta here," Ben said.

"Maybe you oughta call Quinn on your way home and fill him in," Brandt suggested with a snarl. "I agree with my brothers, Ben. You should've handled this better and now we're all payin' for it."

Rage and regret formed a toxic cocktail and Ben knew if he stayed here another minute, he'd lose his mind. This wasn't solely his fault. And fuck them all if they expected him to shoulder all the blame.

But he knew he'd never hear the end of it.

"These two are gonna tell me every fuckin' thing they kept from me while we clean up the shit piles in Dad's house since he ain't here for awhile."

When Dalton opened his mouth to protest, Brandt sent him a death glare.

Fun times.

Ben did call Quinn. He was pissy, in that silent, simmering silent way of his, which bothered Ben far worse than if Quinn had yelled and screamed.

Chapter Twenty-Six

The Wetzlers' place was in view and against his better judgment, Ben pulled into the drive.

The trio of dogs yapped, but he shooed them aside, as he started up the porch steps.

Rielle stepped outside, and leaned against the porch support, her expression a mix of annoyance and wariness.

"I thought we had a deal, Rielle."

"We had no deal." She folded her arms over her chest. "I thought what we talked about was confidential."

"It was."

"Then how come your McKay cousins showed up, all charming cowboy smiles, with the aw-shucks, we're all just neighbors attitude as they were mentally leveling my goddamn creek front and trying to decide how many cows they could run?"

"I'm not my cousins, Ree. You know that. I thought we were friends."

"I thought so too." She tossed her head, trying to keep the wind from her face. "But you have enough friends these days. New friends."

"What?"

"Don't play that game. I know you're sleeping with Ainsley Hamilton. I've seen her car at your place several times in the last few weeks. And isn't it a coincidence the bank she runs wouldn't lend me the money I needed to keep my land? But I'll bet she was more than happy to loan money to you so you could buy it."

"So you're what? Punishing me?"

"This isn't about you, McKay."

"I didn't get you into the financial mess you're in," he retorted hotly, "and you don't honestly believe I had dishonorable intentions when I offered to help bail you out of that situation."

Rielle shivered. "I didn't know what to believe. That was the problem."

"Who'd you sell to?"

It appeared she wouldn't answer and then she said, "I sold it to Gavin."

Ben's mouth nearly hit the porch slats. "Gavin? As in my brother Gavin?"

"Yes. He made me an offer...the same day you did, actually. I told him the same thing I told you. I'd think about it. Your cousins coming by last week made my decision. I called Gavin, we came to a verbal agreement and he paid off my note, that day, in its entirely, in cash. He's having his real estate lawyer draw up the terms of sale."

"Jesus. And you just trust him? You don't know him, Ree. Not like you know us."

She glared at him. "I'm not stupid, Ben. I've hired my own attorney to look over the agreement, and you can bet your ass that lawyer is not Ginger McKay." Rielle shook her head. "Sorry. That was uncalled for. You have no idea how hard this has been on me."

"Didn't hafta be."

Her eyes connected with a point over his shoulder. "Did I ever tell you the last thing my daddy said to me? Don't sell the land to the McKays."

"But you did anyway."

"No, I sold it to Gavin. That man is about as far from a McKay as you can get."

Stung by her cutting words, he shot back, "Sorry we've been such horrible neighbors for the last thirty years. Bet you won't miss that."

"Don't say that," she implored. "This is just business."

Hadn't Dalton and Tell said the same thing?

"Besides, I'm not going anywhere."

"What?" Ben stared at her suspiciously. "You're not moving out and Gavin is moving in?"

"No. Gavin agreed to divide the land. The creek front is mine so eventually I'll be able to build on it. Since he's not sure of his plans, long-term or short-term, I'll continue living in the house just like I've been."

"So nothin' has changed for you," he said dully.

"*Everything* has changed for me."

Ben was at a loss. Feeling betrayed on many levels, by his cousin's accusations, by his longtime friend, and by his brother. And since he didn't know what to say, he turned and walked away.

Rielle's shouted offer to finally pay him for the beds fell on deaf ears.

So he'd called his father to share the love. "Ben. What's up?"

"My curiosity mostly."

"Well, your tone don't match your words. You sound mad as hell, son."

"I am." He counted to fifty. "I just left Uncle Casper's house where I had to keep Brandt, Tell and Dalton from beating the tar outta Colt."

No response.

"And you don't seem particularly surprised about that."

"Not much surprises me these days."

"It sure shocked the shit outta us," he snapped.

"Before you chew my ass, lemme say Casper's private business is not mine to share with you or with them." A pause and Ben heard the squeak of his dad's office chair. "So I take it Casper's boys just found out?"

Ben's knuckles turned white on the steering wheel. "Yeah. Kane called me to run interference and keep fists from flying."

"That responsibility always seems to fall to you, don't it? Bein' the one to smooth things over and calm them hotheads down."

He was surprised his father had noticed.

"Look, none of us have been on the best terms with Casper, especially in the last year. But he is my brother. You know you'd keep your brother's secrets too."

"Some of my brothers are better at keeping secrets than others, aren't they," he snarled. "Did you know?"

"Do I know what?"

"Don't play stupid, it just pisses me off."

"Like you calling me, throwing accusations left and right is pissin' me off? Why don't you just spit it the hell out."

"Did you know Gavin bought the Wetzler place?"

"What? Gavin? Wait. Since when has it been for sale?"

"It wasn't." Ben explained what'd gone down. His dad stayed silent

259

for so long Ben wondered if they'd gotten cut off. "You there?"

He cleared his throat. "Yeah. I'm just stunned. Gavin hasn't said a word about it to me or to Vi." Ben's relief was short lived, however, when his dad said, "But I'm takin' this as a good sign."

"You consider it a good sign that Gavin would purposely fuck us over?"

"I'm gonna ignore that smartass remark bein's you're not acting at all like yourself. What I meant was I'm takin' this as a sign that Gavin wants to be closer to us. He's interested in becoming part of the family."

"Family doesn't do shit like this to each other, and if he's that type of guy, then I sure as fuck don't want him as part of my family."

A deep paternal sigh. "You don't mean that. Have you talked to Gavin about any of this?"

"No. I don't care if I ever talk to Gavin again."

"Son—"

"Don't tell me I don't mean it, because I do. This day has been a clusterfuck of epic proportions and I need a goddamn drink. Later." He hung up.

When Ben reached his house, his temper had pegged overload. Needing to blow off steam, he roughhoused with his dogs. He chopped and stacked firewood. After a long, hot shower, he'd calmed down and poured himself a hefty shot of Pendleton whiskey.

Ace and Deuce dozed by the woodstove. Ben had always kept his shit moods to himself, dealt with them himself. It worked for him.

But wouldn't it be nice to have someone to share this with? Someone to listen to you, verbally soothe you and then you could lose yourself in the heat, softness and surrender of her body to yours?

Just another fucked up situation in his life. Taking out the damn loan in the first place is what had caused him to lose Ainsley. All because he wanted to do something good, something helpful for his family. All his family saw was the loss of the land. There's no way he could make them understand he'd lost something far more valuable.

Grabbing the bottle, he flopped in front of the TV and flipped the channel to *Wheel of Fortune*. But he'd gotten so used to watching the show with Ainsley in the last month, it felt pathetic sitting by himself, guessing the puzzles out loud.

Halfway through the program his phone buzzed. He didn't

recognize the number, but he answered it anyway. "Ben McKay."

"Ben? Gavin."

"Fuck."

"Don't hang up. Please hear me out."

"Start that fast talking bullshit you do so well, cause you've got about thirty seconds."

"Charlie called me, mad as hell, and chewed my ass. I assure you I didn't want any of you to find out this way."

"What way were we supposed to find out? The McKays are a big family in a small community. Word gets around."

"Look, I overheard your conversation with Rielle the morning after Chase's event. You made her a fair offer."

"But you swooped in and made her a better one."

"Yes. But not for the reason you think. I bought it as an investment."

Ben laughed harshly. "So you're giving up life as an Arizona real estate tycoon to run a B&B in nowhere Wyoming?"

"Not hardly. I'm not big on repeating others mistakes. I've seen Rielle struggling with the B&B since I first stayed with her. When she asked for advice I gave it."

"Big surprise that your advice to her was to sell...to you."

Gavin sighed. "I'm in real estate. I make decisions like this all the time. It's nothing personal."

"It's goddamned personal to me. My family has been tryin' to buy that for three decades and once again it's in a stranger's hands. Now you're giving my folks the impression that you're moving to Wyoming, changing your last name to McKay, which we both know ain't true."

When silence burned his ear, Ben wished he could take the words back.

"I never meant to give Charlie and Vi false hope."

"Too late. And know what sucks? Mom and Dad will take any kind of hope when it comes to you, and I don't wanna see them hurt."

"I'm not a bad guy, Ben."

"Prove it." Ben drained his whiskey. "And by my clock your thirty seconds are up." He hung up and poured himself another drink.

Everything in his life had gone to hell in the last two days and he saw no clear way to fix any of it.

Chapter Twenty-Seven

Not a good sign when a smug Turton knocked on her office door before quitting time on Tuesday and made himself comfortable. "Glad to see you've recovered from your illness."

What the heck? He didn't give a rip about her health. "You're lucky you didn't get it."

"Well, some of us have a stronger constitution than others. I make it a point to take good care of myself so I don't catch every bug that crawls along."

Yes, Turton, you are the picture of health with your bony-assed body and pasty complexion. "Was there something you needed?"

"Yes. I'm not sure how to approach this. Saturday evening I stopped into the Golden Boot. Our Jenny was there and she and I started talking..." He picked lint off his sport coat before continuing. "Then I ran into Steve Talbot at the diner Sunday morning. We had breakfast together, which included a pretty interesting conversation."

She did not like the turd's need to talk around the subject to build suspense before he got to the point. She really didn't like that he'd become so friendly with Jenny.

"Interestingly enough, both Jenny and Steve posed the same question to me. A question about you."

"Me? Why on earth would I be a topic of conversation?"

"That's what I asked myself. I've been so busy doing my job here at the bank, that I pay little attention to office gossip, and even less attention to the small town gossip about the citizens of Sundance."

Doing my job here at the bank. As if she'd been sitting in the employee break room checking her Facebook page all day rather than working.

"So I'll admit to being perplexed that both Jenny and Steve mentioned the same thing. Numerous times."

"Which was?"

"That you are involved with Ben McKay."

Ainsley's lungs seized up.

"Which wouldn't be a big deal, since you are both single adults. And if you prefer to sneak around and see him on the sly because he's got a...questionable reputation with the ladies, that's your business. So that, in and of itself, didn't bother me. But when Jenny informed me that Ben McKay had applied for a loan, through you, not through Leslie? And that no one in the office was aware of this loan but you? And you immediately sent the loan application to Denver for approval and priority processing? Well, that did bother me. Quite a bit actually. So much that I spent the entire morning verifying those facts.

"When Steve suggested that you've been intimately involved with Ben McKay to get the McKays' banking business away from Settler's First...I really didn't know how to respond, except to agree with him it's very unprofessional on your part, but not necessarily unethical. Then Steve said he saw you and Ben together, late at night after Chase McKay's event, and early the next morning, which by my estimation is about a week prior to Ben applying for a loan. And that also brings up the question if you were involved with Ben McKay *before* you helped arrange the community event for his brother, and if that involvement swayed your recommendation for the bank to donate five thousand dollars to Chase McKay's foundation."

This couldn't be happening.

"I'll admit I'm shocked, Ainsley. You have a solid reputation."

"Here's where you'll make this supposed scandal go away and allow me to keep my solid reputation intact if I...what? Quit and recommend you take over as bank president?"

His eyes gleamed with pure spite. "I'd never stoop to blackmail. I truly feel this situation needs to be brought to the attention of the management team at the corporate office in Denver."

Ainsley was infuriated because everything that'd been done on the up and up would now be brought into question. All her actions would be scrutinized. With the bank's avoidance of scandal, after the fiasco with a nonprofit group that'd felled the man tapped to take the president's position, she suspected she'd be fired. With jobs so hard to come by in the financial world, she'd be lucky to find another job anywhere in the banking industry.

And admitting her sexual relationship with Ben had ended the day he applied for the loan would be a moot point. Another moot point would be defending her decision to process the loan herself because Leslie had left the office that day due to illness. And yet another moot point would be mentioning she'd sent loan paperwork through herself all the time in her previous bank position. It wasn't like Ben McKay hadn't met all the criteria required of every other person who applied for a loan.

All valid points that wouldn't make a damn bit of difference now.

"I've set up a conference call for Thursday."

Turton stood, wearing a look of fake sympathy she wanted to smack right off his face.

Great plan, Ainsley. Add assault to your charges.

"And not to worry, I will have the utmost discretion with this matter." *But only until it's resolved and then I'll gossip with glee,* was heavily implied.

She closed the computer programs. Tidied up the papers on her desk. Made a stack of filing to finish so Turton could easily find the files after she got canned. She was half tempted to track down a box for easy transport of her measly personal belongings, so she wouldn't have to paw through the damn Dumpster on Thursday afternoon.

Jenny knocked on the door. "I'm leaving. Do you need anything else?"

"No."

A pause. Then, "Is everything okay?"

You know damn well it isn't.

"Fine." Ainsley didn't look up. While she knew this situation wasn't Jenny's fault, she'd definitely played a part in bringing it about.

The door closed quietly.

Ainsley drove home on autopilot. She slipped on pajamas and snuggled with her cats. But even they tired of her tears after a while. Miserable, her red-rimmed gaze swept over her living room. She still had stuff in boxes. That'd make moving easier.

Easier. Right. This was the hardest thing she'd ever have to do.

Ainsley debated on answering the door when Ben knocked. She'd spent the last twenty-four hours in misery, coming to some harsh realizations—about herself, her life and Ben. But she couldn't postpone the inevitable so she flipped the locks and let him in.

Ben blew right past her. "I went by the bank today but you weren't there."

Great. Like she needed more fuel added to the fire by Ben casually stopping by. "I took a personal day."

"Huh." Ben yanked off his duster and draped it across the back of the couch.

Huh? That was it? For a man who claimed to be so in tune with her, why hadn't he noticed her distraction? Her haggard appearance?

Then he was right there, peering into her face with raptness that made her feel as transparent as glass. "Tell me what's wrong."

"I might be about to lose my job."

Ben went motionless. "What? Why?"

"It's about your loan. Turton, the VP, confronted me about it. He got ahold of the paperwork and said it was bogus."

"When?"

"Yesterday."

"Was that why you didn't go into work today?"

"Yes."

"How did he find out? Not that it matters now, but I should've told you the real reason I applied for the loan."

"What?" Ainsley fought a sense of dread. "What real reason? What did you intend to use the money for if not for furniture equipment and supplies?"

Distractedly, he said, "A down payment on Rielle's land, actually. She was in a financial bind. Doesn't hold true now."

"You lied to me? You lied on the loan application?"

His head snapped up. "Isn't that what you meant?"

"No! I meant the loan itself was bogus, not the reason for the loan. But my God, this makes it ten times worse!"

"Angel—"

"Don't call me that! Don't you understand? Turton questioned why I sent your loan paperwork to the head office myself, instead of running it through our loan officer. Like I was trying to hide it because we've been sneaking around. Then he brought up Chase's event. How I pushed for the bank's sponsorship and donation, and now my motives would be construed as dishonest, given our intimate relationship."

"This is all bullshit, Ainsley."

"Is it?" she shot back. "We have been sexually involved on a level that isn't normal...which makes me even more paranoid because what if people found out what I let you do to me—"

"*Let* me do to you?" he repeated incredulously. "What the fuck is that supposed to mean?

"You know what that means, Bennett." She paced and the cats scattered. "I wasn't thinking clearly. Dammit. I haven't been acting responsibly since the second I donned that stupid wig and waltzed into the Rawhide Club pretending to be someone I'm not."

"Are you sayin' you're sorry we met?"

Ainsley didn't answer that—she couldn't. "All Turton's accusations have a grain of truth that once piled up makes a damn convincing argument about my poor judgment. As bank president, I can't have poor financial judgment."

"This Turton guy is just tryin' to scare you because I—"

"He has scared me. He's already set up a phone conference with the district manager for tomorrow. So it's not like he's blackmailing me. He intends to get me fired." She continued pacing. "I'll have to move back to Denver. Although I'm not sure where I'll live or what I'll do."

"Ainsley. Listen to me. There's another option."

A hollow feeling filled her chest and belly when she looked at him. She'd dreaded this. But she'd known it was coming. "What?"

"Would you stay if I asked you?"

"Stay where? In Sundance?"

"Yeah."

"And do what?" She froze when he continued staring at her with that Dom look. "I can't ever...be that."

Ben frowned. "Be what?"

"A lifestyle submissive. Like Layla. With the collar, the full subservience and the discipline whippings."

"For Christsake!" he bellowed. "*That's* what you think I want from you?"

He never bellowed and Ainsley shrank back.

"God, Ainsley, do you really think I'm some kind of controlling monster? That I purposely set out to fuck up your professional life so I could force you into a lifestyle that you're not suited for, for my own selfish purposes?"

When he put it like that, she felt petty. Bitchy. Ben knew all her vulnerabilities. And he'd never used them against her. Not once.

But you've used his against him. You're about to use them now.

"No. But this circumstance has driven home the point I didn't know what I was getting into with this Dom/sub thing."

"And now?"

"Now I know I was naïve. Stupidly hopeful. Nothing but a tourist."

"What are you saying?" Ben demanded.

Ainsley didn't want to give him false hope. Confess what the last few weeks had meant to her. Confess what he meant to her. She had to take a hard stance and make a clean break, no matter if it would break her. "I knew exactly what you were when I met you, Bennett. A Dom. My job crisis changes nothing for you. You're still a Dom. You still need the club. The friendships you've made and acceptance you've gotten at the Rawhide are important to you. I'd never ask you to give that up."

Realization dawned in his eyes. His jaw went rigid. "But it's changed everything for you. You can't be a part of it. At all."

"No. Even if by some miracle this loan fiasco blows over, I can't be in a relationship, even casually, with a man who frequents a sex club. Banking is a conservative industry and women have an even harder row to hoe than men."

"That sounds like an excuse."

"An excuse? Right. Because no one has ever lost their job due to a sex scandal," she snapped.

That shut him down for a minute or so. "It doesn't have to be this way."

"Yes, it does." Ainsley briefly squeezed her eyes shut against the tears and the pain. "I don't want to change you. But you need to understand I can't do this."

When she looked into his wounded blue eyes, her heart went into free fall.

"So this is it? You're cutting me loose? Because of what I am?"

"You're taking this the wrong way, Ben, it's not—"

"Just stop. Please. Stop justifying it. This...fuck...it's..." His voice caught. "I can't..."

With an economy of movement, Ben slipped on the black duster. He grabbed his hat off the sofa table.

He didn't look broken-hearted when he walked out. He just looked broken.

Thursday was the longest day in the history of the world.

She'd put a couple of contingency plans in place on the off chance it'd work in her favor.

Ten minutes before the phone conference was scheduled to start, she left her office. Turton left his office at the same time. Not a coincidence and she felt manipulated.

"Ainsley? Turton?"

They turned and looked at Leslie. "I know you've got a conference call scheduled with the district manager in a few minutes. And because this call is regarding a loan situation, as the sole loan officer in this branch, I want to lead the call."

Turton harrumphed and walked into the conference room.

Ainsley and Leslie followed.

"Frankly, Leslie, I'm a little disappointed that you are rushing to Ainsley's defense. I imagine the district manager won't see it as a smart judgment call for you either."

"On the contrary, Turton. I'm not rushing to Ainsley's defense. I merely want the chance to explain why I didn't originate these loans. My part—or lack thereof—should be clarified because I need this job."

Turton's beady eyes narrowed behind his glasses. "Loans?" he said sharply. "As in Ainsley's tried to circumvent normal channels to slide *another* loan through?"

Leslie sat at the head of the table. "No. To be honest, I would've processed Ben McKay's loan, had he come to me, and it would've netted the same result. The loan I'm questioning is the one you originated for Jenny, our bank receptionist, for a new car."

His lips flattened.

"Is there a reason you didn't tell me about this loan, Turton? Why you circumvented normal channels to slide it through? Given the fact Jenny is an employee and she has no assets? Plus, a few employees have questioned whether there's more going on between you and Jenny than just a working relationship."

"This is outrageous!"

Even-tempered Leslie vanished. She slapped the file folders on the table. "Any more outrageous than you accusing Ainsley of having more than a working relationship with Ben McKay? I find it outrageous you expect to run Ainsley out on a rail for making one bad judgment call, when you've done exactly the same thing. You're both in the wrong here. Neither of you followed proper procedure."

Ainsley stared at Leslie, both impressed and scared by her ability to ferret out information.

"So you're going to blackmail me?" Turton sneered.

"No. You're both going to let me handle the phone call with management. Where I will bring up the general question of loan origination. Who has the authority to do it? Then I'll point out you both originated loans without going through me. Since we're a new branch, and this hasn't come up before, I wanted to be the one to ask for clarification with both the president and the vice president in attendance so there'd be no disputes."

"And if I refuse?"

Do not lunge across the conference table and wrap your hands around his scrawny throat.

"You won't. Because if you continue with your accusations about Ainsley's involvement with Ben McKay prior to the loan, I have documentation of times you were spotted with Jenny Timsdale, outside of banking hours, prior to her loan application too."

Turton's face immediately went bright red. He seemed too angry to speak.

But Leslie wasn't finished. "I strongly advise you allow me to handle this phone conference. That way we can all keep our jobs and continue to work together as one big, happy family here at National West Bank."

For the first time in two days, Ainsley felt like the world wasn't crumbling beneath her feet. On a professional level anyway.

Leslie looked at them each in turn. "So. What's it going to be?"

Turton wouldn't meet Ainsley's gaze. "Make the call."

The district manager was notoriously cranky. After listening to Leslie's question, he let fly. Chewing out both Ainsley and Turton for overstepping their bounds and reminding them National West assigned a loan officer at that location for a reason. Then he reminded them of their responsibilities and if they were too busy doing someone else's job, they were neglecting their own. In a totally surprising move, he insisted Ainsley and Turton attend an interpersonal management skills workshop in Denver. Over the weekend. He commended Leslie for her attention to detail. All in all, the phone call was short and to the point.

Ainsley sat in stunned silence when the dial tone echoed in the conference room. Turton didn't say a word. He just left but he'd seemed to have lost some of the cock-of-the-walk attitude.

Leslie gathered up her papers.

"Thank you," Ainsley said. "I expected I'd be packing up my office and turning in my pass key today."

"You're welcome. I didn't do this for you, Ainsley. You and Turton were both in the wrong, professionally, and I didn't want to get caught in the middle. I need this job and I've seen it happen before, where the lower level employee gets fired for a mistake the boss made."

She knew Leslie had worked for Steve Talbot at Settler's First for a few years before getting laid off.

"On a personal level, I hated Turton's double standard. He expected you to get fired for a personal relationship crossing the line, when he was doing the same thing." She shook her head. "The bizarre part of it was Turton wasn't drawing those parallels."

Ainsley knew trying to find common ground with Turton would be nearly impossible now.

Leslie paused at the door and looked over her shoulder. "Just so you know. Ben McKay came by yesterday to see me and formally dropped his loan request."

Her heart jumped into her throat. "He did?"

"Yes."

The door shut behind her.

She didn't move for the longest time. Mostly because she wasn't sure what her next move should be.

Chapter Twenty-Eight

As soon as Ben finished chores on Friday he drove to the Rawhide Club. After Ainsley's stinging dismissal, he'd needed to be in a place where people looked at him with respect. Where he was liked for being exactly who he was.

But his haven didn't offer him the usual validation. And that confused the hell out of him. So he'd found a spot in the back corner and brooded. About Ainsley. About her refusal to listen to reason and his attempt to fix his mistake. For the first time since they'd started a relationship, she'd looked at him with pity. Like he was a freak.

When Cody straddled the chair around across from him, Ben bit back a leave-me-the-fuck alone snarl. Cody would snap right back, demanding to know why Ben came to the club if he'd wanted solitude.

"Looks like you're doing some deep thinking."

"I am. It's very taxing on my pea-sized brain."

He laughed. "Bullshit. Spill the details, man. Especially since you ain't been here in a month again. What's going on?"

"Fuck, Cody, I don't know where to start."

"I see I had reason to be worried about you. Come on, Ben. It's me. We've talked about everything over the years. And I mean everything."

"I know that," he said softly. In some ways, Ben was closer to the guys at the Rawhide Club than he was with his brothers.

"Then talk to me."

"Remember that friend of Layla's?" Cody nodded. "We ran into each other in Sundance after that weekend at the club. She's just moved there, so we've been playin' at my house, on a trial basis because she's not convinced she's cut out for a Dom/sub relationship. It's ended up complicated. Even more than I'm letting on because I have feelings for her. Like hardcore I-think-I'm-in-fucking-love-with-her feelings."

Cody whistled. "Did you tell her?"

"No." Ben knocked back a swallow of beer. "Because I know she doesn't feel the same way. I was an experiment. A failed one; she wanted me because I was a Dom, and now she doesn't want me because I'm a Dom."

"We came to terms with who we are a long time ago, Ben."

"I thought I had. Now I don't know."

Cody clapped him on the back. "I'm gonna give you the same advice you gave me when Kristin gave me back my collar, get over it, get on with it."

Ben snorted. "And that's worked for you...how? You're still fucking in love with Kristin. You're still waiting for her to walk back through that door."

"And hell will freeze over before that happens, so don't be a dumb fucker like me. There are plenty of woman who wanna get with Bennett. Line up another sub. That'll take the sting out of it."

But I don't want another sub. I want Ainsley.

"I recognize that look. Listen to me. Don't be a pathetic motherfucker. Move on. Because we both know once a sub's made her mind up she's not really a sub, or she's got an excuse not to be with you as you really are, there's no going back." Cody squeezed his shoulder and left him to consider his advice.

What sucked? Cody was exactly right. Which was why Ben hadn't wanted to talk to him in the first place.

Sometime later Mary Jane and Cliff braved the gloomy cloud surrounding Ben and took seats at his table. The couple had been married thirty years and recently committed to a dominant and submissive relationship.

Mary Jane liked a bite of pain. Cliff, a novice with brute strength, had gotten comfortable with a flogger and a cane, but shied away from the single tail whip. So Ben helped them out, using the whip on Mary Jane while Cliff watched. When Mary Jane reached her happy place, Ben left the scene. No hard-on, no hard feelings.

"Bennett. Haven't seen you in a while."

"It's been a few. How are things with you?" He addressed his comments to Cliff, since they followed traditional protocol in the club and Mary Jane kept her eyes averted.

"Good. Is everything all right?" Cliff asked.

He sighed. "I've got a few things on my mind."

"Anything we can help with?"

Ben looked from Cliff to Mary Jane. Maybe it was fated they ended up at his table tonight, given the last couple days. He knew Mary Jane had a high-powered job as an oil company executive, so maybe she could shed light on what'd happened with Ainsley. "Would you allow me to speak freely to your sub, Cliff?"

"Mary Jane? You have permission to speak to Bennett."

"Thank you, Sir." Mary Jane raised her eyes to Ben's. "What may I help you with?"

"This might sound like a strange question, but would your job be affected if anyone you worked with discovered you were a sexual submissive?"

"In my job right now? Probably not."

See? Ainsley was just making up excuses not to be with you.

"But bear in mind I'm five years from retirement. If I was a young woman just starting out? Especially in a male-dominated industry? That would be the kiss of death for my career."

Ben froze.

"Also remember I'm a sexual submissive to my husband of three decades. I'm not a single woman being passed from Dom to Dom in this sex club. That's also an entirely different situation."

Ben's hopes that the obstacles he and Ainsley faced would somehow magically work out, given time and distance, began to fade.

Mary Jane tapped her fingernails on the table. "The reason Cliff and I insist on almost total privacy here is because of my professional position. I wouldn't be keen on anyone finding out I liked to be whipped by a stranger. And I'm sure your outside friends don't know that you get...something from whipping the crap out of women you have no sexual interest in."

Ben frowned.

"No offense, Bennett, but I don't want to get to know you. Emotional ties change things. I'm fine with Cliff spanking or flogging me. But there's something sadistic about telling the man I love to whip me until I almost pass out."

"But it's different when I wield the whip?"

"Yes. Because when you're landing strikes on my body I bear

them for him. To show him I can take it. I share the joy and pain with Cliff, not with you. To put it in the simplest terms, you're the bad guy beating me and Cliff is the good guy who will take care of me when it's all done."

Holy shit. Was that really how she saw him? As the bad guy?

"Mary Jane. Apologize to Bennett for insulting him," Cliff demanded.

He said, "It's all right, Cliff," even when it wasn't. Fuck. He felt he'd just been kicked in the teeth and kneed in the nads.

"I'll be honest, Bennett. Your blows sting like hell. I've been tempted to run, especially in the beginning. Me getting whipped does nothing for Cliff, but he understands it does something for me."

"Would you miss it if you didn't have it?" Ben asked.

"Maybe. Would you miss it if you didn't do it?"

I don't know.

But he hadn't missed it in the month he'd been involved with Ainsley.

Cliff said, "We hoped to utilize your whip skills tonight. But given what you're wrestling with, we'd understand if you opt not to."

In his frame of mind, he'd take validation where he could get it. "Which room?"

"Seven. In about thirty minutes?"

"I'll be there."

Sending out bad vibes kept subs at bay as Ben attempted to get his head in the game. Holding his whip, he bypassed a public scene where the woman getting flogged looked totally bored.

Ah hell. Was that...Zoe?

He ducked from view and hustled down the hallway. He peeked in the window to see if they were ready for him and stepped inside.

Mary Jane was blindfolded, naked and secured facedown to the bed.

Cliff gave Ben the instructions in low tones. The scene went better for Mary Jane if she didn't know where the blows would strike or how many.

Ben walked the perimeter of the bed. That too, heightened her senses. The fall of his boots on the carpet. The jostling of the bed as he bumped into it. And then that first whip crack. Rarely did he land the first blow. He loved the sound it made, the leather whistling through the air before the end connected with solid mass and a sharp *crack*.

That's when he found his headspace. The intense focus needed to keep his aim true and please both Cliff and Mary Jane.

But what had he gotten from the scene?

Ben's shirt was sweat-soaked and he floated on the buzz of adrenaline when Cliff said, "Red. She's done in, Bennett. Thank you."

He nodded and slipped from the room, the edgy feeling still riding him hard. As he skirted the crowd, he couldn't believe Zoe's scene was still playing out. Their eyes met.

Hers held a look of frustration. She said, "Please. Bennett. Show him. Help me."

The weight of onlookers' stares didn't faze him. He crossed his arms over his chest and let the whip dangle. "Say your safe word."

"No. Just help me." She didn't even flinch when her Dom landed two hard swats on the backs of her legs.

"Rules are rules. Say your safe word and I'll step in."

Zoe screamed, "Red! Red! Goddammit!"

The guy halted mid-swat. The same frustration burned in his eyes as in Zoe's when Ben stepped from the edge of the crowd. "You're in charge of this scene?"

"Yes. Who the hell are you?"

"Bennett. And you?"

"Brian."

"Well, Brian, I hafta ask. Have you played in public with her before?"

"Only once."

"Is this a pain with sex scene or just pain?"

"Pain with sex."

"I have history with Zoe, and I might be able to help you both out. I'll give her the pain if you'll handle the sex and aftercare."

Brian actually looked relieved. "Sounds fair."

Ben kept his gaze on Brian's as he spoke to the sub. "Zoe, I've already warmed up with the single tail. You ready?"

"Yes. Sir. Please, Sir."

"How many?" he murmured to Brian.

"Twenty-three," Brian whispered back. "You choose the spots. If she stops counting then you stop."

"Agreed." Ben walked forward and slowly ran the whip handle down Zoe's spine and the crack of her ass. Her whole body jerked, the chains rattled and she strained to look over her shoulder at him.

When he moved, her head tried to follow his movement.

"You oughten be watchin' me, Zoe. You oughta be focused on how you're gonna breathe through the first blow. 'Cause I guarantee it's gonna hurt."

The crowd murmured behind them.

"Blindfold her."

Zoe gasped and turned to glare at Ben. "What? No, you can't—"

Ben grabbed her jaw, tilting her face up. "I most certainly can, because you're the one trussed up in chains, not me. And if you don't show me respect, since this is now *my* scene? When I've deemed that you are done with the pain portion? I won't let Brian touch you. At all. All you'll feel is pain. Nothin' else. So choose."

She lowered her eyes. "I apologize for my behavior, Sir."

Brian tied on the blindfold.

At the first whip crack, the crowd moved back.

"Brian. Distract her."

As soon as Brian's lips touched hers, Zoe relaxed. She arched into him, making soft noises as he broke the kiss.

"Count. Starting from one." Ben placed the first blow on the fleshy part of Zoe's right shoulder.

"One. Thank you, Sir."

Ben kept moving, walking closer, letting Brian offer soothing words and caresses as he marked her skin with random stinging blows. He concentrated the hits on her buttocks and the backs of her thighs, remembering those as her hot spots. But he felt no stirring of arousal. No need to caress her skin or take her to the next level. He felt...tired. Maybe a little used. More than ready to be done with this night.

At Zoe's full body slump, he let his whip fall to the side. Brian moved in and gave his sub what she needed.

The crowd parted for him, but all eyes returned to the action at the front.

Ben wanted a shot of whiskey and the comfort of his own bed. He cut down the hallway when a hand landed on his shoulder, jerking him to a stop. He whirled around and his cousin Dalton was in his face, wearing a look of disgust.

"What the fuck was that I just saw, Bennett?"

"Dalton?" Ben glanced at the crowd to see if a monitor was close by. "How did you get in here?"

"I dropped your name at the door. They let me in with a guest pass."

He'd asked for that pass for Ainsley. The fact she'd never use it made him lash out. "Go away. I ain't in the mood to deal with you right now." Ben sidestepped him.

But Dalton anticipated the move. "What are you in the mood for? Beating on another helpless woman? With a fucking bullwhip, for Christsake?"

"Keep your goddamn voice down."

"The fuck I will. I want some fuckin' answers on why you get off whipping women as they cry out for you to stop hitting them! I couldn't believe my eyes when I saw you with that older couple. I looked in the window and watched you beat her. And then I saw you immediately jump at the chance to beat another chick. Jesus. What did either of those women do to you?"

Dalton was more muscle bound, but Ben had more experience dealing with hotheads, so he grabbed his cousin by his shirt and shoved him into room three.

Ben would've welcomed Dalton taking a swing at him. But Dalton paced. Muttered to himself. Ben had wondered how he'd handle it if this day came. How he'd explain. If he even wanted to try.

Then Dalton invaded his space. "How long have you been comin' to this place?"

"I helped start this club six years ago."

"So how many women have you tortured and raped during that time?"

Ben shoved Dalton and held the whip handle against his throat. "Back the fuck off, Dalton. You don't have the first fuckin' clue what you're talking about. You're just flapping your gums, spouting bullshit and proving your ignorance."

"I know what I saw."

"Do you? If what I was doing was so unwanted or wrong, then why the hell didn't the woman's husband stop me? Then why didn't any one of the fifty other members watching the last scene step in and stop me? Not because they were scared I'd turn the whip on them. They didn't stop it because they understood what I was doin'. You don't."

"You're goddamned right I don't," Dalton retorted. "What kind of man does this? And do you know the really sick part? You didn't get off doin' it."

"So you're saying you'd understand it more if I would've fucked those women afterward?"

"Yes. No. Maybe. Fuck, I don't know. This makes no sense to me." Dalton paced to the back of the room and jammed a hand through his hair. "I don't get it. Why?"

Ben dropped into the chair. "You think I can explain it enough to satisfy you? I recognize that look in your eyes, Dalton and that is the reason I don't broadcast this. Here at the club I find women who are looking for the same thing."

"Lookin' to get their asses whaled on?" Dalton sneered.

"Sometimes."

"So you're tellin' me this private club is a real freak parade."

"This place is no more a freak parade than the Golden Boot, where you troll for pussy every weekend."

Dalton took a belligerent stance, arms crossed over his chest, feet braced wide. "Wrong. This ain't normal."

"You've never tied a woman up during sex?"

"Ah. Sure. Who hasn't?" Dalton shifted his stance, then his eyes. "So I oughta be afraid the next step will be shackling a woman in chains and beating on her in front of a room full of strangers?"

He sank into the closest chair. "This is pointless."

"Does your family know?"

Ben shook his head.

"They should. Maybe they can get you some help, cuz, 'cause this is seriously fucked up."

He thought he'd conquered the fear of being outed to his family. But the idea of his brothers and parents staring at him, with Dalton's same judgmental eyes, made him physically ill. His voice came out a hoarse whisper. "You gonna take it upon yourself to tell them?"

"I don't know. But you can't deny the reason *you* haven't told them is because you know it's wrong."

Now he had to worry that Dalton would blab to the entire McKay family.

"Look at yourself, Ben. Sitting there holding a whip, a whip that you used on not one, but two women tonight. And you're tellin' me *I'm* the one with the problem." He shook his head. "It'd be funny if it wasn't so sad." Dalton stormed out.

There was the game-ending blow. It'd been ages since he'd felt such a wash of shame. Since he'd felt like an outcast. And then he topped off those failings with the fear that no decent woman—like Ainsley—would ever love him because of his tendencies. Hidden fears that smacked him in the face today from his cousin's accusations.

Ben remained in the room a long time, emotions warring. He fingered the beautifully made whip. Device of torture? Instrument of pleasure? His supposed expertise gnawed at him. He'd honed his skills on cattle. What would his family say if they knew he regularly used it on people? On women? Would they be ashamed? Should he be ashamed?

So Dalton hadn't been totally off base.

Ben felt raw. Used. Confused. Lonely. As much as he'd broadened Ainsley's horizon, she'd broadened his too. He glanced around the room. He felt nothing. No pride, or excitement or anger. No anticipation for what might be in store for him for future nights with future subs. He just wanted to go home.

Chapter Twenty-Nine

Ainsley dreamt of Bennett every night. Images so vivid she couldn't tell the difference between fantasy and reality until she woke up alone.

After last night's dream she'd leapt out of bed and stared out the hotel window across the freeway to the Denver skyline. She'd hoped she wouldn't dream of him here, as she had the last two nights in her bed in Sundance.

Wrong.

Which begged the question: were her regrets about her decision haunting her?

Yes.

But there wasn't anything she could do about it. She was miserable. Trying to stave off the dreams that left her feeling bereft, she drank four strong gin and tonics at the hotel bar before she stumbled back to her room.

But not even booze kept him from overtaking her thoughts.

A rough-skinned hand brushed her forehead and she shot straight up in bed. She couldn't see anything it was so dark. "Who's there?"

The echo of heavy breathing was the only response.

She scrambled backward, even when she recognized the warm, earthy scent of her dominant's aftershave. "What do you want?"

A deep, male chuckle. "You know what I want."

That initial spike of fear faded. She shouldn't be surprised he'd taken it upon himself to make her bedroom stranger sexual fantasy a reality.

Or was this a dream? It was so vivid, the sound of his feet shuffling on the carpet. The scent of his skin so close she could taste his sweat on her tongue. The way her body was wound tight with anticipation whenever he was near.

"I've been watchin' you. I know what you do when you're alone in your bedroom."

"I-I don't know what you're talking about."

"Do you know how many times I've watched you jerk up your nightgown and reach for your vibrator? You grab a couple of your favorite naughty books. You've used them so many times the pages fall open to your favorite scenes. I know which scenes get you hot," he said, much closer to her than he'd been. "Which scenes make you turn that vibrator on high. Which scenes made your pussy dripping wet.

"You imagine yourself trussed up. Subject to a man's whim, maybe his to mercy, but always to his pleasure. However he wants to fuck you, in as many positions as his greedy, depraved brain can create, as many times as he can get it up." His hot breath stuttered across her ear. "But here's where your fantasy is mine. Here's where the dream becomes real. Because this man, this dream lover, wants to prove he can be the man to give you what no man ever has before."

She blurted, "What are you going to do to me?"

"Make you scream."

Ainsley shrieked when his strong hands gripped her ankles and she was flipped onto her belly. Her arms were jerked together behind her back and cool metal circled her wrists.

Then his mouth was by her temple. "Be still. Be quiet or I'll gag you. Understand?"

"Yes."

"On your knees."

Heart racing, she scooted back, focusing on the feel of her cotton sheets against the side of her face as her shoulders were pressed into the mattress. Metal grinding on metal sounded above her head. Then her arms were lifted off the small of her back. "What's that?"

"To ensure you cooperate. If you fight me I'll pull this chain and it lifts your arms until I get your attention." Her Dom's familiar touch floated down her arms, and his breath drifted across her nape. His callused fingertips traced her knuckles and fingers as he tested the tightness of the cuffs. His touch was efficient, but tender. Insistent, but elusive.

He was a study in contradiction tonight.

Why wouldn't he let her see his face?

He stroked and teased. When a thick finger smeared cold

lubricant into her asshole, her heartbeat sped up. She sucked in a sharp breath when an anal plug breached the ring of muscle. She involuntarily clenched around it.

His hands caressed her ass. Then he delivered a hard smack on each cheek, growling, "Mine. Every part of you is mine tonight. Say it."

"I'm yours."

"I'll fuck any part of this body I want to." The coarse hair of his calves brushed the inside of hers as he moved in behind her. He draped his warm body across her back, his weight pushing her chest deeper into the mattress. Panic filled her. She was trapped. She thrashed. A simple gentle touch on her neck stopped her frantic movements.

"Stop. Remember you're safe with me. You're always safe with me, Ainsley."

She turned her head but she couldn't see him.

Isn't that what you wanted in your fantasy?

No. I want to see him. I want to know it's him.

Then his big, capable hands squeezed her breasts. His fingers twirled, tugged and tweaked her nipples. Between the squeezing, the pinching and her complete immobilization, her breath was coming in short bursts of air that left her light headed. She started to drift into her floaty headspace.

His hand floated down her belly and his fingers traced her clit. "I wanna get you off like you do when you're alone in your bed." He stroked, working one, then two fingers inside her. Plunging deep, knowing exactly how much pressure to exert to keep her whimpering for more. To make her pussy moisten and swell for him.

Just as she could almost taste that sweet climax, he withdrew. She groaned, turning her head to wipe the sweat gathered on her brow. To try and see him. "Please."

The bed wiggled. "Maybe you'd rather get off with a vibrator."

"Your hand is fine."

"You sure?" A loud mechanical buzz sounded next to her ear. "Because I found this on your nightstand."

"I didn't plan to use it. I swear."

"Such a liar." He nibbled on the back of her neck, sending a shudder through her. "I think you planned to give yourself a little treat before you fell asleep."

"No."

"Let's see how this works." He'd lubed up her rabbit vibrator; the cool silicone easily slipped inside her. He turned on all the moving parts at once—a total blitz on her senses. She'd already teetered on that elusive point and this would kick her right over the edge.

When he started pinching the tender skin on the inside of her thighs, she tried to close her legs against the intense pleasure.

He hissed, "Don't deny yourself this. Don't lie to yourself that you don't like what I'm doin' to you."

Why did that feel so good? Was she a masochist for craving more of that pain?

Light pinches on her thicker folds of skin gave way to smaller, faster pinches. As she spiraled closer to orgasm a line of liquid heat shot from those pinpoints.

"Oh. Please."

He flipped the vibrator on high, holding it in place. The phallus spun inside her, hitting her G-spot every third rotation. The plastic cage around her clit stopped vibrating at random intervals and stayed steady. That tingling, buzzing sensation tormented every nerve ending in her body. Her sex, her nipples, even her skin throbbed. She forgot how to breathe, how to think, she could only focus on that desperate need.

"Lemme hear you come." One last hard pinch on her inner thigh and Ainsley unraveled. Her pussy muscles clamped down around the vibrator, increasing the intensity of the pressure against her clit. A long wail poured from her mouth.

She fell flat on the mattress, after he withdrew the vibrator, her body trembling violently. She closed her eyes, vaguely aware of the gentle tugging of the plug from her ass. She wanted to beg him not to leave, but her tongue and lips weren't responding.

Chains rattled and she was rolled to her back. She couldn't make her eyes open. Her arms were useless. A determined pair of hands pushed her thighs apart. Hot kisses seared her belly. A warm mouth followed the edge of her ribcage and outlined the lower swell of her breasts. Soft suckling and delicate licks on her nipples brought about her contented sigh.

His mouth snared hers in a kiss as he eased his cock inside her, filling her with one smooth stroke. Realizing just how boneless she was, he brought her legs around his waist.

When his cock nudged her cervix, her lower half bowed off the mattress.

His lips clung to hers with sweet, sweet kisses. "I need to feel you wrapped around me like this. Let me have you. Let me have you like this forever."

Ainsley managed a soft, "Yes," and arched her neck for him in a show of full submission.

Then his weight disappeared from her body. His scent vanished. She opened her eyes and found herself alone. "Bennett? Where are you?"

His voice came out of nowhere, but it was everywhere. "Gone." A ghostly breeze drifted across her face. "Too late. I'm already gone."

Ainsley woke up sobbing, "No," over and over with an acute sense of loss.

She threw back the covers and patted the mattress as if she'd find Ben there.

But he wasn't.

And that's always when she woke up.

Chapter Thirty

Late Sunday afternoon, Ben had just racked up the balls to shoot another game of pool—by himself, how pathetic—when his dogs started barking. By the time he reached the door to check out the ruckus, he was looking through the door into his brother's faces. Quinn, and Chase, with Gavin behind them. And off to the left, Dalton.

He had a bad feeling about this. He quieted the dogs. "Did someone die?"

Quinn shook his head and came inside.

Ben asked, "Did I forget I was throwing a party?"

Chase shook his head and came inside.

"Is this about the sale of the Wetzler place?" Ben asked.

Gavin shook his head and came inside.

But Ben blocked Dalton from coming in. "Did you do this?"

Dalton gave him a somber look. "Yes."

"Who else did you tell?"

"Just them." Dalton shouldered past and Ben let him.

No words were exchanged as outerwear was discarded. Everyone wandered to the TV area instead of the bar.

Ben's heart thundered in his temples. He felt his cheeks burning as he joined them, sitting in the chair furthest away from his family.

"So, Dalton, you gonna tell us why we're here? And why you think Ben needs an intervention?" Quinn asked.

Dalton wiped his hands on his jeans. When he realized the action hinted at nerves, he folded his arms across his chest. "Ben's never been one to talk about the women in his life. He's always says that a gentleman never kisses and tells, which never rang true for me, because all guys brag on the chicks they're banging. Then I couldn't remember the last time I saw Ben out at the bar or heard about him on a date with a woman. I thought it was weird he drove to his buddy's bar in Gillette. That made me wonder if Ben was gay and hidin' it.

"That also made me wonder if the bar in Gillette was a gay hangout, especially since not one person in our family has ever been there. After the bullshit with us not getting the Wetzler place, and the rumors I'd heard from Jenny that Ben was involved with the president of the new bank, well, I suspected if he was gay he'd slept with her just to get a loan."

Dalton had a high opinion of him.

"I call bullshit on that, Dalton," Chase snapped. "Ben ain't the type of guy to use women and discard them."

"That just shows how much you *don't* know about him. See, I went to the Rawhide Bar Friday night. Dropped Ben's name and I was escorted to a different door. A private club. A sex club. But the thing I saw that knocked me to my knees? My cousin using a whip on not one, but two different women. Women who were tied up so they couldn't get away. These woman begged him to stop and he didn't. He just kept hurting them."

Ben studied his hands in the silence.

"That's why I called you guys. Ben's out of control. He's got a problem with violence against women. I know a violent streak runs in the McKay family. Brandt struggles with it. Kane and Colt deal with it by beatin' the shit out of each other. I figured Quinn had it in your family. Makes me sick to think Ben's had it all this time and we didn't notice. Add in the kinky sex stuff I saw? And it's all kinds of wrong. We need to intervene and get him away from that kinda behavior. We need to help him." Dalton finally looked at Ben pleadingly. "If my dad, who's been a binge drinker his whole life, can admit at his age that he's got a problem, I know we can find a way to help you."

He'd be touched by Dalton's concern if he wasn't so fucking mad. If he wasn't so fucking mortified he'd have to look his brothers in the eye and admit, yes, part of what Dalton said was true.

Ben expected silence as his brothers tried to process Dalton's accusations.

But Quinn started to laugh. His older brother, who defined restrained, laughed so hysterically tears rolled down his face. He laughed so hard he doubled over on the couch. He'd look up at Dalton, then at Ben, and cackle, giggle and wheeze with laughter.

Not the reaction Ben had predicted.

Finally, Quinn calmed down. He wiped his eyes. He addressed

Dalton, who'd taken a seat during Quinn's laughing fit. "I understand your concern, okay? I don't know how I would've reacted seein' Ben in that situation. But you've taken it totally out of context."

"Bullshit."

"So you ever been to a bar or a club in a big city like what you seen in Gillette?"

"That don't matter. This ain't about me."

"You're laying all Ben's secrets bare. I'm expecting the same thing from you."

"Fine. Whatever."

"You've lied about how many women you've fucked, haven't you?"

Dalton squirmed. "Huh-uh."

"Come on, Dalton. Admit bein' a McKay sometimes makes you feel you've gotta live up to that man-whore reputation," Quinn cajoled. "You ain't the stud you pretend to be are you?"

Took a solid minute, but Dalton blushed and shook his head.

"How old are you again?"

"Twenty-four."

"You're awful damn naïve," Chase answered. "I wish you'da told us your suspicions besides the vague *Ben needs help and he's too proud to admit he has a problem* line that got us to haul ass to Wyoming."

"Wait," Ben inserted. "Dalton didn't tell you guys anything?"

Gavin said, "No. Just that it was urgent and Ben's brothers needed to intervene."

Ben wasn't sure which shocked him more; that they'd all come, including Gavin, or that they hadn't questioned *why* they should come.

"Why aren't you guys takin' this seriously?" Dalton demanded. "It's some heavy shit."

Quinn lifted a brow at Ben. "I'm sure you would've preferred to keep this quiet as you have for years, but given the circumstances, you wanna explain? In plain terms so Mr. Naïve over there gets a decent grasp on it?"

"I'm what's called a sexual dominant. That means in sex play, I'm in charge. But in order to be dominant I need a submissive. A submissive chooses to give herself, her body, her will, to the Dom. A Dom does not take what isn't offered. There isn't rape. There isn't

287

torture. At least not in my scenes. I don't expect my subs to be lifestyle subs twenty-four/seven. I'm a Dom strictly in sexual situations." He gave Dalton a pointed look. "With women."

Dalton had the grace to be flustered.

"On the surface, the Dom/sub relationship is about sex. And I ain't gonna lie, the sex is what drew me to it. It still does. That exchange of power is heady stuff. But when I'm in my dominant role, I'm completely attuned to my sub. To her needs, her fears, her pleasure."

"How long have you been a dominant?" Quinn asked.

"Officially? About eight years."

"But what about the whippings?" Dalton blurted out. "That ain't right."

"That's not for you to judge." Ben looked at his brothers. "What bothered Dalton was I wasn't sexually involved with those submissives. Because it's not always about sex. I used the single tail whip on the sub at the request of the sub's Dom. That Dom decides when I stop."

Chase asked, "Do you do that a lot?"

"Whip another Dom's sub? Only because they know I'm awful damn good with a whip. The new Doms learn from me. Some Doms don't like usin' the single tail but their sub really gets off on it. So I fill a need."

"So you like beatin' on women," Dalton said.

Snapping at his clueless cousin would serve no purpose. "Only if they ask me real nice."

"That ain't funny."

Gavin laughed. "Yes, it is. I'm getting quite the education. I'm impressed, Ben. Shocked, but relieved."

"Not me. I sort of suspected," Chase said, "when I noticed instruments of the trade Ben accidentally left on his bar last summer. And the missus says sometimes when she looks into Ben's eyes, she has the urge to do whatever he tells her."

Ben's eyebrows went up. "Ava said that? Really?"

"Yep. Now I'm wonderin' if you can teach me that trick." Chase smiled slyly. "Because, bro, the 'be a man' advice really worked."

"He gave you the 'be a man' advice? Hell, when me'n Libby were havin' problems he told me I needed to romance her. Be a different man than I'd been."

"And it worked, didn't it?" Chase said.

"Best thing I ever did."

"Maybe when I'm not so pissed that I took my marriage vows seriously and my ex-wife did not, and I'm ready to dip a toe into the dating pool, I'll come to you for advice, Ben."

That acceptance, coupled with the fact Gavin had flown up here out of concern, was sort of an olive branch. "Sure. Will I be giving the advice over the phone? Or in person over at the B&B?"

"Only time will answer that question."

"So what now?" Dalton asked Quinn, Chase and Gavin. "I'm the village idiot because I didn't know this was...what did you call it? A lifestyle? A real lifestyle out of the movies and shit. You guys are on board with Ben's *whole tie 'em up, whip 'em and fuck 'em* attitude toward women?"

Ben ran his hands through his hair. "What do you want from me, Dalton? I don't talk about this part of my life. I don't need your acceptance or your approval. I just need your promise this won't go any farther than you. I don't want members of the McKay family lookin' at me like I'm an abuser. Or wondering if the woman I'm with has no self-esteem because she is submissive to me in the bedroom."

"Fine. I ain't gonna tell anyone, because Christ, who'd believe me?" Dalton stood, confusion warring on his face, looking like a twelve-year-old boy who'd just watched his first porn flick.

"What?" Ben asked wearily.

"Are you pissed that I told them?"

I'm more pissed about the shitty things you said to me regarding the land deal. "I'll get over it. Eventually."

"Well, that's...good, I guess. I'll see you around." Dalton practically ran out.

Ben sort of felt sorry for him. Sort of.

Quinn stepped behind the bar. Ben sat on the barstool between Gavin and Chase. Which was strange because Ben usually kept the bar as a buffer between himself and those he served.

Maybe that's an indication of how you view the world.

"Drinks all around, boys," Quinn said lining up four shot glasses and filling them with Scotch. He raised his glass. Paused. "What the hell are we drinking to?"

"To Dalton bein' a dumbass," Chase drawled.

They laughed and clinked their glasses together.

Gavin motioned for Quinn to set 'em up again. "As much as you won't apologize for the lifestyle you lead behind closed doors, I won't apologize for buying Rielle's place. So if you want to berate me, go ahead. But I don't want it to be a point of contention between us forever, Ben."

"I've no interest in beatin' that horse anymore. It's dead. And buried."

"Fair enough."

"I can't believe you all showed up." Ben looked at Chase and Gavin. "Do Mom and Dad know you're here?"

"Nah. We didn't wanna worry them. Now that we know you ain't some psycho killer, we'll probably just take off without telling them. It'll stay between us."

Ben fiddled with his full shot glass. "Ah, thanks."

"I'll admit it's a slippery concept to grasp, pain as foreplay. But as long as I don't gotta watch you in action? It ain't none of my business," Chase said.

"In all seriousness. The reason I laughed so fucking hard when Dalton said you were outta control? Because I know you, Ben. I work with you every goddamn day. You have more control, more cool-headedness and more compassion, in any situation, than anyone I know."

Ben had no idea what to say to that.

They bullshitted about nothing. But it didn't seem forced. Or like they were all trying to avoid the elephant in the room.

Quinn and Chase took off, cracking jokes about examining Ben's collection of chains, whips and sex toys. Ben would've been worried if they hadn't given him a rash of shit about being a pervert.

But Gavin wasn't in a hurry to leave.

"So was Sierra covered in body piercings when you picked her up a few weeks back?"

"No. Luckily for her mother. She's a piece of work. It's no wonder I steer clear of anything resembling a date."

"Your ex-wife has ruined you for all other women?"

"Christ, she'd have a field day thinking she still had that much power over me." Gavin sighed. "I just don't have the...hell if I know. Desire? Patience? Time? Balls? My excuses change every week. It isn't so much Ellen's fault anymore as it is I find reasons not to meet women, let alone get mixed up with one." He sipped the Scotch. "What about you? Still involved with that new banker?"

Ben shot him a sideways glance. "Bein' involved with Ainsley wasn't common knowledge, so where'd you hear it?"

"Rielle said her car was here a lot."

"Yeah, well, it's over."

"Why? Because you came clean to her about your club life as a dominant?"

How did he phrase this and keep Ainsley's experimentation as a sub a secret?

Gavin whistled. "She's into the life too, isn't she? I'm guessing she's your sub?"

"She *was* my sub."

"For how long?"

Not nearly long enough. "A month."

"She ended it?"

"Yeah."

"So what if she wouldn't have?"

"I'd still be with her. The ironic thing about Dalton seeing me at the club? I hadn't been there for the month I'd been with Ainsley. As I walked around? I felt nothing. I just fucking missed her. Missed who I was with her." And it all poured out. "Since the night I met her I felt our relationship would be different. Club subs want good times and the anything-goes sex. Bringing them out of that world and into mine wouldn't work. But Ainsley...works. She's smart and sexy. She challenges me. She gets me. She goes from bein' the bank prez, to hanging out with me, to bein' my sub, all in one night. Almost seamlessly. She's amazing."

"So what did you do to fuck it up?"

"She's the bank president. No one can know she associates with lowlife sexual degenerates like me who belong to the Rawhide Club," he said with a slightly bitter edge.

Gavin shook his head and chuckled.

"What?"

"You. All 'I'm the dominant, I'm in charge', and yet, here you are, moping around in your house with your dogs. You're not that guy, Ben. *I'm* that guy and trust me, it's beyond fucking pathetic. So I'm going to mimic the 'be a man' advice you gave our brothers. If you want this woman for the long haul, make it happen. Screw the club. You haven't needed it the last month, you don't need it now. Play with her here. Or at her place. Set your own rules. Or change the rules."

Ben was as flustered by the admonishment as he was by Gavin's admission of brotherly ties. "It's not that easy."

Or was it?

Chapter Thirty-One

Ben had come inside from cleaning out the cattle truck when she burst through his front door. The dogs went berserk. Barking and jumping until she threw two rawhide chews out the door and slammed it shut behind them.

Christ. His mother was mad as a wet hen. She angrily pulled off her purple gloves finger by finger. Only after she'd shed the outer layer did she seem calm enough to speak. "Hello, son."

"Mom. It'd be nice if you didn't banish my dogs from their home every time you come over."

"Those mutts belong outside. I'll take a cup of coffee if it's fresh."

He poured a cup, refilled his mug and faced her.

"You look like hell, Bennett."

"Gee, thanks. What brings you by?"

"This and that."

She curled her hands around the coffee mug and wandered to the kitchen window, appearing to gather her thoughts.

Not good.

Finally she looked at him. "I heard something a little disturbing today."

His gut roiled. Goddamn Dalton. Hadn't he stressed the importance of keeping his big mouth shut? Was it a coincidence that one day after Dalton's accusations, Ben's mother showed up, hot under the collar? How was he supposed to look her in the eye when she questioned him about the rumor? Would she be disappointed? Would she ask where she'd gone wrong raising him?

Ben managed a nonchalant, "What did you hear?"

She blew across her cup, expecting him to fess up like a ten-year-old boy.

Not happening.

She sighed. "Tell me about the woman you took out for lunch last week."

Why did she give a rip about that?

"Just answer the damn question, Bennett."

He was punchy if he hadn't realized he'd uttered that out loud. His thoughts backtracked. Last week? Right. A last minute lunch with his client from Jackson Hole who'd been driving through town to give him an overdue payment. "You mean Dani? She's a friend. That's it."

"That's it?" she mimicked. "You move fast, which I find disturbing."

This conversation wasn't about Dalton's intervention? His relief was short lived.

"What happened between you and Ainsley? Weren't you two an item just last week? Because I like her."

I like her too. A lot. In fact, I fell in love with her.

"Bennett?"

"Ah, well, it's sort of complicated and—"

"What did you do to her?"

Ben's gaze hooked hers. "Me? Why does the problem have to be from my end?"

His mother rolled her eyes. "Because you're a McKay."

"Like that makes me a defective man or something?"

"Watch your tone, Mister," she warned. "It's my job as your mother to find out if you're being a jackass to the only decent woman to come into your life in years."

He snorted.

"Were you trying to make Ainsley jealous by having lunch with another woman? Right under her nose?"

Jesus. Was his mother on crack? "I'm tired of everyone in this family poking their nose into my personal business—"

"Bennett Andrew McKay." Her cup hit the counter and liquid sloshed everywhere. "My God. Sometimes your pigheadedness is astounding."

Thoroughly reprimanded, Ben sponged up the mess with a paper towel and waited for the lecture, because guaranteed she had one prepared.

"You brought Ainsley to our attention, by inviting her to a family party. I drive by your house every day. I know she's been an overnight guest." She peered at him over the tops of her glasses. "On many occasions. I'm pretty sure you two weren't playing Parcheesi."

He blushed. Goddammit. He never blushed.

"So I'm a big enough person to admit my visit the weekend you were sick—and don't get me started on how I had to find out that my own son was sick from Rielle—was to check this woman out for myself. Because heaven knows *you'd* never tell me if you were involved with someone. But when I asked her, she insisted there wasn't anything between you."

Why did that sting?

"Of course I didn't believe her. So when Carolyn called me today because she saw you cozied up to that ex-stripper last week—"

"Dani is not a stripper!"

"Hence the term *ex*-stripper." She drained her coffee and lifted an eyebrow. "Not going to deny it?"

Ben counted to fifteen. "Mom. What does this have to do with anything? Why are you here?"

"To meddle, naturally."

"Doesn't Dad get after you for that? I thought you promised to knock that crap off."

"Ah ah ah. I promised no more meddling in Quinn and Libby's life. Chase and Ava aren't around enough for me to meddle. So that leaves you, my dear middle son, as my man in the meddle."

"Great."

"So no bullshit. What happened between you and Ainsley?"

Defeated, and tired of playing the denial game, he ducked his face from her probing gaze. "We were involved but she..." *Brought everything inside me alive. Created hope in me I hadn't felt in years. Then she validated my biggest fear: no woman I wanted would ever want me, as I am, long-term.*

"Bennett. Look at me please."

Maybe he'd gotten his Dom tendencies from his mother, not his father. He glanced up and she was standing in front of him. "Oh, son, come here." She opened her arms and Ben walked into her embrace without hesitation. He might tower over her now, but her hugs hadn't changed from when he was a little boy. There was fierceness in her hugs. Protectiveness. Unconditional love. Funny how he'd forgotten that. Ironic how she'd known he'd needed the reminder.

"You are a good man. If she can't see that..." She eased back and fussed with his collar. "Then she's a blind fool."

"Thanks."

Ben expected her to leave. But she chatted away about Adam and Amelia's latest antics. His father's upcoming birthday. Chase and Ava. Quinn and Libby. Gavin and his daughter. The situation with Casper. When she talked about tattoos, Ben tuned her out. He had a shit ton to do and daylight was wasting.

"And so I have to go...but I have a confession to make. There's another reason I stopped by today."

Here it comes.

"I don't want you to get upset if I pursue a friendship with Ainsley."

His jaw dropped. "What? How can you be buddy-buddy with a woman you just called a blind fool?" *With the woman who rejected me?*

"Because she and I have a lot in common. Besides, I've been trying to widen my social circle. Vaudette can be such a self-righteous pain in the patootie."

Typical of his mother to carry on three conversations at once and expect him to follow each one. What the devil did her best friend Vaudette Dickens have to do with anything? Wait. Was she trying to tell him something? "When did you talk to Ainsley?"

"I had lunch with her today."

Stunned, he just stared at her.

"I got the impression she's looking for people to connect with outside her job as bank president." She shrugged on her coat. "Sounds like she's under a lot of stress. She'll be busy in the next six months trying to bring new business into National West."

So Ainsley hadn't lost her job? A weird, wonderful kind of hope began to overtake his feeling of defeat. If Ainsley was living in Sundance, he had a chance with her. Until he remembered why he didn't have a chance with her.

His mother clucked her tongue. "The poor girl sounded so lonely."

That tore at him. "How the hell can she be lonely?" Ben demanded. "When up until last week, she was with me most nights for the past four weeks?"

"Why are you asking me? Maybe you should trot yourself to town and ask her. Because God knows, I would never hear the end of it if I poked my nose into your personal business."

Unreal.

His mother threw a gaudy sequined scarf over her shoulder like a Hollywood diva. She placed her hands on Ben's cheeks and stood on tiptoe to peck him on the mouth. "I love you. So here's some advice, and please don't take this the wrong way. You are a strong, independent man. A good man. A man who deserves happiness. But don't be a stubborn man. It doesn't make you weak to want to rely on someone or to want someone in your life who understands you fully. Who accepts you completely. Who gives you something you can't get from anyone else. Everything in life is about compromise. If it's worth it, you'll change to get it. Changing things about your life that don't fit who you are anymore doesn't mean you have to change who you are inside."

He stared at her with his mouth hanging open.

"It's scary how well I know you, isn't it, son? We're a lot alike." She laughed. "And that absolutely horrifies you, doesn't it?"

The door slammed behind her and she yelled at his dogs before she sped off.

Smart woman, his mother. Between her advice, and Gavin's, he'd finally found the answer he'd been looking for.

Without changing clothes, without giving himself a chance to change his mind, he jumped in his truck and headed for Gillette.

Chapter Thirty-Two

Late Tuesday morning Layla showed up at the bank, practically spitting fire.

As soon as Ainsley shut her office door, Layla was in her face. "What did you do to Bennett?"

"Me? Nothing." Panic surfaced. "Why? What happened to him? Is he all right?"

"No, he's not all right. He resigned from the Rawhide Club."

Her stomach lurched. "He did? When?"

"Last night." Layla poked her in the chest. "We're friends, A, but if you did something to hurt him, I swear I'll—"

"Hold up. Why do you assume it was something I did?"

"Because he told me it was."

"Sit and start from the beginning."

Layla flopped into the chair. "I just happened to be at the club last night."

"The club was open last night?"

"No. The guys have a meeting every couple months to deal with schedules, new members, any problems. Ben showed up, which he almost never does. But he looked awful. He had bags under his eyes. I think he came in wearing cow-poop-covered clothes. That isn't the Bennett I know. He gave no input during the meeting. As soon as it ended, he stood and announced he was canceling his membership. He'd appreciated their friendship and support over the years, but sometimes a man had to make a choice and he'd made his."

Ainsley couldn't believe her ears. "What did the other guys—his friends—say?"

"What could they say? They were stunned. So I followed Bennett out to his truck and asked him why he was leaving the club. He said being with you changed his life."

Anger rose. Bennett could tell Layla that, but not her?

You have no right to the anger. You gave him no choice but to keep his feelings from you when you told him it was over.

Layla tapped on the desk to get her attention. "Tell me what happened between you two."

Despite her distraction, Ainsley gave Layla the rundown. She tried for detachment in the telling, but by the time she finished, the pressure and misery from the past couple of days nearly had her in tears.

"So everything with him was all just an experiment to you and you can just walk away like nothing happened?"

"No!" She jabbed her finger at Layla. "You're the one who said I should give the club a try. I did. You're the one who said I should embrace my sexuality. I did. It was supposed to be one weekend out of my life and nothing more."

"But it wasn't enough, was it?" Layla said softly. "I had nothing to do with you agreeing to be Bennett's sub, outside the club for a month. So don't pretend you were coerced."

"I know that, Layla. I'm not denying it. I've learned...I've accepted that I prefer to be submissive when it comes to sex."

"But?"

"But after seeing how I jeopardized my job with one misstep, regarding Ben, I knew it had to end. All of it." *Even when I didn't want it to.*

"Why? What you do in a private club isn't anyone's business but yours."

"Wrong. What would happen if my coworkers or bosses found out I'm a sexual submissive? That I do whatever Bennett demands of me, without question? That I'm involved with a man who's a sexual dominant at a sex club? And please don't tell me it doesn't matter because it does. Maybe not in all lines of work, but definitely in this one and definitely in this part of the country. And Bennett keeps the Dom side of himself hidden from his family and friends too, so it's not just me who knows the risks of our preferences becoming common knowledge."

Ainsley sank back in her chair.

"I get that, A, but don't you see how much Bennett cares about you? He's removing the big obstacle that prevents you two from being together."

"I don't want that burden from him."

"Too bad, you've got it," Layla snapped, "and now you have to deal with it. So tell me how you plan to?"

Stung, she retorted, "How long do you think before Bennett gets bored with me and misses the sexual variety that defined his time as a Dom at the Rawhide?"

"Bennett has always been very committed to the club. Making it a place where everyone who's a member is comfortable because he struggled for years with accepting who he was as a Dom. So for him to walk away for good? I know he's even more committed to making this work with you."

That brought tears to her eyes again. "Damn him. I didn't want this."

"Didn't want what?"

Didn't want to fall for him.

"Ainsley, do you love him?"

Yes. "What if my feelings are from the sex that rocks my world? What if I've latched onto the convenience of being with Ben because he lives here? What if I've confused submission with love?"

"What if it is love and you're making all these lame excuses because you don't believe you can fall in love in a month?" Layla countered.

"That's not it."

"Then are you worried Bennett will expect you to become a lifestyle sub like me if you're outside the club?"

She remembered exchanging harsh words about that very thing the last night they'd seen each other. "No. I know that's not what he wants. But hearing that he's leaving the club—"*makes me hopeful that maybe we have a chance, "—*makes me wonder if he feels pressured to do it."

"Bennett is a force all his own. He doesn't do a damn thing he doesn't want to. He is willingly walking away from the club because he wants you, A, for the long haul. He found something more meaningful than he was getting with random hookups at the club. He found it with you." She shook her finger at Ainsley. "But don't for a second think he'll become some pussified girly man because he's no longer wielding a whip at the Rawhide. Bennett is a Dom through and through. That part of him won't change. Ever. He'll still want a sexual Dom/sub relationship with you, and not temporarily this time."

"I don't want that part of him to change."

"Good." A long sigh echoed. "I know you, Ainsley. Don't talk yourself out of what could be the best thing that's ever happened to you because you're scared."

"I *am* scared. Aren't you the one who warned me not to fall for Bennett because he wasn't a long-term guy? You told me I'd be an idiot for taking up with the first Dom I met."

Layla leveled her with an uncompromising stare. "I was wrong. I can admit it. Can you?" She stood. "Don't be an idiot. Accept him as he is. Accept yourself for what you are to him. Accept what you two can have together."

Ainsley watched Layla flounce out of her office. Her friend's words swirling around in her head.

Accept him as he is.

Accept yourself for what you are to him.

Bennett made no apologies about who he was. He'd given her all of himself while helping her get in tune with a side of herself she hadn't acknowledged. He'd respected her boundaries, even while pushing them at every opportunity.

And now she wanted to bring those boundaries back in because *she* was scared? She wanted to use what he was—unapologetically sexually dominant—against him because she was freaked out about what she'd discovered about herself?

Why couldn't she just accept that she admired the sexual woman she'd become because of Bennett? She liked that he challenged her. She liked handing control to him, knowing he'd never abuse it. She liked how he looked at her, not only the admiring gazes he gave her body, but when he locked his eyes to hers and seemed to see into her soul. He saw the real her. He acknowledged the woman she was—in and out of the bedroom—not just as who she was as his submissive.

Ainsley let her head fall back and stared at the ceiling.

So what to do now?

Call Ben and share the news she hadn't gotten canned?

Confess she'd fallen in love with him? Not only as Bennett the Dom, but as Ben the man? That she wanted them both?

Or would he believe her confession was only a knee-jerk reaction to her relief at not losing her job?

Or would he think she'd only come to him because he'd quit the Rawhide Club?

Don't think about it now. Get back to work.

But the rest of the afternoon was a total wash.

So many thoughts bounced in her brain, she pled a headache to her staff and shut off the lights in her office. Her mind kept drifting to sex, specifically the night she'd shown up at Ben's house to seduce him with plain old vanilla sex. Intending to prove they didn't need foreplay in the form of ropes, cuffs, vibrators or restraints. They could get naked, roll around between the sheets, until hungry kisses and fevered touches weren't enough. Then Ben could pin her body beneath his and gaze into her eyes as he slowly slipped inside her. Loving her as fiercely and hotly as he always did.

It could've happened that way.

But it hadn't.

He'd gotten off. She'd gotten off. It wasn't bad sex; it just wasn't great sex.

Afterward, she laid beside him, feeling like she used to before, during, and after sex—awkward. Anxious. Self-conscious.

Then his hot body had spooned behind hers, because he'd sensed her retreat and he hadn't allowed it. "So while that was fun, what the hell has gotten into you, Ainsley?"

"I came here to prove I can seduce you. We can have sex anytime we want without all the kinky accoutrements."

"And?"

"And I realized I couldn't have seduced you if you hadn't let me."

He'd laughed. "You accept that I'm a Dom, but you're still fighting the idea you're submissive."

A statement. "Maybe. When I'm with you, when we're in the moment, I don't think about anything but how you make me feel or how much my surrender pleases you. But when I'm by myself, or at work, those feelings of...wrongness pop up. Like there's something wrong with me for loving when you dominate me. There's something wrong with me for liking that you use cuffs, ropes and handcuffs on me. There's something wrong with me for wanting to get my butt paddled or to feel the flogger on my skin or the riding crop connecting with my flesh. I wonder why I can't be satisfied with—"

"Vanilla sex?" he supplied.

"Yes. Then when we have vanilla sex...it's not as satisfying and I wonder why I want to give up fantastic sex because what we do behind closed bedroom doors isn't the norm."

"It's a vicious circle, angel."

Then he'd just held her. Stroked her. Let her wrestle with her thoughts, until she'd asked, "Does the level of kink increase the longer a Dom/sub are together?"

"I wouldn't know." He'd placed a soft kiss behind her ear. "You're the first woman who's tempted me to find out."

That's when she'd squirmed away and reminded him she'd only signed on for a month.

That's when he'd grabbed her, pinned her, tied her up and fucked her twice, reminding her that the month wasn't up yet.

It hit her then. Ben had been telling her before the loan fiasco, before her disastrous plan to force him into just accepting her friendship, before walking away from the club...that he'd wanted more with her.

And she wanted more with him. She wanted it all.

After all he'd shown her, after all he'd been to her, and now proving—in his typical Dom way—what he wanted to be to her, did she really think she could let him go?

No.

Hell no.

She gathered her things and left the bank early.

Ben's truck wasn't in his driveway.

And where were his pesky dogs?

Maybe his truck was in the shop and he'd let the dogs in his haven since it was so cold outside. She shivered as snowflakes whirled around her head and she sought shelter in his woodshop.

Although he'd gotten pissy the one time she'd violated his woodworking sanctuary, she hoped he'd forgive her today.

But what if her making the first move wasn't enough?

Shoving aside her doubts, Ainsley marched through the door. "Ben? Are you in here? We need to talk."

No answer.

She flipped on the lights. No sign of him. She knew he hadn't been in recently because the woodstove was cold. So Ainsley snooped. Animal skins of different colors and textures hung on the wall. Three barrels filled with a smelly solution lined the back wall and she vaguely remembered him talking about the process of tanning hides.

In the main room, various pieces of finished furniture were lined up, ready for assembly. She ran her hands into the grooves his hands had created. The man was amazingly talented. No wonder she'd believed his loan request; he could easily turn his hobby into a fulltime business, despite his claims of just being a simple rancher.

Several hand-carved pieces were spread on the long workbench that looked like toppers for bedposts and chairs. A few wooden sculptures were in different phases of completion. She recognized a small bird, a thick stem of a flower. Another funky cat. She let her fingers trace the jagged edges, not bothering to hold back her tears when she saw three shelves full of finished pieces. All these beautiful works of art were just lying around, gathering dust, not out in view where they could be admired. Cherished. He'd hidden this part of himself from his family too. Was there anyone who knew all sides of Bennett McKay?

You do.

That's when every doubt vanished. When Ainsley understood she'd do whatever it took to have Ben in her life. To make him understand that she appreciated and celebrated everything about him. Everything he was.

When she exited the building she noticed another car had parked in the drive. Pulling her coat more securely against the Wyoming wind, she hustled toward the house. She looked up when the front door slammed.

Rielle stared back at her. "Ainsley."

"Rielle."

"Ben's not around."

"So I gathered." She glanced at the keys dangling from Rielle's hand. "What are you doing here?"

"Bein' neighborly." Rielle smirked. "Oh, it gets your panties in a twist that I have a key to his house and you don't, doesn't it?"

Ainsley bit back a retort.

"I see the venom in your eyes. So why don't you ask me if there's anything going on between me and Ben."

"Fine. What the hell is going on between you and Ben?"

"Not a damn thing." Rielle paused. "Because the man is in love with you."

Ainsley couldn't breathe.

"I see you're surprised to hear that."

She nodded.

"You're both idiots," Rielle muttered. "That makes me marginally less pissed off at you."

"Why would you be pissed off at me? Because you've had your eye on him?"

Rielle rolled her eyes. "Are you kidding me? Ben is a great guy but I've never had any interest in him."

"Still not understanding why you would be mad at me."

"Because I knew you two were sneaking around. I recognized something was going on between you two the first day at the bank. I watched you two having lunch at Fields. Ben couldn't take his eyes off you. When he held your hand? And you shook him off when I approached? I figured you didn't want the Sundance townsfolk to know the new bank president was getting down and dirty with a local rancher. So yeah, I blamed you."

"Our reasons for keeping our relationship quiet are private. And since you don't know me, maybe I understand why you'd jump to the worst conclusion first. But you are wrong."

"Ben is a very private guy. He rarely has female overnight guests. So the fact you were here all the damn time?" Rielle shook her head, sending her baby-fine blonde hair flying against the bitterly cold wind. "I knew it wasn't casual. And I like Ben. He's a good guy. I don't want to see him get hurt. He deserves a woman who isn't embarrassed to be seen with him."

"Well, I am that woman." Ainsley didn't need to prove it to Rielle; she needed to prove it to Ben.

They measured one another.

"So where is he?"

Rielle's eyes narrowed. "Why don't you know where he is?"

"Because Ben and I had a...fight and I haven't talked to him since last week."

"You're here to kiss and make up?"

Snoopy thing, aren't you Mrs. Kravitz?

Rielle laughed. "Mrs. Kravitz? Did you really just compare me to the nosy, annoying neighbor from *Bewitched*?"

Ainsley notched her chin higher, because she hadn't meant to say that out loud. "Yes."

"Seeing how protective you are of Ben might make me change my mind about you."

Oh, goodie. That's what she needed. Rielle's approval.

"The McKays are taking cattle to market. He's supposed to be home Friday night."

So much for getting this all straightened out today.

"Did your fight with Ben have anything to do with the land issues coming to a head?"

"Land issues?" Ainsley repeated.

"Him and his cousins made a fair play for my land by offering to catch up my payments at Settler's First. I appreciated Ben's offer. But Gavin's was better."

Ainsley squinted at her. "Wait a second. I'm confused."

Rielle explained and Ainsley felt guiltier and guiltier. Ben been dealing with such a shit storm in his life the last night they'd seen each other and she hadn't noticed. She'd just added to it.

"But it was the best way for me to save face, keep out of bankruptcy and not be beholden to a McKay."

Her gaze snapped up. Had she said that to Ben? Impugned his family name? "You are talking about Ben's brother Gavin, right?"

"Yes. But he isn't anything like the rest of them."

"Didn't your decision cause problems between you and Ben?"

She tossed her head. "Yes, Ben is pissy with me. Which is why I came over and checked on his place. It's a neighborly thing. You wouldn't understand."

Ainsley wasn't about to back down. "I understand perfectly. You're expecting the betrayal of your friendship with him will just go away if you show up with a pan of homemade muffins? Wrong." She held her hand out. "Give me the damn key."

"But—"

"Right now." Surprisingly, Rielle slapped it in her hand. Then

Ainsley got in her face. "Go home. Your relationship with Ben will never be the same."

"Because of you? Now that you're in the picture you're warning me off?"

"I'm telling you that I know Ben on a level you never will. You were his friend. And now you're just another person in a long line of people who have used and hurt him. Well, guess what, Rielle? I'll never be that person. Ever. And yes, I plan on being in the picture for a long, damn time. So get used to it."

Rielle didn't utter a word. She drove off.

Ainsley would make it right with Ben, no matter what she had to do.

She called Layla on her way home. "I've been thinking a lot about what you said today. Yes. I agree." She laughed. "Well, funny you should ask...I need a huge favor."

Chapter Thirty-Three

Dead tired after four days of loading cattle, taking them to market, and making the drive back, all Ben wanted was a shot of whiskey, a hot shower and a solid night's sleep.

And his soft Ainsley curled beside him.

Might as well wish for a million bucks.

Ben trudged to his front door and shoved his key in the lock. Ace and Deuce saw something by the barn and raced off. After being cooped up in the truck for the past few days, the dogs needed to lose their rowdiness before the impending blizzard restricted their antics indoors.

He knew he'd loaded enough wood in the outside stack by the backdoor to last through the storm. Absentmindedly he shucked his outerwear and piled it by the chair. He'd expected the house to be cold, so the fire burning in the woodstove shocked him. As did the stack of split logs filling the woodbin. He noticed a flash of red out of the corner of his eye and whipped his head toward the kitchen.

Ben had never understood the phrase gob smacked until he saw Ainsley perched on his kitchen counter. In the same clothes she'd worn at the club the first night he'd met her.

Then he had the overwhelming fear this was a fantasy playing out in his mind as he snoozed in the truck.

His breath stalled. His heart raced, every beat a two-part recitation of her name. Nothing existed in that blur of space known as the universe except for her.

A primal voice inside his head roared *mine.*

Ben erased the distance separating them. He didn't say a word. He didn't take the kiss he craved. He simply grabbed her by the hips and threw her over his shoulder.

She shrieked, "Oh my God, Bennett, what are you doing?"

"Hush." He swatted her ass as he marched to his bedroom. "We're gonna have this out right now. But since you showed up on my turf, my rules apply."

"Your rules always apply, no matter where we are."

"True." He tossed her on the bed. Before she could scramble away, he pounced on her, pinning her flat to the mattress. Her arms above her head, his knees by her hips to keep her from bucking.

"I cannot believe you just dumped me on the bed—"

"Yes, you can." He inhaled a deep breath, bringing her scent inside him, allowing it to calm him. "You're here." *Brilliant observation.* "How did you get in?"

"Rielle gave up her key. For good."

"*Why* are you here?"

Ainsley tried to act put out, but she couldn't quite pull it off. "I came to grovel, but I figured the beastly Dom would take it the wrong way if he came home and found me naked on my knees."

Ben smiled. "You know me so well." He watched as her eyes turned somber. "I know you too, angel. Talk to me. Start from that night when everything went to hell between us."

"I'm sorry. I was damn near hysterical at the thought of losing my job when you came to see me."

"You blamed me." Not a question.

She nodded. "Made it worse when you admitted you lied to me."

"I know, baby. I'm sorry too. I never should've applied for the loan through National West. It all turned to shit anyway, but I regret putting you through that. Regret putting us both through that."

"I wanted to hurt you back. So I stupidly made a couple of horrible accusations, and I am so, so sorry."

He'd felt like he'd been gut shot that night. Knowing he loved her and he'd probably lost her for opening up to her. For hoping she'd accept him, everything about him and having her reject him.

"Yet, you tried to make it right. You tried to tell me you attempted to fix it by withdrawing the loan request. But I was too incensed." She swallowed hard. "Too...hurt and too busy lashing out at you to listen to what you were saying."

"You do seem to pay better attention when you're tied up," he murmured.

Ainsley's full lips curved slightly. "You like that far too much,

Bennett."

"No lie." He grinned without shame.

"I missed that smile of yours. I missed you in the last week."

"Did you miss Ben? Or Bennett?"

"I've figured out they're one in the same. I can't have one without the other. I don't want one without the other."

Hope nearly blindsided him and he fought to retain control. Ben released her arms so he could touch her. "I gathered from my mom that you didn't get fired."

Ainsley blinked at him. "Vi? How would she know about my job at the bank?"

"Didn't you have lunch with her on Monday?"

"No. I was in Denver Friday night through Monday. That's why I didn't swing by this weekend and talk about what'd happened. The district manager got pissy after the phone call and forced me and Turton to attend a weekend seminar in Denver about interpersonal team management."

Ben tugged Ainsley upright and took her mouth in a savage kiss. He owned each breath, each exhalation, each tongue tangling thrust. And when he thought his head might explode, he broke his lips free from hers. "That little taste isn't enough."

"Ben—"

"God, woman, I'm dyin' for you, but not until we talk this through. All of it."

"You and that blasted talking." She nuzzled his cheek. "Okay. But let's talk fast. Rielle told me what happened. You should know...I had words with her."

"What kind of words?"

"Words that made it plain I wouldn't stand for her hurting you." Ainsley's fingers were gently scraping against three days worth of beard growth on his face. "I know you, Ben. Her betrayal of your friendship hurt worse than Gavin buying the land."

This woman saw so much, she knew him so much better than he'd imagined.

"Been a rough week for you. I cut you loose. You were let down by your brother and your friend." She paused. "And you resigned from the Rawhide Club."

"News travels fast. Layla must've told you?"

"Told me? No. She confronted me, accused me, and threatened me...so it'd be redundant if I asked why you quit. But I want to know if you're sure you want to quit?"

Ben turned his head and kissed her palm. "I'm positive." When she didn't say anything else, he prompted. "And?"

"And now will you ask me if I'd be here if you hadn't resigned from the club?"

"No. When you told me that we couldn't be together because of what I was—it pissed me off. You knew I was a Dom, you knew that I belonged to a club when we met. It chapped my ass you were using that as an excuse to break it off with me—because you were scared of embracing your submissive nature permanently."

"While that is partially true—"

Ben stopped her protest with his fingers. "But once my anger and pride cleared, I understood it wasn't me bein' a Dom that was the issue. Or you not accepting being submissive. It was the Rawhide Club itself. You weren't passing judgment on it or on people who belong to it. Not on me either. And to some extent, not on yourself."

Her eyes lit up. "You do understand."

"Took me a couple days, and a bad night at the club, but I finally got it."

"A bad night at the club? You went to the club last weekend?" she said sharply.

"Don't look at me like that, angel. I wasn't there for a hookup. After everything came to a head with us, the Rawhide has always been my go-to place for support, consolation, acceptance, whatever. Long story short, my cousin Dalton showed up and his accusations brought out some questions I'd not dealt with for quite a while."

"What kind of questions?"

"Why I needed the club. Why I needed certain aspects of it and not others, which really made me think."

"Are you okay?" Her eyes narrowed. "What accusations did your cousin make? Because you shouldn't have to explain who you are to anyone." She snapped, "Did he threaten to tell your family that you're a Dom? Is that why you resigned from the club?"

He loved how she jumped to his defense. "He told my brothers. Which got Chase and Gavin here right away." Ben still couldn't believe they'd shown up. "We had a talk about that part of my life and they didn't pass judgment."

"I'm glad, Ben. I'm really, really glad for you. That's got to be a huge relief."

"Dalton promised to keep my...proclivities under his hat. But in some ways his questions were good for me. A big reason I kept going to the Rawhide, aside from my friendships with the guys, is I found acceptance. I'd never had that before."

"But now?"

"Now?" His eyes searched hers and his heart rate spiked. "You tell me."

"Tell you what?"

"Why you're here. What you want from me."

Ainsley didn't hold back. "I want it all. More time with you and me together. With you as my Dom. With every part, each facet, all sides of yourself that you want to share with me."

Everything in him that'd been wound tight...loosened. "I hoped you'd want that. "

"I do. More than anything."

"I knew I'd have to choose."

"Choose what?"

"Choose between the club and you."

She went utterly still.

"And I chose you. I've got your acceptance and I don't need to go anywhere else. I'm not giving anything up by leaving the club, Ainsley, I feel like I'm gaining so much more than I'd ever hoped for."

"What are you saying?" she whispered, trailing her fingers across the stubble on his jaw.

Ben's mouth went dry as the words he'd never said to a woman poured from his mouth, from his heart. "I love you."

"Oh. God. Ben."

"I feel whole with you. Before I kept the two halves of myself separated. But when I'm with you, I'm a whole man. I'm the man I want to be. I'm the man I was meant to be. You are everything I've ever wanted in a woman but thought I'd never find. And here you are."

She laughed, sniffing against the tears leaking from the corners of her eyes. "I love you. The whole you. The Dom side. The rancher side.

The intuitive side. The sweet side. The raunchy side."

Ben kissed her with a lingering smooch as he tried to slow the thundering of his heart. "I like who I am when I'm with you, angel."

"Ben."

"I want to be with you. All of you. I want to pick you up at the bank, take you out for lunch and let everyone know we're together. I want to support your community events. I want you to come to my family deals as my woman, not my friend. I want to take you dancing, and horseback riding, and then I want to tie you up, turn your ass pink before I fuck you hard." He traced her jawline. "I want to be with you every damn day. I want this angelic face to be the first thing I see in the morning and the last thing I see at night. If I had my way, I'd move all your stuff over here tonight."

"But?"

"But I understand that you probably wanna take it slow. You're still trying to find your place in a new town. In a new job. In a new type of relationship. I'm just as shocked as you are that so much has happened between us and it's only been a little over a month."

"Seems longer, doesn't it?"

"Mmm-hmm." Ben peered into her eyes. "I'm here whenever you're ready to take that next step. I'm a patient man."

"Except for when you're not."

He smirked. "Well, there is that."

Ainsley pecked him on the lips. "I want to be with you too, Ben. And I know in my heart we will be together, sooner rather than later. But we have a few serious, major things to discuss before that day comes."

Ben didn't like how she'd dropped her gaze. Instead of commanding her to look at him, he tipped her chin up and saw uneasiness swimming in her eyes. "Give me an example of a major thing."

"Like...you're a dog person and I'm a cat person."

"Well, that *is* a deal breaker. Who ever heard of cats and dogs living together in harmony?" Ben chuckled and smooched her nose. "Try again."

"I don't know anything about ranching."

"I don't know anything about banking so that one's a wash too."

"I'm older than you."

"So?"

"So?" she repeated. "I'm the older, clichéd divorced woman."

"It's not like you're the same age as my mother, for Christsake. You've got five years on me." His eyes gleamed. "Since I'm a dog person, let's say that adds seven years on my age, so I'm actually two years older than you."

"You are crazy."

"Yep. Totally crazy for everything about you. So no more excuses, angel, give me a valid reason why we have to have this discussion again at a later date."

Ainsley blurted, "Because I don't want kids. Ever. And it isn't something I'll change my mind on. I know your family is big on big families—"

"Whoa. One of the first things you need to know about me when it comes to my family is that while I love them, I'm not them. I don't follow their lead. I do things my own way. And with the way my cousins are reproducing? There's no chance the McKay family name will die out." He twined a section of her hair around his finger, loving the silken texture against his coarser skin. "Here's something I've never told anyone. I don't want kids either. Never have. Never will. That's another reason the club worked so well for me. It's also why I didn't date much. Most women want a family. I don't. Wasn't fair to enter into a relationship that was goin' nowhere. And like you, it's unlikely I'll ever change my mind."

"For real? You don't want..."

"Nope. The only ass I wanna paddle now and in the future is yours."

She sighed. "You are the perfect man for me, aren't you?"

"Yep."

"So what now?"

He watched how the curve of her breast begged for the touch of his rough-tipped finger.

"Look at me, please."

Bossy little sub. His eyes hooked hers.

"Answer the question."

Ben lifted a brow. "Getting a bit big for your britches. Just because we're talking don't mean you're calling the shots."

"Ben—"

"Bennett," he corrected. "And I've decided you have entirely too many clothes on. Strip."

"Now?"

"It is gonna be so fun reacquainting your ass with my hand," he growled.

"But, there is one other thing I wanted to bring up." She rolled to her feet and stood by the side of the bed. "I hope I'm not overstepping my bounds, but I'd like...I mean, I asked Layla..."

Why was Ainsley so nervous? "Spit it out."

Her eyes roamed his face and she found what she'd been looking for. "I'm not the type of sub to wear a collar. But I want you to know I'm serious about our relationship, knowing my place in your life, and yours in mine. So I thought..." She pulled out two black bracelets from the Rawhide Club. "When I wear mine, I'll know who I am to you. And when you look at yours, you'll know that I accept everything about you. It's a small symbol that we belong to each other. Maybe it's not much, but it's a start."

He was totally gonna paddle her ass for making him tear up like a fucking girl.

"Too corny?" she asked softly.

"No. It's perfect," he said. He cleared his throat and slipped the bracelet on her left wrist, letting his finger follow the thin band all the way around. Such a simple thing that meant so much. Then held his arm out so she could do the same. When he was dry-eyed, he looked up at her. "Thank you."

"My pleasure."

"Now, weren't you supposed to be getting nekkid?"

"But—"

"Are you really gonna argue with me?"

"No. Looks like the beastly Dom is back."

He grinned. "Darlin', he never left."

Ainsley leaned over and laid a hot, wet, kiss on him. "And I hope he never does."

About the Author

To learn more about Lorelei James, read her Author Notes on this and other titles, and see a McKay family tree, please visit www.loreleijames.com. Send an email to lorelei@loreleijames.com or join her Yahoo! group to join in the fun with other readers as well as Lorelei:

http://groups.yahoo.com/group/LoreleiJamesGang

She wants it. He's got it. And the chase is on...

Chasin' Eight
© 2011 Lorelei James
Rough Riders, Book 11

Bull rider Chase McKay has finally landed in a pile too big to charm his way out of. Caught with his pants down, he finds himself bucked right off the PBR tour until he can get his act together.

Hollywood actress Ava Cooper became the tabloids' favorite target when her longtime boyfriend was outed as gay. Now she wants a place to lay low and a chance to prove to herself that she can satisfy a red-blooded man between the sheets. The sexy, rugged cowboy she finds holed up in her Wyoming hideaway seems like the answer to her every fantasy.

But Chase has sworn off women. Forever. Or at least a month. Whichever comes first.

When they take to the road to get Chase more hands-on bull riding experience, they have every intention of keeping their hands off each other. But the two headstrong stars quickly end up riding a hot and heady rodeo circuit all their own—until the press gets wind of their affair. When the dust clears and the lights of the paparazzi fade, are they ready to give up chasing the dream for a chance of finding forever?

Warning: Strap in, another hot McKay is about to bust out of the gate and this bull rider knows a thing or two about riding hard...

Available now in ebook and print from Samhain Publishing.

Nothing comes easy. You've gotta work for it.

Rocky Mountain Desire
© *2012 Vivian Arend*
Six Pack Ranch, Book 3

Matt Coleman always figured at this point in his life, he'd be settled down with a family. Since his ex split for the big city, though, no way will he give anyone else the chance to drop-kick his heart. Physical pleasure? Hell, yeah, he'll take—and give—with gusto, but nothing more.

Hope Meridan is working long hours to hold on to her new quilt shop, going it alone since her sister/business partner ran off. Sex? Right, like she's got the time. Not that she doesn't have the occasional dirty fantasy about Matt. Fat chance he'd dream of knocking boots with her—the younger sister of the woman who dumped him. Nope, she'll just have to settle for the F-word.

Friends would be far easier if there wasn't something combustible going on between them. And when casual interest starts to grow into something more, their tenuous bond strengthens in the heat of desire. But it may not survive the hurricane-force arrival of the last person either of them ever wanted to see again...

Warning: Small-town rivals, men in pursuit and family meddling— in good and bad ways. Look for a cowboy who knows how to rope, ride and rein in a hell of a lot more than eight seconds of sheer bliss.

Available now in ebook from Samhain Publishing.

It's all about the story...

www.samhainpublishing.com

CPSIA information can be obtained at www.ICGtesting.com
Printed in the USA
LVOW131527260313

326142LV00001B/125/P

9 781609 288143